GENESIS
CODE

Also by Jamie Metzl

Fiction:
The Depths of the Sea

Nonfiction:
Western Responses to Human Rights Abuses in Cambodia, 1975–80

GENESIS CODE

A THRILLER OF THE NEAR FUTURE

JAMIE METZL

Arcade Publishing • New York

First Paperback Edition 2016

Extract from "Monet's Water Lilies" by Robert Hayden, used by the kind permission of W. W. Norton & Company.

Arcade Publishing books may be purchased in bulk at special discounts for sales promotion, corporate gifts, fund-raising, or educational purposes. Special editions can also be created to specifications. For details, contact the Special Sales Department, Arcade Publishing, 307 West 36th Street, 11th Floor, New York, NY 10018 or arcade@skyhorsepublishing.com.

Arcade Publishing® is a registered trademark of Skyhorse Publishing, Inc.®, a Delaware corporation.

Visit our website at www.arcadepub.com.
Visit the author's website at www.jamiemetzl.com.

10 9 8 7 6 5 4 3 2 1

Library of Congress Cataloging-in-Publication Data

Metzl, Jamie Frederic.
    Genesis code : a thriller of the near future / Jamie Metzl. — First edition.
        pages cm
    ISBN 978-1-62872-423-3 (hardcover); ISBN 978-1-62872-608-4 (paperback); ISBN 978-1-62872-465-3 (ebook)
    1. Murder—Fiction. 2. Conspiracies—Fiction. I. Title.
    PS3613.E895G46 2014
    813'.6—dc23
                            2014024917

Jacket design by Erin Seaward-Hiatt
Jacket photo credit: Thinkstock

Printed in the United States of America

GENESIS CODE

1

From the moment we're born we begin learning, creating ourselves in a process that lasts a lifetime, a process that is our life. It's an uplifting thought. But, depressingly, from the same moment the clock starts ticking down on our finite lives. We've already begun to die.

And when you're dead, you're just dead.

I've always hoped that were it my corpse lying on the floor people would hover around drawing lessons from my life, pondering the infinite.

But in this finite world bodies start to stink after a while and MaryLee Stock sadly is not going to be an exception.

Her body rests on its side facing away from me, her long, straight black hair splayed across the ivory carpet. From my vantage point inside her apartment's front door, she looks like she's fallen asleep after coming home drunk from a party. Peaceful.

I lift my wrist toward my mouth and start whispering into my u.D. "Caucasian female, mid-twenties, no signs of struggle, Monet water lilies on wall." I'm not sure what inspires me to focus on the water lilies. Perhaps her cheaply framed poster reminds me of the old Robert Hayden poem where he gets lost in the painting at the Museum of Modern Art, forgetting for a moment about the Vietnam War. *O light beheld as through refracting tears, Here is the aura of that world each of us has lost, Here is the shadow of its joy.*

I wonder if MaryLee had a brief moment of clarity before she died, whether she'd seen light and joy through the refracted tears of life, or if she'd just stopped like a toaster with a pulled plug.

"Hey, Rich," Maurice Henderson says in a no-nonsense tone, "I need you out of here."

"Sure, Inspector," I grumble, grateful he's let me in at all. He and I know he's only doing me this favor because I helped him out when he needed it three months ago.

The story had been horrific. A downtown hipster was pushing Blue Magic, a designer psychedelic hallucinogen that wreaked havoc on young people's brains. Kids taking it would become wildly manic for forty-eight hours before their inevitable crash. The ones who couldn't get enough of a fix from the pill started injecting it pulverized straight into their bloodstreams. Then the bodies started showing up in the morgue with furrowed eyes, purple-tinged skin, and puncture marks dotting their inner arms.

"What a waste," I say.

"Yup," he says curtly, not looking in my direction.

Henderson led the team that tracked down and arrested the supplier, but the drugs were still on the street. When he requested my help, I went above and beyond what he'd asked for my own reasons. My detailed three-part series in the *Star* describing the origins and gruesome dangers of Blue Magic became a key part of KCPD's outreach to schools and colleges around town.

"Anything you can share?" I ask.

"No."

"Any indication of the cause of death?"

"You're seeing what I'm seeing," he snaps with a why-are-you-asking-me-this look on his face. "Good-bye, Rich."

I know that between her u.D, the crime scene, and pathology someone will probably come up with more information. But that will take time and I need to post something an hour from now, "something juicy," as my assignment editor, Martina Hernandez, barked as I'd run out of the newsroom. With the hint of even more layoffs wafting in the air, it didn't take my PhD to construe her words as an implicit threat.

I look around the apartment one last time.

The small one-bedroom is clearly a starter place on someone's journey up the bedroom scale of life. Each space is small enough to be useful but not large enough to be wasteful. The kitchen is spotless, with only different size jars containing flour, sugar, and small packages of peanut M&Ms, a bottle of vitamins, and a small bamboo plant betraying signs of life. The books on the shelf organized by color and size, her plates stacked orderly in the IKEA armoire, the small, golden-clasped cherry box resting on a knitted mat on her shelf, her symmetrically organized framed print of Monet's water lilies, a haloed baby Jesus in the arms of Mary, and of the Country Club Plaza mall lit up by its famous Christmas lights all seem like tiny gestures striving to bring order to the chaos of human existence. So much for that.

"Will you guys put out a statement?" I ask.

Henderson's face contorts with irritation. "Good-bye, Rich."

I know I should be more grateful and just accept the favor Maurice has done me. Of course, I can't. "Maurice," I say solemnly.

His look makes clear I'm pushing my limit.

"Do you mind if I walk across the room?"

"This is a crime scene, Rich, not a damn sidewalk."

I haven't known Maurice for long, just since Martina started putting me on the crime beat four months ago, but I've had a strong sense from the moment I met him that Maurice's sometimes hostile demeanor covers a profound decency.

"I want to see her face," I say. The words carry a deeper meaning. I want to register her as a human being.

Maurice stares at me coldly, but I sense, or convince myself I sense, only on the surface.

I try to see myself as he sees me. Five foot eleven, medium-length black hair parted on the side, rail thin with a long, pensive face, a nose built to hold the glasses I don't yet need, an untucked button-down shirt over faded blue jeans, the beginnings of afternoon scruff, and an ever present dreamy look I can't seem to shake.

Maurice's perfectly starched white shirt, navy suit, and blue tie, lean, muscular body, and military cropped Afro, on the other hand, all project an authority I clearly lack.

"Walk around the perimeter of the room, don't touch a damn thing."

I nod slightly in Maurice's direction.

He glares back.

I skirt the small wooden table and two chairs and almost bump into the far end of her sofa jutting out from the wall.

And then it strikes me.

I'm not sure what I'd thought MaryLee Stock's face would look like. Her pale skin seems almost translucent against the beige carpet, her thin frame and delicate fingers suggest a fragility, an innocence, that life somehow has clearly betrayed. I freeze.

It's not that she looks like Astrid. She doesn't. Astrid's face was fuller, her hair more wild, her body more substantial. But the physical manifestation of purity permeating each of their faces strikes me on an inexplicable, almost metaphysical level as being the same.

MaryLee's right arm extends on the carpet as if reaching for something she will now never find. The lines of her palm tell a story that will now never be realized. My eyes travel down her thin arm. A tiny red dot catches my eye. "Did you see that?" I say, pointing.

"What do you think you're doing here, Rich?"

I feel like an idiot for having thought Maurice was just doing me a favor. "And you think . . ."

"I have to consider the possibility. Twenty-three kids dead in this town over the last six months with needle marks in their arms, this could be twenty-four."

"But you've seen those bodies. You know what they look like when it's Blue Magic."

"We don't know enough to know," Maurice says.

"Fair point," I say. I've become one of the more informed people in Kansas City on Blue Magic, but there's a lot about it, like most everything else in life, I don't fully understand. "No reason for us to speculate—the lab tests will tell us whether it is or it isn't."

"They will, but that'll take time."

I hardly hear Maurice as I stare at MaryLee's arm, emotionally returning to what I'd felt so vividly at Astrid's wake seventeen years ago—desperate, alone, helpless, inadequate, guilty. A deep nausea rises up inside of me. I have no idea how much time has passed when Maurice's command pierces my fog.

"Now I need you to leave."

I hesitantly retrace my steps toward the door, passing just close enough to the kitchenette to see the top of the white plastic trash bag folded in her IKEA garbage bin. I peek in, looking for a syringe. It's empty.

I glance at the body one last time, then stumble out the small apartment building past the hubbub of television reporters and police while trying to shake off what I know is an irrational connection in my clouded head between the dead girl in apartment 33 and my precious little Astrid. Every big picture is made of countless tiny dots, and the needle mark on MaryLee's arm, like a similar dot I'd seen obscured by makeup on Astrid's arm almost two decades ago, like the puncture holes I'd seen on the kids who'd done themselves in with Blue Magic, won't let me go.

MaryLee Stock didn't look to me like a Blue Magic victim, but if that's what the dot on her arm represents then there's got to be a syringe somewhere. As I turn right on to Oak Street, my usual Clark Kent inevitably gives way to my inner superhero—Garbageman.

For as long as I can remember, I've been garbage obsessed. Maybe it's because one of my earliest memories is my father bringing home bits and pieces from other people's garbage we'd glue and weld into stationary robots that stood guard over our play room. "Look what my little garbageman dragged in," he'd said the first time I brought home a discarded toaster oven, the cracked base of a blender, four short pieces of pipe, and a dead Sony Discman for the head. I'd beamed, sensing that Garbageman must be a new superhero to add to the pantheon. After then, we'd gone on garbage requisition missions together and our ever larger robots had spilled into the garage.

Or maybe I'm garbage obsessed because growing up in a shrinking Armenian family who never threw anything away I've become afraid that people can just vanish. Maybe garbage has become some kind of obscene record of our otherwise ephemeral existence. I don't know.

I do know that if there's a syringe there's at least a decent chance I can find it in MaryLee's garbage. I turn right on Brookside Boulevard and follow the walking trail around the corner of Cleaver Boulevard through the Winstead's parking lot, then limbo under the gate back into the Whitehall apartment complex.

Locating the central garbage chute is easy. Climbing in and inhaling the putrid air, I wonder yet again why I always find myself thrashing around in the messy under-regions of human existence, even if my curiosity about people's detritus has served me reasonably well in my seven years at the *Star*.

Analysis. It's 4 p.m. and MaryLee's been dead for at least four hours since the police first got called. Her bag, if it's here, can't be toward the front. I count six white garbage bags in the middle of the pile and untie them in succession.

I've always believed that any person's garbage at any time of the day reveals a snapshot of the person's life. As Garbageman, my job is to find it. The first bag has five beer bottles—out. The next, McDonalds—out. The third, an empty bag of sliced turkey—maybe. The next smells of curry—out. The fifth, a tube of toothpaste methodically squeezed from the bottom up—could be. The sixth, the *Kansas City Star* embedded video magazine with pizza stains—out.

I don't see a syringe, but I take my two most promising options and climb back through the chute, slide under the gate, saunter through the Winstead's parking lot, and stash the bags behind the dumpster. I scurry around the block to my Hyundai then drive to the lot, throw the garbage bags in my trunk, and drive away trying to look innocuous.

A twinge of conscience strikes me as I go. Maurice has done me a favor, and now I may be whisking away evidence. But if I find a syringe, I'll just let him know. My job is to find the story and hauling away trash is not a crime.

Unless, of course, I actually do have MaryLee Stock's garbage in my trunk.

2

Decay, perhaps, is our inevitable fate.

Heading down Main toward the *Kansas City Star* building, I pass forty crumbling years of failed urban renewal, the empty, new streetcars rolling by yet another reminder of good intentions gone awry.

Some call the *Star* building a Georgian revival masterpiece. I'm sure it once was. The only appropriate word to describe it today is "dump." Although things are just starting to turn around in this country, the building feels like a metaphor for what America has done to itself over the last forty years—failed to invest in our future and let decay set in just when a rising China was challenging us and our way of life like never before.

Decay greets me as I pull in to the cracked parking lot, as I walk past the peeling Formica guard station at the entrance, the uninterested, slovenly guards mumbling into the universal.Devices—u.Ds—wrapped around their forearms. I wonder if anyone in America actually works or if the whole country is messaging each other or quite literally playing with themselves on their u.Ds. No wonder China's been cleaning our clocks. The sense of pervasive decay greets me most acutely when the elevator opens to the sprawling, chaotic newsroom floor.

Whoever invented the cubicle was probably intending to give everyone a little corner of the world for themselves. Now that the interior of each cubicle is covered from top to bottom with digital screens, each person has designed a little universe all of their own—a mountain scene here, coral reef there, a Parisian café around the corner—but none of this comes even close to providing anyone the slightest sanctuary on the crowded floor. Colleagues' aggressively wafting conversations spread collective doom like sprawling ivy across this labyrinth of communal isolation.

The doom is not hard to understand in our struggling industry. No matter how many jobs were shed, bureaus closed, costs reduced, it was mathematically impossible for the old-form newspapers and magazines to compete in the new environment. Every dental plan, every sheet of paper, every union contract was a dead weight around our necks. The legacy media business has been in a freefall for twenty years that even the great Jeff Bezos couldn't slow. If not for Uncle Sam, we'd have splattered years ago.

The isolation is more personal, so I always keep my head down and try to glide unnoticed through the maze. Somehow I've never felt anything that good was heading my way here.

"Yo, Jorge."

Cringing inwardly, I maintain my forward momentum.

"Don't be such a killjoy," Martina says. "Rich-ie," she sings as if calling a preschooler in from recess or a dog back to the house.

I straighten my torso and turn slowly to face her. A part of me wants to tell her to stop calling me Jorge, but I know this will only make things worse.

Just north of fifty with frizzy salt and pepper hair, having internalized the *Star's* hierarchy and fought her way to the top, living every day as if she's crawling through the jungle with a knife between her teeth, Martina may have once been a looker but now just looks . . . tough. Every wrinkle on her face seems a battle line, a notch demarcating a vanquished foe.

Why on earth had I ever told her I'd been inspired by Jorge Luis Borges' mind-altering book, *Ficciones*, which explores the deep interconnectivity between fact and fiction, the boundary where the "real world" ends and surreality begins, where we dream fantastic dreams that slowly overtake our previous realities? Perhaps in my early days at the *Star* I'd been trying to show off my literary fluency. Perhaps I never really wanted to belong here. I don't know. I do know that calling me Jorge is her way of poking me for my worldview perched somewhere between fantasy and reality. I approach her, fighting the sour lemon look on my face.

"I liked the teledildonics piece," she says dryly, referencing the article I wrote and embedded multimedia platform we created last week about the new Get Luckey 2300 full body Enhanced Virtual Reality suit and the intersection between telecommunications, long-distance relationships, and remote-controlled sexual devices. "Very stimulating."

"I'm sure you can do better than that," I say, wondering if I'm sometimes selling my soul by following Martina's threatening orders to file ever more "juicy" stories. For every one Blue Magic story there are ten teledildonics, and I get the sense from Martina that my Blue Magic success has already been all but forgotten.

"Let me think about it," she says, putting two fingers to her right temple in faux contemplation. "It's coming."

I smirk painfully, shake my head, and turn to walk away, sensing that Martina is just marking territory like an alpha dog. I'm not in the mood to get pissed on.

"Richie," she says in a softer tone, "I'm teasing you."

Despite her perpetual antagonism, I have to admit, grudgingly, that I like Martina Hernandez in spite of myself. She may not be well educated, but she is dogged and has worked her way up from answering phones in circulation to being a senior editor, no small feat even in a dying industry like this.

"What did you find out?"

"Not much. Dead body of young girl. Needle mark on her arm, so it could be Blue Magic, but she doesn't look like any of the others I've seen."

Martina's ears perk up. "When can you confirm?"

"The autopsy should take a few days, but I'm trying to figure things out earlier than that."

I can see Martina weighing the options of whether this is a

Blue Magic case and therefore a worthwhile story, or not and probably in her mind just a waste of our time. "All right," she says deliberately, tilting her head to the side, "just do a short piece for now. We'll only need more if there's a story."

"Yes'm," I say sarcastically, making an oblique reference to my subservient status that she ignores.

"The clock's ticking, Jorge. We don't need a dissertation. Some things are what they are."

I ignore the dissertation comment, shake my head, then walk toward my cubicle, following the route I probably should have selected in the first place and wondering how I got here and what the hell I'm doing.

After Astrid's death I'd drifted through life without a destination, doing odd jobs around Davis to keep me in my run-down apartment and away from Glendale, passing through a series of almost relationships with a series of women I now hardly remember, listening obsessively to Bach, smoking marijuana when I felt particularly shitty, and pretending with the few of my friends who'd stuck around that college had never really ended and the terrifying expanse of life was not looming before us.

Some drifters stay up all night drinking, others dissolve into video games. I became obsessed with voraciously reading everything I came across as if getting lost in a book, any book, was better than facing the abyss of my little sister's murder or playing the scene over in my mind again and again, wondering whether I could have saved her. I read my way through mountains of crappy thrillers, heaps of biographies, stacks of manga, reading with a fervor to take me anywhere but where I was. But nowhere could I get as ecstatically lost as in the most obscure of philosophy books. Schopenhauer, Nietzsche, Kant, Rawls, Spinoza—nothing was too dense. I dove in as if exploring an underwater cave, only half wanting to ever make it back to the surface.

As I started on my PhD at Davis, philosophy became even more of a new world for me to inhabit, a series of existential puzzles that kept my painful memories of Astrid, my sense of guilt, life itself at a safe distance. But without a bridge between that world and the world that any child could recognize as the real one, my work left me no way back once I began to heal. Over the five years getting my degree and three years as a postdoc writing obscure articles on the subjective nature of existence, my world of escape began to feel increasingly like a glass prison separating me from life in a more real world I felt an increasing yearning to revisit.

So I escaped to what I'd thought was a more concrete existence, but I'm not sure if coming to the *Star* was a landing or if I'm still falling without realizing it, the way our planet feels stable enough when you're standing on it but is in fact hurtling through space at a fantastic speed.

But if I feel bad about it, I can't help but offload the feeling as I approach Joseph Abraham's desk.

Shit flows downhill and only scientists call it gravity.

3

"Abraham," I bark in my best drill sergeant voice.

He straightens in his chair with a jolt.

"Yes, sir."

I feel guilty. Clearly I've triggered some kind of atavistic response drilled into Indian schoolchildren by the distant legacies of harsh nuns wielding sticks.

I place my hand on his shoulder. "I need your help," I say in a softer voice.

He exhales.

Joseph Abraham is on a work visa from India. He'd graduated from Mizzou with a Master's degree in journalism and needed a job to keep from being sent home. We'd hired him for little more than minimum wage and he was grateful.

Short and pudgy yet sturdy like a bulldog, Joseph has thousand-year-old eyes that nestle deep in his round honey-brown face topped by a mop of curly jet-black hair, collectively somehow creating the impression he's been molded from the earth or emerged organically as the reincarnation of an ancient tree. I'd teased him in the beginning about having two first names and taking everything so seriously, but the earnestness of his responses eventually sucked the fun out of the whole teasing enterprise. It also changed things that I've become ever more dependent on this quiet, resourceful, thoroughly decent young-old man. In spite of his twenty-seven years of age, there is nothing about Joseph— the way he sits, stands, walks, his clothes, his overall demeanor— that suggests youth. Joseph carries the weight of the world on his shoulders, which, in a perverse way, connects him firmly to the ground.

"What did you find?" I'd sent Joseph MaryLee's name from my car and asked him to dig up everything he could on her.

"MaryLee Stock," he says in his lyrically accented English, "age twenty-four, from Springfield, Missouri, attended Springfield High School, 640/680/690 SAT scores, right field for the Springfield Tigers women's softball team, only child. MaryLee is . . . was, getting her Master's in pharmacy at the University of Missouri–Kansas City, second year, section four. Adopted from Romania when she was three years old, no information on her biological parents. Adoptive father died when she was twelve. Her mother never remarried, works at the YMCA."

I have no idea what they taught guys like Joseph at the Indian Institute of Technology, but I am always amazed at how much information he can gather so quickly from sources I can't imagine are open to the public. Of course, I made him promise to always work through anonymizing web portals and to feel free to "work from home" when he needed "extra time with the wife and kids" he doesn't have.

"Here is the Galileo GPS image of her mother's house in Springfield. The address is at the bottom. This is her class schedule. Here are her grades for the last three semesters."

"What kind of images do you have of her?" I ask.

"Surprisingly little," Joseph says, tapping up the photos on his wall screen. "These are from the Springfield High yearbooks from 2014 to 2017. Here's the photo in the UMKC system."

I feel uneasily voyeuristic as I look into MaryLee's wide blue eyes shining brightly above her kind half smile. How could she have known when taking this photo that such a tragic fate awaited her?

"I couldn't find much video," Joseph adds, "only this clip from the Springfield School of Dance tap recital when she was ten in

2009." He rolls his finger along his u.D, and a video box appears on his cubicle wall.

"*Somewhere beyond the sea . . .*" The music starts playing as the three young girls tap across the podium in glittery blue halter tops and green skirts. It's immediately clear that MaryLee is the one in the middle. Her long, black hair flows a moment behind each of her movements. At first, her smile is self-conscious as her attention points inward to count each step, but she warms up as the music plays, releasing herself to the joy of the music and movement. By the end of the short song her feet are tapping like whips, her arms flowing with abandon. She and the others reach their hands into the air as the music stops and the muffled applause is heard in the background. I watch her scan the audience with a wide, jubilant smile as the clip cuts.

I shake my head from side to side. "Anything else?"

"That's it, boss."

"Great start," I say.

Joseph looks up.

"Thank you," I add.

His mouth twitches up at the edges for a quick moment then recedes.

I take the papers and settle into my cubicle to dictate my first story. Just the facts, ma'am. Young woman found dead, no comment from police, name withheld by police request, police investigating. The story doesn't seem like much, definitely neither reflecting the loss nor "juicy" enough to make me feel confident about my future.

Not that anyone in this business has much right to feel confident no matter what we do.

Few of us were big fans of the News Protection Act of 2021, but the struggling newspapers across the country simply could not survive without financial support, and only the federal government was willing to provide it. Sure, we mocked the requirement pushed by the AARP and the unions that subsidized news organizations continue their paper editions and hated the idea of a national security exemption in exchange for the subsidies, but that was the final offer and no one wanted to face the alternative.

Even with all of us straying into new territory because of shrinking staffs from the budget cuts, I'd been pretty cautious when Martina asked me to start covering crime stories a few months ago. But I know all too well, as the rounds of layoffs continue, that a journalist with a job is a lucky one.

An image on the wall catches my eye as I head toward the newsroom exit.

The south wall is one enormous screen divided into four quadrants. The two bottom sections show native Great Plains prairie grasses blowing in the wind, but the image in the top left has become strangely familiar these past months. Senator Carlton King is addressing yet another rally of the faithful at a prayer vigil in yet another stop of his relentless bus tour around the country. The images are always the same—the weeping men and women, the hands in the air, the stoic, contained voice of Senator King as he lays out his indictment of America's highway to hell and charts the path out of darkness.

"When God created the earth, did he want us to poison it with dangerous chemicals, to bake our planet in greenhouse gases?"

"No," the assembled voices reply.

"Did he want us to murder the most precious of his creations when they were defenseless babies held in the protective embrace of their mothers' wombs?"

"No," the voices wail.

"Did he want us to create new life in laboratories, to challenge the sanctity of the world he so lovingly created?"

"No!" they shriek.

I stand absorbed in this strange conservative revival spreading across the country.

Who would have thought, I wonder, that a religious movement could have become so powerful in 2023 America? But then again, who could have thought the mighty United States could have defaulted on its debts in 2019, or that China, America's biggest rival, could have led the International Monetary Fund and a group of creditor nations in demanding such major reforms in order to keep lending us money? Most shocking of all, who could have imagined that instead of fighting against these tough conditions, the centrist wings of the Democratic and Republican parties would have come together to field a national unity slate of candidates for the 2020 elections based on the twin themes of national competitiveness and national revival, or that the first bill passed by the new team, the National Competitiveness Act, could have done so much to start turning things around? It's been almost three years, and I still can hardly believe it myself.

The national unity platform was good news for America, but not every American perceived it that way. The 2020 Republican primary split the Republican party right down the middle, with Senator Carlton King, the powerful Missouri senator and ultimate political operator desperately seeking the Republican presidential nomination, denouncing then Ohio governor and soon-to-be-president Bart Lewis for selling out Republican and American moral values by making common cause with the Democrats.

"Or did he want us to follow a path of righteousness?" King asks, his tirade escalating, "to love and respect the great bounty he has provided, to remake, to reincarnate America once again as the great beacon on the hill?"

The collective "Yes" sounds almost sexual.

If the nation and the parties were coming together on the big things, perhaps it was inevitable that new fault lines would emerge. King read the political wind of American conservatives, largely evangelical Christians, growing uneasy with rapid technological and social change and blasted Lewis in the 2020 Republican primaries for betraying America's "Christian values" and raised the culture issues—abortion, stem cell, synthetic biology, biotech, genetics research—to a fever pitch, leading religious-tinged marches on biotechnology research centers and abortion clinics around the country. He condemned the National Bioethics Commission as a "servant of sin" and led a successful campaign to have it abolished by Congress.

King lost the 2020 nomination by a hair and entered into an uneasy truce with nominee and then president Lewis and, the ultimate stake in the heart, Lewis's Democratic vice president Jack Alvarez, a declared agnostic. But now, less than four years later, King is charging hard at President Lewis in advance of the April 2024 Republican primary with his army of the righteous marching right behind him.

"Then I need you with me on this great crusade to bring this great country back to God's path. Are you with me?" King yells.

"Yes," the voices proclaim.

King drops his voice to a near whisper. "Are you with me?" he says powerfully, staring directly into the camera.

The assembled follow his tone, now completely under his control. "Yes."

The scene sends shivers down my spine.

The camera scans the weeping crowd that looks far more like faithful at a religious revival than party advocates at a political rally.

"Then we march on together," King says quietly, his body becoming more erect with each word. "God Bless America," he bellows, then pauses for a dramatic moment before delivering, once again, his movement's thundering punch line. "God—shall—overcome."

The assembled stand silent until the familiar music starts playing and the singing begins.

I feel myself almost moved but fight the impulse. If I who loathe what King stands for am feeling this, I wonder how the average American Christian must be responding. The polls are starting to show the answer. Positively.

I may be marching on, but only out to my car to head home.

My little place on Thirty-Sixth and Charlotte in Hyde Park isn't much, Adirondack style with an exposed deck I hardly use and a central atrium that always feels empty to me.

The neighborhood was once the proud domain of blue-collar whites, then it became part of the hood after desegregation, and it's been slowly creeping back over the past years. It's ironic that crappy neighborhoods like this can reintegrate as formerly wealthier people drop down the income scale. Leaving this neighborhood was once an aspiration; now just staying here is.

I pop the trunk and grab my two bags. Everyone else in the world is taking the garbage out. I must be the only guy taking the garbage in.

My u.D vibrates as I push open the door. I tap my wrist and feel the silence.

"Mom," I say after a few moments, "are you okay?" I know the answer but always ask anyway.

"I'm okay, *janum*," she says unconvincingly. The rapid-fire blows of my sister's murder and my father's death knocked the wind out of her. She's a strong woman at her core, but it always takes her a few moments when we talk to gather her momentum.

My mind scrambles to fill the void. What can I say? That I'm investigating the senseless death of a young woman? I revert to our cultural default. "Are you eating, Mother?" Seventeen years ago, before everything, she must have been a good thirty pounds heavier.

"Yes, *janum*," she says.

I know she's lying.

Her maternal instinct kicks in. "How are you, *jeegarus*?"

"I'm good, Mother," I say, slightly concerned she's still calling me her liver after all these years and not sure whether I am okay or not but happy to shift the conversation toward me.

When I speak with my mother, I feel even more acutely that somehow my life seems to dangle over a precipice dividing my painful past and unknown future. I remain wracked with guilt that I am living away and only bring myself to visit her in California once every couple of years, yet am painfully aware during my occasional visits that my mother's mournful love has the potential to smother me.

"How is Shoonig?" I ask stupidly. Shoonig, the high-strung shih tzu I bought for my mother as an unsuspecting puppy six years ago, has become my yapping alter ego, pathetically standing in for my absent presence.

Her voice picks up as if mention of the dog has reconnected her to life. "He's a good dog. It's our fate to keep each other company."

I feel a twinge of guilt at my mother's subtle barb, painfully aware that I've outsourced the task of minding my mother to a fur ball with the IQ of a two-year-old.

"No one is an island, my *janum*." My mother catches me off guard with her pivot.

"I know, Mother," I say, sensing where she is heading.

"Life is difficult sometimes, and it's okay to lean on people who love you," she continues. "Did you know that married people live longer than single people, that people with pets live longer than people who don't have them?"

"I know, Mother." I'm not sure she hears me.

"Even people with plants live longer than people without them."

I don't answer. I don't have to for this line of argument to arrive at its conclusion.

"Have you heard anything from Toni?" she asks.

"Mother, you know we split up six months ago." I try to keep a measured voice but sense she's not convinced.

"She sounded to me like a *dandeegin*. Nobody is perfect. Even you, my *janum*, are not 100 percent completely perfect."

Don't I know it?

I remain silent. It's not worth making it again clear that Toni's the one who left me.

"Dikran, are you there?" she says.

I'm thirty-nine years old, but I still cringe at the sound of my real name. To this day, it brings haunting memories of being teased on the bus to my new school. Dikran had been a perfectly respectable name at the Chamlian Armenian School. Two days of being called Dickwad after I transferred to the Woodrow Wilson Middle School in Glendale had inspired my supersonic switch to the English version of the name, Richard.

"Can I call you back, Mother?"

"Of course, *janum*," she says in her motherly tone. "You know I say these things because I love you and don't want you to be alone."

"I know, Mom," I say as I push open the door and begin dragging my bags of garbage down the stairs. "I'll call you."

The words have hardly left my mouth and I already feel guilty that I probably won't.

4

The earth, by most accounts, has existed for four and a half billion years. Life emerged more than three billion years ago. Humans, at least in our current form, have been around for two hundred and fifty thousand years. What, I can't help but constantly wonder, do any of us leave behind?

We have babies and pass on our DNA, capture our thoughts in words or images, or simply accrue nonbiodegradable junk that outlasts us. None of these feel capable of shaking the sense of absolute impermanence that haunts me.

Maybe I should have learned when we lost Astrid that even the most precious things can be lost for no discernible reason. Perhaps had we known who killed my baby sister in the senseless drive-by shooting seventeen years ago, I could have more peace.

I remind myself every day over and over that I was self-indulgently hanging around post-graduation Davis the day Astrid was killed, that if I'd have been home the flow of that day would have been altered, the butterfly effect would have guided the stray bullet elsewhere. I remind myself that I knew and my parents didn't that Astrid was getting herself into trouble, that she was hiding the track marks on her arms, hanging out in parts of town where she should never have been and with people with whom she should never have associated.

Undoing the tie on the first bag of garbage before me, I feel the sad contradiction that we live our lives moving forward but only begin to understand them in retrospect, the urge to do for MaryLee what I was never able to do for Astrid. I begin the process of excavating a life to illuminate a death.

A part of me wants to find the syringe I'm looking for, to complete this strange parallel I've drawn in my head between Astrid and MaryLee. Another part wants to leave MaryLee as innocent and at peace as she seemed when I first saw her earlier today.

I'm sure there are official procedures, but I'm too inexperienced to know them. My process is more intuitive. I spread a large sheet of white butcher paper over my basement table and draw grid lines across both axes, dividing the sheet into twelve squares. I number each, put on my rubber gloves, open the first garbage bag, and place each individual item into one of the squares. No syringe.

My analysis begins. The Healthy Choice lemon chicken with pasta in square two suggests someone watching what she eats but not fully informed about how to do it. Could be. But the chopsticks in square three don't feel completely like Springfield, and the pink woman's sock in square seven looks a little small for a healthy sized Caucasian like MaryLee. The crumpled turkey bag from Cosentino's market also doesn't seem to jibe with the methodical feel of MaryLee's apartment. Her world had the peace of the water lilies; this garbage does not.

The receipt from 7-Eleven in square ten itemizes the gallon of two percent milk and a dozen eggs, and, more importantly, lists the last four digits of the credit card used to pay. I call out the numbers to my u.D, put the garbage into numbered Ziploc bags, and place them in my basement refrigerator.

As I unpack and spread the contents of the second garbage bag, I still don't see a syringe but begin to sense a story. The stem of iceberg lettuce with the leaves cut, not ripped, the sliced-off white bread crusts, and the VitaMix cereal in the first few of my squares give me the impression I'm looking at a careful female's garbage. The recycled paper coffee cup in square seven conjures someone who progresses slowly in her drinking. I lift the lid and inhale the scent of hazelnut. The dental floss, methodically squeezed toothpaste container, and spent jar of Radiant Light face cream in my next few squares suggest to me the kind of meticulousness I associate with MaryLee's tidy apartment.

My pulse quickens as I examine the coffee receipt for $2.42 from the UMKC Hospital Hill Café in square eleven, dated October 16, 2023—yesterday—at 3:37 p.m. MaryLee might not have been the only UMKC student in her building, but a link to UMKC certainly narrows the field. Square twelve holds an empty envelope from Softbank Mobile and a receipt from Corner Drug from yesterday at 4:41 p.m. listing items costing $10.95, $24.95, and $1.65 each. I wish the receipt had come from a chain like Rite Aid or Nepstar that would have itemized, but it is what it is. I dictate the figures to my u.D.

Of course, I realize, it would be far easier to just do a DNA test on the coffee cup rather than go through my highly unscientific process of weighing my prejudices and preconceptions. If I had DNA processing equipment in my basement, I surely would be following that tried-and-true approach. But the police certainly aren't going to tell me what they find any time soon, so I have to do my own work with the means at my disposal.

I come back up to my kitchen to think. No syringe, no other evidence of Blue Magic, but still the basic problem of a dead girl. I imagine Martina would probably now want me to drop the story and move on to something "juicier." But juicy or not, I somehow can't seem to get the image of MaryLee Stock lying dead on the floor out of my mind. I open the file Joseph has sent me.

Nothing jumps out from his notes on MaryLee's parents, Carol and Greg Stock. Two working people raising their adopted daughter until he passes away and she goes to work for the YMCA. They, and then she, paid their taxes on time every year, paid their monthly dues at the YMCA without fail, and, like most of us, left only a minimal public trail.

The photos, however, haunt me. The first is of the young, earnest couple in the wedding announcement from the *Springfield News-Leader*. The next, from the same paper, shows the two of them, slightly older, holding a young girl between them. The family looks slightly stiff, as if being posed in a shopping mall photo studio. The grip of each parent's hand on MaryLee's shoulder brings to mind jumper cables connected to a car battery. The final photo, from the Springfield YMCA newsletter, shows a slightly older but more frightened Carol Stock, alone, announcing she has joined the YMCA accounting office.

The satellite photograph of the Stock house in Springfield is just what I'd have expected, compact and rectangular with a small yard.

I don't know how to read the adoption papers, but nothing jumps out. I uSearch the agency, All Blessings International, and look through their website thinking of the poor woman in Romania giving up her child for adoption, not knowing her baby would one day wind up dead on the floor of a Kansas City apartment.

The next three documents are from the UMKC—pretty much Bs across the board with a few As sprinkled in. This semester she'd been taking Organic Chemistry II, Organic Chemistry lab, Mammalian Physiology lecture and lab, and Introduction to Pharmacy.

The Monday schedule shows that Organic Chemistry lab, her last class of the day, ended at 3:30. Hypothesizing for a moment the second garbage bag is hers, the 3:37 hazelnut coffee fits this timetable perfectly. I still don't know what she would have done between 3:37 and 4:41, when she, or whoever, made purchases at Corner Drug. If she'd sat and drank her coffee during that time, how would the coffee cup wind up in her garbage at home? Even a patient coffee drinker would hardly nurse a coffee for more than an hour. I always drink mine in about three minutes. Mammalian Physiology lab is scheduled for tomorrow from 8:30 to 10:30, with Intro to Pharmacy starting at 11.

I tap my u.D. "Call Joseph."

"Boss?" he answers.

"I need the contact information for Carol Stock. Find out if there are surveillance cameras in the Whitehill apartment complex, the

UMKC Pharmacy School coffee shop, and the Corner Drug on Forty-Eighth and Troost. See if you can find MaryLee's Visa number."

I hear Joseph gasp. Even he knows that credit numbers are sacrosanct in our world of near-zero privacy. I reframe.

"See if you can determine if the last four digits of her Visa Digital Authorization Code were"—I pause to look at the numbers on my u.D—"3927. I'm going to UMKC tomorrow, so see what you can tell me about her classmates. Also, try to find out if MaryLee had blood drawn in the last couple of days at the UKMC clinic."

I start to feel guilty about overloading poor Joseph. "And Joseph."

"Boss?"

"Feel free to work from home on this one." I must not be feeling that guilty.

I wait for Joseph to respond until it becomes aggressively clear he has no intention to.

"Thank you, Joseph."

"Yeah," he says as the call drops.

My freezerator's door display springs to life as I approach.

I turned off the digital avatar four months ago after the cheap thrill of the Manga vixen I programmed to call me "master" had worn off. Voiceless and faceless, my Haier Jeeves 2300 now struggles to communicate with me with text display, the one tool left at its disposal. ALERT: YOUR DAIRYLAND MILK IS TWELVE DAYS PAST EXPIRATION. THE SIX EGGS IN THE DOOR COMPARTMENT ARE SEVENTEEN DAYS PAST EXPIRATION AND SHOULD NOT BE EATEN. KIRKLAND CARROTS ARE SHOWING SIGNS OF DECAY AND SHOULD BE DISCARDED. The door becomes clear as I touch it, revealing among other things the carrots that even a starving rabbit would be smart to avoid. It's easier to work around these items, so I go for the manual option and pop a couple of frozen pitas into the toaster, take my Costco hummus from the fridge, toss a frozen chicken breast on a plate, cover it with Gates Bar-B-Q sauce, and stick it in the microwave for seven minutes.

The exchange with my freezerator reminds me, like so many other things these days, of Toni.

She'd harassed me when we first started dating about all the expired items in my kitchen, rejecting my stated philosophy that expiration dates were mostly a scam by food companies to get consumers to buy more. Her early-morning raid on my kitchen the third night she'd stayed over had made my internal commitment meter go off, but I never missed the items she'd thrown away. Perhaps it was poetic justice that my old refrigerator-freezer had broken down two weeks after we split and I replaced it with a new model freezerator that adopted Toni's crusade against expired food where she left off.

Of course, there's a lot more to what I'm feeling than that.

It's funny how people end up residing in each other—knocking on the door at first, staying a few days, sometimes, metaphorically at least, moving in. Then they move out and the internal space they once occupied leaves a void, like a paper cutout, only the angels holding hands are gone and the cut-up paper is the only evidence they once were.

Antonia Hewitt, Toni, had been a great partner, girlfriend, Chiquita banana—I was never sure of the right word—for the eight months we dated. I loved the silly hats she sometimes wore, the special place she had in her heart for underdogs. I loved the way her mouth would go crooked when she was really laughing. I loved waking up in the middle of the night and just feeling her there.

But amazing as she was, is, I was never able to completely give myself over to the relationship. As much as I tried, I could never fully accept that she took life as she experienced it in her day-to-day and didn't see its ultimate goal as challenging every concept and pushing herself in a lifelong process of reinvention. I'd feared our growth trajectories would diverge and as my fears accrued I became more cautious.

Toni's frustration, of course, grew with my caution. I answered her questions as honestly as I could muster but couldn't counter the sadness that grew in her with each difficult conversation. I didn't want her to go but couldn't muster enough of a response when she told me she was leaving. Part of me sensed it was the right answer.

"You'll see," she'd said angrily then, "you think you need someone flying next to you but what you really need is ground control."

Would I have cared she didn't see life morphing like a spore but instead as a prix fixe meal to be slowly enjoyed if we'd had two or three kids and all the practicalities that would have entailed? Was I just hiding behind abstract principles to avoid embracing the real life staring me in the face? I didn't know, and not knowing itself became my problem.

I tap my u.D. "Call Toni," I say.

My finger races to the red icon before I hear the first ring.

5

My 6:30 a.m. u.D alarm feels merely inspirational.

I'd hoped to go to the gym but end up grumbling "snooze" six times and barely making it out of bed. I settle for a few quick sit-ups and push-ups before sauntering to the shower.

Maybe my Armenian athletic role models were not quite inspiring enough, I think, as I wander down to the kitchen and pour myself some VitaCharms. Sure everyone's heard of Andre Agassi, Agassian as he's lovingly called in Glendale, but you know you're in trouble when Garry Kasparov and the Maleeva sisters top the pantheon of your group's sports heroes.

I put Joseph on my dashboard screen as I head to UMKC Pharmacy School.

"Boss," he says, "can't find any record of MaryLee Stock going to the university clinic or giving blood, but I'm still looking. Also, a reservation has been made in the name of Carol Stock at the downtown Marriott. They have room 825 reserved for her. She's expected to check in today."

"How do you get this shit, Joseph?" I mumble to myself, not really wanting to know. "And who should I look for at the pharmacy school?"

"Hold on a second, boss," he says, "I'm calling up the names of her lab mates now." He begins reading from the screen. "Anil Sharma, third year medical student, born Creve Coeur, Missouri. Min Zhao, Chinese national, from Wuhan, China. Undergraduate degree from Lanxiang University, member of UMKC Chinese Students Association, second year pharmacy student. Neary

Savang, Cambodian-American, born in Kansas City, Missouri, valedictorian of Don Bosco High School in Kansas City, second year pharmacy student. Joyce Rodriguez, born Juarez, Mexico, attended college and high school in Tucson, Arizona, American citizen."

"Got it. Thanks." I tap out.

America has fallen from its former heights in so many areas as China has surged, but for a local school that once educated Missourians and now also trains third-tier elites from around the world, UMKC is more than adequate.

I don't know what to expect as I enter the uninspired yellow faux-brick building. The police still haven't officially released the name, but it somehow feels that news of MaryLee's death must have begun to circulate. The school is functioning, but something seems amiss.

I walk up one flight of stairs looking for room 205. It is 10:18 and Mammalian Physiology is scheduled to end in twelve minutes. I wait outside the door feeling slightly nauseous from the wafting smell of formaldehyde.

Perhaps time just moves more slowly in places that feel like high school, but the twelve minutes seem like an eternity. As the first students start trickling out, I realize I don't have any pictures of the people I'm looking for. I ask a young Asian woman with a head scarf if she can tell me who Anil Sharma is. She points tentatively. The group of four is packing up.

"Are you Anil?" I ask.

He looks up cautiously. The three women around him fit my perception of what a Min, Neary, and a J-Rod ought to look like.

"I'm Rich Azadian from the *Kansas City Star*."

He doesn't respond.

"I want to ask you about MaryLee Stock," I say quietly.

The group freezes.

"What do you know about MaryLee?" he asks suspiciously.

The woman I believe to be Joyce begins to tear.

"What do you know?" he asks, this time more aggressively.

I'm not sure what to say. I need to confirm their obvious suspicions that something's wrong before I can ask them about MaryLee, but something seems inappropriate about doing so. I shake my head slightly from side to side. We stand facing each other in silence.

"Excuse me!" I hear a voice with authority coming from across the room. "Who are you?"

"Rich Azadian from the *Kansas City Star*."

"I am Dr. Marc Solomon. What the hell are you doing in my lab?"

"I'm asking some questions."

"On UMKC property? Have you cleared this with school administration?"

"No," I say, perturbed.

"Then get the hell out," he says in a trembling voice. "You have no right to be here. Get out. Now."

I'm fighting for this story but know that Solomon is right. If the police haven't yet released the name, then the university can't make an official announcement. If the university can't make an announcement, they can't start grief counseling. I've clearly disrupted the process.

"Now," Solomon says, firmly placing his hand on my back and aggressively ushering me out of the classroom, down the stairs, and out the front door. I don't resist. I walk to my car, not sure exactly how to proceed.

"Mr. Azadian."

I turn to see the woman I think is Neary running toward me. She is short and compact. Her waist-length black hair trails behind her like a blowing scarf.

"I'm Neary Savang. MaryLee was my friend. Is she dead?"

I'm a little surprised by the directness of her question, but her earnest tone and pleading eyes force an honest response.

"I'm so sorry," I say softly.

Neary's shoulders collapse inward.

"I'm so sorry," I repeat pathetically.

I stand awkwardly as she struggles to pull herself together.

"What happened?" she says through her tears after a few minutes.

"I don't know," I say as gently as I can. "That's what I'm trying to figure out. She died at home yesterday. The police are investigating." My staccato statement of facts feels brutally practical.

Neary shudders. "What're the police doing?"

"Trying to figure out how she died."

"Do you know?"

"I don't, but I have questions."

"Like?"

"Can I ask you about MaryLee?"

She nods tentatively.

"Do you know if she ever experimented with any kinds of drugs? Did she ever mention Blue Magic?"

Neary pulls her head back in surprise. "Impossible. MaryLee didn't drink alcohol, she didn't even drink Coca-Cola."

"Did she ever do anything out of the ordinary? Was there anything about her that stuck out?"

Neary pauses to think. "She did the right thing for everybody. She would do anything for her friends."

"Like?"

"Like helping with my school work or driving me home at the end of the day. She brought me a care package when I had the flu a couple of months ago."

"Can you tell me what kind of car she drove?"

Neary gives me a funny look. "A blue Kia Curve."

"Did she have a lot of friends?"

"Just normal. She wasn't one of those people who goes to parties or to the bars in Westport."

"Did she have a boyfriend?"

Neary looks surprised. "Not that I knew of. It would have been hard to imagine."

"Why?"

"She was waiting for 'the one.'"

"The one?"

"The person who was meant to be."

"Meant to be by . . ."

"By God, by Jesus. She was very religious, completely committed to her church in Springfield, where she's from. I think Reverend Becker was very important to her."

"Cobalt Becker?" I say, surprised. "*The* Cobalt Becker?"

Reverend Cobalt Becker had merely been an evangelical superpastor before the 2020 elections. Politics had made him much more over the past few years.

Neary nods. "She didn't talk much about it, but once she did mention that it was a lot of pressure to be 'the chosen one.'"

"What do you think she meant by that?"

"I asked but she didn't really say."

"Anything else about her that stood out?"

"I don't know, Mr. Azadian. She was just a really good person, a kind and giving person." Neary is shaking and holding back tears.

"Can I call you Neary?" I ask, switching tack to try to calm her.

She nods apprehensively.

"Neary, I am trying to find out what happened. Most likely she died of some kind of health condition. People die of strange things all the time—brain aneurysms, SDS, all sorts of things."

I hear my words but I'm not convinced I believe them. Something about the dot on MaryLee's arm has been giving me the unsettling feeling this isn't just a natural causes story. But there's no need to torture this poor girl with unsubstantiated suspicions.

"Can I ask you one more question?"

Neary nods.

"Had MaryLee shown any signs of being sick?"

Neary takes a deep breath. "For the last couple of months she just hasn't looked like herself. She looked tired. She tried to hide it, but I could tell. She just didn't seem right."

"Did you have any idea what it was?"

"She told me she was fine, that she must have caught a stomach bug." Neary pauses for a moment. "Maybe somehow I thought this could happen. My parents taught me about these things."

"These things?"

"Impermanence, that people can be lost. They grew up in Cambodia."

"Neary," I say, "can I ask you a favor?"

She nods.

"Can I leave you my u.D contacts and ask you to contact me if you think of anything that might be relevant?"

"What do you think happened to her?" Neary asks.

"I really don't know, but I promise you I'll do my best to find out. Are you going to be okay?"

She nods but I'm not so sure.

We wave our u.Ds toward each other before I get into my car.

I tap in Joseph from the road.

"Abraham," he says.

"Surveillance cameras at UMKC?"

"At the Hospital Hill Café and in the parking lot."

"Can we get the feeds from Monday at around 3:40?"

"I don't think so, boss. They'll only show them to the police."

"Anything else?"

"I called the security company that does the electronic surveillance for from Whitehall. I told them I was calling from the Whitehall Homeowners Association and wanted to see the feeds from Monday. They put me on hold for a moment then told me they'd already told the police that the feeds had been scrambled for about an eight-hour period that day. She said that sometimes happens when there's too much interference in the area."

"Wow," I say, "at just the time MaryLee seems to have died."

"Looks like it," Joseph says. "And Carol Stock just checked in to the downtown Marriott. She was early, so they put her in another room. It's 933."

6

My three gentle knocks barely register on the door.

I hear shuffling inside room 933 but no footsteps approaching.

I knock harder.

"Who is it?"

The harsh male voice throws me. "Rich Azadian from the *Kansas City Star.*"

"What do you want?" the gruff voice asks.

"I'd like to speak with Carol Stock."

I don't know what to make of the ensuing silence.

"Nobody here cares to speak with you," the voice says after a pause.

"With whom do I have the pleasure of speaking?" I ask, unable to contain my inner smart-ass.

"That's none of your concern. Do I need to call security?"

"No need to call security," I say, "I'm leaving now."

Why would someone accompanying a grieving mother not care to identify himself and threaten to call security? I walk down the hall to the small enclave and hide in the shadow beside the ice machine to get a clear line of sight to the room.

After about forty-five minutes the door opens and a man's head pops out, looking right then left down the corridor. Hearing the sound of footsteps walking toward me, I slide deeper into the dark space. I only get a glimpse of the two people walking by, a heavyset woman whom I immediately identify as Carol Stock and a lanky priest with dark hair looking to be in his mid-thirties.

I hear the elevator bell ring and the door open and close before rushing to the elevator bank to follow. I find them just outside the lobby door waiting for the valet to bring a car.

"Hello," I say, unable to think of anything more creative.

Carol Stock looks at the priest as if expecting him to take charge.

He steps between her and me. "I presume you are the reporter from the *Kansas City Star*," he says.

"I am."

"Then you must know why we are here."

"I do."

"And you must understand why we'd like to be left alone."

"I do," I say, remaining where I am.

The priest's angled face contorts as rage passes from his body to his face to his eyes and then at me. "Now," he orders.

I take a step back. "And you are?"

He glares at me for the few moments until the car arrives and the two get in and drive away.

I hit speed dial 3 on my u.D.

"Abraham."

"Joseph, can you find out who else may be staying in room 933?"

"I already have that record up, boss, it's just Carol Stock."

"Then how about anyone else who checked in at around the same time and may be staying in a room near hers?"

"I'll call you back in five minutes."

I wander through the lobby waiting for the call, stopping for a moment in front of the large screen blanketing the bar wall. The AJN reporter is describing yet another aggressive march on Washington by religious leaders and their followers shouting that the emerging field of synthetic biology, making life out of inert elements, is an affront to God's plan. It's not an official King rally, but it may as well be.

The u.D vibrates.

"Room 935," Joseph says, "checked in two minutes after Carol Stock. The name is Ezekial DeWitt."

"And he is?"

"I'm just calling that up on my screen now. Ezekial DeWitt, thirty-five years old, associate pastor of the Holy Virgin Church of Christ, originally from Texas. Graduate of Southern Methodist University with a Master's degree in biology."

"From Cobalt Becker's church?"

"Yes, boss."

"That's interesting," I say. "I just learned from one of MaryLee's classmates at the pharmacy school that MaryLee was involved with Becker's church and mentioned it was difficult being the 'chosen one.'"

"What does that mean, boss?"

"I don't know," I say pensively. "Keep working on the surveillance feeds. We'll talk later."

Images of Cobalt Becker invade my mind as the call drops.

Anyone interested in Missouri politics, let alone political junkies like me, knows about Becker, at least since the 2020 elections. Now, in the run-up to the 2024 presidential race, he's become a key national voice in the raging culture wars and one of Senator King's most important backers.

Being a "spiritual advisor" to King was one thing when it was just politics but another when things started to get really ugly.

Both then Governor Lewis and Senator King had denounced the bombs detonated at two biotech research centers and three abortion clinics that led to fourteen deaths around the time of the 2020 Republican primaries. A secretive group of evangelical zealots called Eden's Army, which had pledged to use "all Godly force necessary" to defend the sanctity of life, was eventually blamed for the attacks. The group had no official tie to King but the experience made clear that many of King's followers were answering to a higher authority.

In spite of the violence, the cause marched on with Becker

right behind Senator King, Bible in hand, leading his dedicated army of salvation. If Lewis and Alvarez's centrist alliance of Democrats and Republicans was calling for the renewal of America, King positioned himself at the vanguard of the religious right by calling for the country's reincarnation. If Lewis finished his speeches with the requisite "God bless America," King took it one step further with "God shall overcome."

People like Cobalt Becker had been almost irrelevant when the country was obsessed with its bond rating or the perceived growing danger of fast-rising China. When culture and morality re-emerged as the great dividing issues in American politics and interpreting God's will once again became an incredible source of power, suddenly they were kingmakers.

Well, I remind myself, almost King-makers. King lost the nomination to Lewis in 2020, but now all bets are off as King, backed by the evangelical surge, prepares to challenge the president once again for the 2024 Republican nomination.

Is it news that someone from Becker's church dies a premature death? Probably not. Is it news that the church sends a minister with the grieving mother down to Kansas City? Doubt it. Is it news that the priest acts suspiciously, refuses to identify himself, and has a mien filled with rage? Add a track mark and scrambled surveillance feed? Is it news that Cobalt Becker is involved in anything even borderline questionable just when his support for Senator King could potentially be the deciding factor in determining the next Republican candidate for the presidency of the United States?

"The question is at least *juicy*," I say to myself as I head down Highway 7 South to Springfield.

Z

There are two shrines in Springfield, Missouri.

The first is the Bass Pro Shop. The magnitude of the 500,000-square-foot log cabin on steroids with its endless departments and indoor fishing stream seems designed to overwhelm the senses.

The second, just a few miles away, is built to inspire a similar awe. Holy Virgin Church of Christ looks from the outside more like a shopping mall than a church. The building leans forward with a central spire reaching for the sky and the two smaller points, one on each side, ready to hug, or perhaps swallow, the Lilliputians approaching the door.

When I'd announced to my friends from U.C. Davis I was moving to Kansas City, all anyone could think of was the Wizard of Oz. This is Missouri, not neighboring Kansas, but maybe, I think, as I enter the oversized glass doors of the Holy Virgin Church of Christ, Oz exists and I've found it.

The full interior wall above the reception desk is a massive screen with the enormous digital image of Reverend Cobalt Becker opening his arms wide then beckoning me in. The image then fades and is overtaken by a bright light. Slowly, bit by bit, new images are woven into the scene. First brown dirt blows and settles on the ground. Then a river begins to trickle through. Vegetation grows under the rising sun until a rabbit hops into the picture and wiggles its nose, followed by birds and deer. It's only when a snake slithers toward an apple tree that I finally recognize what I am witnessing.

"Hi, may I help you?"

I'm so mesmerized by the images that the words startle me.

The receptionist's thick makeup and auburn hair pulled tightly back in a bun give her a severe but attractive Miss America look.

"Yes, ma'am," I say, finally focusing on her. "I'm looking for Reverend Becker."

"We're all looking for Reverend Becker," she says dreamily in a mild Southern accent.

Her comment hangs awkwardly in the air.

"I'm from the *Kansas City Star*. I'm looking into the death of the member of this congregation."

She taps her u.D.

"Becky," she whispers, "there's a gentleman here from the *Kansas City Star* who says he wants to speak with the pastor about the death of a member of the congregation."

The receptionist listens earnestly for a moment to the voice coming through her earpiece. "No, he did not," she says. She nods in response to what she is hearing. "Yes, ma'am," she replies before tapping off. She focuses her eyes on me. "Mister . . . ?"

"Azadian."

She bites her lower lip for a fraction of a second as if trying to figure out what I am. "Mr. Azadian, please have a seat in the waiting room. Rebecca Stevenson will come greet you in a moment."

Our business completed, her face returns to its neutral state of bliss.

The interaction somehow bothers me.

I don't remember when precisely I'd become so suspicious of organized religion, especially on this larger-than-life scale. It hit me early on in Armenian school that no matter how much I valued doing the right thing, the institutions designed to make people do it in the name of one ultimate truth generally ended up corrupting themselves, killing people, or doing bad in the name of good. After Astrid's death, the whole edifice seemed even more ridiculous to me.

On top of that, I could never get over the whole virgin birth thing. My mind rolls through the options I'd so carefully contemplated in Armenian Orthodox Sunday school.

Option one. Mary is visited by the Holy Spirit, a mysterious entity no one has ever before heard of, and impregnated. This Holy Spirit, *I think that's what he said his name was*, transfers a full set of genetic material to link with Mary's and a beautiful baby boy pops out. Which haplogroup did the Holy Spirit belong to again?

Option two. Mary has a fling with a dashing herdsman from down valley or an itinerant carpet salesman from the Bethlehem suburbs. A couple of months later she feels the bulge in her stomach and starts to panic. What is she going to tell her loyal and trusting husband? They've never slept together, so a whole range of excuses are off the table. She frets, she tosses and turns. Then the idea comes to her in a dream. It was a virgin birth, the Holy Spirit visited, that's who.

Poof. A new religion is born and tens of millions of people are slaughtered in the name of this white lie over the next two thousand years. Makes a person want to be careful about what stories they spin to their spouse. *I wasn't having an affair honey, I was out bowling.* Poof. The crusaders are marching with fire in their eyes to punish the pagan heretics who dare defy the magic bowling god.

Or maybe Joseph was just the dad.

Of course, I was kicked out of Sunday school class repeatedly for my irreverence.

My eyes wander around the waiting room.

The large images flashing across the digital wall tell *the* story. A fresh, thin Cobalt Becker, his young wife beside him, hammering a sign into the ground in front of a small, dilapidated church. SERVICES SUNDAY, 10:00, COME HUNGRY, YOUR SOUL WILL BE SERVED.

The next image, clearly taken inside the same church, captures the energy of the long-haired rock band, the rapturous faces of the packed congregants, the confident smirk of the slightly larger Cobalt Becker at the front of the dais.

In the third, a rounder Becker, his wife and two small children beside him, stands with arms outstretched like Moses in front of a bigger church. Congregants wander in the foreground like new homeowners.

The next images are almost a series. Becker with the Republican governor of Missouri, a larger Becker cutting a ribbon in front of an office building with a banner reading INSPIRATION MINISTRIES, a smiling Becker with headphones in a radio studio, Becker in a cowboy hat surrounded by cattle.

At the groundbreaking photo for the current site, I recognize most of the state Republican dignitaries, especially Senator King. King was no dummy. The most successful businessman in the impoverished boot heel of Missouri's southeast corner, he had planted political seeds around the state for years with strategic contributions to Republican candidates, all of whom then backed his election as chairman of the state party. It had been among the state's worst-kept secrets he wanted more. But a business leader with strategic political backing and no political base does not a successful politician make. King probably felt the same. That's when he, so to speak, found Jesus.

King rode the Christian agenda all the way to the US Senate, the evangelical army, Cobalt Becker at its head, charging behind him all the way. King pushed legislation that promoted school prayer, sought to restrict stem cell, cloning, and biotechnology research, tried to block the use of chimeric embryos in research, funded a national media campaign to encourage people to have children through good old-fashioned sex rather than by genetic selection at IVFGS clinics. His fiery rhetoric reignited an evangelical passion previously thought by many Americans to have dimmed and created the environment where secretive evangelical militants like Eden's Army began to thrive. Evangelicals running for slots in local school boards is part of the democratic process, but Eden's Army operatives infiltrating local health systems or even federal government agencies to undermine critical research, was quite another. And that was the gentle stuff.

No one could technically blame King for the bombings and violent protests attributed to these evangelical operatives who fashioned themselves as modern Knights Templar defending the True Faith, but it was abundantly clear that the ideology and political force of his movement had been shifting the American landscape well before the 2020 attacks.

The original Mrs. Becker seems to have vanished from the scene in the groundbreaking photo as a new woman, younger and slimmer, appears in the background.

The last image in the series, with minor changes, could have been from *Rolling Stone*. Viewed from the back of the church, Becker stands triumphantly with one microphoned arm in the air. The congregation is on its feet with the energy from the stage pulsating through their hands. He has arrived.

The series is designed to impress and I'm feeling it as a heavily made-up woman looking to be in her forties marches toward me purposefully.

"Mr. Azadian," she declares pointedly, "I am Rebecca Stevenson, assistant to Revered Becker."

I stand up.

"Please sit down. Miss Taylor tells me you are here investigating the death of a member of our congregation."

"Yes."

"Mr. Azadian, can you tell me the name of the congregant to whom you are referring?"

"MaryLee Stock."

"We have over fifteen thousand members of this congregation and the death of any of our family, in spite of what comes next, is a cause of sadness. What can we do for you, Mr. Azadian?" She speaks officiously and without emotion. Her constant repetition of my name feels somehow creepy.

"I'd like to speak with Reverend Becker," I say.

"Mr. Azadian," she says again, "as you can appreciate, Reverend Becker is a very busy man."

"Yes, but it's important I speak with him."

"If you will please leave me your card I will let you know when the Reverend might be available."

The shopping center sanctimoniousness of this place begins to get to me. "Look," I say sharply, "a member of this church is dead and I'm trying to figure out why. I drove here from Kansas City and," I soften my tone, "I'd like to speak with Reverend Becker."

"Mr. Azadian," she replies brusquely, barely masking her annoyance, "most everyone who lives in this state is a member of one church or another. I will make this request. We will get back to you. Thank you." She opens the door and walks forcefully across the foyer.

I follow her. "Excuse me," I press. "I'm sorry to bother you. This story is coming out soon and I can write that you are being cooperative or I can write that you are not." I know I'm taking a leap but can't think of anything better to do.

Rebecca Stevenson stops in her tracks and turns toward me, barely suppressing the anger on her face. "What are you suggesting, Mr. Azadian?"

"I'm trying to figure out what happened and I need to speak with Reverend Becker."

If I'd been less agitated I might have noticed the shadow approaching from my left. Instead, I'm startled when I hear the familiar bass.

"Shalom, friend."

I've come to his home, but I'm still surprised to encounter him. I've seen his image so many times but never met him in person. He is bigger than I'd imagined, his face rounder, his silver mane more lion-like. His masculine presence radiates through the room. I'm speechless.

"You are here to discuss MaryLee Stock?" Cobalt Becker booms.

My mouth shifts to form words that don't come.

8

"It's a terrible, terrible tragedy," Becker says, opening a side door. "Please step into my office."

As Rebecca Stevenson steps away obsequiously, I pause for a moment, still stunned, before following Becker.

His spacious office is tastefully decorated with more framed photographs of him with famous people and various Christian images. Something inexplicable triggers a sense of alert in my mind.

"Please, have a seat," he says. His voice is strangely reassuring.

The plush ivory sofa almost swallows me in its softness. My mind whirls, trying to figure out what's bothering me.

"Mr. Azadian"—Becker's eyes bear into mine—"I'm glad you are here."

My Wizard of Oz images flow together. Becker the Wizard, Becker the Lion, Becker the Witch—which one? I'd come thinking West. In his presence, I find myself melting toward East.

"You are?" I reply, dumbfounded.

"Of course. I learned of MaryLee's death yesterday. It is a terrible tragedy that someone so young, with such promise, could be taken from us so prematurely."

I nod like an idiot.

"God must have a higher purpose for her," Becker continues, "perhaps one we can never understand."

Becker's words trouble me. "I don't know, Reverend," I say delicately. "I actually saw her dead body yesterday." The body on the apartment floor didn't look to me like a contribution to any cosmic master plan.

I'm not sure why I add the part about the body. Whatever the reason, I notice a shift in his energy, as if the champ has taken a blow to the stomach but knows he shouldn't show it hurts.

Becker crosses his legs and places his hands together on his lap, fingers interlocked. He looks distracted for a moment then regains his composure. "MaryLee was a special girl. She and her mother have been congregants here from the beginning."

The mention of her mother jolts my recognition. My head turns toward an image of Mary and Jesus in a golden frame behind Becker's desk. The blue shawl over Mary's face captures the light shining up from baby Jesus's halo. Her pale skin and white clothing embody an essence of purity within the darker blue shades that form the edges of the painting.

Becker notices my shifting attention. "It's who we are," he says.

My face registers I'm not following.

"That painting. It shows the purity in all of us that can shine when we open ourselves to the illumination of Jesus."

"I see," I say softly.

Becker eyes me suspiciously as I stand and walk over to the painting.

"It's a nice painting," I say slowly, "and this box?" My hands tremble slightly as I reach down toward the gold clasp on the cherry box.

From the corner of my eye I see Becker jump up and move quickly in my direction.

I open the clasp and swing open the lid before he reaches me. The box is lined with red velvet. In the middle rests a small golden ball, with sections for what look like white stones on one side of the ball and brown stones on the other.

Becker slows down and regains his composure. "It's gold, frankincense, and myrrh," he says calmly.

"The gifts of the wise men brought to Mary and Joseph."

"I see you know your Bible, Mr. Azadian," Becker says with a half smile, "there may be hope for you yet."

"MaryLee Stock had the same box and the same picture in her house."

"I know," he says calmly. "We gave them to her as gifts when she started graduate school."

"Is that something you normally do?"

"Sometimes. Why do you ask?"

I change the subject. "I was in Kansas City yesterday and met your associate, Reverend DeWitt."

"Yes," Becker says, "I sent him there to look after Carol Stock."

"You do that normally, too?"

"Sometimes," Becker says again, this time with a slight edge. "Are you getting at something?"

"Just trying to get a fuller picture of her. MaryLee was adopted, yes?"

Becker starts to look annoyed, then tilts back his head and takes a deep breath. "MaryLee has been part of the community since childhood."

"Can you tell me more about her adoption?"

"Nothing really to tell."

"Were you involved in it?"

"What exactly do you mean, Mr. Azadian?"

"All Blessings International. I understand that you were on their board," I say, throwing out another strange coincidence Joseph had sent me during my drive to Springfield.

"I was," Becker says coolly, "and the significance of that?"

"I'm just trying to learn as much about MaryLee as I can. Did you have any role in MaryLee's adoption?"

"Not really. Carol asked me for my counsel and I connected her with All Blessings. She adopted the child."

"From Romania?"

"You obviously know the answer to that question, Mr. Azadian.

Many children were being adopted from Romania then, just like so many are being adopted from Bangladesh today. These things seem to go in waves."

"Were you involved with MaryLee as a child?" I ask clumsily.

"Why are you asking me these questions, Mr. Azadian?"

"I'm trying to learn more about who MaryLee Stock was."

"She was a member of the flock, an active member of our youth group, a special girl, smart, athletic, kind."

"When was the last time you saw her?"

"Around three months ago. She was home visiting her mother at the end of the summer and dropped by."

"Did you notice anything different about her at that time?"

"Such as?" Becker says curtly.

"Like she was sick in some way?"

"I didn't."

"Anything different than what you'd seen previously?"

"What are you getting at, Mr. Azadian?" Becker says sharply, his voice projecting a sense of pity for me. "If you have something to say, say it. MaryLee Stock's death is a cause of sadness. Her life is a cause of celebration. She is now with Our Father." He pauses to let his words sink in before speaking. "Let me ask you a question, Mr. Azadian."

I nod.

"What do you think happened to MaryLee? How do you think she . . . passed?" he says in a softer tone.

"I don't know," I say honestly. "It's not natural for a young, seemingly healthy woman to just die. They're doing an autopsy, but we won't know the results for a few days."

"I see," he says calmly before standing. "I ask that you let me know if you learn anything more about MaryLee. Thank you for your visit."

As he begins to move toward the door I remain where I am.

"Reverend," I say, "I have a few more questions, and I'd like to get another quote from you, if I may."

Becker does not move back in my direction. "I just have a few moments, Mr. Azadian."

"I learned from a friend of hers that MaryLee once said she felt a lot of pressure being the 'chosen one.' Do you have any idea what that might mean?"

"I'm sorry, I don't," Becker says without inflection, his impatience with my refusal to leave growing. "All who believe are chosen by God."

"What can you tell me about Carol Stock?"

Becker sighs. "Carol is a fine woman."

"Was she a good mother?"

"Our church has a long history of pious mothers—Sarah, Rachel, Hannah, Ruth."

"And she was one?"

"In that spirit," he says as if speaking to a child.

I nod like one.

"This is a time of mourning for Mrs. Stock, of shiva," Becker continues. "I think it best for her to be left in peace. The Lord has taken MaryLee Stock. We can never fully understand his ways, and our sadness is tempered by our absolute faith in God's plan. You can use that as your quote, Mr. Azadian."

I want to ask Becker about politics, about abortion and the stem cell debate, about his relationship with Senator King, about where the line between religion and politics should be drawn, but my time is clearly running out.

"Will you preside at the funeral?"

The same blank look flashes across his face for the briefest of moments before his magnanimous composure returns. "I don't know, Mr. Azadian. Bless you." He reaches out his hand.

As I take it, my resolve suddenly disappears. I feel almost overwhelmed by him, uncontrollably sucked into his irresistible orbit. "Thank you, Reverend," I say. I have no idea where my words are coming from.

I rush out the door feeling like an asshole.

2

Stumbling through the parking lot, I feel the irrepressible need to get away from the strange power of Cobalt Becker, to breathe the Kansas City air still trapped in my car to remind me who I am.

What happened there? I ask myself. What came over me?

I take three deep breaths, look out on the garish architecture and the real me resurfaces. The errant synapses fire through my mind, failing to connect but leaving me with an embryonic sense of unease.

I put in my earbud and tap speed dial 3 on my u.D. Joseph's face pops onto my dashboard screen.

"Start digging deeper on Cobalt Becker," I say.

"How do you mean, boss?"

"I don't know. Find out about his past, his businesses, his relationships. See what you can find behind the headlines."

"Um, okay. Yes, boss. I'll see what I can do."

I recognize that my request is not at all focused. "What else did you learn?"

"Well, for one, 3927 doesn't appear to be the last four digits of MaryLee Stock's credit card number."

"And you know this because?"

Joseph sighs. "Because I called the phone company and they wouldn't let me in to the account."

"And the surveillance cameras, can we get the feeds?"

"UMKC needs a warrant. Corner Drug says they don't share."

"Joseph," I say, "do me a favor. Call Corner Drug and say that your blue Kia Curve was broken into when you were parked there two days ago but you didn't realize it until you got home. Tell them that it happened at around 4:40 p.m. Okay?"

"Yes, boss," he says, I'm sure wondering whether a stupid US visa is really worth this aggravation.

The connection drops.

I lean back and take a deep breath. My mind flips through the disparate clues, arranging and rearranging them, waiting for something to pop.

A girl dies. So what? People die all the time. We're born. We kick around for a while. We die leaving scant trace. But who can comprehend the ultimate vastness of time and space, maybe it's enough to treasure the meaning we have, every part of it, every life.

As the strange coincidences pile up, something nags at me, makes me feel increasingly obsessed with adding up the pieces of a lost life to see if anything closer to a coherent or even semi-coherent narrative can be put together. The world may be shattered, but what would it mean to be able to piece a small part of it together?

I tap my u.D to direct me to the Stock house and pull out of the Holy Virgin driveway. Left on Holy Virgin Lane, right on Broad Street, left on Summit Drive. From Virgin to Broad, I think to myself, a quick fall from grace.

The small and rectangular house reminds me of Toni's parents' place in Independence, Missouri. The image of Toni, as usual, starts a cascade in my mind.

How could any two even moderately well-developed adults ever be matched, I wonder. I understand completely how my grandparents had done it in Ottoman times. When you're fifteen and in an arranged marriage, life is not so complicated. You are a stem cell that can grow in thousands of different directions and encounter a vast number of possible matches. When you are thirty-nine with a lifetime of opinions, preferences, delusions, aspirations, fantasies, habits, ideals, idiosyncrasies, and tastes, when you've become comfortable with a life of semi-sociable solitude, you are like a toenail cell, just doing your thing over and over again and increasingly unsuited for compromise.

Maybe the Christians had it right, I think. All of this relationship stuff is challenging. Maybe it's better to find a sweet virgin, let God plant a magic seed in her, and poof, you've got a messiah. It seems a lot easier than dating.

As I begin my drive back to Kansas City, the errant synapses begin to connect, first slowly then with greater and greater intensity. Holy Virgin Church of Christ, MaryLee's sickness, the package of women's vitamins in MaryLee's apartment, the look on Becker's face when I'd mentioned the dead body, frankincense and myrrh, the "chosen one," Becker's masculine energy. Could it be? The idea seems far-fetched.

I tap my u.D frenetically. "Universal image search. Keywords: gold, frankincense, myrrh, box, golden clasp, red velvet." The exact image is the fourteenth option on Alibaba popping up on my dashboard screen. *The ultimate box for welcoming the Messiah, made with Jerusalem Cedar and 24 karat gold.* Somehow I am not surprised when I see the price: $29,950.

How many of those are you giving away, Cobalt Becker? I ask myself.

Now my mind is on fire. "What did Becker say about Carol Stock?" I say aloud. "She was from a history of pious mothers like Sarah, Rachel, and Hannah." My time in the principal's office detracted from my learning in Sunday school, but wasn't Hannah the mother of Virgin Mary?

I tap speed dial 3 on my u.D.

"Yes, boss," he says, with even more exasperation.

"Joseph," I say breathlessly. "I need you to check out something as quickly as possible."

"Boss?"

"Go to Corner Drug. Write down for me the name and cost of every early pregnancy test they have in the store."

10

It hits me as I speed down 13 North through Osceola.

What the hell am I thinking?

Cobalt Becker had almost frightened me with his charismatic power. I'd felt unsteady and unsettled when I'd stumbled to my car. But how had I taken the leap so quickly between Becker seeming sad about MaryLee's death to his potentially being much more intimately involved?

I remember the note my friend Noam Kugelmass once passed me in the U.C. Davis library. "WWWOOD?" It had taken me a few minutes, but I finally figured out his implicit critique of my overactive mind. What would William of Occam do? If the fourteenth-century English theologian were here in my 2018 Hyundai, he wouldn't be encouraging me to conjure up a theory out of whole cloth. He'd apply his principle, Occam's razor to figure out the simplest and most logical explanation.

According to Occam's principle of parsimony, a person trying to solve a problem shouldn't make more assumptions than the minimum number needed. Although the principle has huge consequences for math, science, and philosophy, its practical implications are what my mother has admonished me to do since I was a child. "Don't make your life difficult." The advice didn't stick.

My mind conjures the frocked theologian to the passenger seat.

"Fuhst," Occam says, "isn't it simplest to assume she may have died of Blue Magic, whatever cauldron of sorcery that is, or of natural causes? Second, what makes you think she's pregnant? Thuhd . . ."

"Excuse me, Occam," I say in my head, "we're just passing Burger King. Would you care for anything?"

I actually laugh aloud at my exchange with my mental projection.

"Thuhd, even if she were pregnant," my internal Occam continues, "is Becker the most likely father? Wasn't she a graduate student surrounded by billowing waves of testosterone?"

Occam's razor is making mincemeat of my flimsy theory. I hit speed dial 3.

"Yeah, boss."

"Abraham, where are you?"

"Heading down Troost, will be at Corner Drug in about five minutes."

"One more job for you."

"Yes, boss," he says slowly, bracing himself for yet another illogical demand.

"Can you make a list of everything in the store that costs $10.95 and the same for $24.95?"

I can hear the air pressing out of Joseph's nose, then a grunt as the connection drops.

"Fifth," the struggling-to-be-logical side of my brain now inquires, "are you even positive you've got the right garbage for MaryLee Stock? Aren't you, my good man, putting a lot of weight on a neatly squeezed toothpaste tube?"

Occam, you're killing me.

"Sixth, you gormless scullion," Occam charges on, "have you stopped to consider that surveillance feeds might actually be interrupted from time to time . . ."

"Did they even have surveillance feeds in fourteenth-century England?" my mind fires back.

"Bollocks," Occam replies, "or that the painting of Mary and

Jesus and the gift box were reasonable gifts from a multimillion-aire pastor?"

I speed forward impatiently, accelerating unevenly in contrast with the smooth flow of driverless cars in the AVO, Autonomous Vehicles Only, lanes beside me. The contrast feels like a metaphor for my life.

I read passing electronic billboard screens, trying to distract myself while I wait for Joseph's call.

NEED A NEW LIFE? GOD ACCEPTS TRADE-INS.

IF GOD DOESN'T MATTER TO HIM, say the block letters above the blurry image of a black man with a shaking gun, DO YOU? WWW.ANSWERSINGENESIS.ORG.

A billboard reading RIGHTEOUSNESS EXALTETH A NATION, BUT SIN IS A REPROACH TO ANY PEOPLE: THE BLOOD OF JESUS CLEANSETH US FROM ALL SIN, towers above a large red, white, and blue sign reading KING FOR PRESIDENT, the "T" at the end of the word "President" forming an illuminated cross.

IF YOU DIED TODAY, WHERE WOULD YOU SPEND ETERNITY?, reads another sign. The eyes of Jesus on the cross track my car as I speed past.

JESUS IS COMING—ARE YOU READY?

The signs begin to bother me. Everyone has a right to choose their own religion, but when one group tries to force itself on others is when I start to have problems. The surging evangelicals have every right to live as they please, but not to force the rest of us to live like them. We're not living through the Inquisition in 2023 America but the same quality of intolerance is brewing.

WANDER INTO THE LION'S DEN—WHERE LOVERS SHOP.

Finally, I think, as I pass through Clinton, somebody has a sense of humor or at least recognizes the intimate link between sexual and religious passion.

"Joseph," I say to my windshield, "what the hell is taking so long?"

I tap my u.D just as I feel the vibration. "Talk to me."

Joseph's face appears on the dashboard screen. "Boss, it's going to take me a little while to look at everything in the store, but I thought you'd want to know that the Accu-Clear Early Pregnancy Test costs $10.95."

I breathe in.

"Another thing, boss."

"Yes?"

"They had a look at the surveillance feeds. No one bumped my blue Kia Curve when it was here yesterday at 4:40."

I feel an electric current surge up my spine. "What time does the store close?" I say with a new urgency.

"In ten minutes, at seven."

"Make your lists and email them to me when you have them."

"Yes, boss."

"And Joseph."

"Yes?"

"Thank you."

He stares at me briefly before looking down. The connection drops.

Occam is still holding court inside my head, but if MaryLee's car was at Corner Drug two days ago, then I definitely have her garbage. And if a pregnancy test costs $10.95, there's at least a decent chance . . .

I tap my u.D to place the call.

"Neary, it's Rich Azadian," I say, feeling the urge to bombard her with questions. A better part of me takes hold. "I wanted to see how you are doing."

"It's tough, Mr. Azadian," she says respectfully. "I still can't believe it."

"I'm so sorry," I say awkwardly. I let the silence settle, feeling badly for pushing on. "Do you mind if I ask you a couple more questions."

"It's okay, Mr. Azadian."

"You told me this morning that MaryLee had been feeling sick. Can you tell me more about her symptoms?"

"She just seemed slow, tired. She had a bit of a sour look on her face."

"Was it obvious?"

"Not really. MaryLee was a very positive person."

"Neary, I'm going to ask you a question that may surprise you."

"Okay."

"Do you think that MaryLee could have been pregnant?"

"Oh, no," she says instinctively. "Definitely not."

"Why not?"

"She wasn't dating. She'd taken a chastity pledge."

"Neary," I say, "have you ever been around someone who is pregnant?"

"Yes, of course. Lots of cousins."

"And if you didn't know MaryLee and just observed her symptoms, would you, as a scientist, think she might be pregnant?"

I hear Neary's sigh before she speaks. "As a scientist maybe yes, but I would also observe her as a person, and I can't imagine she was pregnant." Neary pauses. "Do you think she was?"

"I'm starting to think it's possible."

I can hear Neary starting to sniffle.

"I'll let you know if I learn anything. Okay?" I say softly after a pause.

I hear another sniffle. The connection drops.

I make one more call as I speed through Harrisonville.

"Maurice, it's Rich Azadian. I'm driving back from Springfield. I need to talk with you."

11

If I ever carry my anti-establishment bravado to its full conclusion, I'll certainly wind up another middle-aged guy with a graying ponytail dangling from a balding scalp, poorly fitting jeans, an army surplus jacket, and glimpses of faded tattoos peering from the edges of my sleeves in a rundown place like here, the Broadway Café on Forty-First Street.

I look around with a slight feeling of repulsion. I know they had their day, but that was fifty years ago and what has hippie culture really produced? What would Darwin say about this lifestyle? Has it earned a half-century life span?

But a part of me knows I doth protest too much, that I'm probably not as out of place in this island of lost toys as I'd like myself to believe.

No matter how almost hip I may appear to others, I still often feel that the lanky kid I once was is shadowing me, that I command my space and shrink from it at the same time, too geeky to be hip, too almost hip to be geeky.

I order a "medium" latte, still refusing to use the ever escalating Italian terms for big cups, unfold my monitor, tap my u.D, and start reading through the notes Joseph has sent me on Becker.

Born Christian Cobalt Becker in El Paso, Texas, in 1966, graduate of Texas Christian University and student body president. Churches in Lubbock and Wichita, Kansas, before coming to Springfield. Built Holy Virgin into a megachurch with nearly fifteen thousand congregants every Sunday and a political force first in Missouri and then nationally.

The headlines confirm the story. "Becker Builds Megachurch for the Generations," reads the *Springfield News-Leader*; "Becker Emerges as King-maker of the MO Republican Party," says the *St. Louis Post-Dispatch*. "Becker Leads Silent March on State Legislature," the *Jefferson City News Tribune* reports in an article describing the synthetic biology debate. The irreverent title in the *Dallas Morning News*, "God's Rancher Builds His Herd," describes Becker's sprawling, well-protected cattle ranch in Waco, Texas.

It's strange how all of these old-fashioned newspapers have had a renaissance of late. It wasn't that long ago when people were talking about the blogosphere as if it was a disintermediated citizen's news source. But ever since the Chinese government and the big corporations and anyone else with an interest and some money began to hire their own fifty-cent armies to message away on their behalf and the famed global commons became the global propangandosphere, the idea that Twitter and Facebook were once seen almost as news sources has become laughable. It's sad how completely that world has been wiped out.

With so many of the voices compromised and mistrusted, stories come out of the cybercloud like signs of life come from the stars. They may be there, but the chances of our finding them is slim. With the decentralized communication world of the old Internet completely manipulated and compromised, the country suddenly needed news organizations just as the financial model of the traditional news business was collapsing.

Maurice marches in at 8:42 p.m., looking annoyed, and refocuses my wandering mind. His polo shirt tucked tightly into his khakis makes him look official even though not in uniform. I imagine his children calling him sir at the breakfast table.

"What's this all about?" he asks briskly, not sitting down.

"Can I get you some coffee?" My politeness almost, but not quite, mocks his annoyance for the sheer pleasure of it.

Maurice stares at me with wide, intense eyes.

"It's about MaryLee Stock."

"And?" he says, sitting down.

"I know you guys haven't released her name or made a statement."

"We know that too, Rich."

I look at him blankly.

"We're releasing her name tomorrow," he says with an I-don't-know-why-the-hell-I'm-telling-you-this look on his face.

"We've been doing *our* research and I wanted to compare notes," I say.

"You took me away from my family at eight thirty at night because you wanted to compare damn notes?"

"Any trace of Blue Magic?"

Anger rises up Maurice's face. "You called me here to ask *me* questions?"

"I think I may have something."

"Tell me," he orders.

"If I do, I need to know you'll be square with me, that if I give you something you'll help me," I say, mindful that Maurice probably has no intention of letting me know the Whitehall surveillance cameras were dark when MaryLee Stock died.

"I make no promises," he says.

"I'm not looking for promises, Maurice. I'm going to give you a lead. All I ask is that you let me know if this goes anywhere."

"I won't promise," Maurice says again, this time more assertively.

I construe this as a deal. "What do you know of Cobalt Becker?"

Maurice leans against the back of his chair. "Same as everyone else. Telepastor, Republican kingmaker, conservative standard-bearer. Why?"

I take a deep breath. "MaryLee was from Springfield. She was a member of Becker's Holy Virgin Church of Christ."

"This is earth-shattering, Rich. The junior pastor was in my office today."

Maurice is starting to get annoyed. I realize I need to start with the punch line and work backward.

"MaryLee Stock may have been pregnant."

Maurice puts two hands face down on each side of the chair to straighten himself out. "I'm listening."

"You're not going to like this," I add after laying out my pre-liminary case, "but yesterday I found MaryLee Stock's garbage bag at Whitehall."

He flashes me a sharp look.

"I know I shouldn't have done that."

"Damn right you shouldn't have."

"Arrest me later. First let me tell you what I know."

Maurice lifts his eyebrows.

"I didn't find the syringe I was looking for in her garbage, but I did find two receipts. One for the UMKC coffee shop and the other for Corner Drug."

"Did they have her name on them?"

"No," I say, "but I confirmed with Corner Drug that Mary Lee was there at the time the receipt was given."

"How?"

"Her car was there. A blue Kia Curve."

"When?"

"4:41 Monday."

"Go on."

"I spoke with one of her classmates who told me that MaryLee had been feeling nauseous for the past couple of months."

Maurice signals with his head for me to go on.

"The classmate thought she couldn't be pregnant because MaryLee was a committed virgin without a boyfriend."

Maurice nods.

"There were three items on MaryLee's Corner Drug receipt. The receipt didn't say what was sold, just the price."

"Why not?"

"It's a mom-and-pop store. I have no idea. The receipts were for $10.95, $24.95, and $1.65. One of the do-it-yourself pregnancy tests costs $10.95 at Corner Drug."

"And this is your police work?"

I tell him about the wooden box of frankincense and myrrh, the picture of Jesus and Mary, Becker's reactions to my words.

"Are you done?" he says when I stop speaking.

I nod cautiously.

"So you don't trust Becker, MaryLee was sick, she's got a painting of Jesus in her apartment and a damn box, and a pregnancy test costs $10.95," Maurice says, getting more agitated as he speaks. "That's what you called me out to tell me. If jock itch spray also costs $10.95 will you call me back to say she had that?"

I suddenly feel amateurish and insecure. "If they find out that she's pregnant, can we talk more?" I say, trying to hide my newfound lack of confidence.

"If they find out she's pregnant," Maurice says slowly, "I'm coming to you for an astrological reading." He chuckles indignantly then stands to leave.

"You also might want to get the feeds from the UMKC Hospital Hill Café surveillance cameras at 3:40 p.m. on Monday, October 16," I throw out.

Maurice shakes his head from side to side and turns toward the door.

"Any trace of Blue Magic?"

"The autopsy is being released tomorrow," he says over his shoulder as he walks out.

12

As I amble to the car, I feel the first hint of looming winter on my face and see the small red dot blinking on my u.D. I somehow sense intuitively who it represents. I tap my u.D, and the voice flows through my earbud and into my subconscious.

"Dikranigus, *janeegus, gyankus.*"

Janeegus, my dear, is to be expected. *Gyankus*, my life, is often a precursor to something that's going to make me feel inadequate.

It's not just the words. It's not just my mother. It's not just the hundreds of years of history underpinning both. It's all three combined into a sometimes overwhelming mix.

My great-grandparents' little village in Ottoman-ruled Armenia, Sepastia, had been a universe unto itself. The extent of life, by and large, was, at least until genocide and war intervened, the limit of the village. The few who could get out did and came to places like America, where they suppressed their memories of death and created mental replicas of their same little villages inside the large metropolises they put up with but never fully occupied. That generation was passionate about preserving their culture and educating their kids. They did both with great success.

Following in their footsteps, my grandparents put enormous energy into making sure my mother never fully entered the modern world. I remember finding an old photograph from her wedding. She and my dad touching their crowned heads together, symbolic Armenian king and queen harking back to the Middle Ages. I then sensed that the photo represented the only possible future for me as well. In some ways, I've struggled with this legacy all my life, not just the death and destruction from the genocide a century ago, but the fossilization of culture as a historical time capsule that threatened to overtake my individuality if only I'd succumb to its flow. Somehow, my mother's voice always calls me back.

"Dikranigus, I know you're busy, but you said yesterday you'd call."

Yes, I think, then kick myself for thinking, I'm only thirty-nine years old and live half a country away, but of course I should call at least twice a day.

"I know you're a big boy."

Mother.

Even in a prerecorded message, she anticipates my response.

"I'm sorry, Dikranigus, you are a man. But even a man can call his mother from time to time."

I can't help but be drawn into her monologue. Being a now only child of a widowed mother has for the past seventeen years woven us into a sometimes claustrophobic tapestry with the ever-present ghosts of Astrid and my father.

"The Devedjian girl is back in town for a few days."

She knows I remember our ill-fated three dates during a college vacation.

"I know you are a big boy, Dikranigus. Oh, I'm sorry. I said it again. But would it kill you to settle down just a little bit?"

She suddenly seems to realize she's only leaving me a message.

"Oh," she says. I'm not sure who she's talking to, herself or me. "You know I love you. I just worry sometimes. *Bacheegs.*"

The message ends and I'm feeling both love and an almost childlike frustration, the story of my life. I know to my core how much my mother loves me. I know to my core how much I need to be there for her. But I also need to live my own life, to find my own way. The residue is a strange brew of guilt and inadequacy. I fear I am neither supporting my mother enough to be a good son nor making enough progress in finding my own way to justify the cost of my distance.

I pull into my driveway.

In some human form of barn fever, exhaustion takes me as I lumber out of my car and through the back door. The echo of my mother's voice still in my head, Becker's reference to Hannah and other biblical mothers springs forward.

"uSearch Hannah," I mumble to my u.D.

"Text or spoken?" the sexy siren voice I downloaded last year asks.

I know that had I chosen standard male for my u.D voice settings, I'd now be telling the u.D I was too tired to give a fuck, but the female voice somehow soothes me. I take a deep breath, hold it for a few seconds, then exhale. I lift my shoulders and rotate my head in a circle before closing my eyes a few seconds. "Text, please," I say in a fake Indian accent that for some stupid reason makes me smile.

The words pop up in bold print on the screen embedded in my kitchen table.

"The *Apocryphal Gospel of James* describes how Hannah and her husband Joachim, who had suffered years of childlessness, received the visitation of an angel of the Lord who told them they would bear a child. In ultimate gratitude, Hannah dedicated the child to God's service. Joachim and Hannah delivered Mary to the service of the Second Temple in Jerusalem when the girl was three years old. According the church doctrine, Mary was conceived in the normal manner but was protected from the stain of original sin to make her fit to bear Christ."

The number three pulsates through my head as I slip back through my u.D notes. I find it in the first batch of materials Joseph had sent me. MaryLec Stock, adopted from Romania at the age of three by All Blessings International and placed in a family belonging to Becker's church in Springfield.

"You awake?" my dictated message to Joseph reads.

"What do you think?" he replies immediately.

I wonder if it's just my perception or whether Joseph is becoming more of a smart-ass the more reliant on him I become.

"Keep digging on Becker," I mumble into the u.D and watch it shift to text.

"Roger, boss."

"We'll talk in AM. Need you there at seven. Police releasing her name tomorrow."

I sense his groan in the pause before his text reply appears, "Yes, boss."

I know I need to be at work early tomorrow, but I lay in bed unable to sleep. My mind swirls with images of Astrid. She's five years old coming into my room with a plate of sesame cookies she's baked in her Cozy Kitchen Mini Oven. I feel a twinge of guilt as I remember telling her to just leave them on my bed, not looking up from my Nintendo console. I can't remember what I was playing, but for the rest of my life not looking up will remain my personal image for how I failed my little sister. I am thirteen and at soccer practice, trying not to notice my five-year-old baby sister riding her bright red bike in loops around the field. I'm seventeen and forced by my parents to attend her Armenian dance recital, anxious to get the hell out but still noticing how joyously Astrid shakes and prances around the stage dancing the *Kochari*. I'm twenty-two and in a state of shock at the funeral.

The sadness lingers as I start my process of counting backward in my head from one hundred. It's supposed to help me calm my mind, but I always seem to find work-arounds.

Ninety-seven, ninety-six, ninety . . .

I'm sure there are many ways that having such an active mind must have once been a blessing. In prehistoric times they probably stationed people like me near the mouth of caves to be the first to sense an approaching saber-toothed tiger. It must have been a useful skill back then and my ancestors surely got laid repeatedly for having it, passing the now useless restlessness gene down to me.

Eighty-four, eighty-three, eighty . . .

My mind wanders back to MaryLee.

Seventy-two, seventy-one, seventy . . .

"Get to bed, you knotty-pated fool," Occam's voice declares in my head. "You don't even know she was pregnant."

"Oh you, Occam," my voice in my head replies. "I thought you were out clubbing."

13

The 5:30 a.m. alarm only partially penetrates my fog.

I think about running but hit snooze twice before drowsily putting on my running clothes and lumbering unconvincingly down Rainbow, around Penn Valley Park, past Clyde Manor, and back to my place.

Distance: 3.2 miles; Pace: 5.8 mph; Sleep quality: poor, the message on my u.D flashes.

"Don't I know it," I mumble into my wrist, my head still buzzing as I amble down the stairs to my kitchen, ignoring the alerts flashing on my freezerator door and feeling oppressed by my technology. I grab three eggs and two slices of frozen bread for my Haier Breakfast Deluxe machine. I tap the omelet with toast button then place a plate at the mouth of the machine and head upstairs to the shower. In old romantic movies the sounds coming up from my kitchen would be of the beautiful woman whistling, naked but for my business shirt, as she cooks up an omelet. Now, the Chinese machine has stepped in. How strange that the United States and China have such a tense relationship but we live our lives interacting so intimately with so many of the things they make.

The newsroom somehow looks different to me when I arrive at 6:55. Not many people are here, but the few who are seem to me like modern Don Quixotes fighting an unbeatable foe, or at least bearing an unbearable sorrow, for truth. What a difference a day makes.

Joseph, of course, is already at his desk. He starts speaking mid-sentence when he sees me as if he's been conversing with me in his head before I've arrived.

"—UMKC student health records are strongly protected, but the scheduling software is not."

"Have you been here all night?" Joseph looks tired on the best of days, but today looks even worse.

He ignores the question. "I'm not seeing any appointments for MaryLee Stock at the university clinic in the last six months."

"All right."

"There's something else. I was working from home last night," he says without irony, "and I tried to get into her u.M account. I finally got in, and there was nothing there."

"Maybe she didn't use the mail account very much or had a different account," I say.

"Could be," Joseph says, "but I did find records in some of her other classmates' accounts showing they'd sent messages to her at this address."

"Is that odd?"

"Usually when files get erased there's still a record. These ones are gone."

"What do you think that means?"

"I don't know, boss. It's not normal."

"Keep on it, Joseph," I say, catching Martina Hernandez out of the corner of my eye.

"Martina," I yell across the newsroom, "I need to speak with you."

She looks ready to spar but intuits this is not the time. "Come to my office," she says without her usual edge.

I turn back to Joseph.

"Joseph, if she didn't visit the university clinic, where else was she? Did she give blood any time before she died? If she was pregnant, there's got to be an obstetrician or a clinic somewhere in this town that's treated her. I need you to find out who it is."

"Got it, boss," he says softly.

I give him a lot of shit, but there's no one I'd rather have in my corner. I march across the newsroom to Martina's office.

"Talk to me," she says without looking up from the screen covering her desk.

"The police are officially announcing MaryLee Stock's death later this morning. The autopsy is being completed later today."

Martina focuses on her screen.

"I'm willing to bet the autopsy will find she was pregnant," I add.

She looks up.

"And," I continue, "I'm starting to suspect Cobalt Becker could be the father."

I wait for the statement to sink in.

"Fuck." The word seeps from Martina's mouth.

I've rarely seen her so unoriginal.

"Can you prove it?" she asks.

"No."

"What do you have?"

I lay out my findings.

Martina listens intently, but I can't tell if I'm convincing her or not. When I'm done, she stares over my head into a middle distance then speaks as if to herself or to no one.

"King is challenging the president of the United States for control of the Republican party, maybe even for control of the country, and you're telling me that his spiritual advisor and key link to the evangelical community may have gotten a young woman from his church pregnant? Do you have any idea what the implications of this would be? And you think we should just push ahead based on flimflam and conjecture, based on stories made up after stealing a dead woman's garbage? Do you have any clue what it would mean for the *Star* if you got this wrong?" She taps her fingers on the side of her reddened face.

Martina's increasingly agitated response surprises me. After all of the insinuations about what would happen if we didn't bring back "juicy" stories, I could now be on the heels of something big and she suddenly seems cautious.

I try to slow the speeding train. "The autopsy will be completed by the end of the day. If it was Blue Magic or if she was pregnant, at least we should have confirmation soon."

"Let's see what the autopsy says," she says after a deep breath. "Don't take a fucking step without checking with me first. The case you've presented to me so far is bullshit and guesswork."

I quickly turn and rush out of the room before she changes her mind.

14

The magic of life is its imprecision, the multiple narratives constantly unfolding before us. Every step we take, every decision we make, reshuffles the deck of our lives and sets a new trajectory of possibility in motion.

But, here in the KCPD briefing room, life and death get boiled down to their bare essentials.

"Good morning," the public information officer says with a synthetic energy.

The sorry lot of crime reporters doesn't respond. How many of these briefings have they each attended over the years? I've only been at it for three months and am already conditioned to feel disappointed even before the briefing begins.

The officer invites Police Chief Slade Roberts to the podium. Tall and wide, Roberts looks like he had once been an athlete before doughnuts, stakeouts, deskwork, and gravity got the best of him. His expressionless face looks like another victim of glacial melting.

"We announced three days ago that a young woman had been found dead in her apartment at 4704 Oak Street in Kansas City," Roberts drones. "At that time, we were not able to release the name of the deceased. MaryLee Stock, age twenty-four, was a second year Master's student at the University of Missouri Kansas City. We are investigating the cause of her death and will release that information in due course. Thank you."

How much of the poetry of a life is lost in the description Roberts just gave, I wonder.

KCTV9.com's Walter Heming knocks me from my thought. "Is there any indication this was an unnatural death?"

"We are not able to make that determination at this time."

"When will the autopsy results be released?" KCWEB's Barbara Washington asks.

"We are hoping to release them tomorrow or the day after."

The briefing feels like a rerun of an old show. The chief needs to say as little as possible. The reporters need to ask the questions they know won't be answered. Everyone seems half dead. Everyone except for Maurice Henderson and me. Maurice stands behind Chief Roberts saying nothing. I catch his eye for a moment and nod. He doesn't respond.

The chief points at my raised hand.

"Do we know if any evidence of drug use was found in her body?" I ask.

His face remains impassive. "Not that I'm aware of."

The questions keep coming at Roberts, but it's clear that the reporters have to justify their jobs by asking the logical questions and that he's doing his by not budging, raising the question of why the press conference is being held in the first place. After fifteen minutes the chief delivers an inflectionless, "Thank you," and marches out of the room.

All of us reporters head out to file. I may be critical but also know I'm one of them, pushing copy to justify my role in a shrinking corner of a dying industry, following the death of a young white woman when we know full well that young black and Hispanic women in Kansas City die all the time without much fanfare.

I find an empty bench in Ilus Davis Park, tap my u.D, and start dictating. Scanning the park as I speak, I watch a few Latino kids skateboarding a slalom course through the long line of flagpoles. A homeless man with a long beard counts the cans he takes from his shopping cart as he places them in a clear plastic bag. Surrounded by the decay of downtown Kansas City, the green park with its cascading fountains feels like a canyon at the center of yesterday. Then I see her.

Carol Stock sits motionless on a bench looking down. I approach cautiously.

"Excuse me," I say in my softest voice, "Mrs. Stock?"

Her vacant eyes focus slowly and hesitantly on my face.

"I am so terribly sorry about your daughter."

She looks at me with pleading-at-the-universe eyes. Her round body and polyester pantsuit seem wedged into the bench.

"I am Rich Azadian from the *Kansas City Star*. We met Wednesday." I feel guilty for transitioning so quickly from concerned human to cog in the death industry.

The expression on her face becomes even more guarded and inward-looking.

"I really can't talk," she says. "I hope that's okay."

I appreciate her Midwestern graciousness but almost pity her inability to tell me to go to hell.

"I understand, ma'am," I say.

She looks at me blankly, like a wounded bird unable to fly away.

A part of me feels I should just leave her in peace. "Do you mind if I ask you a few questions?"

"Please," she pleads, "just let me be. I'm so sorry."

Her daughter is dead and she is apologizing to me? "Mrs. Stock, I've been assigned to write the story about what happened to your daughter."

"I don't know if we'll ever know," she says hesitantly. "One minute she is a beautiful child and the next minute, the next minute . . ."

"I'm so sorry," I say because I can't think of anything better. "Do you have any idea what happened?"

"I don't understand it." She pauses for a moment then says through her sniffles, "I don't know how this happened to Lee."

My mind takes a moment to readjust. "Lee?"

Carol Stock looks at me as if I'm an alien. "Why are you asking me this? Please."

Constitutionally, I want to leave her alone. Professionally, I can't.

"I'm so sorry, Mrs. Stock," I say the words again, but this time they seem to have a different meaning. I am so sorry to keep pushing when the right thing to do is to stop. "Did you always call her Lee?"

Carol Stock's Eeyore eyes suggest a lifetime of feeling moved by forces beyond her control. "Yes," she says quietly, the words falling from her mouth. "We named her after her grandma Leanne."

"And how did you come up with Mary?"

"The Reverend thought it would be a good name."

"Reverend Becker?"

She nods.

"Did he say why?"

"He said Lee was three when she came to us and Mother Mary was three when she came to the temple in Jerusalem."

My heart begins to pound. "Mrs. Stock, do you know if your daughter had a boyfriend?"

Carol Stock freezes. Then her head jerks back. She stares up at me before her head falls forward as if unsupported by her neck. "She was a good girl," she says softly.

"Mrs. Stock, do you think anyone would want to hurt your daughter, hurt . . . Lee?"

Carol Stock looks at me bewildered. "No, never. Never ever. She was a good person, a kind person. No," she pleads.

An awkward silence descends as Carol hides her face in her hands. "Do you think that's what happened?" she asks softly.

"I don't know, but I promise I will do whatever I can to find out," I say, not sure if my words are noble or predatory. "I'd like to give you my u.D contacts. If you ever want to talk, I hope you'll please call me."

I hold out my u.D. She looks at my hand for a moment then

lifts her right arm. I wave my u.D over hers then pause, wrestling with myself whether I should ask my last question.

As always, charging at the truth wins.

"Mrs. Stock, I know this may be an uncomfortable question for you, but do you think there's any chance MaryLee might have been pregnant?"

Carol Stock looks up at me as if she's been struck by lightning.

"Excuse me?" I hear a man's aggressive voice coming from behind.

Reverend DeWitt is almost running in my direction. "Didn't I tell you to leave us alone?" he fires.

"Nice to see you again, Reverend," I say peevishly.

"Mr. Azadian," he says darkly, pushing uncomfortably into my space, "I've told you to leave us alone. What part of that don't you understand? Have the decency to leave Mrs. Stock alone in her grief."

We stare at each other for a tense moment before I turn my head back toward Carol Stock. "I beg your pardon, Mrs. Stock," I say. "Please let me know if there's anything I can do."

"That's enough, Azadian," DeWitt barks.

I flash DeWitt a barbed scowl, then turn and walk toward my car with one thought in my mind.

The son of a bitch named her Mary.

15

The fact that a true story can never be told does not mean that truth does not exist. Because each of us is unique, we can never fully divorce our observation of something from the thing itself. Just by observing it, we change it and make it our own.

In the Cal philosophy department, this was the central conceit of postmodernism. Texts do not exist in themselves, the French deconstructionist Jacques Derrida told us, we write our own text every time we experience someone else's.

Over time this all seemed like bullshit to me, which may be part of the reason I'm here in Kansas City trying to figure out what happened to MaryLee Stock rather than in Bumblefuck State University trying to convince disinterested jocks that truth is a relative construct, while kids in China are mastering nanobiotics and complex systems engineering.

But maybe, I think, as I arrive at the UMKC's Flarsheim Hall, given the unbelievable complexity of human interactions, the vicissitudes of memory, and the instability of matter, telling an accurate story of what happened in the past is, if not impossible, pretty darn close.

There are so many brazen stereotypes of computer geeks in popular culture. The pasty skin, greasy hair, glasses, ill-fitting clothes, social awkwardness, and up-all-night look of computer experts in Hollywood movies are, I am sure, the bane of many computer professionals who don't have those qualities.

But Jerry Weisberg has most of them. From the moment I met him at the Hyde Park Community Association meeting last year, it was clear that Jerry was pure Dungeons and Dragons. I didn't care that much about how many different bins for various types of recycling people should be required to have, but Jerry was so passionate about it I backed him anyway. It hadn't been a big deal for me, but it somehow meant a lot to him that I'd been on his side, and he'd welcomed me in his awkward sort of way at neighborhood association meetings ever since.

As I open the door to his Department of Computer Science office, I'm not quite sure whether this meager history entitles me to ask him for a favor.

The office feels like a cave. The lights are dim, and the glowing screens covering two of the office's four walls reflect off of Jerry's shiny face. A third is lined by a glass case containing what I instantly recognize as computer equipment from the last century. The room smells like crackers.

"Thanks so much for seeing me, Jerry."

"Sure," he mumbles as he stands and moves toward me. Jerry walks with a half shuffle, bends forward with a half stoop. His brown hair is messy-curly, half covering a receding hairline.

A part of me thinks I should start with small talk about the neighborhood, but I sense it will be more comfortable if I just jump straight in.

"I need your help."

He looks at me blankly, awaiting further data.

"I'm investigating the story of a woman who died three days ago, a UMKC student."

"I read your articles."

I pause to give him the opportunity to say more. An awkward silence ensues.

"It's not completely clear what happened," I push on.

"Mmm," he mumbles, still waiting for more information.

"Just at the time she died, I'm not sure before or after, all the contents of her u.Mail account were erased. We've tried to find out what happened but can't."

He perks up. "She probably erased it herself."

"Could be," I say. "I really don't know."

"There's usually a trail in this sort of thing. It's pretty hard to erase something completely."

"That's what we were thinking."

"Do you have the username and Biometric Authentication Code?"

I tap my u.D to send him the username information and BAC that Joseph hacked from the UMKC system. "How long do you think this will take?"

"I'll probably be able to send you something later today. It's no big deal."

"Talk with you later then?" I say awkwardly, standing to look at the old equipment in his case. The vintage Macintosh looks like a relic from a bygone age. The smattering of old phones, each identified by a neatly printed index card indicating its model and year, makes me wonder if Jerry isn't just a historian of past technologies but also a pack rat.

I turn to ask him about the collection, but Jerry has already reintegrated with his screens. He points and wiggles his hands like a conductor of his own digital symphony, hardly noticing me sliding out the door.

16

"She definitely didn't do it at any of the blood banks," Joseph announces from my dashboard screen, "and definitely didn't go to the university clinic."

"What about the OBs and fertility clinics?"

"There are almost five hundred OBs in Kansas City, and eighteen fertility clinics. The OBs are in ninety-two medical groups, and I've eliminated seventy-eight. I've eliminated all the IVFGS clinics but four."

I'm once again amazed by Joseph's work. "And you're doing this by?"

"Calling to make follow-up appointments. They can't seem to find my wife's file."

Doesn't anyone follow the news, I wonder. He's calling for a follow-up appointment for someone publicly announced dead and nobody raises an eyebrow?

"Keep pushing, Joseph," I say. "At some point soon people may start recognizing the name."

"I know, boss," Joseph says in a less annoyed tone than I probably deserve, "that's why I'm making these calls."

My u.D vibrates. It's Henderson.

"Joseph, gotta run," I blurt as my hand springs to tap my wrist.

"We've got to talk," Maurice says as his stern face appears.

"Is it confirmed?"

"We've got to talk," he repeats. "Broadway Café. Seven thirty."

"Are you releasing the autopsy report?" I say, pushing my luck.

"Seven thirty."

"See you there," I say into the already dropped connection.

I pull over on Gilliam Road, feeling momentarily paralyzed, not sure in what direction I should move. Joseph is tracking down the doctor, Jerry is looking into the u.Mail account, Maurice won't tell me when the autopsy report is going to be released, but I'm guessing it won't be before seven thirty tonight, I can't harass Carol Stock anymore. Should I go home and read the Bible?

The vibration on my wrist knocks me out of my reverie. I tap my u.D and Jerry Weisberg's strangely glowing face appears on my dashboard.

"Um, Rich," he stammers, "you might want to get back here." He nods awkwardly as if to stress his seriousness.

"I'm on my way now. There in ten."

I screech a U-turn then speed down Gilliam in the opposite direction.

Jerry is intensely working all of the images bouncing around his screens at once as I rush into his cave.

"Close the door," he orders.

I follow the instruction.

"Sit down."

I do.

"Do you remember the first struggle between Google and China?" he asks without looking at me, his eyes darting between screens.

"Yes, of course," I answer, "about fifteen years ago."

"Two thousand nine," he declares, as if everyone should know this date. "Just when China was emerging economically, militarily, and politically, becoming the major global player they are today."

"China broke into the Google mainframe," I say, "stole their source code, snuck into people's Gmail accounts. Google found out and threatened to leave China."

"Yeah," Jerry says, "that was the story. But the real story was deeper. We all discovered how vulnerable we were. And then there was a virus called Stuxnet. Do you remember that?"

I nod, not sure where this tutorial is going but eager for it to move forward.

"Stuxnet was the stealth bomber of computer viruses," Jerry says with a patience that bothers me, "smarter than anything anyone had seen before. It was a really a worm designed to infiltrate Iran's computer system and look for very specific computer codes while making it look like everything was normal. The Iranians responded by unleashing the Shamoon and Mallah viruses that targeted the US and Saudi Arabia. Then US intelligence tracked the Byzantine Candor and PLA Shanghai hacker cells back to China and found that the Chinese government was stealing hundreds of billions of dollars of R&D from US companies and Edward Snowden leaked America's cyber-capabilities to the world and America tried to indict Chinese military hackers and the Chinese responded and things went crazy from there. All the hacking and viruses, all the big countries setting up and massively funding cyber commands, the US hack-bombing the secret Iranian cyber-agency as a warning to everyone else, the quiet cyber battle raging ever since."

"I think I remember some Canadians helping," I say.

"Exactly," Jerry says. "A group called the OpenNet consortium based out of the University of Toronto with people pitching in from around the world."

"Good guys?" I ask.

"For us. For the Chinese they're the SOBs."

This is all well and good, I think, but I'm beginning to wonder what I'm doing here. Is Jerry just wanting company? "What's the connection?"

"The Chinese broke into the US Department of Defense System in 2017 and left a Trojan horse, a piece of code that later gets activated to do something sinister."

"And?" I'm still trying to figure out where he's going.

"It became clear to everyone just how easy it was to sneak something into the trillions of lines of code that control our lives."

Control seems like a strong word.

"So?" I ask anxiously.

"Just as the Chinese and the Russians and the Iranians and so many others were getting good at sneaking into systems where they weren't welcome, the good guys were getting smarter and smarter at setting traps to help figure out who was meddling where they didn't belong. They call them 'comments.' Think of it like putting a homing device in a suitcase of cash you think might be stolen."

"Setting traps for the setters of traps?"

"Exactly," Jerry replies excitedly, "even more. Some of the Trojan horses contain Centurions."

"Centurions?"

Jerry looks at me as if I'm hopeless. "Code that reports back about people trying to access its specific location. It watches you watch it. The cat and mouse game goes on and on, a classic arms race situation."

"Jerry, what are you trying to tell me?"

"You need to understand one more thing."

I nod impatiently.

"The OpenNet consortium is always sharing software that helps us figure out when we're being infiltrated. They're fighting the losing battle to save cyberspace. Their work isn't perfect, but it's better than nothing."

I urge Jerry on with my wide eyes and pursed lips.

"I tried logging in to the u.Mail account you gave me, and you were right, nothing was there. I did all of the obvious checks, and there was not a trace that anything had ever been there."

I nod.

"So I thought I'd sweep the account to see if anything popped up," Jerry continues.

Now Jerry's monologue is beginning to make sense.

"So I applied the latest version of OpenNet software and I found the bugger."

"What is it?"

"This," he says, activating one of his screens with the wave of a finger.

A string of code pours across the screens. It means nothing to me.

"I've just had a preliminary look at the code," Jerry says. "The moment you enter this account, the brilliant little Centurion reports back to someone who you are. Hi, little fella."

"Do you know who?"

"It seems to pass through a lot of anonymizing portals. I'll keep looking. It also sends you home with a little Trojan horse of your own to give someone access to your system when the Trojan gets activated."

"So anyone who's been in this account has been compromised?"

"Not everyone," Jerry says. "It's a zoo out there, and I always explore the web through proxy servers and firewalls. I'm pretty sure I haven't been compromised, but you really never know."

My mind races to Joseph Abraham. He's good but is he Jerry good? "So the average person who's been in this account has tipped his hand to someone and probably brought back a Trojan horse."

"Exactly."

"How sophisticated would someone need to be to do this?" I ask breathlessly.

"That's the point," Jerry replies excitedly, "that's why I called you here. There are basic viruses and malware codes everywhere, and they can be easy to deal with if you know what you are doing. Annoying but manageable. I've only just begun studying this code, but some parts of it have incredibly high levels of encryption. There are only a small number of people this good out there."

I put my hands together in front of my face as I try to process what this could mean. Why would someone with this level of sophistication care about MaryLee Stock's u.Mail account?

I feel a surge of vulnerability. But if someone *can* watch me, does it mean they *are* watching me? With all my reliance on technology, I realize what I really need to do is talk to Joseph the old-fashioned way that can't be compromised by Trojan horses, Centurions, and viruses.

"Jerry," I say as I get up to leave, "I don't yet know what it all means, but I do know I need your help. Can you try to find out who the malware is reporting back to?"

I wonder if the miniscule favor I'd done Jerry in the Community Association justifies all I'm asking him to do now.

Jerry seems to pick up on my hesitation. "MaryLee Stock was a student in this university. I don't want to put words in your mouth, but if you're digging like this it makes me think . . ."—Jerry interrupts himself—"it makes me think the least I can do is help you dig."

"And Jerry," I add, "please don't talk about this with anyone."

Jerry flashes me an *of course* look.

"If I've been compromised," I say, "what's the best way for us to communicate?"

"I have a beta program for Cupstring. It's for heavy encrypted communication. I'll also add a button for the GreenTorrent anonymizer. Just tap that first before you access the cloud. In person is safest."

Jerry takes my u.D from my wrist, pulls it apart from the data stick, then plugs it into his system. "This ought to do it for now," he says, handing my u.D back to me after a few moments. "I shared our encryption keys. You should probably get a new u.D when you can and connect with an e-tag that doesn't link back to you."

"Thank you, Jerry," I say, reaching out to shake his hand.

Jerry takes a quick step backward and raises his hands facing outward in front of his chest. "Sorry," he says apologetically, "germs."

Something in my gut tells me we have a lot more to be frightened of.

17

Joseph Abraham is nothing if not predictable. His quiet temperament and diligent presence belie a consistency and inner resourcefulness I've come to rely on. Day and night at all hours I've grown accustomed to seeing the back of his head and finding him peering intensely into his screens or wiggling his hands in the air as he manipulates images across his digital cubicle or bending his head forward talking to someone in a muted voice that travels only a few inches from his mouthpiece.

But as I turn the corner past Arts and Entertainment, I'm startled by what I see.

That Joseph is facing me is surprising enough. That he jumps up the moment he sees me and bounds toward me is downright revolutionary.

"We've got to talk," he says breathlessly.

"That's what I was about to say."

"Martina's looking for you, says she's called you three times and you haven't answered."

"And?"

"She told me to stop working on this story."

"That makes no sense. Where is she?"

Joseph's look over my shoulder answers my question. I turn to see Martina striding toward me with a strange, angry look on her face.

"Where the hell have you been?" Her barbed question is not meant to be answered. "Come into my office," she commands.

I inhale and follow.

Suddenly remembering my original purpose, I turn back to Joseph. "Joseph, don't connect to the cloud."

"Boss?" he replies.

"Don't. I'll be back in a sec."

He looks confused. "Yes, sir."

I expect Martina to slam the door after I enter her office as she generally does when she's in a mood. Instead, she slowly closes the door behind me and looks to confirm the handle has clicked.

"Sit down," she orders.

I still can't read the vibe.

"First," she says, "I want you to know that this is fucking bull-shit."

I rack my brain to figure out what she's talking about and come up empty.

"I've been fucking calling you because I got a visit this morning from Marshal Dickhead."

I can't help but smile. "From whom, madam?"

"Don't be an idiot," she says, flipping a calling card in my direction. *Anderson Gillespie, United States Marshal.*

When she starts apologizing, I realize this can't be good.

"Look," she says, leaning her head toward me, "I've never faced a 39(c). I always knew it was possible, theoretically possible."

"Until now," I say, not sure if I'm asking a question or providing an answer.

She looks at me square in the eye.

"Can you tell me more?" I ask.

"Marshal Dickhead and his creepy sidekick came by after you filed your story this morning. They couldn't have been more polite. To tell you the truth, I hadn't thought about the NPA in years, since the fight over the original law. It hasn't been as bad as we'd thought and God knows we're all living off of the federal money." She pauses for a moment reflectively. "I'd almost forgotten what 39(c) stands for. But he was kind enough to bring a copy of the law with him and reminded me that we'd all made a deal and that the tab had come due."

"On my story?"

"Yes."

"Did he say why?" I ask after a heavy silence.

"He said he didn't have to. He read me the text. It says in black and white that the federal government can instruct a federally subsidized news organization to not cover a particular story for purposes of national security and the news organization must immediately cease coverage or, and he was very clear on this point, after two official notifications, lose NPA funding for a period of at least five years. On top of that, those responsible for any violations face personal criminal liability."

My mind races to integrate this new piece of information with of the other shards I've been collecting. The pieces don't fit. "I can't believe this."

Martina takes a one-page document from a folder on her desk. "This is notice one," she says matter-of-factly as she hands me the document.

> By order of Article 39, Sub-Section C of the News Protection Act of 2021, this notice hereby orders the Kansas City Star to cease and desist immediately from providing any coverage whatsoever to the death of Missouri resident MaryLee Stock. If the Kansas City Star does not fully follow this order, one more official notice will be sent. If, following receipt of a second notice, the Kansas City Star continues to provide coverage of this matter, all NPA funding provided to the Kansas City Star will be terminated immediately, upon receipt of a third notice, for a period of no less than five years and those responsible for violating the cease and desist order will face personal criminal liability as will any other media or other organization that may publish or release this content. Per 39(c)(2) of the NPA of 2021, this order cannot be challenged in any court of law.

"We have this law for two years and nothing and now they want to apply it in a case of a twenty-four-year-old nobody from Springfield?" I say.

Martina and I have the same thought. It's no longer just a case about a twenty-four-year-old from Springfield. She's no longer nobody.

I interlock my fingers in front of my mouth and start biting the tips of my thumbs. "What are we going to do?"

"I spoke with Terry, I spoke with Wes," Martina says. "The answer to that is clear."

Of course she'd had to go to the editor and the publisher.

"They didn't take much time to make the decision."

"And?"

"What choice do they have? What choice do any of us have? Look at all of these people slaving away out there." She points through her glass wall to the newsroom. "If we could afford this on our own, we would. We can't. That was our deal with the devil in 2021. That was everyone's deal. Americans wanted news organizations, but our financial model was broken. We either signed on the dotted line and took the government's money or went bust. We signed. We got the federal subsidies. Now the chickens are coming home to roost."

"That, respectfully," I say, "is bullshit."

"Of course it is, Azadian," she says emphatically. "It's complete bullshit, but it's cost-benefit analysis. Do we risk everything for one story, or do we take a hit in the name of the greater good?"

I shake my head from side to side. "And Terry and Wes said to drop it?"

"Do you really need me to answer that? I thought you were the guy with the PhD."

"And I thought you were the one telling me to find a story. I come back with a list of extremely strange circumstances, something that might be huge, right in the middle of a political crisis that could split our country down the middle, now the federal government is weighing in, for Christ's sake, practically announcing to us that something big is going on, and you're telling me to drop it?" I say heatedly.

"Don't be in idiot," Martina fires back. "We need to fucking exist in order to cover anything. Why would we throw all of it away to chase one story that isn't even proven?"

"I can't believe that you, of all people, can say that."

"Believe it, Azadian," she says fiercely, then pulls herself back. "Believe it," she says again more softly. I'm not sure if I'm picking up a thread of remorse in her voice.

"What percentage of our operating budget comes from NPA funds?" I ask, changing tack.

"That I know precisely. Wes repeated it five times in our conversation. Fifty-three percent."

The number deflates me.

"It's not just the 53 percent," Martina adds. "It's the difference between the *Kansas City Star* existing or not existing, between all of us having jobs and unemployment, between doing what we do, even imperfectly, and doing nothing."

"And the cost is closing our eyes?"

"I'm not even going to answer that, Azadian. Sometimes adults need to close their eyes for a moment so they can open them again."

"And if I keep looking into this anyway?"

"You know the answer to that question. We'd have to fire you to protect the paper."

"And you think that's what I should do?" I say, hardly masking the edge in my voice.

I can read the distant fire in Martina's eyes before she puts her elbows on the desk and leans all the way forward toward me. I can almost see the words "Fuck no" forming in her mind and reaching toward her larynx.

"Yes," she says softly.

<u>18</u>

"I'm going to tell Terry and Wes I've spoken to you and ordered you to drop the story."

I'm feeling less loving toward Martina. "And violating 39(c) is a federal offense."

"It is," she says matter-of-factly.

"Even though I was assigned the story by the *Star*."

"I am officially unassigning you. From my and the paper's perspective, this story is done. We're out of it."

The words hang in the air.

"And," she adds, "I'm assigning you to a new story. The flower show."

"The flower show?" The assignment seems like a cruel hoax. The flower show is truly the most boring, predictable, mind-numbing story imaginable.

"Yup," she says in the same tone as before.

I begin to realize what I think she's saying.

"I don't want to see you or Abraham around here working on the MaryLee Stock story. I don't want to hear a thing about it. Got that?"

I nod.

"Well then. We are clear?"

I hold her gaze for a few extra moments before I repeat her words. "We are clear."

I find Joseph still sitting on his swivel chair facing the wrong direction.

"Walk with me," I say.

I'm not sure where we should go to talk but pick the most obvious and least appealing option simply for a lack of creativity. Joseph goes in first. I join him a few minutes later, locking the door of the special needs restroom behind me.

I tell him about my conversation with Martina, Maurice Henderson's call, and the Centurion and Trojan horse Jerry has discovered. "Joseph, I don't know what I'm going to do but you need to stop working on this story."

He doesn't respond.

"You could get deported for it, or worse. I'm not willing to take that chance."

Joseph pauses and looks at me with his thousand-year-old eyes. "What, and leave show business?" he says with a straight face.

It takes me a few moments to process what he's saying.

When Joseph had first joined the *Star*, I'd made it my mission to make him smile. I was rarely successful. I told him the joke about the elephant manure cleaner at the circus who gets offered a high-paying desk job at a law firm. Joseph hadn't smiled then. Now I want to hug him for repeating the punch line back to me.

"I'm not here for the visa, boss," he says earnestly. "I'm here because I believe in what this country stands for."

Both of us recognize the awkwardness of his idealism in light of what it looks like we're now facing.

"Do you think your system has been compromised?" My words feel like a betrayal of Joseph the moment they leave my mouth. I haven't even fully decided what I'm going to do and I'm already putting him at risk.

"Could be."

"So what do we do?"

"As a start I think we need new u.Ds and new e-tags so we can connect anonymously."

I give him the $242 in my wallet. "We can have Jerry Weisberg synch our keys when you get the new devices. You can also probably use the old computer at the downtown library and the old pay phones for your calls," I say, still amazed that pay phones have found a gasping lease on life, double-hatted as public Wi-Fi spots, one of the few concessions the telecommunication workers union was able to secure in the National Competitiveness Act.

"On it, boss."

Momentum begins to feel like a non-decision decision.

I look at Joseph for a moment, my mind pulling me in the two opposite directions of keeping him on the story because I need him and kicking him off because of the potential risks to him.

"Okay," I say heavily, "find me the doctor, keep digging on Becker, figure out what she could have bought at Corner Drug."

He nods.

I feel undeserving of Joseph's loyalty as I send him out of the bathroom and lock the door.

I tap my u.D as I wait. The blinking red light indicates four messages. Three are frantic messages from Martina escalating from "Where are you?" to "Where the fuck are you?" to "Where the fucking hell are you? Call me immediately." The fourth is less expected.

"Rich, this is Maurice. New plan. Meet at Swope Park picnic area C, eight thirty tonight."

The Swope Park picnic area is no place for a white dude, no place for anyone respectable at eight thirty at night.

Joseph surreptitiously hands me a printout as I walk toward the stairway door. The headline from the police wire tells me all I need to know.

"MaryLee Stock declared dead by natural causes due to heart arrhythmia."

19

There was a time when people believed that humans emerged from a divine spark.

Nonsense.

Science has shown us definitively that organic matter can emerge from alkaline hydrothermal vents at the bottom of the ocean, that life itself can be generated from synthetic nucleotides, that thought and emotion are merely chemical reactions, and that all we ultimately are is a massively but not infinitely complex bag of bones and water with some electrical charges passing through.

Buddhism accepts the transience of this limited physical presence but gussies it up with concepts of transmigrating souls and reincarnation. It would be nice to think I'll be coming back for another round.

I'm not.

The great futurist Ray Kurzweil has been promising for twenty years that anyone who lives ten more years can live forever. He's only seventy-five but now struggling on life support at Mass General Hospital. Hope of overcoming mortality springs eternal but the actuarial tables plod on.

The evangelical Christians now fighting under the banner of Senator King and his army of the righteous have a complete answer to the existential dilemma. Accept God, fully recognize Jesus as his incarnation here on earth, follow all of God's rules, and eternal life can be yours. Oh, and one more thing. Senator King and his colleagues will be the ones to tell you exactly what God wants you to do.

I've always believed, on the other hand and perhaps to a fault, that the path toward knowledge requires chasing truth down its rabbit hole to its deepest, darkest core. So the idea of an autopsy, the word itself derived from the ancient Greek *autopsia*, "to see for oneself," ought to appeal. The opposite feels true as I drive toward Truman Medical.

I uSearch "autopsy procedure." My sexy vixen u.D voice informs me that most states require autopsies for people who die without having been attended by a physician as I absent-mindedly roll through a stop sign. In these cases, the medical examiner doesn't need family consent.

The process described for cutting up the body is disturbingly graphic. A Y-shaped incision is made from shoulder to shoulder and then down toward the navel. The skin is peeled back and the rib cage is pulled from the skeleton. Then the larynx, esophagus, and various arteries and ligaments are taken out. The skull is cut with an electric saw and opened so the brain can be removed.

I'd only met MaryLee, if I can use the word "met" loosely, when she was lying dead on her carpet. I'd seen her presence reflected in the absence on her mother's face. I've only been chasing her down for three days now, but the thought of her being ravaged with a Y-incision nauseates me nonetheless.

It would be nice to believe MaryLee is smiling down from heaven or being reborn in the spirit of a newborn crying in a nursery somewhere. She is not. She is cut up and in a box. The image pains me.

Tucked away in a corner of the pathology department, the medical examiner's office is easy to find. The hall stinks of formaldehyde and Lysol.

"I'm looking for someone with whom I can discuss a, a . . . deceased," I say as I approach the nurses' station.

"And you are?" the receptionist asks, not looking up.

I pause for a moment, unsure who I am. I'm not officially representing the *Star*, I'm not a friend. What am I?

"I'm associated with the family of the deceased," I say.

"Associated?" she asks, her head still pointing down.

"The mother, of the deceased, asked me to come."

"Uh, huh," she says, "and who exactly are you here to inquire about?"

"Ms. MaryLee Stock."

She finally shifts her head upward. "We are not able to provide any information to the public. The report was released earlier today."

"Yes," I say, "I know. I was wondering if there is anyone I can talk with about her situation."

"I'm sorry, sir," she says sharply, "that is not possible. Is there anything else?"

"No, thank you," I say with an ingratiating smile as my mind races to conjure Plan B.

I move back toward the elevators and step into the men's room. I wait a few minutes before exiting and head the other way.

I've spent enough time in this hospital to understand its architectural logic. I trace a figure eight, the opposite direction until I see the door I'm looking for: Martin A. Papadakis, Medical Examiner. I open the door and knock as I enter.

"Excuse me, Dr. Papadakis?" I say.

He looks up from his papers, startled. Jet black hair slicked back over his head, his sunken eyes, and round face give him a panda look but nothing about him seems cuddly.

"I'm Rich Azadian from the *Kansas City Star*."

"And what are you doing in my office?" he asks coldly.

"I'm covering the death of Mary Lee Stock." I tell the truth and lie simultaneously.

"Before I ask you to leave, I'll remind you the official report on that case was released this morning."

"I know."

"Then thank you and good-bye," he says tersely.

"Heart arrhythmia?" I throw the words out.

Papadakis pauses for a moment to absorb my words. I almost

sense a twitch. "Yes, Mr. Azadian," he says calmly. "I did the autopsy myself."

I try to block from my mind the image of him gutting MaryLee like a fish then sawing off the top of her head. "Did you find anything else irregular?"

"Of course I cannot speak to the press, or to anyone other than next of kin for that matter."

"Did you see a needle mark on her arm?"

"This is a hospital, a confidential environment," Papadakis spits, leaning back against his chair.

"I understand," I say. "Can you please tell me if you follow the JCAHO guidelines, Dr. Papadakis?"

He doesn't respond.

"I believe the Joint Commission for Accreditation of Health Organizations sets guidelines for autopsies," I add, "and I just wanted to see if you followed them."

"What are you getting at, Mr. Azadian?"

"You've provided the preliminary report within the required three working days, but I wanted to see if you plan on retaining tissue for additional tests?"

Papadakis's face begins to redden with a growing rage. He takes a deep breath and composes himself. "This is really not appropriate, Mr. Azadian. Are you going to leave my office or would you prefer I call security?" He reaches toward the screen embedded in his desk.

Even from where I'm standing near the door, I notice a slight tremble in his hand. I pause a few moments to test what he will do. His fingers don't move. With all the strange circumstances surrounding this story, why am I not surprised?

"So sorry to bother you," I say, backing out the door.

20

I'm tempted to just drop by the Neonatal Intensive Care Unit to say hello to Toni. I haven't seen her in six months and a little voice in my head tells me that dropping by unannounced is probably not a good idea. I hope she doesn't see me as I dart out the door.

It's mid-afternoon, and I'm itching to meet Henderson but know I need to wait.

All I can think to do is drop by the flower show.

I walk through the massive doors of the American Royal arena. The place smells pleasantly of flowers, greens, and manure. It's a natural, instinctive smell. At some other time I would want to tell the story of what I imagine is really happening here, how the competition feels, what makes the judges tick, the gestalt of the overall event.

Then I think of MaryLee cut up in a box awaiting her burial. Fuck it. I ask the usher to point me to the press room.

The basic principle of public relations is that journalists are lazy. It's only part true. The fact of the matter is that there's a lot we don't give a shit about, and given the choice between learning things in this category from scratch or getting spoon fed by someone we know is using us, we generally prefer the latter.

I identify myself, ask for my packet, and instantly recognize the work of a professional. The press release is basically written so I can practically use the whole thing as my story. I'm not that obvious but see the story in an instant. I tell the flower show press officer, a freckled roly-poly woman probably in her late twenties, that

I have a few questions for the organizer and for the best flower arrangement competition winner from last year. She brings them both over in minutes. I tap the record button on my u.D, ask them each a few questions, and am on my way. Bad journalism is frighteningly easy.

I dictate the story into my u.D sitting in my car in the parking lot. Eight hundred words of predictable crap.

I grab a quick bite at Gates Bar-B-Q on my way to Swope Park, lock my doors, and head in. One of the largest urban parks in the country and once the center of a very fashionable part of town, the park itself is actually a beautiful place. Now the city's energy has moved south and west, and Swope Park at night is dark and scary.

I follow the signs to the picnic area, then the arrows to subsection C. It's pitch dark and eerily quiet but for the occasional chirps of insects. I turn off the car and wait.

A few minutes past eight, the Ford Energi-F gently rolls up beside me. Maurice cuts the ignition then walks over to my car, opens my door, and lowers himself into my passenger seat. The interior light catches his pinched face.

"Tell me again why you thought MaryLee Stock was pregnant?" he says, slowly and deliberately.

I again lay out the case.

He silently broods as I finish talking.

"Heart arrhythmia?" I say, breaking the silence.

Maurice looks almost startled by my question. "Don't you think I know that, Rich? What the hell do you think I'm doing here? But let me be clear with you. I'm here to ask you questions. I have no intention of answering any."

"Yes, sir," I say, with only a dash of smart-ass mixed in.

"So just based on the price of something she bought at Corner Drug, a twinkle in Becker's eye, and her lab partner saying she was sick you came to the conclusion she was pregnant?" he asks.

"Let's call it a hypothesis," I say. "Add vitamins, the matching paintings of the virgin, the thirty-thousand-dollar box with frankincense and myrrh. Was I right?"

He stares at me with an are-you-fucking-kidding-me-didn't-you-hear-what-I-just-said expression on his face. His tapping on the dashboard with his curved fingers gives me the strong impression I was. "And you don't believe the autopsy report, either?"

"It didn't even mention the needle mark. You saw that." I press on. "I also interviewed the medical examiner."

"Papadakis?"

"Yeah. He didn't tell me anything, but that seemed to tell me something."

"What do you mean?"

"What reason does a medical examiner have to be coy, let alone rude?"

"How about protecting himself from jackass journalists?"

"There's more. It turns out that MaryLee's u.Mail account was hacked in a very sophisticated way, using high-level encryption and malware."

Maurice nods.

"And then," I say, finally throwing out the headline, "federal marshals came to the *Star* this morning and ordered us to drop this story."

"Ordered?"

"Under Article 39(c) of the News Protection Act."

Maurice looks confused.

"The bill that bailed out the newspapers with federal money two years ago. Article 39, Section C allows the government to kill stories for national security reasons. No questions asked or askable."

"And you think someone is covering up?" he asks pensively.

"Someone wipes out her u.Mail account and inserts sophisticated malware, then federal marshals order the *Kansas City Star* to drop the story. If that doesn't sounds like a cover-up, I don't know what does."

"If you're right, who do you think is driving this?"

"I don't know," I say, "but if my theory is correct about Cobalt Becker, I could at least come up with a pretty convincing hypothesis."

Maurice stares at me. "So you think if Becker is involved somehow, King's people are doing damage control?"

"They'd at least have a motive," I say. "It'd be hard for King to fight God's battle on earth with his spiritual advisor caught up in a scandal."

Maurice stares intensely out the front windshield into the darkness for a few moments before turning toward me. "That may be a plausible theory, Rich, but that's not enough."

A thick silence weaves itself through the car. Maurice breaks it. "Senator King is hosting a day-long prayer service in the Hammons Arena in Springfield Saturday as part of his national bus tour. He's invited superpastors from around the state, including Becker."

"Maybe we should—"

Maurice cuts me off. "We're not doing anything unless we have a lot more evidence." Maurice pauses. "Until we have any evidence at all."

I move my mouth, starting to talk, then pull myself back. The car returns to silence.

Then Maurice reaches into his shirt pocket and hands me a small Huawei hand phone, the disposable kind that sells for twenty dollars at 7-Eleven. "Use this phone to talk with me. Don't give anyone else the number or use it for anything else. Got it?"

"Aren't these things traceable?" I ask, nervous that talking on the phone might make us even more vulnerable.

"It's from special police stock," Maurice says. "It ought to be okay."

I have so many questions about what's happening at KCPD, the autopsy, what we're doing sneaking around like this. "Maurice," I say, "I need to ask you—"

"Don't."

I roll on nonetheless. "I want to ask you if the track marks I saw on MaryLee's arm meant anything."

Maurice stares at me, deep in thought, not revealing anything.

"I want to ask—" I add.

"Didn't I just say . . . ?"

I hold my ground facing Maurice. He stops mid-sentence. His head moves only a fraction of a centimeter in an almost unrecognizable nod. "We'll be in touch," he then says before getting out of the car. "Call me if you learn anything."

My head feels like a lead weight as I drive the few blocks home. I dictate my message to Joseph into my u.D. *Come over tomorrow morning at eight.*

10-4. The text reply comes back almost instantaneously.

I pull into my driveway, the image of my sofa now fully replaced with a passionate image of my bed. If I can get to sleep, maybe the Borges librarian of my subconscious will configure all of this data in a way my conscious mind is failing to do.

But as the penumbra of light catches a shadow on my front porch, it becomes clear my dream of sleep will be an illusion.

My mind searches for what this can possibly mean. I hadn't at all expected her.

Neary Savang sprints frantically toward my car.

21

"One of my lab partners didn't show up for class today," she says breathlessly through my opening window. Her face seems a mixture of panic, fear, and confusion.

"And?" I say, stepping quickly out of the car.

"At first I thought it was no big deal because we were all so sad about what happened to MaryLee. But then I called her and didn't get an answer."

"Called who?"

"Min, Min. I think I was just extra worried after what happened to MaryLee and what you told me, so I decided to go by her dorm room to check on her."

"And?"

"I got there and she was gone."

"What do you mean?"

"She wasn't there, a bunch of her stuff wasn't there."

"How do you know?"

"I picked the lock," she says a little awkwardly.

"You picked the lock?" I am impressed.

"Her clothes were gone. First MaryLee dies, and now Min disappears in the middle of the semester. She doesn't say anything, just disappears?" Neary is shaking.

"Do you have any idea what could have happened?" I ask.

"I really don't. I thought of reporting it to the police but wasn't sure what to say. Maybe she just went somewhere and didn't tell us. I wanted to talk with you about it."

My mind buzzes with a nervous energy. Every moment seems

to produce a new strange coincidence, a new shard that lays with the others in the mud, identifiable as individual pieces but wholly resistant to being reconstituted as a whole. Min Zhao had hardly been part of my narrative, and now I don't know if she is a shy Chinese girl who found love, is dead somewhere, or is part of a story in some other way.

"I think you need to report this," I say.

"Can you do it?" she asks cautiously.

My mind jumps to Marshal Dickhead. "I really wish I could, Neary, but I can't."

She looks surprised. "What do you mean?"

"It's complicated."

She seems to accept my words at face value.

"What can you tell me about Min?"

"Not so much. She was a quiet girl, conscientious."

"From China, right?" I ask.

"Yeah. She did her college in China and came to UMKC for her Master's. She had credits from China, so they let her transfer in to our class at the beginning of this year. She's really smart."

I tap through my notes from Joseph. *Min Zhao, 26, Chinese national, graduate of Lanxiang University, UMKC Lab Group 4.*

"Neary," I say, trying to calm her, "I'm going to find out what happened, but for now I think all you can do is report what you know. You should probably go the UMKC police and let them handle it."

A disappointed look crosses Neary's face.

"I wish I could do more, Neary. I promise I'll look. Do you need me to drive you back to school?"

Neary walks around to the passenger side of my car and gets in.

The drive back to UMKC is mostly silent.

"I promise you, I'll figure this out, Neary," I say again, feeling wholly inadequate I can't do more. "Please just keep me in the loop."

Neary gets out of the car without a word, a forlorn look on her face. I lower the passenger side window and call after her.

"Neary."

"Yes, Mr. Azadian."

"Please be careful."

She turns and walks toward the station.

22

Joseph, of course, is sitting on my porch when I open the door at 7:30 a.m. after yet another restless night.

Sleep quality: poor, my u.D tells me as if I didn't already know.

It somehow soothes me having Joseph here. I invite him in, peeking nervously out the door in both directions.

"How's the library?" I ask.

"Too crowded. The computers are prehistoric and connected to the wall. They close at eight," he says, handing me my new u.D.

"What do you have?"

"I'm down to five OB doctors and three fertility clinics. The remaining ones are pretty tight with their information and wouldn't tell me anything."

Joseph passes me a handwritten list of items under the three price categories from Corner Drug. Nothing jumps out except for the pregnancy test. I'm glad to see jock itch spray doesn't cost $10.95.

"Joseph, do you remember Min Zhao?"

"One of the UMKC students?"

"Her classmate Neary Savang was here last night. It looks like Min has disappeared."

"Disappeared? What do you want me to do?"

"For starters, find out everything you can about her. After what happened to MaryLee, I fear the worst."

Joseph just mumbles, his rapt attention now focused on my coffee table screen as I head to the kitchen to grab us coffee.

"Hey boss, have a look at this," I hear Joseph yell from the living room.

I rush in.

"Min Zhao, graduate of Lianxing University, undergraduate degree in nursing."

"Yeah," I say, not seeing the significance.

"Look at the wiki selection for Lianxing University. Connected to the Chinese military, a central hub for the infamous Chinese hacker community."

"And you think that could be connected to MaryLee's u.Mail hack?"

"I don't know," Joseph says. "With all of the hacking and computer attacks coming out of China these days, it's at least worth exploring."

"Interesting," I say. "Keep looking." I pick up the bat phone and call Maurice.

"Maurice, it's Rich."

"Hi, baby," Maurice says in a sugary voice I've never before heard.

"Maurice?"

"Sure, baby. I'll meet you for coffee but just for a second."

"Maurice? This is Rich."

I'm starting to wonder if the phone is not working, and then it hits me.

"Just long enough for a coffee and a kiss," he says.

I'm silent.

"Same place at eight thirty? For you, anything. Bye, baby."

The line drops and my world is suddenly even more complicated.

23

Maurice is already parked at picnic area C when I arrive. "What more have you learned?" he barks.

I describe the disappearance of Min and Lianxing University. I feel him stewing as I speak.

"I need to get one thing straight with you, Rich," he says. "I need to trust you, but I need to know you won't screw me."

"I'm in a pretty tough situation myself," I say earnestly. "I could go to jail for staying on this story, and you could probably put me there."

Maurice hesitates before he speaks. "You know this, but the autopsy report that came out yesterday is a sham. I saw the needle mark on her arm just like you did. There wasn't even a reference to it in the full report." Maurice pauses. "This morning, the chief told me to drop the case."

"Did he say why?"

"That federal authorities were taking over and I needed to drop it."

"Are you going to?"

Maurice pauses reflectively. "Given everything we've learned so far, I want to know more about why the chief is asking me to do this. Not every case gets resolved, but I'll be damned if I'll walk away from something like this without knowing why. That's not what I'm about."

"So," I say, assessing the situation, "I'm not covering the story, and you're not investigating the case."

"I'd call it not completely investigating this case," Maurice says.

Maurice and I are suddenly in the same boat, and it's a leaky one. "How does that happen?"

"I don't know, but fish start to stink from the head down," Maurice says.

"And Becker?"

"I started asking around. That's when the storm kicked in."

"And the girl, Min?" I ask.

"UMKC police called us last night. You know that."

"I dropped the girl off who reported it."

"What do you make of it?"

"I don't know," I say. "Could be a lot of things."

"Rich," Maurice says, "The Chinese girl left the country yesterday. Flew from Chicago to Beijing. We tracked her when we got the report from the UMKC police."

"Wow."

"And we did look at the feeds from the UMKC coffee shop. You were right. MaryLee Stock was there, and guess who she was with?"

24

"Mrs. Stock, this is Rich Azadian," I say into my earpiece as I drive toward the flower show. "We met yesterday at the park?"

She doesn't respond.

"I'm so sorry to bother you again, but I was hoping we might talk."

Silence.

"I have some concerns about the autopsy report I was hoping I might be able to discuss with you."

"The autopsy report?" she says quietly. Her voice feels disconnected from the ebb and flow of normal life.

"I don't know quite how to say this, but I have questions about the accuracy of the report, whether it was, correct."

"Correct?" she repeats weakly.

"Whether the report was what actually happened. Is it okay if I ask you a question?"

"Yes?" The creaky vowel drags.

"Mrs. Stock, I don't believe the police are telling the full story about Lee. I think there may be more to what happened. Might you be willing to help me find out?"

"But the police . . ."

"I know, Mrs. Stock, but I have reason to believe they're not telling the full truth."

I hear her breath.

"I don't believe Lee died from a heart arrhythmia," I add, feeling badly for pressing on.

"I don't know, Mr. Azadian. This is all happening so fast."

"I know. I'm so sorry," I say pathetically.

Silence.

"I need to know if you'd be willing to help me find out what really happened."

"I don't know," she stutters, "maybe I should ask Reverend Becker."

"Mrs. Stock, Reverend Becker is a fine man, but maybe it will be best if we take this one step at a time. I just have one small request."

I'm not sure if we are still connected, then I hear her weak voice.

"What?"

"Just to go with me to the hospital and ask them to review the autopsy. They have to keep tissue in the hospital, and by law they'd have to do a review if you request it."

"A review?"

"Have another look at the tissue to see if they can learn more."

"But the funeral is tomorrow," she says in a near whisper.

"I know, Mrs. Stock. I'm so sorry."

Her heavy breathing fills the line.

"Mrs. Stock, I promised you I'd find out what happened to Lee. I believe deeply that the full story of what really happened is somehow not being told."

"What do you want me to do?"

"I can pick you up in thirty minutes to take you to the hospital."

I feel the indecision in the silence.

"I'll be there in thirty minutes. I have a navy blue Hyundai Sonata. If you're willing to help, just please come out. If not, I completely understand. Okay?" I feel like a jerk for pushing so hard as I tap off the call.

"What do you mean by 'what really happened?'" she asks through dead eyes as she gets in to my car thirty minutes later.

"I just think there's more to the story than what the police are saying." I fight with myself about how much to tell but decide to leave it at that. "And I think there's more to be learned from the autopsy report."

A look of greater pain crosses her face as I explain the autopsy review procedure and how she can make an official request. I wait in the car as she goes in.

Watching this poor woman amble toward the door, I wonder if I'm doing the right thing. Her only child is gone. How much does it matter whether she died of a heart arrhythmia or of something else? How much does it matter if her daughter was pregnant or not, if Becker was involved or not, if Min Zhao is part of the story? Her daughter is lost. Period. Maybe it's just me who cares to tell the story, me burdened by my lost sister, my callous sense of justice, by a million and a half dead Armenians whose stories can never fully be told. Maybe I should just leave her alone.

"They said they can't do it," she says through heavy breaths after opening the car door fifteen minutes later.

"Who said?"

"The doctor, I think his name was Papadoc or something like that."

"Dr. Papadakis."

"Yes."

"What did he say?"

"That he's sorry but that he did the autopsy himself and there's no reason to review it just to find the same thing."

"But that choice isn't his to make if you make the request."

She turns to face me with a pleading look in her eyes. "Please, Mr. Azadian, take me back to the hotel."

Part of me wants to resist, but I know it's not the right thing to do. "I'm so sorry," I say again, stupidly.

I turn gently toward Carol as I pull up the drive toward the hotel entrance. "When I spoke with you on Wednesday, I asked if you thought maybe she might have been pregnant."

Her body stiffens; a strange look comes across her face. "I'm not supposed to talk about it," she says nervously after a long pause.

"Can you say who told you to not talk about it?" I ask gingerly, sensing I may already know the answer.

"He had big plans . . ." She stops herself.

"Big plans for what?" I say as softly as possible, fearing that even the slightest pressure could tip Carol Stock over.

She doesn't respond.

"Mrs. Stock," I almost whisper, "big plans for what?"

Carol Stock stares at me pleadingly, as if asking to be excused from answering my question. "For the Second Coming." The words flow quietly through her lips like gas leaking from a cracked jar.

"Are you telling me that Reverend Becker—"

The smack on my driver's side window reverberates through my head like a sledgehammer. I jerk my head left and instinctively retreat from the enormous hand spread across the glass like a ferocious paw. I cast my gaze upward and cower under the raging gaze of Cobalt Becker.

25

If the God in whom I don't believe is, as the Puritans understood, an angry God, then Cobalt Becker, his self-appointed representative here on earth, is his equally wrathful agent.

Becker's burning eyes reach through my window and grab me. I have only one option. I open the door and stand before him.

He glares through me with laser-like intensity. His shoulders rise and fall with his heavy breath like a bull setting to charge.

I expect a barreling voice when he begins moving his mouth, but his intense whisper, more like a hiss, is even more chilling. "What in God's name are you doing?"

My mind scans for possible answers. There is nothing for me to say.

"Have you no decency," he thunders quietly, "no shame?"

I stand my ground, but only barely.

"How dare you take advantage of this woman? How dare you cause her even more pain in her hour of grief?"

I feel myself shrinking before the fierce charisma of Cobalt Becker.

Then something clicks inside of me.

My voice returns. "Good afternoon, Reverend."

His glower pierces my defenses.

I struggle to hold out. "Everyone feels terrible about what happened to MaryLee Stock," I say, feeling self-conscious that I never actually knew her, "but I am determined to find the full story of what *actually* happened."

My words almost physically push back Cobalt Becker. I press forward. "I don't believe she died of a heart arrhythmia."

Becker's stare almost assaults me.

I press on. "It looks to me like something worse may have happened to her. Her story deserves to be told." My spirit grows beyond my frame like a shadow elongating in a setting sun.

Becker's breath quickens, his chest lifts, his eyes grow wider. Then his look softens like a car shifting down a gear. "Tell me exactly what you mean."

His shift puts me again off balance. "I think the autopsy was a sham," I say quickly. "I think MaryLee's death was connected to something bigger than her. I think there are a lot of questions that need to be answered."

Becker then turns his attention to Carol Stock.

"Carol," he says softly, "please go inside. Revered DeWitt is there to take care of you."

Carol Stock gets out of the car and shuffles toward the hotel entrance as if she's become a bit player in her own daughter's death.

"I have no idea what you are talking about," Becker whispers, "but this is not right. Look at her. You must leave her in peace."

He places one hand on each of my shoulders. I fear he's going to strangle me but then feel the warmth of his massive hands almost merging with my muscles as if he's melting me. He leans his head toward mine as if offering a benediction.

"Leave us in peace, Mr. Azadian," he says in a whisper that washes through my body. "Whatever you are looking for, you will not find it here."

He peers into my eyes and then deeper, into the soul I've always doubted I possess. I am overpowered.

Becker removes his hands then walks slowly to the hotel entrance, not looking back.

I stand paralyzed, as if this brief encounter has scrambled the controls to my nervous system.

Who is Cobalt Becker? I ask myself, stunned. What strange power does he have over me? I can't read him. Somehow I fear him. Something inside me is inexplicably drawn to him. I stumble to my car, feeling anger boiling up inside of me.

I tap through my u.D. Joseph Abraham and Jerry Weisberg's faces pop up on my split screen dashboard. "Are we secure?" I ask.

"Think so," Jerry answers.

"Jerry, could Cobalt Becker possibly build a Centurion or a Trojan horse?"

Jerry nods. "You'd need resources to do it, but he seems to have them."

"Anything more on the malware?"

"We're working on it, but it's some really impressive work. It'll take more time."

"Joseph, what about the doctors and clinics?"

"I'm down to two fertility clinics and three OBs, but I'm having a hard time getting it down from there."

"Let me try," I say. "Send me the contact information."

"Will do, boss."

"Thanks, to both of you. We'll connect later."

The screen reverts to the shifting collage of photographs sent randomly from my u.D.

The image of Toni and me on horseback watching the annual burning of the Kansas prairie in Cottonwood Falls flashes by. The sun casts an orange spell on the reflecting grasses, the quiet joy flows from our faces. Should I have deleted these photos? I ask myself. Then the idea hits me. I hate to ask. I know how she'll feel when I do. But I know to my core that I cannot leave MaryLee's death, like Astrid's, unexplored and unexplained. And who else do I know who can help me get to the bottom of this?

I stupidly tap the text icon on my u.D.

T—need to speak, can we meet?

I pause for a moment, realizing how she will read these words and feeling like a jerk. Then I add *work related*. I know this will piss her off. I also know she'll be there.

The response comes in seconds.

Can meet in 30 near hospital.

1:00 at Tofu Bell on 32nd, I dictate, picking the least romantic place possible, trying, however feebly, to not give mixed signals.

CU, she replies.

I call Maurice on the bat phone and update him on Carol Stock and my total failure to get access to the tissue. I think about telling him of my unfolding plans but decide against it. If he didn't like my stealing garbage . . .

26

Tofu Bell is my dirty little secret.

A big part of me believes that to be great, something must be unique. If everyone embraces any fashion or view, chances are there's a better path they are missing available to those who challenge the orthodoxy.

"Whoso would be a man," my hero Ralph Waldo Emerson writes, "must be a nonconformist." But whoso would like a veggie bowl with quinoa, kale, sesame tofu, black beans, chia seeds, diced broccoli, and jicama for $9.95 must eat at Tofu Bell. That it's in every airport in the United States is somebody else's problem.

I take a seat facing the door and can't help feeling jittery as I wait.

Six months ago I was torn between my strong feelings for her and my constant sense there was another destiny awaiting me. Maybe Toni had been right when she'd told me that happiness wasn't a grand plan but a continuous series of small acts, each insignificant in itself, banding together to make a life, that the image of happiness was not staying up all night talking but her coming into the house with grass stains on her knees after playing with our hypothetical kids in our hypothetical backyard. Maybe the big picture, life itself, is made up of small dots, the pixels of our daily lives. Maybe, I wonder as I momentarily stop breathing as I see Toni gliding through the door, marking off the entire universe is the same as laying claim to nothing.

A mix of excitement, warmth, nervousness, attraction, and trepidation surges through my veins.

Five foot seven and too thin to be curvy, her long flowing arms sway with her stride like willow branches blowing in a gentle breeze. The sculpted bob of her jet-black hair curves in to frame her oval face. Her green eyes dance from her almond skin. She radiates.

I smile inwardly and gulp at the same time as I stand and move awkwardly in her direction. Not sure if I should hug her or just say hello, I end up in a strange no-man's land between the two. "Hi," I say. The small word struggles to carry layers of imperfectly defined meaning.

She looks at me and smiles unevenly, her smile impulse seeming blocked by better sense. I step back.

As I have from the moment I met her, I feel the desire to pull her to me. I don't. "Can I get you something?"

She glances at me with a knowing look on her face, challenging me to explain what she's doing here.

I pull out a seat for her. "It's good to see you," I say, racking my brain for something more creative.

"It's nice to see you, Rich," she says, sitting.

In our eight months of dating she almost never once called me Rich, Dikran, or any proper name. Her words confirm our new status.

"How have you been?" I ask, kicking myself for my predictability.

"I've been fine. How's your mom?" she says, throwing me a bone.

"She's good."

"Still worried about you?"

"Do you need to ask?"

"Still showing her photos of Shoonig?"

"Do you really need to ask?"

"The Janissary?" she adds with a slight smile.

Every word, every gesture with Toni has a history, tells a story that simultaneously pushes us together and pulls us apart.

It had been our third date, the Kansas City Symphony playing Rachmaninoff in front of the magnificent Union Station. Toni noticed the look on my face when she leaned over from our picnic and petted the dachshund puppy passing our blanket.

"Look at the baby," she'd said, an unbridled love in her voice.

It was hard for me to pretend. The first two dates had gone so well I didn't feel the need to. My mistake.

The dog passed and she gave me a look I'd later learn much better how to interpret. Then, I didn't know it was a warning sign to stop.

"You know, psychopaths don't like dogs," she'd said.

"I could have sworn it's that kids who abuse their pets can end up as psychopaths," I'd replied, dipping a baby carrot into the Costco hummus.

She'd wiggled her nose, in retrospect another sign I should have left well enough alone.

"I know people say a dog is a man's best friend," I'd prattled on, "but who are the other friends?"

She'd bit her lower lip. Of course, yet another missed sign.

"And people feel like their dogs love them, but what else are the dogs going to do?" I'd jabbered on. "They have one evolutionary skill of kissing their owners' asses in exchange for food and shelter. What other options do they have? How many Chihuahuas would make it on their own in the wild? How many Chihuahuas does it take to bring down a wildebeest?"

Now Toni was visibly starting to get annoyed. It was hard to miss but I was on a roll.

"And on top of that these dogs' lives start with a crime. We steal them away from their mothers and then force them to live with the people responsible for this theft. If any dog ever got full awareness of its life situation the first thing it would do is attack its owner. It's like the Janissaries during the Ottoman Empire, Christian babies stolen from their parents and forced to fight for the Sultan."

She'd stuck out her tongue in a playful way that sucked the wind out of my monologue.

"But that was a cute dog," I surrendered.

She shook her head from side to side.

In retrospect, I'm not sure I'd sufficiently appreciated how nice it was for someone to look at a puppy and simply feel love, or what an ass I'd been to push on with my point so obliviously. Maybe nothing about love is simple.

Toni smiles gently.

"Fine," I say, "the Janissary is fine." I tilt my head to suggest she hasn't answered my question.

"I'm good, Rich," she says, this time meaning it.

"Your parents, your sister, the nieces, guitar lessons?"

"Everyone's good," she says suspiciously, again challenging me to say what's going on before she decides how to respond.

I look at her for a moment too long then turn my eyes away. We speak for a while, skimming the surface but each mining in our different ways the many currents that lie below.

I know I need to tell her why I've asked her to meet me and that doing so will kill our small reconnection. I let the conversation flow until the two images of MaryLee's body, first still beautiful on the apartment floor and then dissected under Papadakis's scalpel, begin to invade my thoughts.

"I need to ask you a favor," I blurt out of seemingly nowhere.

Her body stiffens as I'd known it would. "That's why I'm here?"

"I wanted to see you," I say earnestly, "but yes."

"What do you need?" she asks in a functional voice that makes my shoulders drop.

"It's just that . . ."

"What do you need, Rich, just tell me." She enunciates each word in barely disguised anger.

"It's a complicated story. May I?"

She looks at me like a parent waiting to hear an excuse from an errant child.

As I tell her the story, beginning with MaryLee Stock's body on the apartment floor and ending with the suspicious autopsy, Carol Stock, and Cobalt Becker hissing in front of the downtown Marriott, her demeanor slowly changes.

"Are you sure you want to go forward with this?" she says in a tone that feels warmer.

She knows me well enough to already know the answer.

"What do you need from me?" she asks.

How many people do each of us have in our lives who are in our corner? How many can the universe ultimately provide? "I need you to steal a tissue sample from MaryLee Stock's autopsy," I say, trying not to sound squeamish.

Toni blanches. "You know what that means, don't you?"

"I think I do."

"You can't just steal tissue. It's illegal. People get fired for a lot less than that."

"I know," I say quietly.

"But," she says, finishing my sentence, "you can't rest until you find out what really happened to the girl."

"Do I need to answer that question?"

"But there's something more?" she asks intuitively.

"What do you mean?" I say, already knowing my evasion will be useless.

She looks at me without flinching.

I hesitate before speaking. "Something about her reminded me of Astrid," I say quietly, looking down.

The words hang in the air.

"I saw her dead body and something told me I needed to figure out why," I continue, "that I couldn't let another young woman just go without any rhyme or reason, that—"

"You know this is bullshit, don't you?"

She knows and I know that she can't really turn me down now that I've mentioned my sister. I'd been cautious about mentioning Astrid to Toni when we'd first started dating. Something about sharing the crisis that had shaped so much of my world had felt like a river that, once crossed, I'd never be able to cross back again. But once I'd begun Toni had coaxed the pain out of me in her gentle way.

"Six months ago you couldn't figure out how you felt and now that you need me you're asking me to risk my career?"

I try to speak but can't think of anything valid to say.

"To be or not to be," she had said six months ago in one of our final painful conversations. All of my convoluted words sounded like thinking to her. That was why she left.

What if life is never meant to be lived between these two poles? I'd then thought, between being here physically and everywhere metaphysically, between being present for the day-to-day and simultaneously observing the philosophical absurdities of our existence from above? Toni lived her life at the near pole. I floated, as always, somewhere in between.

"And you want me to sneak into the pathology lab, steal the tissue, and then what?" she says angrily.

"Then I need you to put it into a small refrigerated cooler and bring it to me."

"And what exactly will *you* do with it?" she asks.

"Give it to Maurice Henderson," I say, "the police inspector I'm working with."

Toni looks at me and doesn't need to say it. *If the police want the tissue, they can pretty well get it themselves.*

I shake my head slightly to reject the thought.

She breathes in deeply then blows the breath out through her mouth.

27

It's a lot of pressure being an only child, even worse one who didn't always have that status from a family and a people overburdened by the memory of loss. I'd always known it was expected of me to bring new life into the world to rekindle the tiniest bit of what has been lost and plant a seed for the future. But with each failed relationship the possibility of actually doing this has declined and my barely suppressed anxiety about failing some kind of ancestral mission has edged up.

That's why I'd considered the possibility before as some kind of insurance policy. I'd just never quite followed through.

I'd thought about this a lot. Doing it is another matter.

"Hi. May I help you?"

The Hope Parkway receptionist's words throw me for a loop. What is this, Burger King? I've knocked all five OBs and one fertility clinic off of Joseph's list with creative phone shenanigans, but the last two fertility clinics on the list have proven harder nuts to crack, so I'm stepping up my game in person.

It's sometimes hard to remember the days when fertility clinics were places where older women went trying to have children when nature alone wasn't playing along. In those days sex was the primary act leading to children and people only came to places like this when there was a problem. But that was before we learned how to read the human genome and before Preimplantation Genetic Diagnosis and Selection, PGDS, gave parents the ability to decide which of their many fertilized eggs they wanted to have implanted in the mother.

With parents having the increasing ability to choose which

of their potential children had the best chance of success, only the desperately poor and religious zealots choose to do things the old-fashioned way. For most everyone else sex is becoming a highly enjoyable recreation but an unnecessary risk for procreation, and in vitro fertilization and genetic selection clinics like this have become the norm, at least until the Christian right began to fight back, declaring the IVFGS baby industry contrary to "God's plan."

"I'm, um, here to freeze my sperm," I say haltingly.

"Oh," she says as if I'd said that I was there to deliver office supplies. "Have you been here before?"

"First time," I say with a silly look on my face.

"You'll need to read these materials then fill out the six forms." She hands me an e-tablet. "This isn't covered by insurance. I'll need to get your credit information."

"Um, okay," I say, waving my u.D over the reader.

The charge for $495 appears on my screen. Ouch. Could I have done this at home, I wonder. I have a Ziploc and extra freezer space. I tap the green icon to confirm.

"You can go in that door," she says.

I do.

"Sir." The deep voice comes from behind the nurses' station. I look over.

I hadn't expected a male nurse, let alone one built like a football player.

I must look a bit startled as I read his name tag, NURSE DWAYNE RICHARDSON.

"No problem, man," he says, reading my look, "I get that sometimes."

His words dispel some of the awkwardness but not all.

"Okay," I say in a caricature of a sporty voice, "let's get this show on the road." I cringe at my awkwardness.

"This is one of the easiest jobs you'll ever have," Richardson says calmly. I can't tell if this is some form of male bonding.

"Here's the receptacle, there's the room. Go in and lock the door. Magazines are in the top drawer. You can also download some virtual stuff on your u.D. Just wave it over the reader if you like. We also have virtual reality goggles. When you're done, leave the specimen in the cabinet."

"Tallyho," I say in an overwrought British accent, trying to be funny but immediately feeling like an even bigger idiot.

"Just take the time you need," he says with a coolness that makes me feel even more like crawling into a hole.

The room could have been any medical examination room in any city in America. Had I expected incense and soft music?

I don't dare even touch the outdated Oculus Rift goggles and am tempted to go for the u.D app, but I don't fully trust the privacy settings and am not much of a porn guy anyway.

I leaf through the embedded magazines and see something for everyone. In addition to *Playboy*, they have *Buttmaster*, *Sexy over Sixty*, *Gazongas Maximus*, *Spicy Latinas*, and *Va China*. I sense I must be more old-fashioned than I think as I pick up *Playboy* and start leafing through.

I find myself drawn to an article describing the growing conflict in Siberia as the Russians fight the losing battle to stop China from stealing fresh water via the massive underground cross-border tunnels they've dug into Siberia's Lake Baikal. I get lost in the article until I remind myself of the mission at hand. Or, perhaps, not yet in hand.

I look at the women in the photos, but they all look like children to me. Beautiful, sexy, but kids. I must be getting older. I don't remember having such concerns leafing through the pornos in Billy Gregorian's basement during middle school. I'm not feeling much stirring. This approach isn't going to work.

I close the magazine, lean my back against the wall, and shut my eyes. I don't have to scan long to find the image. It's Toni, just sleeping in my bed. Her head is faced away from me, her black hair rolling over the pillow, her small ribcage gently rising and falling with her breath. I watch her for a while from my side of the bed, feel her warmth, smell her scent. Slowly, I slide behind her, my body following the curve of hers, my arm softly gliding over her stomach. She stirs ever so slightly and her hand reaches up to hold my wrist, pulling me closer into her. She rolls her head in my direction and kisses my shoulder while making an almost imperceptible whine. Our bodies slowly revolve together and settle into each other, fitting perfectly as if mine has an inversion for each protrusion of hers and vice versa.

I unzip my pants and screw the lid off the container.

I close my eyes and enter her. Our bodies rub against each other, into each other, deeper and deeper. They merge.

I release then open my eyes again, dizzy, confused.

What am I doing with my life? I ask myself.

Two billion years of evolution, my life story from a horny protozoan to an angst-ridden thirty-nine-year-old hominid, all collected in a plastic container left in a stainless steel cabinet.

"I have a question for you," I say to football Nurse Dwayne Richardson as I exit the room.

"Shoot."

I refrain from making the obvious joke.

"My wife said after I'm done I should ask about when you are going to fertilize the eggs and what more you need from us?"

"Your wife?" He looks confused.

"She said you had her eggs and now this is what you need." I point back to the examination room.

Nurse Richardson picks up my file.

"You didn't mention that in your forms."

"I thought you knew. That's why I'm here."

"Sorry, man," Richardson says, "this is above my pay grade. You'll need to talk to the doctor for that."

"Can I speak to her now?"

"Sorry, man," Nurse Richardson says, "doesn't work like that. You need to make an appointment."

"Ugh, God, really?" I say. "My wife told me that everything was set and all I need to do is this. We've already met with the doctor two times."

"I don't see that on your file," he says, again leafing through my papers. "Which doctor did you meet with?"

"Dr. Chaudhury," I say.

"Don't see it."

"I don't know," I say. "There's definitely a file. Maybe it's under my wife's name."

"All right," Richardson says cautiously, "let me have a look."

"Last name is Stock," I say, "MaryLee Stock."

He walks up to the reception then comes back a few minutes later. "I don't know what to tell you, man," he says, "we've looked through our all of our files and nothing under that name."

"Oh, shit," I say.

"Sorry man," he says supportively, "we can still freeze your sperm if you want. I see you've already paid for that."

My strong breath out makes my closed lips flap. "Why don't you just do that for now," I say, projecting dejection.

"Sorry man."

This is not the place I'm looking for, but the Azadian legacy is secure until the next power outage.

It's 4:15 p.m. on a Friday and I race toward the next name on the list hoping the drive will be long enough to let the same trick work once more.

Oh, to be twenty again.

28

I pull into the Bright Horizons parking lot twenty minutes before five.

I'd thought Hope Parkway was like a Burger King, but this place is even more corporatized, designed to a T. The Hope Parkway walls seemed painted with army surplus. Here, a Pantone consultant has obviously earned big bucks to come up with a soothing aquamarine and caramel color scheme. The elegant signs on the wall and subdued track lighting seem designed to create an impression—competent, professional, comfortable, safe.

Again the receptionist gives me the e-tablet to fill out, scans my u.D for payment, and sends me through a door. Again a nurse hands me a plastic container, directs me to a room in the back, and gives me instructions. Again I feel awkward.

I still can't get it through my thick head that what was once the result of wild sex in the back of a teenager's car now comes from a man shooting in a plastic container, a woman having her eggs extracted surgically, and the couple coming back a few days later to select from among their twenty or so fertilized eggs based on genetic predictors of future traits. It's even more shocking to me that scientists are on the verge of being able to produce unlimited eggs from induced stem cells that will blow this process wide open.

The room here at Bright Horizons is far better designed for the task than the one at Hope Parkway. The lights are less glaring, the Oculus Rift VR glasses are the latest model and apps can download into them without touching anything. Someone even had the foresight to provide Handi Wipes just in case. How thoughtful, I think, a pump dispenser of Sinoglide.

I must have gotten warmed up at Hope Parkway because I slide on the virtual reality glasses and tap the car wash app. It's as if I am between the young woman and the car, as if I am a soap bubble. Up and down, up and down. This is going to be one fucking clean car. Up and down, now sideways. Her body provides a lot of extra surface area to the cleaning process. The hose . . .

Maybe, I think, as I screw the top back on the filled container, I'm not as complicated as I'd led myself to believe an hour ago.

I leave the specimen in the cabinet then come outside to pull the same trick.

The nurse, a not so spicy thirty-something Latina, stiffens when I mention MaryLee Stock's name then excuses herself and scurries away awkwardly.

I wait for ten minutes.

Nothing.

Ten minutes more.

Nothing.

Then a rail-thin, highly made-up woman who appears to be in her fifties emerges from around the corner where the nurse had disappeared. Her face looks like she's just come through a wind tunnel. Her hair is pulled back in a tight bun. Her gait and expression are all business.

"Mr. Azadian, my name is Jessica Crandell. I'm the general manager here. Can you please step into my office?" She speaks reluctantly, as if retracting each word before she has fully offered it.

She gestures for me to take a seat.

"You say that your wife has had her eggs extracted here. Is that correct?"

"Yes, ma'am,"

"And the name of your wife is?"

"Stock, MaryLee Stock."

"I see," she says slowly. "And do you have documentation of your marital status?"

"Not with me," I say. "Do I need it?"

"As you can imagine, Mr. Azadian, the work we do here at Bright Horizons is highly confidential. We are bound by law and corporate ethics to maintain the utmost secrecy of our records."

"But can't you just look in MaryLee's file? You'll just see my name listed and then I can show you my driver's license to confirm my identity?"

"But Mr. Azadian, I'm sure you will understand I am not at liberty to say if there is a file or not."

"I completely understand," I say, lifting my wrist and starting to tap my u.D, "why don't I just call MaryLee and put you on with her."

A strange, almost smug look comes over Jessica Crandell's face. She leans slightly toward me. "Why don't you just do that, Mr. Azadian," she says, her eyes glaring into mine before a forced almost-smile presses up the edges of her lips.

My suspicion radar is pinging.

"Speed dial five," I dictate to my u.D. I'm not sure what inspires me to pick this number. Maybe it's the one most likely to go straight to voice mail. Maybe I'm a masochist. The voice streams through my earpiece.

"This is Martina Hernandez. I've missed your call. Leave your name and number."

"Baby it's me," I say. "I'm at Bright Horizons and they're having a hard time accessing your file. Can you please call me when you get this? You can also," I look up at the impassive Jessica Crandell, "call Jessica Crandell at . . ."

I revel in the hint of suppressed anger on her face as she spits out the ten digits.

"At nine one three, two seven four, thirty-seven thirty-three," I repeat. "Please call as soon as you can. Love you, baby," I add as I tap off.

A more composed look comes across Crandell's face.

"She'll call any minute," I say.

"It doesn't really matter," she says calmly, "we wouldn't be able to divulge information about any of our, our potential clients by a phone call anyway."

"But didn't you just say that I should just call my wife?" I ask, projecting innocence.

She doesn't miss a beat. "I was saying that you had every right to do that, not that a phone message would have any determinative status."

The words "determinative status" somehow jar me. "I see," I say slowly, "that's what you meant?"

The undercurrent of tension rages below our formal conversation.

"Well, I'll just have to bring her in with me on Monday then."

"You do that, Mr. Azadian," she says, standing with an unconvincing half smile. "We'll look forward to seeing you then." Her demeanor doesn't suggest she's looking forward to anything.

I stand and take a few steps toward the door before turning back. "Oh," I say deliberately, "I see you have the *Kansas City Star* on your coffee table? Are you a reader?"

She is smooth, but I can almost see the calculations in her head. My article on MaryLee Stock's death is on page A3 of this edition of the paper. If she says no, what is the uncreased paper doing on her coffee table? If she says yes and she's as on the ball as she seems, what's the likelihood that MaryLee Stock's name has rung a bell? I enjoy watching her squirm.

"It gets delivered," she says calmly, "but I hardly ever have time to read it."

Bingo.

"Thank you so much, Ms. Crandell. MaryLee and I look forward to getting this straightened out on Monday," I say.

I hold my gaze at Jessica Crandell.

As she stares back, suppressed anger almost pulsates beneath the surface calm of her studied professionalism.

After five or so long seconds I turn and walk out the door with the strange feeling that MaryLee Stock may well have walked these steps before.

29

"I think we may have found it," I say breathlessly into my dashboard screen.

"Are you sure, boss?" Joseph looks startled.

"Pretty sure."

"Which one?" he asks.

"Bright Horizons, 103rd and Mission."

"Now what?"

"Whoever's the father, the information is in their records. That's the link."

"Can we get it?"

"Good question," I say. "I'm not sure. Either we get it or we pretend we have it, either way this could be our blue dress."

"Blue dress, boss?"

"The Clinton sex scandal. I was in middle school when President Clinton denied he'd been with Monica Lewinsky until word got out about a stained blue dress. They never had to produce the dress. The idea of it forced Clinton to confess."

"And you think that's what we have here?"

"Maybe," I say reflectively.

"And if they call the bluff and ask for evidence?"

"If they do that, Joseph, we're, I'm pretty much screwed. I need you to find out what you can about Bright Horizons. Who owns them, how do they protect their records, what kinds of people can access them, do they have surveillance cameras in their parking lot, who can access the tapes? See what you can dig up about the general manager, Jessica Crandell. There's got to be a crack in the wall somewhere."

"On it, boss."

My mind shifts back to Toni as the line drops. I've been fantasizing about her all afternoon but still haven't heard from her.

You OK? I dictate to text.

Do you really want to know? Her reply comes immediately.

Yes!

Not OK.

Talk? I write, navigating the strange strata of intimacy between text, voice, video, and real-life.

I guess.

Meet? I write. *Loose Park tennis court in 15?*

Ugh, she replies, which I interpret as an angry yes.

I'd expected to find her sitting on the park bench near the water fountain but am surprised to see her stewing in her car. I open the passenger door and get in.

"I am really pissed at you," she says in her coldest of tones.

I don't know how to respond without more information. I look at her apologetically. The silence hovers.

"I am really, really pissed at you," she repeats.

I'm still not sure how to respond.

"Talk," she orders.

"What happened?"

"Let me see," she says, "you send me prying around the pathology lab. How much did you care if I got caught? How much did it concern you that I could be fired?"

"I'm so sorry." I realize I keep apologizing to everyone around me and keep pushing them into harm's way nonetheless. "Please tell me what happened," I say softly.

She takes a deep breath then pauses and looks at me angrily. "It was easy to find where the tissue was supposed to be on the hospital computer. We had an infant mortality in the NICU yesterday. At the end of my shift, I told the path people I wanted to see the body one last time before it was sent for burial. I said the case had gotten personal for me. They let me in and pulled out the container with the body. I told the attendant I wanted to be alone with the baby's body for a few moments and asked if he'd excuse me."

Toni pauses to calm herself.

"He said they didn't normally allow that, but because I was on staff he guessed it was okay. When he left, I started to open the drawer with the tissue you wanted. I opened it." Toni's eyes begin to tear. "Then I heard the door flying open. I pushed the drawer closed as quickly as I could, but he saw me."

"He?"

"The chief pathologist, Papadakis, he started screaming, asking me what the hell I was doing, saying he was going to have me fired. He grabbed my ID badge and pulled it off my neck then told me to get out."

"And?"

"And I did. I left the hospital and drove home. And I didn't hear from you and thought it was so typical of you to send me to do something so dangerous for me and to not even call to see how I was."

"I'm so sorry."

Toni shakes her head in disbelief. "I even knew you would say that. You probably even mean it. You just weren't there."

She's right and I know it. Part of me wants to tell her that I've been fighting to find out what happened to an innocent murdered girl, that I'd fantasized about her in the IVFGS clinic when nothing else worked, that it means the world that she was there when I needed her and she is here now. But I know that any of these words will only dig my hole deeper, that all of them are about what she's doing for me. No wonder I'm still alone.

"Can I ask you . . . ?" I say in my softest voice.

Her eyes shift between expectancy and anger.

"What was in the drawer?"

She puts both hands on the steering wheel and looks out the front window with the distant face that had always frightened me when we were together, always signified a chasm I wondered if I could ever overcome.

"I caught a glimpse just as Papadakis was storming in."

"And?" I press on, knowing I'm angering her even more.

She stares at me for a moment then shifts her gaze out the front window.

"It was empty," she says softly.

30

It would be one thing if tissue samples had never been retained, but they had. Papadakis had all but confirmed that in my brief encounter with him. And the samples were logged into the hospital computer system. How could they disappear? Where could they go? Why did Papadakis fly into such a rage when he found Toni in the lab?

Somebody is working incredibly hard to cover up. They erased MaryLee's u.Mail account, officially forced me off the story, took the case away from the KCPD, and now probably stole the remaining tissue that could have told how MaryLee Stock actually died.

Toni looks at me disdainfully. She knows I'm not thinking of her.

My eyes can only be described as sheepish.

"I did what you asked," she says. "Now I think you should go."

I look at her with pleading eyes as I try to formulate a response. "Toni, I'm—"

"Don't," she cuts me off.

I nod my head sadly then slowly get out of the car. I feel the wind on my face as I stand, lost in the small parking area as she pulls away.

Then I feel the vibration on my wrist.

"Azadian, I have no idea what your phone message is about, but it's obvious you're not doing what I told you to do," I hear through my earpiece. "I'm calling to make myself completely clear."

"Not sure if it's a good idea on the u.D," I say.

"Why?"

"Because others might be listening."

"That's the whole point," she says sharply. "I want you and anyone else to hear what I'm about to tell you. Drop the story, Rich."

"You mean the flower show?"

"Don't be a smart-ass. I am telling you, drop the fucking story. Drop the story now. And if you don't understand that, let me put it to you this way. We are suspending you from the paper."

"What?"

"Suspending you. You are suspended. How much clearer can I make this?"

"Martina, I don't understand," I stammer.

"I am here with Wes and Terry. We just had another visit from Marshal Gillespie and his sidekick, who handed us our second NPA notice. Do you know what that means?"

I hesitate.

"Do you?" she asks in an even harsher voice.

"Yes," I say sharply, "that NPA funds will get cut off next."

"That's right. It means that the *Star* will be shut down unless you stop and I, we, are ordering you to do it now. I can't say this any more clearly. Do you understand?"

"Yeah."

"Do you?"

"Yes," I say dejectedly, "I do." My voice trails off.

"Good. Human Resources will be in touch with you about your status, your lack of status."

The call drops.

Whatever I think Martina's personal views may be, this time it's the paper talking.

My mind feels like a sputtering engine randomly spewing sparks as I sink into my car seat and lift my heavy hand to the ignition. All of my passion, all of my drive, feels almost conquered by the darkness coming over me. This could be the story of a lifetime and also the story of a single life, and the *Kansas City Star* wants me to drop it just like that? If I keep going, they will get shut down and I'll go to jail. If I try to get this published somewhere else, I'll still go to jail and that other news organization will face the same NPA pressures as the *Star*.

I'm so lost in my thoughts, I almost miss the ring coming from the bat phone.

"Rich," the furtive voice declares, "it's Henderson. Where are you?"

"In my car, heading home," I say.

"Don't."

"What?"

"Don't go home."

"Why?"

"Trust me, Rich. I already shouldn't be telling you this." His voice drops to a near whisper. "They're there now. Don't go home. Got it? And meet me tomorrow morning at seven thirty. Same place. And Rich."

"Yeah?"

"Be careful," Maurice whispers.

The call drops.

I feel a surge from inside me I can't completely define. Perhaps it's shock that I've just been suspended from my job, perhaps anger at strangers violating my home. I imagine them digging through my piles of crap, shaking my instruments, wiggling their fingers through my socks and underpants. Part of me is enraged, part is a bit frightened. But my secret database is in my head, and to find it they'll need to pull it out from where it is lodged. Halfway, it feels right now, jammed up my ass. And my immediate priority is simply finding a place to go.

My home is out of the question. I sense intuitively I have no other choice.

I tap my u.D for speed dial 2.
She picks up after the first ring.
"It's me," I say softly.
Toni doesn't respond.

31

I must be emitting some kind of cosmic distress signal as I drive toward Toni's place, because just when I think I can't take any more confusion, my mother calls.

"Dikranigus."

I cringe. "Hi, Mom," I say, trying to mask my voice.

My mother's emotional Geiger counter can't be so easily fooled. "Dikran, I hear it in your voice," she says in a more serious tone, "are you okay?"

"I think I am," I say, then kick myself for not resisting.

"What does *that* mean?"

"I'm fine, Mother."

"*Janeegus*, talk to your mother."

"Mom," I say, "please believe me, I can't."

My mother surprises me by uncharacteristically backing off. "Just know I love you and that I'm here for you."

"I know that."

"Where are you now, Dikran?" she asks.

"In my car."

"Going?"

I know I shouldn't answer honestly but don't have the energy to make something up.

"To someone's house," I say after a few seconds.

"Well, I'm not saying anything, Dikranigus, but that's a good direction for you."

"Thanks, Mom," I say without much inflection.

She picks up my tone, or lack of it, immediately. "What did I say?"

"Nothing, Mom. I love you."

"I love you, Dikran, if you want to talk, you know I am always here."

"I know, Ma."

"Bye, Dikran. Say hello to someone for me."

I tap off the call knowing she's still waiting on the line.

I arrive at Toni's small house with a growing sense I'm losing control of my life. I've not been back to Glendale for two years, but my relationship with my mother remains unchanged. I'm separated from Toni but now feel myself drawn back to her. I'm wavering about dropping the story, but with the feds searching my place right now the story is being drawn to me. And I'm exhausted.

I still have her key in my glove compartment but knock anyway. Toni opens the door and walks away without saying a word. I follow her into her kitchen.

"So tell me," she says in her all-business voice, her full defenses deployed.

I explain to her that I've been suspended from the paper, that federal marshals are probably searching my place right now, that I may have to drop the story.

"Are you going to?"

"I don't know."

She thinks for a moment before speaking. "Do you want some tea?"

Her question surprises me. "Thanks," I say, conscious that our new distance forces us to articulate what, when we were together, had increasingly been communicated through gradations of silence.

She fills a mug with water and sticks it in the microwave.

"How can I let go of this when I saw the girl's body on the

floor and when I think that what really happened, whatever that is, is being covered up? But how can I keep going when doing so could so easily kill the paper and land me in jail? And I've already gotten you into so much trouble at work."

I read Toni's face and beat her to the punch. "To be or not to be."

She only half smiles. How many times had she accused me of living my life and observing it from afar at the same time? "Do you have to decide now?"

I think about her question for a moment. "Pretty much."

"Why don't you sleep on it for the night? I hate to say it, but the girl is already dead."

I pause to consider her words.

"Just take the guest room and think about it."

I still don't move.

"Go on up," she orders. "I'll bring you some dinner later or you can eat down here if you like. Either way."

"Thanks," I say, marveling at how many different meanings we cram into these simple, imprecise words.

I lumber up the stairs, passing the door to her bedroom that had taken so much initial effort to enter, then proceeding down the short hall to the guest room. The lavender walls and silver transom hardly match my mood. I throw myself on the bed.

Breathing in deeply, I remember the two yoga classes Toni had dragged me to at her gym. Everybody else sat up at the end of the class with serene looks on their faces and together recited "Namaste." My mind had raced the whole time. I try to watch my breath going in and out. It doesn't seem to help.

Thoughts of William of Occam invade my head. Lay down the facts, weigh the options, find the simple truths on the far side of complexity.

I picture a grid in my mind and place a key piece of the story in each box, then I separate the boxes into a series of free-floating squares, moving them around to see what can match with what, where Occam's simple story emerges. Should I walk away? I wonder. Maybe some stories can't or shouldn't be told.

Toni's words come back to me. Do I really need to make this decision now? What if I just sleep on it? And my meeting with Henderson tomorrow morning in Swope Park? Can I just not show up and call it a day?

Breathe in, breathe out. I watch my breath inside of me and can almost see it.

The knock startles me.

She opens the door slightly and peeks her head in through the crack. "I made some pasta. Want me to bring it up?"

"I'll come down," I say. "Give me a sec."

"Yeah," she says, closing to door.

More silly little words carrying so heavy a load.

The normality of our dinner—pasta, salad, and Perrier around her kitchen table—feels hauntingly familiar, a scene from a past life fast blurring into the present.

We talk about MaryLee Stock, about the hospital, about the comings and goings of her mother and her sister, but the real conversation happens in the spaces between the words.

My mind wanders to a conversation we'd had when we'd just started dating as I walk up the stairs after cleaning the kitchen.

"What's your favorite pet?" she'd asked me as we strolled through the Plaza.

My don't-answer-honestly meter had started beeping in my head. As always, I didn't listen.

"Probably a dolphin," I'd said.

"A dolphin?"

"Yeah, I'd live on the beach and go swimming in the mornings. The dolphin could come swim with me when it wanted then we'd do our own thing until we met the next time."

She'd dropped my hand. It didn't take a mind reader to guess what she'd been thinking.

So much for honesty, I'd thought at the time.

Now I think I'm an asshole.

I get ready for bed and crawl under the covers. I toss and turn, trying unsuccessfully to watch my breath coming in and going out. If I can't make a decision that impacts one other person, how can I make a decision that impacts all 674 employees of the *Kansas City Star*?

32

My u.D alarm only half wakes me because I can't be more than half asleep. I tap off the message from my u.D, annoyed that it keeps reminding me my sleep quality is, don't I know it, *poor*.

An hour before I'm scheduled to meet Maurice I twist out of bed and make my way to the guest bathroom. A bag with socks, underpants, and a couple of shirts hangs from the knob outside my door.

I thought these things had been thrown away when we split. Being here, eating at the kitchen table, having these clothes, makes me feel, confusingly, like I've never left.

Toni is up and reading the news on her counter screen when I come down the stairs. The sight of her sitting erect in her barstool behind the counter, her head tilted slightly to the right as she focuses intensely on the words, her bobbed black hair dangling and exposing the full length of her slender neck, the way her T-shirt rolls over her body make me gasp. I pause and try to hide it, feeling like an actor entering a scene from the wrong part of the stage or from a different play altogether.

"Good morning," she says.

"Thanks for the clothes," I say.

She smiles slightly but doesn't answer.

"I need to ask you for a favor," I say.

She tilts her head and looks at me with wide eyes. *Well?*

"If they're searching my house, it may be best for me to not be driving my car," I say guiltily. It's obvious to both of us that I have already dragged her into this mess far more than I should have, that I've already put her job in danger, and that the federal agents snooping around my house might well be on their way here.

"And so you want to switch?"

"Kind of. I don't like the idea of you driving my car either. What if we switch for today but then maybe you can get a friend to rent a car and we can switch again at the end of the day? I'll take the rental car and you take your car back."

"You know you're drawing me into this, Richie?" she says, staring at me intently.

I don't have an answer.

She looks slowly across the room as she thinks. "Okay," she says after a short pause as if we both know she's already drawn in.

I feel like reaching out to her but look down as she fumbles through her purse. She hands me her keys.

The words *I owe you one* form in my mind but hardly seem worth saying. All I can come up with is the same stale "Thank you."

I head out the door still feeling somehow awkward. "I'll see you later," I say, then kick myself for saying it.

I call Joseph and Jerry as I drive toward Swope Park.

"Guys," I say into my dashboard screen, "federal marshals went through my house last night."

Neither of them looks surprised.

"I just want to let you know I won't blame you if you want to step back."

Joseph seems annoyed that I'm asking this question again. On the other half of the screen, Jerry simply looks distracted.

"They're threatening to pull funding from the paper," I add.

"If you don't drop the story?" Jerry asks.

"Yeah."

"How do they know you're on it?" Jerry says.

"I'm betting the visit to Bright Horizons tipped them off. Joseph, anything on them?"

"I couldn't find any records for Jessica Crandell."

"Is that strange?"

"Is to me, boss. People usually show up somewhere."

"What about their records?"

"Seem to be air-tight," Joseph says.

"Who owns the company?"

"They're owned by a company called Bright Horizons Holdings LLC."

"Who are they?"

"A holding company, boss. There are five Bright Horizons clinics around the US, in Kansas City, Oklahoma City, Atlanta, Denver, and Nashville."

"And what do we know about the LLC?" I ask.

"That's the point, boss. There's no information. I looked everywhere. All I can find is that it's a Delaware holding company held by another holding company in the Cayman Islands."

"Why would a fertility clinic be registered in the Cayman Islands?"

"That's easy," Jerry says. "You register in the Cayman Islands if you don't want anyone to know who you are. All the porn and online gambling sites do it."

"But for a fertility clinic?"

33

I'm starting to feel like a drug addict.

Who else races back and forth to Swope Park at all hours to meet secretly in an obscure picnic area?

Maurice is waiting for me as I pull up. He looks calm and collected. I sense I look like shit.

"Thanks for last night," I say, then add awkwardly, "for warning me."

"What have you learned?"

I pause for a moment feeling a bit uncomfortable about the pattern that's emerging of Maurice asking me all the questions, me telling him everything I know, and him sharing so little with me.

"I'm pretty sure MaryLee was a patient at the Bright Horizons fertility clinic."

"How confident?"

"I was pretty confident when I was there. Then, pretty soon after I left, the federal marshals came to the *Kansas City Star* and issued their second News Protection Act notice. Then you called to say the marshals were coming to my place just after that. Made me think I'd hit a tripwire or something."

"What do you know about Bright Horizons?"

"It's owned by a shell company in the Cayman Islands. Whoever owns Bright Horizons doesn't want anyone to know who they are."

"Go on."

"I told you I was going to ask Carol Stock to request the tissue samples be reviewed."

"Yes."

"She went to the hospital and got turned away by Papadakis."

"I'm not surprised," Maurice says.

"So then I asked someone who works at the hospital to check into it."

Maurice's eyes perk up.

"And that person went to have a look where the samples were supposed to be."

"And?" Maurice asks.

"The samples were gone. Missing."

Maurice nods his head again pensively. "I see," he says softly.

His lack of surprise at this major piece of potential evidence I've just given him finally pushes me over the edge. "What's going on here, Maurice?" I say tersely. "You keep inviting me to this God-forsaken park and asking me to tell you everything I know. I've got my ass flapping in the wind, my friends are in danger, the *Star* is on the line. You ask me to trust you but you're holding back."

Maurice looks at me, but his eyes are unfocused, as if he's weighing options in his head. "What do you want to know?" he says after a pause.

"Everything, dammit."

Maurice stares at me intently. "Let's get a few ground rules straight," he says. "Everything we say doesn't go beyond this car. If I'm ever asked about any of this, I'll deny it. If you're ever asked, you'd better damn well deny it, too."

I nod slightly.

Maurice pauses once again as if not sure whether opening his mouth is the right thing to do.

"Another woman died in Olathe, Kansas, eighteen days ago. Her name was Megan Fogerty. It's outside of KCPD's jurisdiction, and I didn't think anything of it at first, but after the autopsy report came out and after our meeting at the café a couple days ago, I started to wonder if it could just be coincidence two young healthy women about the same age drop dead in the same metropolitan area. I started poking around and found out she was cremated without an autopsy. Then you told me that MaryLee Stock was pregnant when she died."

"And you confirmed it."

"I didn't," Maurice says, "I just refrained from disabusing you of the notion."

My mind tracks back to Maurice's subtle nod I interpreted as confirmation. "What the hell was that about?"

"Keep your shirt on, Rich. I didn't trust what I was seeing at KCPD and needed you to keep going. If the chief wasn't going to allow a proper investigation, you were the only one digging."

I'm annoyed at his manipulation but grudgingly accept the logic. "So tell me why you're so blasé to learn the tissue samples are missing?"

A mischievous grin crosses Maurice's face. "Because I've got the tissues."

34

"Joseph," I say, staring into my dashboard screen, "I need you to dig up everything you can about Megan Fogerty. She's a young woman who died two and a half weeks ago in Olathe. See if you can find any parallels between what happened to her and what happened to MaryLee Stock."

"On it, boss," he says. "There's another thing you should know. King's people just started a flash vigil at City Hall."

The pieces don't yet fit together in my head, but I still can't get over the strange connection between MaryLee Stock and Cobalt Becker, especially in light of Becker's critical relationship with Senator King. "I'm heading over now."

The traffic starts slowing at 17th and Locust. By 15th Street it's not moving at all. I pull in to a lot then start walking rapidly toward the noise. The din that first sounded like electronic static clarifies into thundering words as I near City Hall.

"A cold night is descending on this country," the unmistakable voice booms. "If we continue on the path of sin, if we continue to interfere with God's plan and challenge our Creator through the manipulation of life itself, then we are sowing the seeds of our own destruction, we are paving the road for our descent into hell."

By 12th Street, the full scene comes into view. Hundreds of people are holding hands in three concentric circles surrounding the City Hall building. All are wearing the same e-shirt, each digital shirt broadcasting the same live image on the front and back of Senator King speaking at yet another rally. The sound emitted by each of the shirts alone is small, but together they almost shake the building.

"I did not ask to follow this path," Senator King declares from the hundreds of shirts, "but the Lord sometimes calls upon all of us to take a stand, to do what is right in his name. The Bible tells us to render unto Caesar all things that are Caesar's. My friends, my brothers and sisters, we are all Caesars and God's word commands us to get this great ship of state heading once again in the right direction."

I am amazed at how completely Senator King, the brilliant political tactician with such a keen sense of the prevailing winds, has morphed himself from the rational conservative Republican he was to the quasi-religious figure he has now become. I despise what King and this movement stand for, but it's hard not to feel the power of his words, the strength of the bond he has created with his band of believers.

I walk around the outside of the circle, noting the wide-eyed conviction of the righteous army, contrasting it in my mind with the mild agreement so many of my friends feel when listening to the measured words of President Lewis and Vice President Alvarez. The president may be right, but I sense something possibly even more powerful in the electric energy that binds these people to each other and to King's Republican primary charge.

"And so my fellow Americans, my fellow children of God, I ask you. Will you stand for what you know in your heart to be true? Will you stand to cleanse our country through God's will? Will you stand with me and stand together?"

The ralliers are now weeping. They let go of each other and raise their hands in the air. Their singing starts softly then gains intensity. "God shall overcome, God shall overcome, God shall overcome someday."

Senator King's amped voice trumpets through the song. "Together, we will reincarnate our great country through God's will. God bless you. God bless America. God shall overcome."

The scene is stunning. I feel moved in spite of myself, the electricity of this politically charged zealotry moving through me.

Until I feel the vibration on my wrist.

"I need to see you. Now," Maurice's voice booms through my earpiece with a tone I've never heard from him.

35

The look on Maurice Henderson's face is bewildered with a strong dose of furious.

He stomps over to my car and gets in, slamming the door behind him.

"Potassium cyanide looks like sugar. At about three hundred milligrams, it's deadly," he barks.

"And that's—"

"Yes." He cuts me short. "In doses over three hundred milligrams, it leads to heart block and death. It wasn't Blue Magic. That's how MaryLee Stock died."

"And—"

"Potassium cyanide clears the bloodstream within a few hours, leaving almost no trace. Someone killing themselves probably wouldn't care so much about that and would have a lot of other options."

"But if it clears the bloodstream so fast," I say, "how do we know that's what killed her?"

"A regular autopsy wouldn't catch it. I had the deputy coroner do every possible test after he 'borrowed' the tissue samples. Trace amounts of potassium cyanide showed up in the tissue."

"And a dose that high would need to be ingested or injected," I say.

Maurice taps on the dashboard with an intensity and urgency that frightens me. A long, heavy silence fills the car. There's something more.

"Maurice, tell me," I say exasperatedly.

"How many chromosomes does a normal person have?"

"Forty-six."

Maurice stares at me with an intense focus. "MaryLee Stock was pregnant," he says after a pause.

My face tells Maurice, *I know, so what?*

He stares at me before speaking. "Her fetus had forty-seven."

My eyes pop as my brain processes the magnitude of this new information. "And if she was impregnated at an IVFGS clinic," I say feverishly, "then the various fertilized eggs were all screened before one got inserted."

"Yes."

"And so a decision was made at Bright Horizons to impregnate her with an abnormal fetus."

"Yes," Maurice says softly.

"Holy mother of God." I only realize the irony of my words after they escape my mouth. "And so either the father has a genetic abnormality and the clinic agreed to use his DNA regardless or something else is going on."

Maurice nods pensively.

"But IVFGS clinics don't impregnate people with abnormalities like that. The Supreme Court settled that," I continue.

"Yup."

"And we're dealing with something a lot more serious than we thought."

"Yes."

The silence feels thick as fog.

"So why would an IVFGS clinic impregnate a woman with a defective chain of chromosomes?"

"Defective?" Maurice asks.

"If I remember my biology, people born with too many or too few chromosomes can end up kind of freaky."

"What do you know about genetic enhancement?"

The words stop me in my tracks. "Biology 101," I say. "Viruses carry replacement genes into the nucleus."

"That's right," Maurice says. "I spoke with the deputy coroner about this. Apparently a forty-seventh chromosome can work as a docking station for additional genes."

My mind shifts into overdrive. News reports from past years on the miraculous advances in genetics and reproductive biology position and reposition themselves like jigsaw pieces in my head. "So why don't you just go to your boss and tell him what's going on?"

"I've been thinking about that," Maurice says. "I don't trust him. Nothing about this case has smelled right from the beginning. It's obvious the official autopsy report was a sham. It's one thing to miss potassium cyanide traces, but no one misses a pregnancy. There's no way that could've happened without the chief being somehow involved. I have no idea who else might be involved and how high this goes. Reporting this in without first figuring it out could make things ugly."

"And option two is for me to go to my boss and try to get her to run the story, but they're not going to risk the paper for this. And I can't publish elsewhere because the NPA restrictions apply to me, and any news organization in the US that runs it will be shut down and any foreign news organization immediately taken down by the US government."

"Which leaves us with option three," Maurice says. "Finding out what the hell is going on before more bad things happen, so we can figure out what to do without getting fired, imprisoned, or killed."

Maurice's words hit me. When this story hinged on computer code, the stakes were high enough. The stakes now are, quite literally, existential. Whoever killed MaryLee Stock won't necessarily stop there. "So what now?"

"We need more information on Megan Fogerty and Becker."

"I've got my team working on that already," I say. "The Becker connection is eating at me. His 'chosen one' is murdered pregnant, then I start questioning him and the feds jump in. It's too many coincidences. I feel like I should I go back to Springfield."

"So he can tell you the same thing again? You've done that already," Maurice says, "we need to start probing him from different angles, approach him from a different place." He pauses a moment to think. "Didn't you say Becker has a home in Texas?"

"I'm not sure about a home, but he seems to have a big cattle ranch."

"Is that strange?"

"I don't know. One of the newspaper articles called him God's rancher building his herd."

"Sounds pretty strange to me," Maurice says wryly.

"Hmm," I mumble, the preliminary thought forming in my mind.

"What does that mean?"

"I'm not sure," I say, the neurons not fully connecting. "Something about building a herd, building a congregation, building a movement."

"Maybe you should go have a look."

36

"MaryLee Stock died from a dose of potassium cyanide. Her fetus had an extra chromosome."

Joseph's shock comes through the screen. "An extra chromosome, boss?" He looks as if he hasn't heard me correctly.

"A mutation, possibly an enhancement."

"An enhancement?" Joseph says, going through the stages of shock I went through earlier in the morning.

Joseph starts to mumble indecipherably. "*Thayolee.*"

"What are you saying Joseph?"

"It's Malayalam. You don't want to know."

"A parking station for genetic enhancements."

"I've read about the possibility of using an extra chromosome as part of a genetic enhancement process, boss. We used it in India to make our rice drought resistant when the aquifers started to dry."

"Well, we need to know a lot more," I say, wiping my sweaty palms on my jeans. "We need to know the possibilities for an embryo with an extra chromosome."

"Yeah, boss, and how it got there."

"That's the key, Joseph." I'm almost numb from the potential implications. "What do you have on Megan Fogerty?"

"There's not much on her, but I'm sending you what I have right now. Twenty-six years old, not married, worked as an art therapist in the Willard Knox Village retirement complex."

"Was she involved with a church?"

"I didn't see anything, boss."

I tap my u.D, and the side of Jerry Weisberg's head appears on my dashboard.

"Mmm," he says, not looking up from his bank of computer screens.

"Jerry, it's Rich and Joseph," I say.

"Mmm," Jerry says.

"Jerry," I say, trying to get his attention, "we need to talk with you."

"Mmm," he says again, still not looking up from his screens.

I tell him what we've found.

Jerry's head snaps toward the screen. "Holy shit," he says with the face of someone who's just seen a UFO. "And if she got it at Bright Horizons, then—"

"Yes," I say, cutting him off. The PGDS revolution had changed everyone's thinking but not far enough to fathom the implications of this new fact.

"We're going to need help," Jerry says.

"Help?" I say.

"You both are smart guys and everything, but if you think IT code is complicated, wait till you get to the code of life."

"I'm sure you're right, Jerry," I say after a pause, "but we're what we've got right now, so I need—"

"There's a professor in the UMKC biology department who's also on the faculty at the Sowers Institute. Franklin Chou. Good guy. I think it would be worthwhile talking with him."

"Maybe, Jerry, but I'm just about to head out of town and—"

Joseph cuts me off. "I can do it, boss."

In the two years that Joseph has worked for me, I've been the front man out in the world, he the back office supporting me with research from the rear.

"If you can't do it, I can," Joseph says with surprising assertiveness. "I will."

It takes a moment for me to reassemble the pieces in my mind. "Can we trust Professor Chou?"

"Yes," Jerry says, "he's a friend. We don't need to tell him everything, just ask him about the science. He'll help."

"Can you arrange it, Jerry?"

"Will do."

"All right then, if computer code is so simple, what are you finding?" I ask.

Jerry scoffs. "It's simple compared to life, pretty darn complicated compared to everything else. This could be the best encryption program I've ever seen."

"That tells us something," I say. "At least we know we're dealing with experts. A state?"

"Could be. Any of the big guys could do this—China, Russia, Brazil, India, the US—they've all got major cyber commands."

"How about an individual?"

"They'd need to be really good. Really, really good. The Open-Net guys are coming at this thing from a lot of different angles. Does look like it's coming from a server in China, but it's hard to tell if it started there or someone else just hacked in."

"So it's either coming from China or coming from someone who wants people to think it's coming from China," I say.

"You could say that."

"And Bright Horizons?" I ask. "What can we do to find out who owns it?"

"I'm trying," Jerry says, "Cayman Islands are tough, their records are completely private."

"Completely?"

"Supposed to be. Sometimes people can be sloppy."

"What do you mean?"

"To register a company you need legal help, maybe an accountant, maybe you travel there and a hotel records where you're coming from. There are a thousand different angles. I'm probing. Nothing yet."

"All right," I say. "Keep on it."

As I tap off, five messages from Toni reach me at once on the screen.

Call me.

Call me.

Call me.

Where are you???

Dulce de leche.

Intimacy is a precious thing. Private language extracts words that have one meaning for everyone else and stamps new meanings on them that two people share. I get a warm sensation that I actually know what Toni is saying.

Almost a year ago, we were out shopping for a little dinner party for our friends we were having at her place. I grabbed the dulce de leche, her favorite, from the freezer at Price Chopper.

"I'm the only one who likes that," Toni said.

"I know," I told her, "that's why I'm getting it."

"But there are five other people. Put that back," Toni ordered. "Chocolate and vanilla."

When we'd been splitting up the scene had come back to my mind as a metaphor for our different ways of thinking. I was more about the individual. She was more about the group.

Six months later the memory has morphed into something entirely different, our private GPS.

15 minutes, I text back. I drive down 63rd Street then back left toward Meyer Boulevard. I pull into the Price Chopper parking lot and check the time on my u.D. I come around the corner into the frozen foods section and see her. She's wearing a long coat and a large beach hat. She looks ridiculously like someone hiding.

"Are you okay?" I whisper.

"You're the one they're after," she says nervously.

"What happened?"

"They came to my place looking for you."

"They?"

"The guy named Gillespie and another guy, Collins. Federal marshals." She hands me Gillespie's now familiar business card.

I wish this guy would leave me alone. "And?"

"I told him I didn't know where you were."

"And?"

"He said 'but you're letting him drive your car.'" She exhales. The sheepish look returns to my face. *Oh shit.*

"I'm so sorry," I say. "Do you think you were followed here?"

"I went to Ward Parkway and walked all through the mall. If they were following me I think I would have seen them."

"Hope so. And then?"

"I called my mom and told her to leave her car just outside of Trader Joe's and that I'd leave the keys to mine in the freezer section underneath the curry chicken. Then I texted you and drove here."

"I don't think your mom's car is that safe."

"Should we trade again?"

"Probably."

"Excuse me," I say to a long-haired Asian kid in a skateboard getup. "Hey man," I say, "can I borrow your phone for a sec?"

"No prob, dude," he says nonchalantly. I wonder whether American complacency has overcome yet another Asian tiger mom as I hand the phone to Toni who makes the call.

"Thanks, man," I say handing the phone back.

"Hang loose," he says.

I make the hand sign with my thumb and pinkie stretched in opposite directions and feel immediately like an idiot.

He looks at me with a funny expression. I am far too old to be cool.

We drive Toni's mother's car to Brookside and swap it out for Toni's friend Michaela's Honda.

"That was easy," she says, "now what?"

I look at her then flutter my eyes coquettishly before speaking. "Texas?"

37

Am I taking her with me to keep her safe or to keep me company, I argue with myself as I speed south on I-35. Texas is the ultimate destination, but there's a stop I need to make along the way.

According to Joseph's notes, Megan Fogerty had lived on her own in a one-bedroom in the Ridgeview apartment complex in Olathe. It's not even three weeks since she died and they've already rented the place to someone else. I'm tempted to go there and start sleuthing but guess that the garbage has long since been thrown away and the apartment scrubbed. For now, I want to speak with her parents.

I ask Toni to wait in the car when I go in, but she only gives me a look it's not hard for me to read. *You think you're better off approaching a stranger in her own home on your own?*

All of the houses in the Raven Crest subdivision look exactly the same, but how, I wonder as I knock on the front door of the Fogerty home, did the angel of death choose this one?

The door opens partly, and a woman's head leans into the space. Her coiffed blond hair and thick makeup accent her round face and pleasant features, but the makeup can't camouflage the bags under her puffy eyes.

"Christine Fogerty?" I say.

She looks at me blankly.

"My name is Rich Azadian. I've come to ask you a few questions about your daughter."

I feel a heel digging in to my right foot.

"Mrs. Fogerty, my name is Antonia Hewitt," Toni says, stepping in front of me. "I'm a nurse in Kansas City. Rich is a reporter. I know this must be a terrible time for you, and I can't tell you how sorry we are, but we would really appreciate it if we could please come in to ask you a few questions about Megan."

Christine Fogerty looks at Toni, then me, then slowly pulls the door open.

Toni holds me back with her hand and steps in before me. "Thank you, Mrs. Fogerty. We wouldn't be here if this weren't important."

Christine Fogerty leads us silently to her living room and gestures for us to sit on the couch.

"Rich," Toni says, giving me the cue it's okay for me to start talking.

"I'm covering the story of a young woman who died in Kansas City a few days ago. I don't want to alarm you, but there's a chance there could be some similarities between how the young woman in Kansas City and your daughter"—I fumble to find the right word—"passed."

Pain blankets Christine Fogerty's face. "Like what?"

"They were both about the same age, they both seemed to be healthy, they both died with no real explanation at around the same time." Each word feels like an additional dagger into Christine Fogerty's heart.

"I'm not sure what you're getting at," she says heavily.

"Mrs. Fogerty, can you please tell me what the doctors told you and your husband about what happened to Megan?"

"They said they thought she died from Sudden Adult Death Syndrome."

"Had she been sick at all before she died?"

Christine Fogerty fidgets in her chair. "No. They said that's what SADS looks like."

"This is a strange question, but can you please tell me if Megan was involved in the church?"

A nonplussed look crosses her face. "I don't know why you're asking that, but the answer is no. She probably went once a year at Christmas, if that." She looks at me nervously. "Maybe this was a bad idea," she says, standing.

Toni rises slowly to match her.

"Just one more question if I may, Mrs. Fogerty," I say.

She tilts her head slightly.

"Can you please tell me if there's any chance your daughter was pregnant when she died?"

Christine Fogerty stares at me as if I am the angel of death, then staggers backward and collapses into the chair. Toni moves over and crouches next to her, taking her hand.

"How did you know that?" Christine Fogerty whispers through her tears. "Only Megan and I knew. I was going to tell her father when she . . ."

Toni holds on to Christine Fogerty's hand with both of hers.

"I need to ask you to trust me," I say. "I'm trying to get to the bottom of this, but there are still a lot of questions we need to answer."

Christine Fogarty nods gently, struggling to pull herself together.

"I know this is difficult," I say, "but do you know how she got pregnant?"

Christine shakes her head from side to side. "She wouldn't tell me." She seems to shrink with each word I draw from her, as if our very presence is unraveling whatever she's done to begin pulling herself together over the past three weeks.

Toni looks up at me and twitches her head almost imperceptibly. *That's enough.*

We stay for a few more minutes trying to be comforting but aware that our very presence is the primary cause of discomfort.

"We are so sorry, Mrs. Fogerty, so deeply sorry," Toni says as we slowly backstep toward the door.

38

By eleven, I can't drive any more.

Five hours of driving, of briefing Maurice on the bat phone about Megan Fogerty's pregnancy, of pushing Jerry to find a way into the Bright Horizons database, and of reconnecting with Toni in a manner not possible for the past six months has left me drained.

As I swipe the key card on the door of room 431 in the Comfort Inn in Pauls Valley, Oklahoma, I feel a strange mix of fear and excitement. It can be easy to open a door. It's what comes after that gets complicated.

We act normally. We each shower. We brush our teeth. We strip down to our undergarments and climb into opposite sides of the king-size bed.

"You okay?" Toni asks.

"Yeah." I kick myself. A 160,000-word PhD dissertation and all I can come up with is that? "Thanks for being here," I add. The words don't seem to express what I mean.

"You know you don't need to thank me," she says softly.

The words warm me and remind me, as if I need reminding, how grounding an influence Toni had been in my life. Being with her had made me start to wonder whether an astronaut who never lands is simply lost in space. "Should I turn out the light?"

I didn't mean it that way, but the question is fraught with meaning. I always liked making love with the lights on. Before me, she'd always preferred the lights off.

Toni half laughs.

I can't quite read her. Is she making fun of my awkwardness or laughing at my question?

"Good night, Richie," she says, makings things clear.

She rolls onto her stomach, her head facing away from me.

I turn out the light and roll onto my stomach with my head facing the back of hers. We drift into sleep.

I awake, startled, wondering where I am for a moment before feeling the familiar warmth of her body next to mine as if I'd never forgotten.

Semi-conscious, I ease gently into her space. She feels my arm moving around her waist and pulls it in to her.

I can never quite figure out whether life is complicated or simple, whether all our concepts and words only muck up the few basic drives that actually give meaning to our transient existence. I don't know the answer, but this small gesture seems part of it. I sink back to sleep.

My u.D alarm finds us in the same position when it goes off at six thirty. I reach to tap it off and glimpse the message. *Sleep quality: average.*

"Hi," I grumble with a bit of irony.

She rolls over to face me. I can almost read the conflicted look in her eyes.

I want to be with her, here. My body says it loudly.

I rub my index finger down the line of her cheek then kiss her under her chin. Our lips reach toward each other with an inevitable longing, our kiss deepening as our bodies slide together with ever greater power, driving to leave no space between us. Our arms wrap us together.

"Stop, Richie, stop," she whispers, pulling her head away from mine.

I do.

"Six months ago you didn't know what you wanted and couldn't fight for it, and now you're drawing me into all of this. I'm here because I care for you. You know that. But you can't just stumble back into my life without asking me what I want, without telling me what you want."

I know she's right.

"I'm with you, Richie, I'm here," she says, "but I'm not sure either of us is ready for this."

I don't respond. Silence settles in between us then becomes awkward. Our bodies pull slowly apart.

"What would it take for a woman to agree to be impregnated with a genetically enhanced embryo?" I say after a long pause, consciously changing the subject to match the wanderings of my mind, then feeling stupid for navigating toward such dangerous shoals.

Toni plays along graciously. "How do you know she agreed?"

"It's a good question. I don't."

"I don't think I'd do it," she says.

"Why not?"

"For one, I trust nature. Human beings are so complicated, and I don't think we really know much about how the whole system works. Look at all the strange mutations that show up in the animal research. You know I don't agree with Senator King and the crazies, but there's still something frightening about tinkering with systems we don't understand."

"Hmm," I say.

"What does that mean?"

"It means that I can see the pieces, but they just aren't coming together. Should we get dressed?" I ask, then kick myself again for my awkwardness.

"Sure, Mr. Dolphin," she says with an ironic wink.

39

The Rite-Aid in downtown Waco spurs the idea.

"What the hell are you doing?" Toni shrieks as I swerve across two lanes of traffic into the parking lot.

I tell her about the women I'd met in Becker's Church in Springfield.

"Yes, Mr. Azadian," she says with a slight Southern accent as she gets out of the car.

I wait, tapping the small clock icon on the corner of my u.D.

Twenty minutes later she emerges a picture of Southern charm. Her black hair is sprayed to solid perfection. Her face is pancaked, her eyelids a milky shade of blue, her lashes roll up toward the heavens. Her lips are the red of Eve's apple.

"How do you do, sir," she says.

"Ma'am."

"You know," she says, pretending to rub the back of her hand against her forehead, "I just cannot stand to be in these clothes for one more minute."

"Well, ma'am," I say, "I see that there's a fine establishment just down the street. May I interest you in their wares?"

"I'd be much obliged," she says, then the Southern accent stops abruptly. "And you owe me for dressing me up like a hooker."

"You mean like a daughter of Christ?"

"Fuck yourself."

The temper. She'd always said it came from the eighth of Cherokee on her father's side. There were times when I felt she'd have thrown a hatchet if she had one.

Toni emerges from Goodwill in a white silk blouse and a slightly faded blue pinstripe skirt. A string of costume pearls hangs low from her neck, but everything else pushes up from her black high heels.

"On second thought, I will join your church, madam," I say.

"Drive," she orders.

We practice lines as we get closer to the Rocket Café. Joseph called every large animal veterinarian in Waco from a rerouted Springfield number, saying he was calling on Reverend Becker's behalf and wanted to get together. Dr. Martin Barkley was the only one who knew what Joseph was talking about and agreed to a meeting. I have Toni enter the number of my bat phone on her u.D just in case.

The Rocket Café looks nicer than I'd imagined, more an organic granola kind of place than the biscuits and gravy I'd expected. I still feel a bit strange as Toni gets out of the car and walks the block back toward the restaurant.

I've always thought that if we live lives on our own, self-reliant in the best Emersonian sort of way, we can just take responsibility for ourselves. But as I watch Toni walk toward the Rocket Café, I recognize yet again that I'm wrong. The moment we want to protect someone is the moment we put them in danger by connecting them to us, by breaking the hermetic seal of our individual self-reliance. No wonder my mother calls me all the time. Caring for someone is a terrifying thing.

I wait.

Ten minutes, twenty, thirty. I tap on the dashboard and look at the bat phone lying dormant on the passenger seat.

She's just meeting a veterinarian, I remind myself. I'm lost in thought when I hear the first click of the opening door.

She steps into the car with a formality I've never before seen from her. She has become the part. She straightens her back, interlaces her fingers, and places them palms down on her left thigh as she turns her entire torso to face me.

"That," she says slowly, "is an interesting man."

I bend my head down slightly, my eyes still fixed on hers. She'll tell me when she wants to.

"He did fall for it. He's never actually met Becker, only dealt with his assistants from time to time, so it was easy to convince him I was one of them. I told him we were concerned we weren't making enough progress."

"Did he know what you were talking about?" I ask.

"That's what I wanted to test. He said he was concerned, too. I think he was nervous."

"Why?"

"That he wasn't delivering. He started to talk about Dolly."

"Dolly the sheep?" I ask, the synapses firing in my mind. Becker experimenting with genetic manipulation on his ranch, his "chosen one" murdered carrying a genetically enhanced embryo?

"He said that they'd never really perfected nuclear transfer, and the problem with copies is that they're slightly off from the originals, that 227 sheep embryos didn't make it when they were trying to produce Dolly."

I'm speechless.

"The way he spoke about the ranch, I don't think he's the one leading things, just the person they call when something doesn't work."

"One of the leaders of the anti-science evangelical wave sweeping the country is cloning cattle on a well-guarded ranch?" I say incredulously.

Toni nods. "I told him how concerned we were and that Reverend Becker was beginning to think he was partly to blame for the lack of success."

I'm impressed with her technique.

"He got pretty nervous. I think the ranch may be his biggest client. He said most people didn't understand how difficult it is to make a cow a specific color, especially when it's not normal."

"Did you ask . . ."

Toni looks at me and I stop speaking.

"Red," she declares.

My body stiffens. I feel a spark igniting in the depths of my subconscious, lighting a fuse that traverses my central nervous system. The idea had struck me as odd when I was ten years old in Bible class but somehow had lodged in my brain undisturbed for twenty-nine years. Until now.

"Search red heifer," I bark into my u.D.

Options pop up, then the vixen u.D voice purrs through the car speakers. "In the days of the Holy Temple, all who sought to enter were required to be spiritually cleansed by being sprinkled with the ashes of a flawless red heifer burned in its third year. According to messianic sources, the procurement of a red heifer for this purpose is a necessary precondition for the rebuilding of the Temple, itself a precursor to the Second Coming of Christ. Rabbinical sources assert that no flawless red heifer has been born in Israel since the fall of Jerusalem in 70 AD, nearly two thousand years ago."

The idea seems insane. "Tell me more," I order.

A screen pops up with options.

"Read me the scripture."

The voice options flash and I choose the obvious one. The God in whom I don't believe surely has a pronounced British accent.

"Now the Lord said to Moses and to Aaron, tell the people of Israel to bring you a red heifer without defect, in which there is no blemish, and upon which a yoke has never come. And you shall give her to Eleazar the priest, and she shall be taken outside the camp and slaughtered before him; and Eleazar the priest, and shall take some of her blood with his finger, and sprinkle some of her blood toward the front of the tent of meeting seven times. And the heifer shall be burned in his sight; her skin, her flesh, and her blood, with her dung, shall be burned; and the priest shall take cedarwood and hyssop and scarlet stuff, and cast them into the midst of the burning of the heifer. Then the priest shall wash his clothes and bathe his body in water, and afterward he shall come into the camp; and the priest shall be unclean until evening. He who burns the heifer shall wash his clothes in water and bathe his body in water, and shall be unclean until evening. And a man who is clean shall gather up the ashes of the heifer, and deposit them outside the camp in a clean place; and they shall be kept for the congregation of the people of Israel for the water for impurity, for the removal of sin."

Toni and I sit, stunned. What kind of lunatic would want to breed an extinct cow then burn it in a dung fire to pave the way for the Second Coming? My mind races back to my conversation with Carol Stock about Becker's big plans for the Second Coming of Christ. The pieces fly together as the image congeals. The young girl adopted at the same age that Virgin Mary was given to God, the girl initially named Lee whom Becker renames MaryLee, the gifts of the three Kings, the genetically enhanced embryo. It's almost too big to believe, yet the pieces glide together with shocking precision.

"We've got to learn more," I say feverishly. "Did he give you any information about what's happening at the ranch?"

"He said that they didn't even allow him in to what he called 'the lab,' and that he was doing everything he could."

"Did you ask him what he knew about the lab?"

"He said if I wanted to know more I should talk with Dr. Allison."

"Who's that?"

"I acted like I knew. I'm guessing it's the head of the lab."

"How did you leave things?"

"I told him we're going to be keeping a close eye on him and then walked out in a huff."

I'm still shaking as we drive toward the ranch. Finding the ranch isn't hard. The *Dallas Morning News* article mentioned the name and general location. A few people we approach on the side of the road point us in the right direction.

When we get to the entrance, a small sign on the locked gate connected on two sides by a tall electric fence reads RAPTURE GROVE RANCH.

I SatMap our current location to see if there's another entrance. There isn't. The satellite image shows a barn and a medium-sized white shed I assume is "the lab" at the center of a vast property.

"I guess we wait to see what happens," I say, settling in.

Forty minutes later the gate opens and a large white Hyundai pickup drives through. The truck turns left at the road. I hit the gas and squeeze through the gate just before it closes.

"Think they saw us?" I ask Toni.

"I don't know," she says. "I have a feeling we'll find out."

We pass acres of grazing cattle before seeing the barn and white shed in the distance.

The roar startles me before I see the three pickups screeching toward us from behind the barn.

The trucks race forward as if they are going to ram us.

I throw my right arm over to cover Toni as I slam the brakes. She instinctively grabs it and pulls it toward her as I jam the car in reverse and the trucks close in.

Two of them bear down toward me from the front as another speeds past to block my retreat from behind.

I slam the brakes again to spin in a new direction but the trucks are now closing in from three sides.

Just before impact, all three trucks skid to a halt around me, blocking my exit in every direction. A massive cloud of dust swirls around the vehicles. My heart is pounding, my left hand is clenched around the steering wheel, my right stretched stiff holding Toni across her shoulders.

"There's our answer," I say breathlessly.

A tall, lean man looking to be in his early fifties jumps from one of the trucks in front of me and marches in our direction. His jeans, cowboy boots and hat, and furrowed face say cowboy, but his blue blazer and focused gaze say executive and his eyes say "danger." No one ever said the rapture would be pain-free. Three men approach behind him, each with a pistol on his waist. I roll down my window.

"What the hell are you doin'?" he demands in a thick Texas accent.

"Sorry, sir," I say, "my wife and I are lost and we were coming for directions."

Toni leans forward and bats her fake lashes. It doesn't work.

"The hell you are," he says menacingly. "We saw you enter the compound before the gate closed. Now are you goin' to tell us what you're doin' here, or—"

I don't want to hear the next part of the sentence. Given the menacing animosity on his face, it can't be good. "Look, I don't know what you're talking about. So sorry if we've disturbed you."

I wonder if I should mention Cobalt Becker and Dr. Barkley but decide to leave well enough alone.

"If you can just point us in the direction of Fort Worth, we'll be on our way."

"Fort Worth," he repeats, clearly not believing a word.

I have a sinking gut feeling he's thinking of ways of disposing of us.

He lifts his arm and starts snapping pictures of Toni and me, our car, and our license plates from the u.D around his wrist. He stares at me with terrifying other-worldly eyes.

"Let me put it to you this way," he says, the words slithering through his teeth, "to get to Fort Worth you take a right out the gate, left on Route 6, and merge onto I-35 North."

"Thank you," I say with overblown earnestness.

"But if I ever see you back on this property, you're not goin' to get out this easily, not this easily at all."

I don't doubt him for a second.

"Got that?" The words are not a question.

I nod to cover my inner gulp.

He points at the truck behind us then moves his finger to the right. The truck moves.

I pull back carefully. If my driving makes a statement, it is submission. The gate opens as I approach, then closes behind me.

Toni and I drive silently for a few minutes.

She breaks the heavy silence first. "That guy was not kidding."

"I know," I say.

"I guess the rapture has an army."

40

"Joseph, you look terrible."

Even traveling up I-35 at seventy miles an hour, it's impossible not to notice his eyes sunken even more deeply, his hair even more disheveled, his skin more sallow. I worry I'm asking too much of Joseph, throwing him an unlimited number of urgent research requests while he's still doing who knows what in his day job since being tossed into general research pool at the *Star*.

"Thanks, boss," Joseph replies.

"Did you meet with Professor Chou?"

"I did, boss."

"And?"

"Jerry was right. This stuff is unbelievably complicated."

"Was he helpful?"

Joseph ignores the question. "The forty-seventh chromosome," he says.

"Tell me," I say.

"From where?"

"From the start."

"The start is Gregor Mendel."

"After that."

"Is Louise Brown."

"The first test tube baby?"

"Yes," Joseph says, "then the decoding of the human genome."

"I'm with you," I say. "Go on."

"Then the Preimplantation Genetic Diagnosis and Selection procedure, PGDS. They fertilize multiple eggs and let each begin dividing, then extract one cell from each embryo and read its full genome. They pick the one or two embryos they want, extract another cell from each of those, then stimulate those cells to start dividing before implanting them into the mother or the surrogate. And as doctors get better at understanding the genes taken from the fertilized eggs during PGDS, parents know more and more about what they are selecting," Joseph says.

"Yup," I say curtly, trying to push Joseph forward. That having kids through old-fashioned sex leaves too much to chance is something privileged mothers-to-be around the world are fast realizing. "The forty-seventh chromosome?" I ask, frantic to figure out if MaryLee is Cobalt Becker's Dolly.

"Every person has around twenty-three thousand genes, all of them carried on the forty-six chromosomes arranged in the famous double helix connecting them."

Toni can't take it anymore. She shakes her head wildly from side to side.

Joseph, of course, can't see this and keeps marching forward like the diligent Indian Institute of Technology graduate he is.

"Any two people have genomes that are 99.9 percent the same, but the .1 percent accounts for most all the genetic differences between us."

"Joseph," I say impatiently, "everyone knows this."

He ignores me like a trial lawyer dismissing the entreaties of opposing counsel as he lays the foundation of his case.

"From everything we know, most people with extra chromosomes have problems. Down Syndrome is just an extra copy of chromosome twenty-one. Doctors have gotten pretty good at replacing mutated genes with normal ones for single gene mutations for things like cystic fibrosis, but Professor Chou says we probably still don't know enough about complex functions, like intelligence, determined by multiple genes working together. On top of that, all people are different and the same genes can mean different things in different people or even change because of environmental factors, they call it epigenetics. Of course, part of us is also formed through our experiences after we're born."

"Joseph!"

"Almost there, boss. There are different ways to insert new genes into the cell nucleus. By far the most popular way is by using a modified virus to carry a new gene into a cell, but genes inserted this way don't tend to be stable and can often be rejected by the immune system. The second way is to replace one gene with another in a lab. The third—"

"Let me guess," I say.

"Ten years ago, a plant biologist in Korea figured out how to use a synthetic additional chromosome process to add new traits to plants."

"The forty-seventh chromosome?" I repeat impatiently.

"Kind of, boss," he says earnestly. "Different plants have different numbers of chromosomes, but she showed it was possible to meaningfully introduce multiple genes into a cell by creating an artificial additional chromosome."

"In plants. How about humans?"

"I asked Chou about that. It seems like we're a long way from there. The next step up the chain is mice, and a few scientists are starting to experiment with the same technique at Cornell Medical College in New York. They created an extra chromosome in mice and used it to induce pituitary dwarfism."

"Humans, Joseph?"

"Four years ago, a scientist in China found a way to correct the problem of extra copy chromosomes in monkey fetuses during the PGDS process by adding an additional chromosome with synthetic genes to improve cellular functions, but as far as we know artificial forty-seventh chromosomes have not been inserted into humans. Professor Chou said the pieces are coming together to help scientists decipher the vast complexity of each person's genome and then try to figure out how problems might be fixed. As enormously complex as our individual genomes are, they are not random, which means they are ultimately knowable and manipulable. It's just that we haven't figured this all out yet in mice and monkeys, so the jump to humans would be too great a leap for years, that's not even taking into account the ethical issues."

The implication rocks me. In spite of all the promise of this incredible technology, something about manipulating the human genome makes me instinctively uneasy on some kind of deep, primal level. "So either Bright Horizons knowingly impregnated MaryLee with an embryo they knew had a natural mutation or they did it with an extra chromosome introduced with a technology that, as far as we know, doesn't exist for human use?"

"That's it, boss, but if it's the first, no clinic would impregnate someone with an embryo that had been selected in order to be defective. The US Supreme Court held," Joseph pauses to slide through documents on his wall, "in 2018 that genetically deaf parents couldn't select an embryo in the PGDS process to make sure their kid was deaf. So how could they implant someone with an extra chromosome?"

"I guess if the chromosome carried genes people thought were good."

"But that's theoretically illegal too, boss, even though no one's ever done it before. And besides, understanding what genes to load on an extra chromosome seems a lot more sophisticated than we know how to do, even though the Chinese have been working on this for years."

"Maybe they know more than we think. Maybe it's an experiment."

"Two more pieces of the story you need to understand, boss, DNA decoding and synthetic biology."

"Go on."

"Twenty years ago it cost $3 billion to sequence the human genome for the first time. Now we're doing it using the same techniques they used to make semiconductors before most of them went organic. It costs about fifty dollars a pop and can be done on a jacked-up u.D with a nanopore microsequencer."

"I know, Joseph."

Joseph rolls on. "But it was a lot easier and cheaper to sequence the genome than to analyze it until labs started using the same graphics chips used in video consoles."

Joseph pauses to make sure I am following him.

I nod.

"So with so many people getting sequenced around the world and the data being pooled," he continues, "scientists are learning more and more about what each gene does and how they interact to form complex human traits. It's the ultimate big-data challenge."

"And synthetic biology?"

"Is about humans manipulating biology at the genetic level for our own ends."

"Tell me more."

"There are two schools of synthetic biology. The first is what they call whole genome synthesis, the process of designing and building cells from scratch using the natural building blocks of guanine, adenine, thymine, and cytosine. They started with a bacterium that infected goats and worked from there. Now they're making a lot of progress in what they call xenobiology, adding additional chemical units to DNA beyond the regular four, the G, A, T, and C."

"Go on," I say impatiently. If anyone in America hadn't known about synthetic biology before, they do now that Senator King has made it his first piece of evidence that President Lewis and the pagan Alvarez are violating God's plan and leading the country down a path to purgatory.

"The other group was a couple of Harvard biologists who developed a way of making hundreds of changes to a genome at the same time."

"Hijacking."

"Right, boss. They try to take control of the genetic code of a microbe and then reprogram it. They started almost a decade ago with *E. coli* but said they were going to learn how to reprogram forty thousand DNA markers in an elephant fetus to turn it into a wooly mammoth. Now they're making even more progress through reprogramming what they call clustered palindromic repeats. It's essentially gene editing."

"Obviously they didn't get there."

"Right, boss, but they learned a lot by trying. Between the semiconductor sequencing, gene editing and hijacking, 3D microvalve printing of bacteria, and developing an endless supply of induced human embryonic stem cells from scratch to test the new hypothesis, they're starting to make exponential progress."

"Exponential?"

"Everything builds on everything else, the pace of innovation isn't linear."

"And the data is distributed through global networks."

"Right, boss. So how it gets used can't really be controlled, and everyone's still figuring out what it can be used for. The human genome has three billion base pairs of nucleotides, so there's still a lot that's not known about how everything works, but the science seems to be progressing a lot faster than the applications."

I'm not sure if I should be more impressed by what Franklin Chou taught or what Joseph Abraham seems to have absorbed. My mind struggles to connect this new information with everything else I'm learning. "What did the vet say about dealing with the mistakes from 'the lab'?"

Joseph looks confused.

"Sorry, Joseph," I say, "I'm talking to Toni."

Toni leans her head in front of the dashboard screen. "Hi, Joseph," she says sweetly.

Joseph smiles awkwardly. "Are . . . ?" he says before becoming tongue-tied.

Toni responds warmly, then gets down to business. "When I

met with Barkley yesterday, he said some of the cows from their breeding program didn't quite work out the way they were supposed to."

"And there's still the issue of how she got the extra chromosome in the first place. And that leads us, well," I add, "back where we were."

"Bright Horizons?" Joseph asks.

"Figuring out if there's a connection between what seems to be going on there and at Rapture Grove."

The side of Jerry's face pops up as I tap him in. He's wearing the same shirt as yesterday and, from the looks of it, hasn't moved from his chair.

"Jerry," I say, "Bright Horizons?"

"Sorry, Rich," he says. "We're probing from all sorts of angles, but we can't yet find a way in. People are usually sloppier than this."

"Somewhere there's got to be an answer," I say. "Keep pushing."

"You have no idea," he responds exasperatedly. "If we can't figure this out, maybe no one can."

"What about King's day of prayer in Springfield?" I ask.

"I've had it minimized on one of my screens," Jerry says.

"And?"

"A lot of Jesus, a lot of hand-waving, a lot of—"

"Becker?" I interject.

"Is right there by King's side."

"Like Aaron to King's Moses."

"Something like that."

"Thanks, guys," I say.

Jerry looks briefly at the camera. Joseph nods. I hit the red button and the video cuts.

"You know I'm proud of you," Toni says after a pause.

I look over at her.

"You're a pain in the ass," she continues, "you never leave well enough alone, and you're always looking for something you'll probably never find."

The arrows hit but don't sting.

"But," she continues, "I'm proud of you. That girl, MaryLee, didn't have anyone looking out for her. Sure her mom loved her, but you're the one who won't drop it."

Maybe I should feel more proud, but the emotion hitting me is anxiety.

I'm worried that if someone killed MaryLee Stock and maybe even Megan Fogerty to cover something up, they're probably going to track me down too once they realize what I'm up to. And if they find me, they find Toni. And I'm worried that my half-assed efforts to hide my tracks are only likely to fool the most unsophisticated of bad guys. Anyone messing with a forty-seventh chromosome is certainly not that.

"Thanks," I say unconvincingly.

Toni reaches over and gently squeezes the back of my neck. I feel a warmth emanating from her hand. I think of all the genetic cues that make the feeling possible, of me as a mess of conflicting emotions, a long chain of genetic base pairs. Is Toni entering my heart, I wonder, or cracking my code?

By Wichita I can't drive another mile. We pull over and check into La Quinta.

We are silent as we step into the room, as if silence is the only path to where we both know we are going.

Toni's fake pearls were long ago flung to the backseat of the car, but I gently unbutton her blouse, unzip her skirt, unhook her bra.

I feel her body like a blind man.

The tips of my fingers end at her face. I trace the curve of her eyelids, the tips of her nose, the curve of her neck. Our lips hardly touch on our first kiss then press together in countless variations of hard and soft. At the same moment, we stop kissing each other and hug tightly, needily.

"I missed you," she whispers.

As I pull her ever closer to me, I realize how very much I've missed her, too.

And how much I need her in a way I've never felt before.

41

I reflexively grab my wrist, startled and disoriented, to try to shut up my beeping u.D. Where am I? I feel the warmth to my right and remember. So much for geography as a physical sensation. My map of the Wichita darkness is emotional.

I nudge my body into her space. She moans gently and moves into mine. We drift.

"What time is it?" I hear her say as if from a distance.

"Shit, I'm sorry," I say looking over. "Seven forty-five."

"Grrr," she moans adorably.

"What time does your shift start?"

"Nine, if I still have a job, that is."

"You're going to be late."

"I know," she says.

I probably read way too much into her words as I slide my body back into hers. "Thank you for being here, baby," I say again.

"I told you, I'm here because I choose to be here."

I wrap my arms around her. With all of our passion last night, it was almost a more intense connection that we didn't, in fact, make love.

"And," she adds mischievously, "because you tricked me into being here."

I smile. "You have no idea how expensive it is to hire all of these actors."

I feel a twinge of guilt for joking about something so serious.

Toni reads the expression on my face. "I wouldn't be anywhere else," she says. "I feel like an idiot for saying that, but you really opened my world and now, whether I like it or not, probably even both, I associate those parts of myself with you. All I wanted was for you to give us a real chance, but you couldn't seem to get over yourself."

"I'm sorry," I whisper, knowing she's right and feeling stupid for it.

"But if I'm honest, I have to admit I never really gave up on you." Toni puts her hand on my left shoulder and guides me on to my back. She doesn't kiss me but instead reaches down between my legs and grabs me. My body stiffens. "Even if I should have." She squeezes.

I look into her eyes and open my mouth to speak but she stops me with an almost imperceptible shake of her head. *Stop talking for once.* When she climbs on top of me I'm not really sure if I'm entering her, she's engulfing me, or both.

Our bodies lock and unlock together, pulling closer and closer, minimizing the distance between us with each embrace. We match each other's rhythms, drive into each other with what seems like greater intensity and greater softness at the same time.

We climax in unison and she collapses on top of me, glides into me over a thin film of our combined sweat. We hold each other tightly and drift back into a half sleep.

I awake not knowing how far we've drifted when I feel her sliding off of me.

She kisses me and looks me in the eyes. Her loving look frightens me a little. She smiles and lifts her body up slightly. Then she delivers a lightning punch that connects with my left bicep. It's a real punch, and it hurts.

Words return.

"You know what that's for," she whispers seriously.

I do.

Then I roll on top of her and the whole process starts again, this time upside down. By eight forty I am wide awake and grinning from ear to ear like an idiot.

And now she's going to be even later for work.

"Hand me my u.D, baby," she says. She calls the hospital and tells them her car has broken down and she'll be a couple of hours late, apologizing profusely.

"Is it strange your supervisor didn't mention what happened with Papadakis?" I ask when we're back on the highway.

"I was just thinking that," she says.

"What do you make of it?"

"Maybe he's made a complaint and they need to do an investigation. Maybe he made it at a higher level."

"Could be," I say, "but what would it mean if he didn't make a complaint at all?"

"Why wouldn't he?"

"If he didn't want others to snoop around, making a complaint would only raise questions."

"Maybe," she says, "or maybe I'll just be walking into the storm when I show up at work."

The concept of showing up at work startles me. I tap my u.D and Joseph's face appears on the dashboard screen.

"Boss, you asked me to dig around about Jessica Crandell at Bright Horizons. It's a little strange. She seems completely legit, she has a home address, a cloud profile, even a Universal Network Identifier code, but all of it starts two years ago."

"And?" I ask.

"Usually, there are some references to things people did earlier in their lives. Races they ran, clubs they joined, alumni associations, things like that."

"Maybe she got married and changed her name," I say.

"I thought of that, but her current profile at least says she's not married."

"How long has she worked at Bright Horizons?"

"Looks like two years," Joseph says.

"So she gets a new name and joins at the same time."

"Seems so, boss."

I see a shiny metal object in the background behind Joseph's face. "Where are you, Joseph?" I ask.

"In the men's room, boss."

"At the *Star*?"

"Yes, boss."

"Are people saying they can't live without me?"

"Yes, boss," Joseph says sadly. He forces a half smile, which only makes me feel more pathetic.

"Thanks, Joseph."

The line drops.

It's eleven by the time we reach the hospital. We kiss. Not a hotel kiss, a carpool drop-off kiss. I agree to pick her up at five. A few days of unemployment, and I've already become a *hausfrau*. I pull away from the entrance until my path is obstructed by a black GMC. I tilt my head back against the headrest to wait.

The click of the door startles me. I hardly register what is happening before my passenger door swings open.

"What the—?" I say, nonplussed.

The intensity of the man's raging brown eyes as he slides into my passenger seat jumps out at me first, but it's impossible not to notice his height as he scrunches into the space. His long lean face and sunken cheeks give the impression of a tightly stretched canvas. His brown, closely cropped hair forms a thin film over his head. The scowl on his face somehow extends to his whole body.

"Dikran Azadian," he declares.

"And you are?"

"Gillespie," he spits out venomously, handing me his card.

"What is this about and what are you doing in my car?"

"I think you know, Mr. Azadian."

I look at him blankly, refusing to give in. "Is this about those parking tickets?" I say. "You know I've been meaning to pay them."

"This is not a joke, Mr. Azadian."

"I'm not sure what you mean, Mr. Gillespie."

"Where are you coming from, Mr. Azadian?"

"What business is that of yours? Get out of my car," I say testily.

"Let me put it to you this way, Mr. Azadian," Gillespie's robotic precision and barely suppressed rage coming together, "you need to drop this right now."

"Drop what?"

"You know the stakes, Mr. Azadian. It's up to you," he says chillingly, pausing to let the words sink in.

They do.

He opens the door and steps out, then enters the passenger side of the GMC, which slowly drives away.

How did he know I'd be here?

I take out the bat phone and call Maurice.

42

It's too much driving.

I'm in the passenger seat of Maurice's Energi-F heading to Springfield and feeling like a trucker. In the last fifty hours I've been back and forth to Waco and now this.

And I'm still not convinced we have a plan.

Maurice calls it turning up the temperature, but if our goal is to turn up the heat, we're increasingly ill-equipped to do it. I'm suspended from my job at the *Star*, he's sneaking out of the office, pretending his wife is sick and working a case that is officially not his.

Filing through the doors of the Holy Virgin Church of Christ, the same megalomaniacal digital display of Cobalt Becker and the Garden of Eden mesmerizes me far less than when I'd first seen it. It only seems to annoy Maurice.

"May I help you?" the same receptionist announces peacefully.

"We're here to see Reverend Becker," Maurice says firmly.

I anticipate the same reluctance I encountered on my first visit, but instead a beatific look crosses her face. "He's preaching in the chapel right now."

As we open the thick golden chapel doors, it's as if we are entering a magic kingdom. The lights are low, and stars are projected across the ceiling. Streams of red and blue light illuminate the stage where Cobalt Becker presides through the low layer of smoke hovering around him.

"One day very soon Christ will arrive here on earth, the final proof of God's sovereignty over all people, all countries, and all history. His return will bring the final stage of our redemption, the culmination of all God has promised to those who accept his dominion and embrace Jesus Christ as their personal savior." Becker's deep bass pulsates through the room and refracts with the red and blue lights on the mesmerized faces of the congregants standing in rapt attention.

"In John 14:3, Jesus himself declares that he will come back. The Second Coming of Christ will be with great power and great glory, it will end the abominations that cause desolation. Jesus said he would come back, and fear not, the day is near," Becker thunders. "He hasn't forgotten you. The Messiah is coming, do you believe it?"

"Yes!" the believers reply.

"The Messiah is coming, do you believe it?" Becker says more forcefully.

"Yes!" the enthralled cry.

"The Messiah is coming and our job as believers is clear to all who open their eyes. We must pray for his coming, we must watch for his coming." Becker escalates the intensity of his words with each phrase, leading the faithful to ever higher states of rapture. "We must expect he is coming, must look for his coming." Becker's booming voice dominates every air molecule in the sanctuary.

The congregants are crying, reaching their hands into the sky as if picking apples of salvation.

"And above all else, we must make his coming possible." Becker's two hands extend to the sky like light sticks on a celestial runway as electric guitar riffs joins the fiery organ in a rock instrumental of "God shall overcome" that wraps itself around every person in the room, including Maurice and me.

The smoke rises across the stage as the red and blue lights, now joined by lasers, whirl across the hall. The music intensifies to a crescendo then slows itself one measure at a time as the pulsating light slows and the room gradually becomes brighter. As the fog clears, Becker is gone. The music stops, the lights are on, and the stunned congregants begin the process of stepping back from their collective hypnosis.

The scene is so overwhelming, I look around the room to see how people are responding.

Then I see her.

Carol Stock looks very different from the woman I'd seen in Kansas City. She is glowing.

I glance at Maurice before approaching her. "Mrs. Stock, may I have a word with you?"

She looks at me as if lost between two worlds. "You wouldn't understand, you can't," she says nervously.

"Understand what?"

"That there are forces bigger than all of us, that God's plan will lead us." Her words echo Becker's power.

I am floored, unable to imagine how her daughter's death could be part of that plan.

Maurice steps in. "Thank you so much for your time, Mrs. Stock. Godspeed," he says, pulling me away.

Panic overtakes the receptionist's face as we march past her toward the hidden door to Becker's office. "You can't go in there," she orders. We beat her to the door, open it, and walk through.

"Come back here right now. You cannot go in there," she shrieks frantically.

By the time she reaches us, we are already in. I'm almost surprised to see Becker at his desk, transformed from the charismatic magician he seemed just minutes before into a man. He looks up calmly and assuredly, then stands.

"Mr. Azadian," he says, his voice resonates through my head. "To what do I owe the pleasure of your visit?" His cold tone undermines the surface generosity of his sentiments.

I can't find the words to answer.

"And you are?" he asks, walking toward Maurice.

"Maurice Henderson, KCPD, sir," Maurice says. I'm not sure where the "sir" is coming from, but somehow it makes me feel even smaller before Becker.

"KCPD," Becker mulls. "And what brings you to Springfield?"

"I'd hoped to make it to the day of prayer with Senator King and you," Maurice says flatly, "but it looks like I'm a day late, so I thought I'd ask you about the death of MaryLee Stock."

"Are you investigating this, Mr. Henderson?" Becker asks. "And you're working with the *Kansas City Star*?" he says, looking at me.

"Look, sir," Maurice says, "MaryLee Stock is dead. You know that."

"I do," Becker says calmly.

"We all want to know what happened to her," Maurice continues.

Becker stares at each of us in turn, then speaks with his ministerial tone. "Can't you let this poor girl rest in peace? Haven't we been through this already? You've obviously seen the autopsy report. I beg of you, show some respect, some decency."

"We think MaryLee Stock was murdered."

Maurice's words halt Becker's momentum.

"She was poisoned with potassium cyanide. She was pregnant," Maurice fires his sentences at Becker in staccato succession.

The words push Becker back. "Have a seat," he says quietly.

The receptionist slinks away as we sit.

"How do you know?" Becker says after a pause.

"Lab results, sir," Maurice says.

"But I thought—"

"They were wrong."

Becker thinks for a moment. "So what brings you here?"

"We are investigating what happened," Maurice says.

"You meaning KCPD and the *Kansas City Star*?"

Maurice hesitates.

Becker senses the shifting momentum and leans forward

forcefully. "If you are here representing KCPD and the *Star*, I'd like to get Chief Roberts and Wes Morton on the phone to confirm." He casually pulls back his sleeve to expose his u.D.

My body tenses.

"Call them if you want," Maurice says coolly, "but they'll just tell you what we'll tell you now."

"And that is?" Becker asks condescendingly, moving his left hand toward the u.D on his right wrist.

"That neither of us is officially on this case. That both of us have been specifically told not to pursue it."

"So why are you here? Why shouldn't I just have you escorted out?"

"Because we think MaryLee Stock's baby may have been yours, sir," Maurice says, the "sir" sounding quite a bit less deferential this time.

A look of disgust flashes across Becker's face. "That's outrageous. Get out of here."

Neither of us moves.

"I don't need to answer your questions," Becker says. His eyes burn like a bull preparing to charge but he still doesn't tap his u.D.

"You don't, sir," Maurice says, then lets the silence hang. "And you might be able to shut us up. But then again you might not."

Becker stares us each in the eye before speaking. "I don't need to explain myself to you, but let me make one thing clear. I did not have relations with MaryLee Stock nor ever would I have. She was like a daughter to me."

I read the anguished look on Becker's face and maybe even believe him, but not enough to pull back. "I visited Rapture Grove Ranch yesterday," I say softly, "but you already know that."

Becker does not respond.

"I spoke with your veterinarian, I believe his name is Dr. Barkley."

Becker glares.

"We know you are trying to breed a red heifer."

"I've nothing to hide about that," Becker says coolly.

"I agree," I say, "but we have reason to believe that the fetus, the baby, inside of MaryLee Stock had also been genetically mutated."

"What does one thing have to do with the other?" Becker spits out. "What are you getting at?"

"It had an extra chromosome."

"What are you saying?"

"Let me put it to you this way, sir," Maurice says. "We have reason to believe that the fetus inside MaryLee Stock may have been your genetic offspring and that you were somehow involved in making this happen through an association with the Bright Horizons fertility center."

"That is outrageous."

"Because we believe this," Maurice escalates, "we can't help but think you may have had something to do with the murder of MaryLee Stock. Does that help explain why we are here, sir?"

Becker's heavy breathing punctuates the silence. "Let me tell you this," he says, controlling his rage and looking down at the coffee table. "These are outrageous and completely unfounded allegations."

I have to admit that I respect the way he handles himself.

"But," he continues, looking me straight in the eye, "I will tell you with everything I am, I had nothing to do with the death, the murder, if that's what you say, of MaryLee Stock, and"—his voice shifts lower and seems to come from the depths of his soul—"I will do everything in my power to help you find out who committed this monstrous act."

Cobalt Becker never ceases to amaze me.

Maurice's tone conveys less amazement. "In that case, sir, we need your help."

Becker focuses on Maurice and lifts his eyebrows.

"We need you to get the feds off our backs," Maurice says.

"What feds?" Becker asks.

The question startles Maurice. I step into the gap. "The feds who have taken the case from the KUPD and forced the *Star* to drop the story. We need you to reverse that."

"I have no idea what you are talking about, but I can try," Becker says.

I don't know if I believe Becker or not.

"I need you to do better than that," Maurice says, getting up to leave.

I follow.

At the door, Maurice turns back. "But if we find out that you were involved in this murder, I will personally haul you in."

Becker stands erect and defiant, his fierce eyes fixed upon us as we march out the door.

43

"We've got to talk right away," Jerry says nervously. His voice is frazzled.

"Okay. So let's talk," I say into my earpiece as Maurice drives us back to Kansas City.

"This is, is big. It's a big deal."

"Jerry," I say, frustrated, "tell me."

"We need to talk in person."

"We're in Belton. We can meet you in forty-five minutes."

"We?" Jerry asks.

"I'm with Maurice Henderson. We can meet you at—"

"Stop," Jerry orders. "I'm sending you a Frankly message on your u.D. It will disappear in ten seconds. So will your response."

That Jerry is being so cautious when he'd earlier been so confident about our encrypted u.Ds sends a cascade of worry through my mind.

The message arrives on my u.D.

Lewis and Clark statue, 8th and Jefferson. The message vanishes.

"Got it," I say as I tap off the call.

"What the hell was that?" Maurice asks.

"I have no idea, but it doesn't sound good."

I don't see Jerry when we arrive. Maurice's car idles in the circle surrounding the statue of Lewis and Clark surveying what was once the wilds of the Great Plains. The explorers are surrounded by a mournful Sacajawea, a nondescript black guy with a gun, and a trusty and loyal dog, all now condemned to gaze in perpetuity over the crumbling highway, a series of abandoned factories and underused warehouses, and the semiretired Wheeler municipal airport.

The sound of Jerry's Tata Neo screeching to a stop pulls me back from 1804.

Jerry jumps from his car, his right hand waving wildly over his tablet as if he's controlling a marionette dance routine inside the machine.

I reach back to open the door and he jumps in.

"I told you that Bright Horizons clinic is owned by Bright Horizons Holdings LLC, a Delaware Limited Liability Corporation," Jerry says feverishly, "which is 100 percent owned by Sunrise Holdings, the Cayman Island shell company."

"Go on."

"But the real question is who owns that. I've been trying to crack the code for the Cayman Island company registration. It's impregnable."

"You said."

"I found the date when the company officially started doing business and when references to the company started appearing."

"Go on," Maurice says.

"So I looked for law firms and accounting firms that handle this kind of work to see if I could cross-reference dates. I found that there was one main registration service. Their computer system was well defended but not perfect."

"So you hacked it?" Maurice asks.

Jerry looks at Maurice and keeps going with this narrative. "In the three days before the new company was established thirteen new requests were made to the registration service. I tracked these thirteen companies and eleven of them were actually real companies setting up subsidiaries in the Cayman Islands."

"And this means?" Maurice says.

"That anyone trying to hide something would at least try to be more careful."

"Which leaves two," I say.

"So I tracked the two and one led me to a home computer I easily cracked. It was a guy in Long Beach, New York, registering a porn site. The other was protected with SHA eight."

"What's that?" Maurice asks.

"Secure Hash Algorithm version eight, the most sophisticated encryption algorithm in the world. Someone has gone to great lengths to protect this thing."

"Just like the malware on MaryLee's computer," I add.

"But there was one glitch. They didn't erase their acquisition code for the encryption program."

Maurice and I perk up.

"The newest encryption algorithms come from the National Institute of Standards and Technology. When someone downloads the program from them, a code gets attached to the downloaded copy as a tracker. Smart users then erase it."

"So do we know who downloaded it?" Maurice asks.

"The trail led me to the office of a tax attorney in Switzerland, Viktor Brueller."

"Why is a Swiss tax attorney using highest-end encryption systems to transfer money to a Cayman Islands holding company?" I ask.

I interpret Maurice's look as telling me not to be an idiot.

"But Brueller was sloppy," Jerry says. "I had one of the guys from OpenNet probe his system, and it didn't take that long to find the vulnerabilities."

"And?" I say impatiently, annoyed that Jerry keeps pausing at the end of his sentences.

Jerry hardly hears me. "We went through his records and found that two days before the Cayman Islands holding company had been created $280 million were transferred to his office by a private company in Wilmington, Delaware, called Talonsmark," he says breathlessly. "Talonsmark, it turns out, only existed for a month. It was an office with no people. The names listed on their office lease forms don't even match records of people living in the Delaware region or anywhere."

"Which means . . . ?" I say.

Jerry completes my sentence. "That someone is trying to set up two front companies."

He lets the words hang in the air for a moment. "But that's harder to do in these days of electronic records than it used to be."

Maurice has had enough. "Tell us what you know," he commands.

"A $280 million money transfer is hard to mask."

Maurice's look could wilt lettuce.

Jerry breathes in again as if preparing to drag the information out from deep inside of him. He looks at us, making sure we are prepared to hear what he is about to say. "I won't bore you with the details of how we figured this out—"

"Don't," Maurice commands in his voice of God.

Jerry nods, lost in his thought before snapping to attention. "It came from the US Department of National Competitiveness."

44

There are moments in life when something hits you with a force so profound it almost alters your constitution. It scrambles you. They don't happen often.

I've had three the past week.

That MaryLee Stock was carrying a genetically enhanced embryo was one. That I may just love Antonia Hewitt was two. That the genetically enhanced embryo was inserted into MaryLee Stock at a fertility clinic owned by a front company apparently controlled by the United States government is a whopping number three.

The revelation is too big to be swallowed in one gulp.

The word slowly leaks through Maurice's clenched lips. "Why?"

I put my palms together and hold them in front of my face. "What do we know about the DNC?"

"Created by Congress through the National Competitiveness Act of 2021 to help America compete with China," Jerry pipes in. "Bundles reform recommendations vetted through the National Competitiveness Board for an up-or-down vote by Congress . . ."

Maurice and I both zone out from this civics lesson that anyone who lives at all consciously in America could repeat. The National Competitiveness Act was the signature act of President Lewis and Vice President Alvarez's national unity government. Before it, America seemed to be on a path of inevitable decline in the face of China's rise. The grand bargain of the National Competitiveness Act had begun to turn things around. Each year, the Department of National Competitiveness puts together a list of necessary fixes, Congress holds hearings and debates the substance, and the entire list is voted on in an up-or-down vote. And what a difference it's started to make.

In the two years since the act was passed, the US has pushed back the retirement age for Social Security, allowed all Americans to buy in to Medicare, limited the power of unions, eliminated unfair loopholes from the tax code, massively expanded opportunities for skilled immigration, and instituted world-class educational standards. We slapped tariffs on targeted Chinese goods and made it clear that they would go up unless China started actively protecting US intellectual property rights and guaranteed reciprocal market access. People once said it could never be done, but America instituted a carbon tax that's helping alternative energy investment boom in the US. If there is one government agency that is a hero of this process, it is the Department of National Competitiveness.

And now this.

"We may think that the DNC owned the clinic," Maurice says matter-of-factly, "that MaryLee got impregnated there, but we still don't know who killed her. Until we do, all we'll be able to say is that the US government may own a chain of fertility clinics, which we can only try to prove circumstantially based on illegal hacking. It's not much to go on." Maurice pauses reflectively. "It's just enough rope for *us* to get hanged with. We need more information." He takes out his u.D.

"Who are you calling?"

"Your friend," he says to me before speaking into the earpiece. "Put Reverend Becker on," he orders gruffly.

I watch Maurice listening intensely to the response. "Hmm," he says insincerely. "Well, I'm just going to tell you this once, ma'am," he continues. "This is Kansas City Police Department Inspector Maurice Henderson, and if you don't get Reverend Becker on the line in one minute I can guarantee you'll be hearing the sirens any moment now."

His voice softens after a short pause. "Why, of course I'll wait. Thank you, ma'am."

Another pause.

"Hello, sir . . . Sorry, sir, I needed to get their attention . . . I'm sure that's true, sir, but that's not my concern right now . . . Maybe you're right, maybe you're wrong. Only you can decide how you want to play your hand. . . . That's a better approach, I think. What have you done so far to get the feds to stand down? . . . Really? I find that hard to believe. We've actually met the federal marshal . . . I hear you . . . Call me when you know more."

Maurice taps off.

"What was that?" I ask.

"He says Senator King's chief of staff called the Justice Department."

"And?"

"They didn't know anything about a News Protection Act enforcement action."

45

"Somebody out there is showing a complete willingness to kill," I tell Maurice as he drives me back to Toni's friend's car, "and your plan is for us to announce ourselves?"

"Not us," Maurice says dryly, "you."

"So you want me to be a goat tied to a stake to attract predators?"

"This isn't about finding out what happened to MaryLee anymore. If there's a link—"

"I know, Maurice," I say, cutting him off.

Maurice squints. "I think they call it a lamb in this context. We've got to learn more about Gillespie and we're not going to know if there are other MaryLees out there until we figure out what happened here."

Maurice's argument makes sense; it's his technique that concerns me. I'm not sure what they teach at the police academy, but there's got to be something more sophisticated than this.

"Seven a.m., Clyde Manor, apartment 802. You'll get your people there?"

"I will," I say softly, not sure how I'll get everyone together with all of my fears of compromised vehicles and devices.

As I begin to get out of his car, Maurice reaches over and pulls me back. "One more thing," he says with a mischievous half grin I've seen once before, "I've got something to show you."

He reaches inside the left pocket of his blazer and peels off a four-inch piece of masking tape. Specs of dust are affixed to the sticky side.

"What's that?"

He points to an almost imperceptible golden line across the tape as he speaks. "A strand of Cobalt Becker's hair."

I want to hug Maurice Henderson. Instead, I look him in the eye and smile. "You're a good man, Maurice," I say. "How long will it take?"

"I can know by tomorrow morning if it's a genetic match. I'll see you then."

I drive over to pick up Toni from the back entrance of the hospital.

"You look awful," she says, getting into the car. "What's going on?"

I ask her about her day and am somehow surprised it was uneventful. Then I tell her about mine. With each word, I feel I'm simultaneously drawing her in and casting her overboard. I wish I had a better plan, but I explain the rough outline of the one we have.

We drive to her friend's house and pick up her mother's car.

Driving back to Toni's place, I feel sullen. I've been in constant motion since the day MaryLee Stock died, but now that I pause for a moment all of my doubts seem to catch up with me. Have I gone too far with Toni, exposed her to harm, risked too much?

"I'll see you in the morning, baby," I say, walking over to my car.

"Come in?" she says.

I pull her to me, a different embrace than early this morning, and hope it doesn't betray my existential exhaustion and growing unease. Right now I need to be in my own home, sleep in my own bed, refuel my private tank. I feel guilty. "Clyde Manor, room 802. Seven o'clock?"

"Aye aye, sir," she says, trying to lighten the mood.

I smile.

I instruct my Haier kitchenette from my u.D to toast a sesame bagel and cook a veggie burger as I drive home. It's hot and ready when I take it from the cooker, but the freezerator screen senses I'm approaching and flashes the words in bold it wants to shout at me but can't since I've disabled its voice. "Hey, moron," it probably wants to say, "your milk is now fifteen days past expiration and you're going to be praying to the porcelain god if you even think about eating these salmonella-ridden eggs." Instead, the words flash in bold across the screen. ALERT: MILK FIFTEEN DAYS PAST EXPIRY. EGGS FORTY-ONE DAYS PAST EXPIRY. DO NOT CONSUME.

"*Xie xie*," I say, carrying my veggie burger up the steps. I devour it in six bites then collapse into bed without washing up. The thought that strangers have been wandering through my house only vaguely registers. The place seems no more messy than it already was.

My u.D alarm vibrates me awake from a fitful sleep at six fifteen. Waking in my own bed, I feel, for a moment, safe. Then the illusion fades.

The others are there when I arrive at Clyde Manor. The apartment belongs to Maurice's neighbor, a temporarily unoccupied rental unit. Maurice is already going through the paces.

Toni looks at me, shakes her head slightly from side to side, then winks.

Maurice turns his head my way and nods slightly. I can't say I'm surprised, but my heart skips a beat nonetheless when he takes me aside to give me the news from the genetic test of Becker's hair.

Joseph focuses in rapt attention.

"The first element of surveillance is to know whom you are following," Maurice says without an ounce if irony. "The second key principle is, don't get caught. Don't be obvious, don't make jarring moves. Third, coordinate. A one-man surveillance is far less likely to succeed than one with two or three people. Fourth, never take your eyes off the target. Fifth, if the target sees you three times, you are burnt, out of it."

Maurice traces different techniques on sheets of white paper he's taped to the wall.

"Can't we just put a GPS tracker on the guy's car?" Jerry asks.

"Anyone sophisticated would do a scan," Maurice responds.

"Gillespie has met Rich and me, and he probably knows who you are," Toni says.

"Yes," Maurice responds.

"So that leaves Jerry and Joseph."

"That's our team," Maurice says. "The rest of us are support."

I look around the room. The plan makes me uneasy.

After forty-five minutes of training, I take out my phone and call the number on Gillespie's card. He answers after two rings.

"Mr. Gillespie, this is Rich Azadian. We need to talk."

"Where?"

"Why don't you come *back* to my place?"

Toni makes a face at me. *You really can't help yourself, can you?* I raise my eyebrows and smile.

Forty-five minutes later, the familiar black GMC pulls in front of my house.

"Welcome back," I say, inviting him and his colleague in the door.

Gillespie's dead eyes don't respond to the attempted humor. He gruffly introduces his colleague, Marshal Collins. Short and wiry, with close-cropped hair, Collins's forehead juts over a face that looks more like an eagle's beak. His hawkish eyes dart around the room as if hunting for prey.

"What do you want to say?" Gillespie pushes his words at me.

"I've been thinking about our meeting yesterday," I say with a false innocence.

"Thinking?" Gillespie repeats suspiciously.

"Thinking. Not looking into the story, of course."

He glares at me as I continue.

"But I received a very strange message on my u.D from an unknown address and I don't know what to do with it."

"Let me see it," Gillespie says.

"I need to ask you something first."

"What?" Gillespie fumes.

"I feel like I'm in a strange position. I wrote the initial story and, I admit, kept going when I shouldn't have. Now that the NPA letter has been delivered to the *Star*, I've been suspended and stopped investigating."

Gillespie glares at me. Collins paces menacingly around the room, suspiciously eying every corner of it.

"But now," I continue, "I've received this anonymous text and I don't know what to do. I don't want to pass it to anyone or create the impression I'm investigating and put my colleagues at risk. But I know you're looking into this, and I also don't want to interfere with your work. So what's the right thing to do?"

"Show me," Gillespie orders.

I lift my wrist to show him the text on my u.D.

He pulls it hostilely off my arm.

"The part about the extra chromosome really struck me. I know it's none of my business, but do you think that could be true?" I ask, pretending sheepishness.

Collins strides over and stands behind Gillespie, reading the text. The negative energy running through both of them could power the house for months.

"Let me put it to you this way," Gillespie hisses, looking straight through me. "You just stay away from all of this. Do you hear me?" His last sentence is pure threat.

"Yes, sir."

He stares at me for a few seconds more than feels comfortable, hands me my u.D without breaking his stare, then walks out the door.

Collins scans the room one last time before glaring at me with a crooked, pitying half smile. "We're so sorry to bother you, Mr. Azadian." His voice is higher pitched than I'd imagined, his accent betraying a hint of country. But his hawkish eyes are flinty and unflinching. "Have a nice day." The menacingly polite words seem the closing lines of Gillespie's threat. They send a chill down my spine.

Collins holds his intense glare for what feels like an uncomfortable eternity but must only be a few moments, smiles coldly, then turns and strides out the door.

46

"Target turning left on Southwest Trafficway, over," I hear Joseph say.

"I have visual," Jerry responds. "Taking lead. Drop back, over."

Listening to the chatter on the radios Maurice has provided, my mind wanders into the surreal labyrinth of overlapping codes surrounding me.

Borges writes of humanity searching endlessly for a lost catalogue of catalogues that will provide a map of all knowledge that we, the imperfect librarians, are destined to never find. If the human genome is the library of Babel, I wonder if we'll ever be able to understand the catalogue well enough to reorder our nucleotides with even the slightest level of responsibility.

The second code is almost as central to our lives. For some, the history of FORTRAN, Basic, Java, HTML, and Netsperanto has become a modern creation myth, like Abraham, Isaac, and Jacob, like Moses coming down from Sinai. Most everything in our lives has a computer chip embedded somewhere in it, regulated by an endless number of computer programs. If a person had to count the number of lines of computer code that in some way touch him or her on a daily basis, how high would that number be? Trillions?

With all of these lines of code around us, it's incredible we can even define what we mean by a virus, that we have so much faith in the orderly running of things that something violating that structure can earn itself a special name. Can anything rationally be called a weed in such a vast and diversified forest? We live in a world defined by uniformity but still identify ourselves by our mutations.

"Entering 435 East. Backing off, over." The stakeout chatter continues on the base station.

"Got him. Tracking target, over."

I drive to Broadway Café and put two quarters in the pay phone.

"Martina Hernandez's office," Justina Morris says after two rings.

I freeze.

"Miss Hernandez, please," I say in a ridiculous low voice. I was never meant for this kind of subterfuge.

"Who may I say is calling?"

"Tell her it's Mr. Borges."

"Hold the line a moment."

"What the fuck, Azadian?" I hear a moment later. "Why are you calling me?"

"We need to talk. I need you to meet me at the Penn Valley Park Indian statue at noon."

"Listen, Az—"

"I need you to trust me. Meet me." I hang up.

A few minutes before noon, buzzed from my triple espresso, I'm back looking at the Indian statue and waiting for Martina. This poor soul, naked but for his loin cloth in the autumn chill. Astride his horse, his hand shields his eyes from the sun as he surveys the crumbling bridges and rotting houses in the valley below. Stuck forever imagining what it would be like to move forward but never quite getting there, surveilling the evidence of his own failure, he feels depressingly familiar.

At twelve fifteen Martina screeches to a halt beside me. Annoyance defines her face. She rolls down her passenger window reluctantly as I approach.

"Get in," she orders. "Do you know how much you are putting at risk by calling me, by asking me to come here?"

"I do."

"So what the fuck?"

"There's a lot happening. Big things."

"Listen to me Azadian. I know that for whatever fucked up reason you don't want to drop this. But there's a lot more than you at risk here. I'm not going fight this battle and lose the war."

"This battle is a war, Martina," I say.

"Maybe for you it is, but what do you think it means that the *Kansas City Star* exists? It's not just that all the people who work there get dental. It's that we're the only ones around with the resources to hold people accountable for their actions. Who else is keeping the City Council, the mayor honest? Every government in the world, every company, is paying a small army of people to blog and tweet and cloud about how great they are. Every citizen feels empowered, and because everyone has a voice no one does. This town would be a hell of a lot worse if it weren't for what we do."

"And if you have to throw a dead woman, maybe two, maybe more overboard to keep it that way, then that's a price you've got to pay?" I spit out.

"Goddam right it is. What would you rather have us do, the opposite?"

"Accountability?"

"Is an aggregate fucking term," Martina fires back.

"I can take this story somewhere else, you know."

Marina pulls her head back. "And get them shut down, too? You know what the fucking law says, and until you got the story nailed down, airtight, any news organization would be insane to publish it, suicidal. The story would be dead in minutes. They'd be shut down and you'd be in jail."

"I can get there, Martina."

"Are you there now?" she says fiercely.

"No," I say softly, "I'm not."

I can see Martina preparing to charge in for the kill. Then she stops herself. Her lips purse. "Tell me what you mean," she says, after a pause, "but then don't call me, don't call the *Star*, don't represent to the rest of the world that you're connected to us in any way."

I collect my thoughts.

"Talk," she orders.

"MaryLee Stock was murdered by a fatal dose of potassium cyanide. She was pregnant when she died. The police know that but didn't release the information. Cobalt Becker was the genetic father."

"Stop there. Can you prove it?"

I can almost see the political calculations in her head as she processes what this could mean to Senator King's campaign.

"Yes."

"Go on."

"She'd been impregnated through an IVFGS clinic in KC owned by the US Department of National Competitiveness."

Martina's eyes widen. "How concrete is all of this?" she says quietly, her manner changed completely.

"Most of it," I say. "Some of the evidence is circumstantial, and I don't have the whole story nailed down."

"What are you doing now?"

"Trying to confirm."

She taps her right fist with her left open palm for about fifteen seconds. She fixes her sharp eyes on me. "I'm not going to bring anyone else in on this until you tell me that you've got all of this 100 percent. They'd kill it, kill you, kill the *Star*."

I nod.

"Even then," she continues, "they may kill it just the same, but at least we'll be able to have the debate. Right now we wouldn't get that far."

"We need to find a way to communicate."

"How do you mean?"

"I think they're tracking me. I called you from a pay phone.

There's one at the Lukoil station at Fourteenth and Main. I can call you there every day at three o'clock."

She tilts her head slightly to the right and shakes it slowly from side to side as if to say she can't believe she's letting herself be drawn into this. "I'll be there."

"Thanks, Martina," I say to try to seal the deal before she changes her mind.

"Ahora vea por esos hijos de puta!"

My Spanish is not great, but I know enough to understand. *Now let's get those bastards.*

47

"I do," I respond to Maurice as the image flashes across the wall screen, "that's Jessica Crandell."

The room goes silent.

The combined photos that Jerry and Joseph have taken over the course of the day hadn't, until this moment, told much of a story. Gillespie stopping for coffee, Gillespie driving to the downtown federal building and staying put most of the day, Collins leaving at four. Then this photo of Gillespie with Jessica Crandell.

"So if the US government owns Bright Horizons, then what?" Maurice asks.

"Someone knows a lot more than they are telling us. The chances of this being somehow connected to the murder become pretty overwhelming," I say.

"And now that we have more information, it's time to go on the offensive."

Maurice outlines his plan. I can't say I'm convinced. He says it beats sitting around, that we need to catch him off guard and push our momentum. We map out our plan of attack before we head out of Clyde Manor one at a time.

I pause a moment beside her car in the parking lot before scribbling a note I leave under her windshield wiper. *Come over?*

I race home, not entirely certain what she'll do. I wash my face, brush my teeth, and spray the place with Lysol just in case.

"It smells like the hospital in here," she announces, pushing through the door. My face and teeth are clean, the house does not smell as bad as it did a few minutes ago. Looks are another matter.

"And you did all this for me?"

My house has more of an accumulated feel. Shelves that once must have held art objects and perfectly organized decorative tomes under the old occupants now strain under the weight of disheveled old books, pots where a few plants once lived, unused cookware, garbage sculptures, and out-of-date electrical equipment. The Scooba 8600 home bot I purchased two years ago had promised to hover around my house cleaning the floors with the dedication of a sorcerer's apprentice. Trapped between a chair and an empty flowerpot four months ago and unable to make it back to the charging station, the dusty hubcap has become just another part of the problem it was initially recruited to fix.

"I've been a little preoccupied," I say sheepishly.

"That's for sure," she says, moving into the kitchen. The freezerator must sense its opportunity for some TLC. It flashes its milk and eggs warning.

Toni shakes her head as she empties the milk carton in the sink, then tosses it and the offending eggs into the garbage bin.

Really, Rich? she says with her eyes as she starts to transfer dishes from the sink to the dishwasher.

I try to stop myself from feeling alarmed at her kind gestures.

"You don't have to do that," I say, moving behind her and placing my hands on her shoulders.

"It's okay," she says softly.

"I'm sorry I dragged you into this mess," I whisper into her ear.

She turns to face me. "I made my own choice."

"Because I asked?"

"Probably," she says reflectively. "Mostly. I see death all the time at work, but there's something significant about deciding one person is important, for whatever reason. Sometimes one baby dying at the NICU hits hard. I don't always know even why one death reaches me more than others."

I hold her to me.

"Sometimes we just pick one thing to care about, one person, because that's all we can do," she continues, her message to me clear. "That's our statement to the universe that our lives don't just amount to birth and death statistics even though in the big picture they might."

Toni's words reach me. Maybe we each have to just mark off a corner of the universe to call our own, to care for, to project meaning into. Maybe nothing is our destiny except for what we randomly declare to be so.

"Thank you for being here, with me," I say softly.

She reaches for the washcloth to dry her hands and looks me in the eye.

I feel us reconnecting.

Then she smushes the wet washcloth in my face.

I don't move.

She puts the washcloth on the counter and wipes my face with her palm. Her smiling face grows serious. "I'm here, baby."

48

I'm a strange brew of delirious and groggy when I meet Maurice at the I-435 Hilton at 5:45 a.m. Even at this early hour Maurice looks solid and starched.

He preps me one last time then sits in his car as I go in. I chug myself a quick mug from the lobby coffee pot. It tastes like dirt.

I take the elevator to the fifteenth floor then pause a moment in front of room 1527. My heart pounds.

Bam. Bam. Bam. I'm normally not such an aggressive knocker. I count to five, as Maurice and I have practiced.

Bam. Bam. Bam. I hear rustling. One, two, three, four, five.

Bam. Bam. Bam.

"Hold on." Gillespie's words are forceful and angry.

A few moments later the door opens partly and Gillespie reaches his head, turtle-like, into the opening. His hair is messy, his white bathrobe uneven.

"What the fuck are *you* doing here?" Gillespie's words only technically constitute a question.

"We need to talk," I say calmly.

"How did you find me?"

"I don't have time for this," I say. "I wouldn't be here if I weren't serious."

Gillespie stares at me, trying, it seems, to assess if I am. "I'll meet you in the coffee shop in twenty minutes."

This is one of the responses I'd prepared for.

"No," I say. "I need to talk with you now."

"Fuck yourself," Gillespie says. "Twenty minutes."

The door pushes shut.

So much for seizing the momentum.

I amble back to the elevator, feeling like I've failed my first test, then slide into a booth in the coffee shop and wait.

The Gillespie who sits across from me is very different from the mess of raw emotion I'd encountered twenty minutes before. This Gillespie is back in suit and tie, his eyes awakened. He is back, in other words, in control.

"So," he says, his eyes bearing down on mine, "I'll ask you again. What the fuck are you doing here?"

I stare back for a moment before speaking. "Yesterday morning I told you about the text message I received."

"And I told you to back off. What about 'fuck off' don't you understand?"

"I got another text. This one said that MaryLee Stock was impregnated at a fertility clinic called Bright Horizons. Have you heard of it?"

"Fuck you."

"I'm sensing a lot of hostility from you. Are you sure you should be taking caffeine?"

Gillespie's nostrils flare. Something about harassing him is starting to give me pleasure. "It said she was impregnated at Bright Horizons with a mutated embryo, and it said that Bright Horizons is owned by a front company that belongs to the United States Department of National Competitiveness. I'm just feeling torn. I'm trying to drop this case, but I keep getting these messages and I want to do everything I can to help your investigation."

Gillespie looks like he's going to kill me.

"And it said there's a woman at Bright Horizons named Jessica Crandell who is involved in this who has a lot of information about what's going on."

Gillespie is on the verge of boiling over. He stares through me with venomous eyes. "Are you done?"

I nod slightly.

"You can cut the bullshit about the text messages," he hisses. "I know what you're doing. I know you don't give a shit about what happens to the *Kansas City Star*."

"Not that much."

Gillespie shakes his head. "But I'd imagine you care about what might happen to you. I think you know, or you should know, that once you've started covering a story, the News Protection Act applies to you, even if you no longer work for the same organization. You are personally, criminally liable. Everything you're telling me now can and probably will be used against you in a court of law. It's not a regular court. It's a FISA court. Do you know what that is?"

I don't respond.

"Foreign Intelligence Surveillance Act. It's where we try people connected to state secrets. It's not a good place to be. Do you know how long it will take me to get a warrant for your arrest?"

"State secrets?" I ask.

"Fuck off." He stares at me, awaiting my answer.

My position is weakening, but I'm not going to indulge him with an answer.

"I can arrest you now. I can get retrospective FISA approval in an hour. You know why I'm not doing that?"

"Why?"

"Because I think you have no idea what the hell you're doing, what you're interfering with."

"Which is what exactly?"

"I know you think you're being clever, but I'm actually going to tell you. Do you know why?"

I'm afraid to ask. "Why?"

"For two reasons. First, because you have uncovered some useful information for us."

The words surprise me. Who have I compromised?

"You're a smart guy, Azadian," Gillespie continues, "but we're both smart. I can have you locked up right now, but believe it or not, I respect you enough to think that once I tell you what's actually going on here you'll realize you're barking up the wrong tree and back the fuck off. Or you'll be smart enough to recognize how painful this will be for you and the people around you if you keep going. I can haul you in, but even I understand it's never possible to completely muzzle someone."

He looks me straight in the eye and then adds calmly, "No matter how much I would want to do so."

The words send a chill through my body.

"Do you want to know the second reason?"

My internal radar says no.

"I'm telling you so I'll know that if anything on this leaks, you're the one responsible. It's like swallowing dye before an MRI. If this gets out, I'll know that my first reason didn't pan out and I'll have the *Star* shut down and"—his eyes lock on mine—"I'll have you shut down. Am I clear?"

My swallow reflex betrays me.

"Good," he says. "You're right about MaryLee Stock," he adds after a pause to let his words sink in. "That's why I'm here. You already know that."

"I do."

"You're right about the extra chromosome. When someone is born naturally with an extra chromosome, it's a mutation. When someone is conceived that way through IVFGS at a fertility clinic, it's a crime."

I'm trying to figure out where he is going with this.

"You're right that Bright Horizons was involved. That's why we've been tracking them. That's why we are shutting them down. I met with Jessica Crandell about this yesterday."

I stare at him blankly.

"You're wrong about the US government owning Bright Horizons. We've been tracking them for months. They're owned by a front company in the Cayman Islands. We've been trying to hack into their computer network but haven't succeeded, which is why we've had to do things the old-fashioned way."

"Which is?"

"Watching. Which is why I know where you were last Saturday, Dikran. May I call you Dikran?"

May I call you asshole? I want to say.

"So you should be grateful we've let you enjoy your weekend away with your girlfriend. We wanted to see what you were up to."

Now I'm the one seething.

"We lost you for a while, but then you came back on the grid. Which leads us back to the same three questions."

"Which are?"

"Who owns Bright Horizons, why was MaryLee Stock killed, and why was Chinese intelligence monitoring this so closely?"

"Chinese intelligence?"

"Don't be that surprised. Your little friend was the one who alerted us that she'd slipped away."

"She?"

"The Chinese girl, the pharmacy student, Min Zhao."

"And you think—?" I stammer.

"I think they knew something about Bright Horizons. Do I think the Chinese girl killed MaryLee Stock? Could be."

"Why would they do that?" I ask. Looking over Gillespie's shoulder, I notice Collins at a corner table. I have no idea how long he's been there, which is all the more unsettling. His unflinching, hawkish glare locked on me with an eerie intensity I can feel acutely from fifty feet away.

"I'll ask you a question," Gillespie says.

I shift my eyes and nod apprehensively.

He lifts his mug and takes a long, slow sip before placing it back on the table. "Have you ever heard of Yao Ming?"

49

I don't even know how to begin responding to the question.

"The old basketball player?" I stammer.

Gillespie just looks at me.

My mouth begins to form a question, but I'm not quite sure what to ask.

"Where do you think Yao Ming came from?" Gillespie asks. The words shoot from his mouth like bullets from an automatic.

"Um, China."

"Yao Ming was bred," Gillespie declares.

I'm not sure where he's heading, or what it possibly has to do with the murder of MaryLee Stock. I hold my gaze.

"In the 1970s China decided they wanted to compete in international sports like basketball. They sent scouts around the country looking for people with the right physical attributes. Kids with incredible coordination for diving, strength for weight lifting, speed for running—"

"And height," I say, trying to stay on my game by cutting short his pedantry.

"Yao Ming's parents were each recruited by the government." Gillespie scowls. "His dad was the star center for the men's team. The mom was the same for the women. The lead sports official decided to put them together to breed the next superstar for the state. He was born into the national basketball academy. His training started when he was a little kid."

"And you're telling me this because . . ."

Gillespie doesn't listen, only launches into another annoying rhetorical question. "Do you know how many gold medals China won three years ago in the 2020 Olympics?"

"In Tokyo?"

"Yes."

"A lot. They kicked our asses."

"The answer is sixty-two," Gillespie says without inflection. "How many did they win in the eighty-eight Olympics?"

"How many?" My tone conveys how sick I'm getting of this what-am-I-thinking game.

"Five. Twelve years later they won twenty-eight in the 2000 games. Eight years after, fifty-one in Beijing."

"And?" I say, hardly hiding my annoyance at being given a sports trivia lesson.

"The point is that China is getting stronger and stronger. Why?"

I don't respond. If he wants to tell me, let him.

"Because they've been finding the kids with all the right physical characteristics, taking them away from their families, and putting them in sports schools around the country where they spend all their time training. Most of the kids don't make it, but in a country of over a billion people they can find the superstars."

"So what does this have to do with MaryLee Stock?"

Gillespie ignores me and marches on. "Have you ever heard of a Sweeney mouse?"

The pedantry is getting to me. "No."

Gillespie shakes his head slightly as if to suggest I'm a hopeless idiot. "It's a genetically altered mouse, actually a bunch of mice, created at the University of Pennsylvania. Sweeney mice all have a forty-seventh chromosome. Some of them have genes that make them stronger, some of them smarter, and down the line."

Gillespie's words suddenly became a lot more interesting. I sit up in my chair.

"The logical thing would be to explore whether the technology could apply to humans," Gillespie says, "but we can't."

"Politics?" I say, starting to imagine options for where he might be going.

"Yes. Political battles here, but not in China."

Gillespie pauses for dramatic effect. "I'm guessing you also haven't heard of the mouse called Wu."

I don't answer.

Gillespie gives the same you're-an-idiot head shake. "It's named after a Yale University professor named Wu Tian who moved back to China sixteen years ago. He started a lab in Shanghai financed by the Chinese government doing genetic research on knockout mice on a scale never been done before."

"What's that?"

"A mouse with a special moth gene that can be used to turn off one gene at a time, and a jellyfish gene that lights up to show which offspring carries the mutation."

I'm amazed a federal marshal knows this much about genetics.

"I don't expect you to understand this, but they isolated thousands of genes that governed specific traits and began to figure out what small changes to the mouse genome actually meant, then they started experimenting with different combinations of simultaneous genetic manipulations to see what patterns would emerge."

I nod cautiously, mindful of how completely I'm being pulled into Gillespie's story.

"Next, they built an automated factory to genetically alter and test tens of thousands of mice a day and integrated that data with the data they were stealing from the genome sequencing and synthetic biology labs around the world. The Chinese government put tens of billions of dollars toward becoming the world leader in applied genomics with a very specific goal."

The pieces begin to come together in my mind. "And because the mouse genome and the human genome are essentially the same—"

Gillespie cuts me off. "They have essentially the same sets of genes, just organized in a different order, but yes, the three pieces come together. Yao Ming tells us that the Chinese are perfectly comfortable using selective breeding to advance the goals of the state. They are a country run by engineers. For them, the genome is just another system to be rigged. The sports schools tell us that China will take these kids away from their families to train them for their one purpose in life. But the big part of the puzzle is what we've begun to learn about China's plans to use the kind of genetic enhancements applied to the Sweeney and Wu mice to create new human champions of the Chinese state."

"Athletes?"

Gillespie's look says *you're dumber than I thought.* "Scientists, inventors, business leaders, engineers, mathematicians, computer experts, musicians. Anything where China is competing with the rest of the world, anything to give them a competitive advantage."

"And how do you know that?"

"Let's just say we do."

"And we is?" I ask.

"You already know the answer to that question, Dikran. The US Department of National Competitiveness. That's our job."

Stop calling me fucking Dikran. "So why not just go public?"

"Because we don't have all the information. Because we probably won't be able to stop them. That's why we've been monitoring them."

"Them?"

"The Tianjin Genomics Institute, the Ministry of State Security, a unit of military intelligence called 8341. We don't know what they *can* do. We only know what they *want* to do. They started a massive cognitive genomics program a decade ago to try to map the genetic footprint of genius, run by a quirky genius named Zhao Bo Wu. They've got all the systems in place, the genomics institute, the elite schools for all sorts of things based on the sports school model. Right now they're funneling their best and brightest kids into those schools, and the results are impressive. First Yao Ming, then He Shiwen who demolished her own world records in the swimming pool in Tokyo, now the pianist Ying Lang. I guarantee you that the kids in their science schools will be winning Nobel Prizes for decades, even without genetic enhancement. If they're making as much progress on genetic enhancement as we think they are, then all bets are off once those kids enter the system. If it works, there might be no way for us to compete down the line."

"But you don't know whether there's a Chinese Sweeney yet?"

Gillespie drives his index finger into the table. "*That* is the point. We know they're making huge progress. We know they've isolated key genetic patterns that make up different types of intelligence in mice and are putting huge resources into figuring out how these patterns can apply in humans. We know they are collecting or stealing the full genomic readings of tens of thousands of the smartest people in the world and comparing their genomes with those of normal people to try and figure out the genetic recipe for intelligence. We know they and others have found specific genes that correlate to thicker gray matter in the brain and the functioning of the cerebral cortex. I'm sure the letters KL-VS, NR2B, and NPTN don't mean much to you, but they're all genes linked to heightened intelligence the Chinese are focusing on. We know the Chinese are setting up systems designed to breed and educate kids with superhuman capabilities. Do we have someone reporting daily from the secret Chinese military intelligence unit overseeing this all? No."

The magnitude of what Gillespie is saying overwhelms me. Genetic engineering. Rewriting the human code. Eugenics. "So then what?"

"We tracked someone we'd identified as a Unit 8341 intelligence officer entering the country. That's your friend Min."

"Hardly my friend."

"She tripped our wire with her fingerprint scan at the LA airport. We watched her move to Kansas City, start her Master's program at UMKC, cozy up to MaryLee Stock."

My mind is now racing a mile a minute. How had I so easily

cast aside the implications of Min's disappearance? Is Neary in danger?

Gillespie pushes on, his eyes bearing into mine. "We didn't know about Bright Horizons until Min Zhao showed up there with MaryLee Stock. Then we started looking at the organization. I'm sure you wondered just as much as we did why a fertility clinic would need to be registered in the Cayman Islands. That's why we've been probing their registration materials."

"Wait a second," I say. "Some of those materials point to you."

"I know you think that," Gillespie says. "That's why I'm telling you this. We've been trying to get at this from all sorts of angles. We even set up a company to try to wire funds to their holding company as a way of getting inside."

"And?"

"We didn't make big progress so we kept watching Min Zhao. Then everything happened at once. MaryLee was found dead. Zhao slipped out of the country. You showed up, and we still don't completely know what's going on."

I can't hide the look my face. I've been sneaking around thinking I've been clever, and he speaks as if he's been residing in my head. "And the autopsy?"

"It's obvious. We needed to figure out what's going on here before we risked making people crazy. This isn't just about one girl. It's about facing the Chinese threat. It's about the future of this country."

Gillespie stares into my skull without a hint of warmth. "That's why we can't have you running around like a chicken with your fucking head cut off," he says sharply. "You've actually done us a service. That's why I'm talking to you now and not just hauling you in."

I nod cautiously.

Gillespie leans closer toward me from across the table as he continues. "But I just want to make one thing completely clear, Dikran." He pauses for effect. "If you tell anyone a thing I've told you, if you keep meddling in this case, I will not hesitate. I will drag you and anyone, anyone helping you into a FISA court, and I guarantee you that your life will be hell. Do I make myself clear?"

A thousand pounds of tension congregates at my sphincter.

"Thanks for the coffee," he says before standing and walking out.

Collins holds his chilling, hawkish gaze on me from afar a few moments longer before following suit.

50

Where does idiot end and shithead begin? I wonder as I stagger out the hotel entrance.

An idiot doesn't appreciate the magnitude of his ignorance. A shithead puts other people at risk in support of his half-baked schemes.

Toni, Joseph, Jerry, Neary: I'd stupidly compromised them all.

I get into my car and drive to the Denny's on 113th and Metcalf. Maurice follows me in and sits across the booth.

"You don't look very good," he says.

I sink into the bench and relay our conversation word for word.

Maurice rubs his temples with a hand stretched across his face after I finish. "Do you believe him?" he asks.

"I don't know."

"Are you going to heed his warning?"

"I'm not sure."

"FISA courts are serious. He's right that he can put you in jail pretty quickly if he wants."

My mind is whirling. "It's Plato's *Republic*," I say softly. "Plato calls on the state to selectively breed the guardian class of Athens. The breeding committee would decide who goes with whom, and then their kids would be taken away from their parents and trained from early on."

"So this would be Plato's *Republic* on steroids?"

"Plato's *Republic* is essentially operation Yao Ming," I say.

"That's basically phase one. Mix it with genetic enhancement and other human augmentation technologies that could, in principle, make people better, smarter, stronger, faster than their natural counterparts ever could be, and it's definitely a step further."

"So where does Becker fit into all of this?'

"I don't know," I say, my mind shifting different configurations together.

"Let's take a step back and play it out," Maurice says.

We explore the various options for the roles the Department of National Competitiveness, the Chinese government, and Becker might play. Each of them is somehow connected, but which of them would have a motive to kill?

Maurice puts his hands together in front of his face as he thinks.

"But if Becker might be responsible because of his link to MaryLee, what does that say about Megan?" I ask.

"All we know right now is that Megan was about the same age as MaryLee, told her mother she was pregnant, then died unexpectedly. If the two deaths are connected, we've got to figure out what the two women had in common."

"And if there are more MaryLees out there who could be already dead or next," I add.

"But to know that, we've got to figure out what it is that we're looking for, and where we look. Put yourself in their shoes."

"Whose?" I ask.

"Whoever killed MaryLee. What were they looking for?"

"Depends on who killed her."

"Start with whoever decided to impregnate her with the mutated embryo."

"If it was Becker, I'd imagine I'd want someone young and virginal, a Christian, single."

"Why single? Wasn't Virgin Mary married?" Maurice asks.

"Not many guys these days would settle for Joseph's deal. Too complicated. I also get the feeling Becker wouldn't want another guy around."

"Go on," Maurice says.

"If I'm the Chinese, it depends on what I'm up to. If I'm just testing a new technology, I'll take pretty much anybody."

"But why do that here when they have a billion people at home they're willing to experiment with? Go on."

"If I'm trying to breed some kind of special person, I guess I'd look for a special kind of mother."

"In what way?" Maurice prods.

"Single, to keep things simple. Young, because that's what biology wants. And I'd pick based on what I was trying to do. I'd go tall if I was looking for a Yao Ming, or musical, or smart."

"But if you were just starting, experimenting?"

"I'd probably just go for single, young, and smart."

"How would you define young?" Maurice fires.

"Under thirty. That's what the risk tables say."

"And smart?"

"It seems like the most generalizable positive trait. And Gillespie told me the Chinese were putting huge resources into identifying the genetic patterns that make up intelligence."

"So how would they find it?"

"Intelligence tests," I say, "but the IQ tests aren't standardized, and most people don't take them."

"So?"

"The best proxy in the US would probably be SAT scores."

"But how do we know how much genetics is responsible for those scores? I did well on those tests because Momma was behind me with a stick," Maurice says with a rare humor.

The growing intensity of our interchange builds toward an idea. "There are probably three databases we'd need to access to try to triangulate all this," Maurice says thoughtfully, "the police database about young women who've died in the last year, the

Bright Horizon's database if we can ever get access to that, and the databases with SAT scores that have got to be somewhere."

"So, what? We cross-reference the databases without the ability to define exactly what it is we're looking for?"

"Seems like the only option we've got to begin narrowing things down," Maurice says urgently, "but we're going to need help. And we're going to need to figure this out before whoever killed MaryLee realizes what we're up to."

51

The two students sitting in front of Jerry look up, startled, as we barge into his office.

"We're going to need to talk later," he says, sending them out the door.

"There may be more than one person who could have been impregnated with a mutated embryo," I say, getting right to the point.

"By Bright Horizons?"

"That's our hunch, but we need to get into the Bright Horizons database to confirm it. What's happening?"

"I'm working on it. Their database is very well protected."

"What are the chances you can get in?" Maurice asks.

"I'm working on it," he snaps. "These things take time."

"I hope we have it," I say. "If there are more women out there, they could be in serious danger. And the more people know that we're poking around— "

"We need to put together a database search to see if there are other MaryLees out there," Maurice interrupts.

"All right," Jerry says. "The basic principles of search are define your terms and define your fields. The more we can do both the better off we'll be."

"Which means?" Maurice asks impatiently.

"We have to decide what we're looking for and where we want to look for it," Jerry says.

"We know that MaryLee Stock went to Bright Horizons and then was killed," I say. "If and when we get into the database, we need to see whether Megan Fogerty's name shows up there too and what they and any others may have in common. If we can build a profile of those two and any others who may also have been killed, we might then be able to understand what kind of women we're looking for who may still be alive."

"So define the terms," Jerry repeats.

"We need to search in the databases for women in the United States under the age of thirty who died in the last year. Let's say that the women are single, have no criminal records—"

"Why no criminal records?" Jerry asks.

"I'm guessing there would be some kind of screening process. We also need to factor out street people and runaways."

Maurice gives me a strange look. I get the feeling he thinks I'm saying that we're looking for white people.

"We're looking for smart people," I continue, "let's say with good SAT scores."

I tap my u.D to start flipping through my notes on my monitor. "Joseph told me that MaryLee had SAT scores of 640 English, 680 math, 640 writing."

"Pretty good," Maurice says.

"So let's make it lower to be safe. Let's say six hundred or above on each section."

"Okay," Jerry says. "What else?"

"I want to say pregnant, but—"

Maurice cuts me off. "MaryLee wouldn't have shown up under that screen. We need to make sure the terms we set would at least apply to her."

"Is that it?" Jerry asks.

"I think so," I say unconvincingly, "for now."

"So the next question is, where do we look?" Jerry says. "The first obvious place is in the police database." We both turn to face Maurice.

"We're going to need a live link," Jerry says. "We need to be able to play with the numbers, move them around to try to find what we're looking for."

"And we do that how?" Maurice asks suspiciously.

"Um, with live access. I need you to plug a PCM stick into your base station when the database is open, then download a file into your network."

"You want me to infect the KCPD computer system with a virus?"

"I guess when you put it that way, yes," Jerry says.

Maurice blows heavy air out through his nose, his by-the-book nature clearly conflicting with our off-the-book needs. "How long would it take to transfer?"

"About a minute," Jerry says. "It's a big file. It directs your network system to share the database with me. That's the easy part. The hard part is for the file to camouflage itself so it doesn't get picked up by the security system."

Maurice shoots me an I-can't-fucking-believe-this look.

Jerry turns to face his screens, his hands dancing in the air, moving code around frantically.

After a few minutes he hands Maurice a tiny cyberstick. "Open the database, plug this in, and open the one file loaded on the drive. After it opens, pull the drive and close the file. Clear?"

Maurice nods.

"What about the SAT scores?" I ask.

"Those are pretty easy. Every student includes them in their college applications," Jerry says.

"So we'll cross-reference the police database with the SAT scores, and Bright Horizons if you get through," I say. "What else?"

"uSN," Jerry says. "Once we start narrowing the list, we can get a lot of information from the universal Search Network, but that will take time and I'll need help."

"Joseph?" I say.

"He'd be great," Jerry replies.

"Jerry, there's another thing," I say. "When I met with Gillespie this morning, it seemed like they've got pretty good access to our communications."

Jerry thinks for a moment before speaking. "We'll have to go *Battlestar Galactica.*"

Huh?

"It's a long story," Jerry says, responding to my surprise. "A sci-fi TV series from twenty years ago about a battle in space between humans and robots."

I never watched but vaguely remember it.

"The robots figured out how to break into the humans' networks," Jerry continues, "and the only defense the humans have is to use old technology. If someone is tracking us on high tech, maybe all we can do is go low tech."

"Carrier pigeon?" I ask.

"Something like that," Jerry says. "Bicycle taxi works just as well. I'll send Joseph a note."

"Maurice," I say, "when can you get that cyberstick into the computer?"

"Within an hour."

"Jerry, how much time will you need after that?"

"It depends. At least all night. Maybe more."

"As quickly as possible," I say with a strange feeling in my gut we may be racing against a clock we can't even see, frantically searching for dead people as signposts pointing toward other young women who might be in mortal danger.

52

There are times when I feel simultaneously awake and asleep, charged yet dulled. I've hardly slept, yet feel a nervous, almost manic energy running through my veins.

The late Czech writer Milan Kundera wrote that we live our lives as a first draft that is also the final text, a dress rehearsal that is itself our final performance. We stitch little pieces of knowledge together to create understanding, but these flashes come too late to prevent the mistakes we've already made along the way. By the time we've learned enough about something to handle it properly, we've probably already fucked it up beyond repair. I'm learning more about MaryLee's death, but at what cost? How many mistakes am I making along the way? How many people am I putting in danger?

And then, of course, my vibrating u.D interrupts my reflection.

"Hi, Mother," I say, trying to cover my tracks.

"Dikranigus, you sound tired," she says. "What's going on?"

"Everything's good, Mom."

"Are you sure you're okay? This is your mother you're talking to."

"How are you?" I say, trying to change the subject.

She won't be so easily diverted. "I'm worried about you, Dikran."

"I'm fine, Mother," I say. "How is Shoonig?"

Neither Shoonig the Second nor Shoonig the First, whom he replaced six years ago, filled the void left by the loss of Astrid and my father, but each yelp, each demand to be walked or fed, each attack on an errant pillow, chases the ghosts, for a brief moment, out of my mother's head.

She plays along grudgingly. "Barking away at the cars as if he's never seen them before. The kids take the mufflers off, which drives him even more crazy." She tacks back. "How was your visit with—"

"Fine, Mother," I say, cutting her off then feeling badly for it. I've always started to worry when my mother latched on to a name of a former girlfriend, even one like Toni, whom she's never met in person. I again feel guilty and alter my tone. "Toni is fine, Mother, thank you for asking. How is Mrs. Gregorian doing?"

My mother ignores the question. "It's just that I don't want you to be alone, my *janeegus*."

"I know, Mother."

"Are you eating enough?"

I translate her words in my head, my mother again channeling her sadness into an intense, loving focus on me.

"Yes, Mother," I say.

"Five servings of fruit and vegetables every day," she says, rallying.

"Yes, Mother. For you, six."

"You're a good boy, Dikran," she says after a pause.

"Thank you, Mom."

"Just call your mother once in a while."

"Love you," I say with all the positive energy I can muster as I tap my u.D. I don't know if I'm more worried about her or she's more worried about me.

The u.D clock reads 2:48 p.m. I want to call Martina from my u.D, but my conscience gets the better of me. I speed toward the Quik Trip convenience store on Forty-Fourth and Main and arrive a few minutes late for the call.

"Where the hell have you been?" she chides belligerently.

"Sorry."

"What have you got for me?"

"Nothing yet. MaryLee may not have been the only young woman impregnated with a modified fetus. We're trying to see if there are more."

"When will you know?"

"Hopefully by tomorrow."

"Look, Azadian," she says, "I've got to tell you something. Wes came to see me this morning. The lawyers told him that it's not enough we've suspended you. We're sending out the letter today. I'm sorry."

I knew this was coming, but it still stings.

"And this means that you're all alone on this. If you choose to go forward, it's even more on your shoulders. No one can help you if you get in trouble with the government," she says, as if her earlier words weren't clear enough.

"Gillespie told me the same this morning," I say.

"You're in touch with him?"

"That's one way to put it."

The pause becomes awkward.

"Look, Azadian . . . Rich," Martina says, "I need to stay away from this. No more calls. I'm sorry."

"And if I can confirm everything?"

"The entire paper is on the line. The headwinds are still pretty fucking strong."

They are almost blowing me away, but if I can nail things down at least I may have options. "I guess that's it, then," I say coldly.

I wait for a hint of remorse until the silence becomes strained.

"Azadian," she then says, "be careful."

53

I only realize I'm asleep when the doorbell wakes me. I'm on the couch, a box of mostly eaten *phad thai* beside me on the floor. My brain takes a moment to focus.

The bell rings two more times in quick succession.

I walk dizzily toward the front door, my mind flipping through the possibilities.

"Rich, it's me, Jerry. Open the door."

He comes charging in.

"Look at this," he says, breathlessly splashing the content from his u.D monitor onto my coffee table monitor. "It took me a little while to figure out how to run the searches once I got into the KCPD database. Here's the list of women between the ages of twenty and thirty who've died in the United States over the past year." He taps his u.D, and the names start scrolling.

"How many are there?" I ask.

"One hundred and thirty-seven thousand two hundred and fourteen."

"All right."

"But you said single women," Jerry adds, tapping the u.D again. "That takes us down to eighty-six thousand six hundred and seventy-nine."

"Okay."

"And you said no criminal record," Jerry taps a few more times, "which brings us down to sixty-seven thousand four hundred and fifty-five."

"At least we're making progress."

"But that gets us to the end of your first set of questions. If you're right that MaryLee was murdered based on being part of a certain group, but we don't know exactly what criteria define her group, we'd need to narrow things down based on a series of deductions. Your first hypothesis was that MaryLee was killed, that's why we're looking in the police database. Your second was that it was because she was a woman, and your third that she was a woman without a criminal record, that she'd become part of the group, whatever it is, by nature of her positive qualities rather than her negative ones."

"I hadn't thought of it like that," I say, "but makes sense."

"So, if we assume that all of these things are true, the next question is, which other search criteria might be true?"

"Keep going."

"You said that there were three potential perpetrators, Cobalt Becker, the Chinese government, and the US Department of National Competitiveness, right?"

"At least that's what we've come up with so far."

"So tell me again. If you are Becker choosing MaryLee, what are the criteria you're using to make your choice and are you choosing one person or more than one?"

"I'm choosing her because she has no history. She's adopted from some faraway place, so in my mind she comes with a clean slate, like a transgenic mouse. She's worthy of being the mother of the messiah because I've watched her grow, she's smart, and because I think she's a good person, and—" I pause. "And I think I might be able to get away with it because everyone around her trusts me."

My mind flashes back to my encounter with Carol Stock at the Holy Virgin Church. If Carol was such a believer that the Second Coming was imminent, how far might she have been willing to go to help make it possible?

"So there can't be so many women that fill all or most of those criteria?"

"If you're a believer, how many Virgin Marys can there really be? Once you go down that thought path, you're pretty much locked in."

"Okay," Jerry says feverishly. "Let's explore option B. Do it again, you are the Chinese government, what are you looking for?"

"I've invested billions in genetic technologies, but somehow my plans aren't working. I'm missing a key technology. I buy a chain of fertility clinics to get it. Or I'm running a genetic enhancement program at home in China and get an inkling that America may be doing something similar. I begin snooping around and send over an agent, maybe more. I discover something is going on and decide to try to block it. I find out which women are getting impregnated with genetically enhanced embryos and start knocking them off. That's option B-1. Option B-2, I send someone over to look around and when the impregnated woman she's monitoring gets killed, I assume that our cover is blown and order her to get out of Dodge as quickly as possible."

"Which still leaves us with the question of how MaryLee was selected," Jerry says. "Why do you choose MaryLee?"

"If we're selecting for intelligence at home in China, I'd imagine we'd at least explore a similar link here."

"Option C?"

"You know option C," I say. "I'm the US Department of National Competitiveness. My mandate is to make sure America gets back its edge as China surges ahead. I have a broad platform of legislative changes I've gotten through Congress, but I know that even with all of my agency's powers there's no way Congress is going to green-light a genetic enhancement program. So I set up a dummy company and buy a small chain of IVFGS clinics to begin seeding the population with genetically enhanced babies."

"So if you had to pick one data set as your highest priority, what would it be?"

"Intelligence for sure," I say, "at least as a start. It's the quality with the greatest applicability across the board. It's also what Gillespie said the Chinese were selecting for."

Jerry nods. "So I hacked the College Board's database and ran a program that searched automatically under each of the sixty-seven thousand four hundred and forty-five names and matched them with scores. I used the 600 across-the-board benchmark, which was still pretty high relative to the general population. A lot of them came up blank. Probably means that they didn't take the test."

"And?"

Jerry taps the screen again. "There are three hundred ninety-seven women who died over the last year between the ages of twenty and thirty who scored six hundred or above on their math, science, and writing SATs."

I grab the u.D monitor from Jerry's hands and start frantically scrolling down.

"What are you doing?" He asks.

I hardly hear him. My fingers can't move quickly enough as I scroll down through the names.

And then I see it.

"Megan Fogerty is on this list," I say, my heart pounding. "What are the chances that two pregnant women about the same age and with similar SAT scores die mysteriously at the same time in the same city?"

"Not impossible but not high," Jerry says solemnly.

"And do we know if any of the other women on this list were pregnant when they died?"

"I'll get Joseph working on that right now," Jerry says.

"Where is he?" I ask.

"In my basement."

"Doors locked?"

Jerry gives me a funny look.

"And what about the Bright Horizons database? We need it

now," I say with a harshness I regret as soon as the words leave my mouth.

"I know," Jerry says dejectedly. "We're getting close. I think we'll get it."

"When?"

"Soon. It's hard to predict."

My heart is pounding. MaryLee Stock and Megan Fogerty are both dead. There may be others like them who are still alive.

And the only thing that may stand between any of them and the list of deceased might very well be Maurice and me and our little ragtag group of helpers.

54

"Henderson," Maurice says in full grog.

"Sorry to wake you," I say.

"It's five thirty in the morning," he grumbles, stating the obvious. "Hold on a second."

I hear rustling and assume he's moving out of his bedroom.

"What do you have?"

"You think we can talk on these phones?"

"Who the hell knows? God dammit. Meet at the usual place in forty-five minutes, six fifteen."

"See you there."

Maurice still looks half asleep when we rendezvous at Swope Park.

"And obviously it can't be a coincidence that Becker tries to use genetic technologies to breed a red heifer in Texas, then gets MaryLee pregnant with a genetically enhanced fetus," I say after briefing him on what we have.

"It's impossible. Becker isn't telling us what he knows." Maurice pauses. "And I'm starting to think we've been too damned nice with the guy." He taps the u.D on his wrist.

"Reverend Becker," Maurice says, "is that you?"

Pause.

"Six thirty-four, actually. You are four minutes off. . . . I'd feel the same if I were you, but then again if I were you I wouldn't know about the forensic evidence implicating me in a crime."

Maurice looks at me as Becker speaks.

"No, I'm not. I'm just telling you how I would feel if I were you . . . You're right. You don't have to listen to this. If you think hanging up is a better option, I encourage you to do it now. See how that strategy goes for you . . . Good, Reverend. I have two things to tell you. I'll tell you both together so you don't need to respond. I just want you to know what we've found. Okay? . . . Good. First, we did a genetic analysis of the tissue from the fetus MaryLee Stock was carrying when she was killed, and we tested it with a hair I took when I met you in your office . . . I'm an inspector. This is what I do for a living. The two matched. You were the father. Congratulations."

Maurice stops speaking, but I don't hear any noise coming from his earpiece.

"Reverend Becker, are you there? . . . You have that right. Of course we can speak with your lawyer. But just to be clear, I'm not charging you with anything. I'm just telling you what we're finding in our investigation. Of course, this doesn't mean we think you were necessarily involved in the murder. But, Reverend . . . It does mean that we're going to need a lot more help from you to prove otherwise."

Maurice looks fiercely annoyed as Becker speaks.

"Yes, Reverend. I told you before. I *am* out of school here. The question for you is whether you think muzzling me is going to work. That's for you to decide. My own sense is that it's a low-probability approach. . . . That's the right question, Reverend. What we need is more information. Here's our working hypothesis. Your people explored using genetic technologies to engineer a red heifer out of your ranch in Texas, Rapture Grove. You then got it in your mind to breed the next messiah, so you selected the purest girl you knew, MaryLee Stock, and somehow had her impregnated with an enhanced fetus incorporating your genetics at the Bright Horizons fertility clinic. Are you still there? Good. We also still don't know about the murder. The idea that you may have done it has certainly crossed our minds, but why would you do that after going to such lengths to get her pregnant? Then again, who am I to know how you think?"

Maurice pauses again.

"So here's where all of this leaves us. I want to learn everything you know about MaryLee Stock, Bright Horizons, and your breeding operation in Texas. You have every right to get Senator King or Chief Roberts to pull me from the case. If you do, I'm sure you'll succeed. But the question for you is whether by doing that you'll kill this story. In fact, I'm sitting here with my friend Rich Azadian. Say hello, Rich."

Maurice holds out the ear piece.

I feel strange piling on, but only for a moment. "Hello, sir," I say.

"You're probably thinking you can kill the police investigation and kill the *Star*'s story," Maurice says, "and you may be right, but that's a lot of faith in your own abilities and, if I can say, a lack of faith in ours. It's up to you. I'm not forcing you to tell us anything. You are under no obligation. I'm not even investigating this case. But I am only calling you to ask you one thing. Of your own volition, are you going to tell us what you know, or are you going to roll the dice in the hope that you can put this genie back in the bottle?"

An impish grin crosses Maurice's face as he listens to Becker.

"I'll only give you a little time. You need to call me at this number by seven tonight. I want everything. If you don't, we'll follow up on our leads in the manner we see fit, and I'm quite sure you won't like where that path leads. Am I clear?"

55

"Got it," Jerry says feverishly as his face pops up on my screen.

"Where are you? I'll come to you."

"At the office, the door is open."

"Lock it," I say. "I'm on my way."

I call Maurice on the bat phone and tell him to meet me at UMKC. We enter the building together.

I knock three times in quick succession on Jerry's door. The latch pops open. I open the door and see Jerry scurrying back to his computer wall.

"It was incredibly well protected," Jerry mutters, "but we probed from a lot of different angles. I'm not sure if we've been detected, so we've got to work fast. I'm downloading the Bright Horizons database, but it's taking time. They have a custom system, so I need to download the whole underlying program infrastructure, not just the data, and chunks of that program are encrypted separately. I'm also accessing the database itself as if I'm one of their internal users. I'm not sure how long that's going to last."

"Jerry, I need you to check whether MaryLee Stock and Megan Fogerty's names are in the Bright Horizons database," I interrupt impatiently.

Jerry dictates in a search function. "MaryLee Stock was there August 29 and October 13, Megan Fogerty on July 12 and August 14."

Maurice and I look at each other.

"Now compare the names of the dead young women from the

police database with names from the Bright Horizons database," I order.

"Yeah," Jerry says. "That's what I'm trying to do."

"And?" I ask.

"I need a little time to set up the search. Give me fifteen minutes."

"How do you mean?"

"I mean there's a Coke machine on the second floor. Please go for a drink."

I marvel at how assertive Jerry has become. Maurice and I make our retreat. Fifteen minutes feels like an hour.

I knock on his locked door. It opens slowly. Jerry's face is ashen, his eyes wide as he steps into the space. "Nine," he says, the word weighing him down. He is shaking.

"Tell us."

Jerry takes a deep breath in as if collecting pieces of himself scattered across the room. "It's pretty simple really. I matched the two databases. Nine women who were clients of Bright Horizons showed up on our list of three hundred and ninety-seven women from the police database."

We stare at the screen. The nine names seem to hover in space. MaryLee Stock, the fourth, pulsates. This beautiful woman who woke up and had breakfast one week ago, who stopped at the Hospital Hill Café for a hazelnut cappuccino, who played second base for the Springfield Tigers Women's softball team and danced herself into joyous abandon *somewhere beyond the sea* is now just another name in a list of the dead.

Nine names. Nine pieces of data. Nine entire life stories crammed into this little space. Kathryn Allison, Dakota Barnes, Lorelei Patterson, MaryLee Stock, Amanda Sullivan, Celia Guttierez, Megan Fogerty, Louise Osten, Sunita Patel. We stand silently before the screen like pallbearers.

Then Maurice breaks the silence. "Now we've got to figure out what we're looking at."

His words seem cold, but he is right. Whatever else they may once have been, these names of the dead may now be our only data sets that can point us in the direction of any women like them who might be in mortal danger but possibly still alive.

"So what qualities do they all possess besides being smart, single women under thirty, patients of the Bright Horizons fertility clinic, and dead?" I say, grabbing a stack of paper from near Jerry's printer. I start writing. *Age, height, education level, SAT scores, marital status.* "What else?"

Jerry starts calling out characteristics, listing where each of the nine fit in compared to the entire database. All of them are between twenty-two and twenty-seven, compared to an overall average of thirty-three. All of them are five six or taller, compared to an average overall height of five foot five.

"Can you bring up anything about education level?" I ask.

"Doesn't look like it," Jerry says, "but can we get Joseph to work on this?"

"Look at those dates." Maurice points to a far right column. "What does date of submission mean?"

"When the last data was inputted," Jerry says tentatively, "when they visited Bright Horizons the last time."

"So for MaryLee Stock we have October 13, 2023, three days before she died. All of the others have been in the last two months."

The inescapable outcome surges through each of our minds.

I say what we are all thinking. "These women are being hunted down one at a time."

Jerry sinks into his chair. "Shit, shit, shit, shit," he repeats.

"Jerry," Maurice says in his calm and reassuring voice. "How many women in the Bright Horizons database are in the same age, height, and marital categories as the nine deceased?"

Jerry wiggles his fingers in the air and a new screen pops up. "One hundred and twenty-seven," he says after a long silence.

"Print out both lists, Jerry," I say. "We've got to reach out to those women."

"And say what?" Maurice asks.

"I don't know," I say breathlessly, "maybe just to be careful."

"We can, but we still need to find out what we're looking for if we're going to help anyone."

"Jerry, keep probing the database and see what you can come up with," I say hurriedly. "Maurice, you and I can go talk with Joseph—"

My words are cut short by the ring of Jerry's office intercom.

Jerry's eyes bulge with bewilderment as he waves his hands in our direction. His signals are unclear. Our situation is not. "Federal marshals just came into the building," he shrieks. "They're on their way down." He's shaking.

Maurice steps in. "That gives us about two minutes," he says coolly. "All three of us can't get pulled in at the same time. Jerry, is there another way out of here?"

"Um," Jerry stutters, "there's a maintenance tunnel that links all the buildings. It ends at the law school."

"Where's the door?"

"Um. Um, left out the door, right at the first corner, first door on the left."

"Good," Maurice says. "Give Rich your ID badge."

Jerry fumbles to detach it from his belt and hands it to me. "Take this, too," he says, opening the glass case and handing me what looks like a brick.

"What's this?"

"A cell phone from the 1990s, part of my antique collection," Jerry stutters, "still works. *Battlestar Galactica.*"

"Rich, see what you can figure out about the names. Go. Jerry, come with me to face these bastards."

Maurice has taken such complete control of the situation it takes me a few moments to compute all of this on my own. On my own, I now realize, is the operative phrase.

"Go, dammit." The force of Maurice's words pushes me out of my paralysis. I grab the printout of names and the prehistoric cell phone and rush down the hall. I lurch right at the corner and left through the maintenance door.

I walk like I know what I'm doing through the basement of the law school, up the steps, and out the door. My heart is pounding so hard I worry I'm going to drop the phone. The downtown Oak Street bus drives by. I run to catch it at the next stop.

Jumping on, my heart is racing, thoughts of the nine dead women swirl through my brain. The key to their deaths, and to any other women unknowingly in line to become the next statistics on the police database, is the wrinkled sheet of paper burning a hole in my jacket pocket.

56

If you can keep your head when all about you are losing theirs,
Kipling wrote, then you are a man. Heading downtown on the
Main Street Express, I am freaking out. What does that make me?

I'd underestimated Gillespie's ability to track my every move.
How could I have been so stupid, I wonder. How much did he
know of Jerry's visit to my place this morning? How did he know
that Maurice and I were at UMKC? The thought that Maurice
had trained our crew in basic surveillance now seems laughable.
We thought we were the ones following Gillespie, but how many
of our moves had been tracked by him?

And if I've been giving away everyone I've been working with,
who is there left whom I can count on now? Joseph, Jerry, Maurice,
Toni, all seem to have been tapped in some cosmic game of freeze
tag. My mind provides the answer even before I've fully formulated
the question. Who else would have the resources to analyze the
list? Who else would I trust? Who is the only bigger pain in the ass
than I am?

I jump off the bus at Union Station and dial the switchboard.
Music begins to play as the call is transferred.

I try to mask my voice so Justina Morris doesn't recognize me.
"I'm calling from the gas company. We're investigating a leak in
Ms. Hernandez's home address, and this is the number we have on
file. Is Ms. Hernandez available?"

"Just one moment," Justina says, concerned.

Martina picks up after a short pause. "This is Martina Hernandez," she says in her steel-cutting voice.

"It's Rich," I say, "I need to meet you now. I'm at Union Station. The Rings of Saturn IMAX film is playing here at eleven o'clock. I'll be in the third row from the back on the right side. Don't say anything to anyone. Meet me there. This is bigger than the *Star*. It could be life or death."

"Dammit, Azadian," she fires. "Are you fucking sure about this?"

"Martina, I need you. I need you now."

I hear her breath through the earpiece.

"I'll be right there."

I wander around the science museum to calm my jittery nerves while I wait. A display on the miracles of genetics catches my eye.

The digital wall text tells of Watson and Crick deciphering the double helix, the Human Genome Project, the decoding of the full Neanderthal genome, the advances in biomedicine, the almost daily breakthroughs being made in genetic science around the world. *At this breathtaking pace of discovery, it is tempting to believe that human beings are now unlocking the secret codes of life that have been held sacred for millennia. But for all that we know about human genetics, our knowledge constitutes only the tiniest fraction of this vast and massively complex system. As human beings surge forward into this new frontier, we can only hope we will do so with levels of humility commensurate with our relative ignorance.*

Humility. What a concept. It seems like a virtue, but what was Icarus's fault? That he learned to fly or ventured too close to the sun?

I buy my ticket and carry my augmented reality eye patches to my seat. Martina comes in already wearing hers just as the doors close. Anger defines her face.

"This better be fucking good," she whispers, her face pointing toward the screen as she sits down.

I sink down in my chair, leaning my head slightly in her direction. "Thank you for coming," I whisper.

Martina doesn't respond. She won't give an inch until I justify myself.

"We got access to the national police database and ran a search for single women between twenty and thirty who died or were killed over the past year. We cross-referenced that to the database from the fertility clinic where MaryLee Stock was impregnated. Nine women from Bright Horizons were on the police list."

"I see." Martina's shoulders stiffen.

"All nine died in the last month, including MaryLee Stock and Megan Fogerty, a young pregnant woman who died in Olathe three weeks ago."

Martina stares at me, her eyes widening.

"There are 127 other women in the Bright Horizons database from five different cities who match the same age and height characteristics of the five women who died. We pulled together this list of them an hour ago just as federal marshals showed up at UMKC looking for Maurice Henderson and me."

"So now you're on the run?"

"Yes."

"And you thought you'd drag me in?"

"Yes."

I take off my enhanced reality eye patches and look directly at Martina.

"Fuck you," she says, giving me the sense she's on board. "And you think I should risk the entire future of the *Star* on this?"

I don't respond. The answer is clear.

She stares at the screen, purposefully not looking at me. "Tell me," she says after a pause.

"Gillespie, the federal marshal, seems to be tracking every move I make."

"Did he track you here?"

"I have no idea, but I've been careful. I took the bus."

"You took the bus? Makes me feel a whole lot safer."

"Martina," I whisper intensely, "nine women are dead. If there are any others, we need to find them fast or they're dead, too. If whoever killed them finds me or the others who've helped me . . ."

She turns away. "Talk," she says with a sigh I sense is only for show.

"I've got two lists of names from the databases. One is of the 127 women from Bright Horizons who fit our preliminary criteria. Someone needs to call these women to tell them to be careful."

"And what?" Martina whispers, perplexed. "Just be careful? Go to the police? Tell them what?"

"I don't know, but I do know we need to figure out more of what the nine women who've died in the last month have in common. They were all single, young, smart, and tall, but we don't know much more than that."

"And your theory is that if you find out what these nine women have in common you can see which of the 127 living ones share those characteristics?"

"Yes, but I can't do the research because everyone I've been working with seems to have been compromised."

"And you think I can?" Martina says.

I don't answer.

"And you think I should drag the *Star* into this against the fucking law, the wishes of the publisher, and the wishes of the editor?"

"Maybe not the whole *Star*," I say.

"You are really impossible, Azadian," Martina says, a hint of admiration almost detectable in her voice. "What criteria would we look for?"

"Who's we?" I ask with a nervous smile.

"Leave that to me."

"Anything. Histories, schools, scores, connections to churches. I'm hoping that we can find patterns that can point us in the right direction."

"And if we find it, then what? What happens to the *Star*?"

"Listen, Martina," I plead, "this can't be about the *Star* anymore."

Martina shakes her head slightly, as if agreeing in spite of herself. We both know that this story, if we can prove it, is almost big enough to blast its way through the NPA.

"When do we need this?" Martina says.

"Whoever killed these nine women obviously knows things could get messy. They probably know we're poking around. If there are more target women out there, my guess is the danger is growing every minute."

57

Waiting is torture.

Momentum surging through my veins, the knowledge that nine women have been killed in the last month and more could be in danger and all I can do is sit in this dark cinema watching space movies makes me crazy. The brick phone on my lap taunts me as I wait for it to ring.

My urge to do something, anything, almost overwhelms me, but I know that acting irrationally, even acting at all before I have more information, can't do much to help and is far more likely to cause harm.

Halfway through my second movie the ridiculously loud, absurdly anachronistic ring fills the theater. The place is two thirds empty, but the few people look at me annoyed.

"Mmm," I mumble into the handset, trying to be quiet.

"It's Maurice. You okay?"

"Mmm hmm," I mumble.

"Do you think anyone knows where you are?"

"No," I whisper.

"Good. Don't tell me. Just listen."

"Mmm."

"Looks like Gillespie and his goon have been tracking us pretty well. Most of our u.Ds are tapped and our cars have been tagged."

"Thought so," I whisper.

"He went to Chief Roberts with evidence I've been working this case without authorization. I've been suspended."

"Sorry," I whisper.

"Doesn't matter. He's trying to make a point. Roberts told me I'll be fired if I keep at it."

"And?"

"I prefer not to be."

"Mmm," I mumble inconclusively.

"But it doesn't matter what I'm doing, the key is those lists of names. Are you working on that?"

"Yes," I whisper, "hoping to have the analysis back very soon. And Becker?"

"Haven't heard from him yet. Gillespie's visit to UMKC could well have been Becker calling our bluff."

"How do I contact you?" I ask.

"I'm calling you from a pay phone. Let me give you my neighbor's u.D number. I'll borrow his for the next few days."

"What about Jerry?"

"They're holding him for questioning. Told him he was interfering with a federal investigation and was subject to criminal penalties. It's your game now."

"Mmm," I mumble again, hardly relishing the thought.

"The rest of us have been so compromised we may be more harm than good. The key to everything is those lists. You've got to figure out where they point. If other women are in danger, you've got to get to them. Don't trust anybody."

"Anybody?"

"The federal government is trying to kill a murder investigation. A major police force is playing along. It's hard to imagine you're going to be able to get law enforcement to do what you want as quickly as we need with everything so tangled. Trust me on this Rich, act like you're alone. If there are any women still on the hit list, that's what's going to save them. It's up to you. Let me know what you need."

The call drops and I am alone.

Come on, Martina. Where are you?

The phone rings halfway through the closing credits.

"There's one more woman who matches the dead ones." Her tone says it all.

My stomach knots, my whole body is on the verge of convulsion. "Shit."

"Maya Armstrong in Oklahoma City. I pulled together a team of three of the old-timers. Made them swear secrecy. We started making lists of everything we could find about the nine dead women."

"And?"

"You were right. They seem to be targeting smart women. All of the dead women on the Bright Horizons list were Brin scholars."

"What does that mean?"

"They all scored an average of 650 and above on their SATs. There's no chance this can be random. That's the essential category. Of the 127 women on your Bright Horizons client list, only Maya Armstrong was a Brin scholar. She matches the dead women in every other way."

"Except maybe one," I say darkly. "Did you try to contact her?"

"I did but it didn't go well."

"At least she's alive. Why not?"

"She had no idea what I was talking about and hung up. Do we call the cops?" Martina asks.

"I just spoke with Henderson about that. The federal marshals and the KCPD are in on this. Henderson has been suspended and my computer guy is in jail. Henderson says we can't trust the police. We need to do it on our own."

"And we don't know how much time we have?"

"Which is why we need to approach her in person. The address was on the Bright Horizons spreadsheet, right?"

"Yes. We double-checked," Martina says. "It's correct."

"I think I'm the one to go," I say.

"You're going to need help. I spoke with Maya. She's a tough girl."

I'm not sure if Martina wants to come along or not, but she's hardly the type of person I'm going to need to get Maya Armstrong to listen. I need someone far more nurturing. The decision takes no thought.

"I need a car."

"How's mine?" Martina offers.

"Better to have a degree of separation. Can you get someone else's?"

"My brother-in-law's."

"Good."

"Can you do it now?"

"Yes."

"And I need my ex-girlfriend, Antonia Hewitt, to come with me."

"Your ex-girlfriend?"

"Just do it."

Martina sighs. "Where do I find her?"

"Her shift at Truman Medical ends at six. Call the main switchboard from somebody else's phone and ask for her. Tell her that *janum* asked you to pick her up."

"*Janum*," Martina says, "that sounds ridiculous."

"It's Armenian. She'll know I've asked you to do this. Then meet me at the Quik Trip on Forty-Fourth and Main at six fifteen. Let Toni drive. You come in to the store and go into the bathroom when she's filling up. I'll walk out and get into the car on the passenger side. Have someone come pick you up afterward. Can you do that?"

"Yes, sir," Martina says half sarcastically. It's not that our roles have reversed, just that we're suddenly so deeply on the same side.

I'm bursting at the seams as I begin movie number three. At five thirty I go outside under the muddy twilight sky to catch the

Main Street Express uptown. I arrive at Quik Trip a little before six and walk around the block to kill time. At six eighteen Toni pulls up. I can see the worried creases on her face as she gets out to plug in and fill the reserve tank. Martina walks past me toward the bathroom. *What the fuck, Azadian?* her look says. It somehow comforts me. I get into the car and Toni starts to drive.

I am able to read the facial expression she flashes me with far more precision than Martina's. *You have sex with me then don't call for two days then have your boss kidnap me?*

Maybe I'm off by a word or two.

She collects herself. "Would you mind telling me where we are going?"

"Didn't Martina tell you?"

No. I'm waiting, Toni says with her eyes.

"Oklahoma City. Turn right at Southwest Trafficway. We've got to get there fast."

58

"So let me get this straight," Toni says after I fill her in on everything I've learned the past two days, "we bang on this poor young woman's door in the middle of the night unannounced and tell her she's probably carrying a genetically enhanced baby, that she should trust us instead of some unknown person who may or may not be stalking her, that she shouldn't go to the police, and that she should drop everything and let us hide her?"

Now driving, I keep my eyes on the road as we speed toward Oklahoma City.

"I'm not sure how I would react if I were in her shoes," Toni continues.

I nod nervously.

"And why are all of these young, single women going to get impregnated in the first place?" she adds. "I get it that the IVFGS clinic is where most women go to get pregnant these days, but young, single women can still freeze their eggs in their twenties and have babies whenever they want. What's the urgency?"

The shrill ring of my prehistoric cell phone cuts through the car like a buzz saw.

"Becker called and said he needs to meet me tomorrow. Says he's coming to Kansas City to do it in person."

"What do you think, Maurice?"

"My gut says he's playing for time."

"You don't think . . . ?" I say, my voice trailing off as I start to hypothesize in my head. I brief Maurice on everything Martina's learned, Maya Armstrong, and our current plans.

"And if Maya is the last one," he says, "I could imagine wanting to hold off meeting me until the last bit of evidence is . . . gone."

I press down on the gas pedal. "Or he could be covering his tracks in other ways, maybe getting Senator King lined up to do something."

"I thought of that," Maurice says.

"So what do we do?"

"You get where you're going. I'll mail a letter to myself before I meet with Becker just to be safe."

It's ironic how old-school we are getting with our technology. "Meet him in public," I say. "We still have no idea whom to trust."

The line drops.

It's twenty minutes after 1 a.m. when we hit the outskirts of Oklahoma City, a quarter to two when we pull up to the Cambridge Landing apartment complex. Despite its highbrow name, Cambridge Landing is a couple of steps above a trailer park.

We drive around until we find apartment 228, park, and race up the exposed cement stairs. I take a few steps back as Toni touches the doorbell. My hand is trembling. We don't hear a sound. Toni knocks, quietly. Nothing. Could we be too late? A little harder. Nothing. Toni's face says she's starting to share my concern. She knocks harder. No sound. Harder.

"God dammit," the muffled voice says, "who the hell is it?"

Toni and I exchange strange, twisted smiles.

"Maya," Toni says in her sweetest voice, "my name is Antonia Hewitt. I'm a nurse. I'm so sorry to bother you this late at night, but we really need to talk with you."

"'bout what?"

Maya, I can tell from her raspy voice, is no wallflower.

"It's about your baby," Toni says, trying to take the edge off of her words.

Silence.

Not knowing what's happening on the other side of the door,

I begin to worry. Then I see the knob turning. The door opens a crack, still tethered to the wall by the chain.

A disheveled mess of sandy blond hair pops into the open space. A shake reveals a small, angular, pasty-white face defined by suspicion.

"Who the hell are you and how do you know about the baby?"

"It's a long story," Toni says sweetly. "You may be in danger. A friend of ours tried to call you yesterday about this. Can we come in?"

Maya looks at Toni intently, then me. "Who's he?"

I begin to answer, but Toni cuts me off.

"He's my boyfriend, Rich Azadian. He's working with me to try to protect you."

Boyfriend? Yikes, my inappropriate synapse fires.

"From what?"

"It's a long story. You need to hear it. Your life may depend on it. Can we come in?"

Maya's eyes fix back on Toni's. She's clearly trying to process what Toni is telling her and get some kind of instinctual sense of whether or not to trust us. Toni gives her the face that had finally convinced me to open up to her about Astrid almost a year ago.

Maya stares a few moments longer. "You know it's two o'clock in the morning. I need to be up at six. This better be good," she says.

"Maya, we drove from Kansas City to talk with you. We may not have much time. Believe me, we wouldn't be here if we didn't think it was important. It's *really* important."

Through the crack in the door, I see Maya's hand reaching for the chain.

59

Maya's apartment is not much. A postage stamp living room with only a nook of a kitchen, what looks like an even smaller bedroom, white walls, cheap white carpet, a few prints that look as if they've come from a Holiday Inn going-out-of-business sale.

Maya herself seems to fit the décor. Her shock of blond hair running halfway down her back seems almost designed to be swinging around a pole in some roadside club. Her triangular, pinkish face looks pinched. Her hazel eyes dart between Toni and me as she opens the door to let us in. Her movements as we enter remind me of a basketball guard on defense.

"We're so sorry to bother you this late," Toni says in her gentlest voice. "I know it must be frightening to have two strangers show up at your door in the middle of the night. There are a lot of terrible things happening, and we're worried you might be in danger."

"But who *are* you?" Maya thrusts in.

"Maya"—I like the way Toni keeps repeating her name in her effort to connect—"I'm a nurse at Truman Medical Center in Kansas City. Rich is, or was I should probably say, a reporter for the *Kansas City Star*. He got fired for looking into this situation."

Maya stretches her neck and pushes her head toward us, turtle-like. "What situation?"

Toni looks over at me.

"Maya," I say, following Toni's lead, "last Tuesday I was covering the death of a young woman about your age in Kansas City named MaryLee Stock. When I saw her, she was lying dead on her floor in an apartment kind of like this one but roped off by the police."

"What's that got to do with me?" Maya asks suspiciously.

"I fear a lot, Maya," I say, "but I need to give you some background to help you better understand. Is that okay?"

"Go on," she says without emotion.

"It's a bit complicated how I did this, but I learned that she'd been pregnant when she was killed. We can give you the details later, but when the Kansas City police announced what had happened they didn't mention her pregnancy or even that she'd been killed."

"But you knew?" Maya asks, getting more interested in the story.

"We figured it out," I say.

Maya nods nervously.

I tense up in advance of what I know I need to say next. "They also discovered that the baby that MaryLee was carrying had been genetically enhanced. Do you know what that is, Maya?"

"I'm not an idiot."

"Sorry, Maya," I say. "We figured out she'd been genetically enhanced on purpose because she'd been impregnated"—the words sound antiseptically cold coming out of my mouth—"at a fertility clinic that would have known what they were doing."

Maya stiffens.

"Am I correct in assuming that you are pregnant and that you got impregnated at the Bright Horizons fertility clinic here in Oklahoma City?"

Maya's eyes dart between Toni and me like those of a cornered animal. "And you think . . . ?" Her tone makes clear she understands what we're saying.

"We do, Maya," Toni says, "but please let Rich tell you more. You need to know. Is that okay, honey?"

"MaryLee was a member of a church in Springfield, Missouri. It's called the Holy Virgin Church of Christ," I say. "Have you ever heard of it?"

Maya shakes her head no.

"Have you ever heard of the pastor who runs it, Reverend Cobalt Becker?"

"No," Maya says quietly.

"And," I say, "am I correct in assuming that you did really well on your SATs, that you are a Brin scholar?"

"You are really freaking me out," she says. "How do you know all this?"

I pause.

"Tell her," Toni orders.

"Maya, we hacked into the national police database and got a list of young women who died in the US over the past year. Then we compared it with names from Bright Horizons database. Nine names came up. MaryLee's was one of them, as was Megan Fogerty, a young woman who was killed in Olathe, Kansas, two weeks before her."

"What about me?"

"That's how we found you. We analyzed what the nine women had in common. All of them were roughly the same age, a little more than average height, and all of them were Brin scholars."

Maya lifts her hand to cover her mouth. Toni rubs the top of Maya's other arm.

"We then looked through the Bright Horizons database to see if there were any other women who fit the same criteria," I continue.

Maya's two hands now cover her face. "Oh fuck. So you think someone is going to try to kill me?"

"We don't know, Maya," Toni says, "but we really don't want to take any chances."

"But how do I know if I can trust *you*?"

"Maybe you don't, honey," Toni says, "but we really hope you will. Whoever killed those women is still out there."

"Shouldn't we just go to the police?"

"We can, but my friend with the KC police thinks it won't help," I say.

"Why not?"

"For the same reason I got fired from the *Star*, the police lied in the autopsy, and they're holding my friend in jail. They're hiding something. If we go to the police now, we'll just make you more of a target and they may not do enough to help. The worst of both worlds. We can't risk it until we know more."

Maya's eyes are in full panic mode. She holds her head steady. "*Mother fucker*," she says, stressing the first syllable of each word. "So now what?"

I look over at Toni.

"Maya, we don't think you are safe here," Toni says. "We'd like to get you out."

"To go where? I've got a job, you know."

"Do you think you can call in sick for maybe a couple of days?" I say.

Maya hesitates.

"We don't want to disrupt your life, and maybe we're wrong about all of this," Toni pleads. "We hope we are. But we really don't want to take any chances."

Maya's body language begins to suggest surrender. "But what do I do, just disappear?"

"I think so, Maya," Toni responds. "For now."

"Where?"

"Probably to a hotel. Somewhere where people won't know how to find you."

"Two random people I've never met come knocking on my door in the middle of the night and want me to go away with them to a hotel?"

I've had enough. We don't have time for this. It's time to be the adult. "Maya," I say sharply, "last Monday I saw MaryLee Stock sprawled out dead on the floor of her apartment. I won't let that happen to you. I'm not leaving you unprotected."

Maya takes in my words. "So why don't the two of you stay here?" she asks after a pause.

"We could," Toni says, "but we'll be a lot safer if we're somewhere a bit tougher to find."

Maya shakes as if caught between movement vectors pointing in opposing directions.

"Maya, it's not safe here. We need to go now," I say.

Toni steps in to take off my edge. "Please," she says in a way few mortals could reject.

Maya twitches. She looks at Toni for a few moments and then me. Her shoulders fall. "I'll pack a few things," she says in a raspy whisper as she shuffles toward her bedroom.

She swivels back toward us just before she reaches the bedroom door. "If this is some of kind of trick, you guys are going to be in a world of hurt."

"Maya honey, please," Toni says, her every word radiating concern and goodwill.

Maya stares at Toni for a moment, then me.

Then she turns toward her bedroom.

60

If there's a thing called monkey mind, Maya Armstrong has it. I can't blame her.

If a couple of strangers banged on my door at two in the morning, told me the baby I was carrying was some kind of genetic mutant, that someone, but they didn't know who, was trying to kill me, and that I needed to go with them to a hotel right away but couldn't tell me where, I'd ask a lot of questions, too.

Maya's body twitches back toward her apartment, worrying, I can tell, she's making a huge mistake as she walks with us to the car.

Front seat or backseat? I start the psychological analysis in my head. Front seat tells Maya we're taking her seriously, that this is all about her. Backseat tells her that we are the adults here and are in charge. Toni beats me to it.

"Maya, honey," she says opening the back door, "why don't you get in here so you'll have more space."

"Where we going?" Maya asks suspiciously as we drive.

"I don't know. Somewhere we'll be harder to find," I say.

"That's the plan?"

"Maya. Honey," Toni steps in, "we're doing our best."

"I want to call my friend to tell her where we are going."

"Maya, look," I say, "we don't really know what we're up against, but you could be in huge danger. I've been underestimating these guys for the last week, and now I won't take any chances. They've been tracking our almost every move, and if you start using your u.D that might give them another way to find us, to find you. Power off the u.D."

I make eye contact with her through the rearview mirror, then hear the beep of her u.D powering off.

"Thank you, Maya," Toni says.

Maya looks annoyed.

I drive north.

"So you think the baby I'm carrying is some kind of mutant?" she says after a long silence.

Clearly, the thought has been weighing on her.

I'm not sure how to answer.

"Mutant is a strong word," Toni slides in. "It's more that we think that your baby may have genetic mutations, even enhancements. Do you know what a chromosome is?"

"I'm not a moron," Maya shoots back.

"Maya, we know that," I say, "that's why you're in danger."

Maya rephrases, speaking like an annoyed adolescent to her clueless parents. "Yes, I know what a chromosome is."

"I thought so," Toni continues, unfazed. "We think your baby has a forty-seventh chromosome that, if we're right, could give it extra capabilities."

"Like Superman shit?"

"Maybe. We don't know," Toni says.

"A forty-seventh chromosome is kind of like an additional parking space in a person's genetic code," I say. "Different genes can be placed there that could give people extra abilities."

"Like what?" Maya says, "Living underwater and shooting fire out of your ass?"

"Actually," I say deadpan, "I do understand a lab in Utah is doing research on the genetic basis of anal thermogenesis."

Silence.

Then a snort bursts from Maya's mouth like an air bubble hitting the surface. She tries to hold it back, but I see in the rearview mirror what almost looks like a smile.

"So what are the options?" Maya asks, her voice now somehow more available.

"I don't know, Maya. It depends on what someone is trying to do," I continue in a more relaxed voice. "They've been doing all sorts of research for years trying to figure out what combinations of genes make up our human capabilities. Scientists have been trying to give special capabilities to mice."

Toni's eyes flash me a warning.

"They seem to be beginning to figure out what genes make up different skills, like intelligence and memory," I say.

I see in the rearview mirror I've caught Maya's attention.

"And you think they're trying to do that with this baby," she says, looking down at her stomach.

The way she refers to the baby strikes me as oddly distant.

"That's what I think, but I don't know for sure."

"Don't know?" Her previous caution returns.

Toni puts her hand on my arm.

"Maya," I say more gently, "let me just tell you what I know. It's not much. We're still trying to figure things out. Maybe you can help."

"Go on," she says impatiently.

"We don't know who is ultimately behind all of this. We've come up with three options." I see Maya's intent stare through the rearview mirror as I lay them out.

Maya interrupts me when I start talking about Becker. "So this guy wants to breed a red cow in Texas, and now I'm supposed to be the Virgin Mary?" she says giddily. It's clear she may be more from the Mary Magdalene mold.

"Hmm," Maya adds as I describe Bright Horizons. "What does Bright Horizons have that's so good?"

"How do you mean?"

"You said that this guy Becker may have figured something out in Texas, and that the government and China all thought that Bright Horizons had some special capabilities. So what were they?"

I'd thought about the question before, but something about the way Maya phrases it jars me.

"We've been trying to figure out who owns Bright Horizons," I say, "but Its pretty important to know what exactly they could do, or maybe were willing to do, that nobody else could."

"Maya," Toni breaks in. I get the sense she's feeling that our conversation is becoming too technical. "Can I ask you a question?"

Maya doesn't answer.

"How did you decide to have a baby?"

"Easy. I got a letter."

"And?" Toni coaxes.

"They said they'd give me $75,000 cash if I had this baby and kept quiet about it, that they'd make sure it had a good home after it was born."

I feel like I've been slapped across the face. So clear. So obvious. I wish I'd had a live woman to ask this question the past week.

"Who did?" I ask.

"Bright Horizons."

It suddenly makes sense why Maya has been trying more to figure out the puzzle than to know how her baby may have been enhanced.

"How?"

"I got a letter in the mail. I thought about it. I needed the money. So I went in. It's not like I hadn't been pregnant before!"

"What did the letter say?" I ask.

"That they would offer me $75,000 to carry a baby. Seemed like a good deal. They sent me twenty-five thousand when I got impregnated. They said I get twenty-five more when the baby is born and twenty-five two years after that if I stayed quiet."

"And who did you meet with at Bright Horizons?"

"Some lady. Jessica."

"Jessica Crandell?"

"Yeah," Maya says, seeming surprised that I know this.

Shards are beginning to come together in my mind. "Maya,

you're right that if Bright Horizons had some kind of technology, they had to get it from somewhere, and maybe . . ." I stop myself.

"Baby," I say, looking at Toni, "call Maurice back on the phone."

The sound emerging from the receiver sounds downright prehistoric, a primordial groan.

"Maurice, it's me."

"Who else calls at four thirteen in the morning?" he mumbles.

"We need to find out if Bright Horizons had licensed any patents. If Becker had some kind of technology, maybe he did a deal with Bright Horizons. Maybe there are footprints out there we can track."

"Mmm," Maurice groans, still not awake, "search?"

"Maurice, track down Joseph Abraham. We need to find out if Becker had any patents or Bright Horizons did any licensing. It's an angle we haven't explored."

"All right," Maurice says, his mind still discombobulated. "Will."

"Call me back when you know, okay?"

"You all right?" he says, pulling himself out of sleep.

"I am."

"Got the girl?"

"I do, we're . . ."

"Don't tell me," Maurice fires back, this time sharply. He's awake. "I'll call you later this morning."

The line drops.

Something inspires me to pull off in Norman, Oklahoma. I drive about fifteen minutes away from the highway until I come across the Sleep Inn Motel. The run-down place looks like it might have been a Howard Johnson's when this road to nowhere had once been a thoroughfare. That must have been decades ago, and clearly no renovations have been made since. The sleepy Sikh takes my cash in advance with no questions. I pay for two rooms for two days, park, then help the two exhausted women up the stairs and into their room.

I open the door to mine and inhale a noxious mixture of smoke and mold. I strip down to my underpants, fling off the slimy bedspread, and melt into the lumpy mattress.

61

The grinding ring of the brick phone wakes me from an impossible half-sleep.

"Yeah," I grumble.

"It's me. I need you to come to Kansas City."

I shoot up. The hotel room looks strange in the daylight, foreign. The image of Toni and Maya sleeping in the next room ricochets through my mind, my masculine need to protect the women in my cave fully activated. "I can't."

"Listen to me, Rich," Maurice says. "Becker is going to be in Kansas City at three this afternoon. I can't meet with him. You need to do it."

"No, Maurice. I've got two women here I need to—"

"Listen to me," Maurice repeats, this time more forcefully. "He's coming to Kansas City and I can't meet with him."

A pit forms in my stomach as I begin to sense where he is heading.

"I'm willing to take the risks I need to on this, but meeting with Becker just isn't one of them."

I don't credit Maurice with an answer.

"You know I've been willing to put my job on the line," he continues in an almost apologetic tone, "but if I'm the one meeting with Becker and Roberts finds out, I'm done. That gives Becker a lot of leverage over me. It's a stupid risk. It doesn't make sense."

"And you think my leaving here does?"

"I don't know where you are right now, Rich. My guess is no one does. My guess is that you are four or five hours away from

KC. If you leave now, you can be here by one or two. Meet with Becker and you'll be back wherever you're going by eight or nine. Who else is going to be able to get what we need out of Becker?"

"*You*, Maurice."

"It's not the right thing to do." Maurice pauses then speaks softly. "I'm not going to do it."

Crackles punctuate the void.

"This is bullshit," I say.

"It's the only option that makes sense."

I hate the idea, I'm not at all convinced, and I'm beyond pissed at Maurice. His argument, however, does have a hint of depressing logic. Becker can definitely get Maurice fired if he decides to, and it's abundantly clear in my mind that we should never underestimate Becker.

"What do you think Becker has been up to the last twenty-four hours?" Maurice presses on.

"I don't know."

"That's the point. There's so much riding on this for him, for Senator King, for the country. I doubt he's been spending the last twenty-four hours twiddling his thumbs. It makes no sense for me to be there with my job and family so clearly on the line and Becker knowing it."

"And I should be because I have so little to lose?" I say heatedly.

"Sorry, Rich. That's what gives you the most leverage. This is really the best way. We both need you to be here this afternoon. There's too much at stake for you not to be."

I weigh the two options in my mind. The nausea I feel at my core tells me the scale is tipping in his favor.

"We're supposed to meet at Café Aixois at three. Do you know where that is?"

"Fifty-Fourth and Brookside Boulevard?" I say hesitantly.

"Fifty-Fifth," Maurice says. "I'll be parked at the Presbyterian church across the street to keep an eye on things, but I want to be sure Becker doesn't see me."

"What about my car?" I say, recognizing that my questions are forming an unstated consent.

"How do you mean?" Maurice asks, luring me into the details.

"If I do come back into the city and meet with Becker, I'm pretty sure someone would be able to track me down in the car I'm driving and follow me back to, to where I am now."

"I'll take care of that. I'll get you a different car when you're here. You'll be there at three?"

I hesitate.

"Rich?"

I hate the idea but recognize the logic. "Yeah," I grunt. I hear the beginnings of the word "good" as the line drops.

The room is silent but for the occasional rumble of cars speeding by. I feel sick.

My jeans and sweater feel like weights as I drag them on. I put on my shoes, trudge a few steps down the balcony, and softly knock on the door of room 24. No answer.

My heart quickens.

I knock harder, trying to balance my sense of panic with my desire to be gentle if I'm waking them from sleep.

Still no answer.

Panic sweeps me. I pound on the door.

"What the fuck?"

The words feel like music.

"Sorry, Maya. Good morning," I fumble, "can you open the door? I need to talk with you guys."

"Morning, baby," I hear muffled through the thin walls. "Just a sec."

"You don't look so good," Toni says as she opens the door a few moments later.

"Thanks," I say. "I look better than I feel."

"Now what?"

"I need to go to Kansas City for the day to meet with Becker."

"I thought Maurice was doing that," Toni says.

"He was, but not anymore. Now apparently I am."

I see the concern on her face. "When will you be back?"

"By eight or nine tonight at the latest," I say. "I didn't really want to go, but I spoke to Maurice this morning and—"

She takes my hand and squeezes it gently. "It's okay, baby. I trust you."

I feel trusted. I'm just not sure I'm worthy of it. "I'll leave you the old phone."

"I don't think you should," Toni says. "Who could know we're here? God knows we're not going anywhere."

"I'll pick up some food for you at the gas station before I go," I say, trying to retain a few qualities of a caretaker.

"Sure, baby," Toni says in an amused tone, as if she's allowing me to take care of her for my own benefit.

"Maya," I add turning toward her, "will you keep an eye on her for me?"

Maya rolls her eyes. Things seem to be getting a little mushy for her taste. "We'll just spend our day practicing our thermo-genesis," she says, half paying attention as she flips through cable channels.

The food I bring back from the Sinopec station is hardly the stuff of a successful caveman protecting his women. Chocolate milk, various candy bars, two large bottles of water, pumpkin seeds, and a smattering of Little Debbie snacks that seem to have arrived in Norman, Oklahoma, through some kind of time warp from the 1950s.

It's the best I can do, I tell Toni with my eyes.

It's okay, get out of here, she tells me with hers.

My silent link to Toni feels ever farther away as I speed north on Highway 70 toward Kansas City.

62

The plan. Get to Kansas City as quickly as possible. Meet with Becker. Change cars. Come back. Then what?

How long, I wonder, will we need to hole up with Maya? What are we waiting for?

Jesus electronic billboards shout at me as I drive past.

ANTI-GOD IS ANTI-AMERICAN, ANTI-AMERICAN IS TREASON, TRAITORS BEWARE.

JUDGMENT DAY IS COMING—CRY MIGHTILY UNTO GOD.

YOUR CHOICE . . . HEAVEN OR HELL. READ JOHN 3:36. The blistering digital flames appear to almost leap from the billboard.

Red, white, and blue KING FOR PRESIDENT signs stand underneath each of these billboards, each now joined by five or six people in KING FOR PRESIDENT e-shirts waving American flags. This level of energy feels like an ominous sign for the coming primary.

The screeching ring of the brick phone breaks my concentration.

"Rich, it's Maurice," he says, "I'm here with Joseph. We checked the patent registry. Genesis Labs, a company owned by the same registered holding company that controls Rapture Grove, applied for three patents to the US Patent Office."

"And?"

"They all deal with techniques for genetic transfer."

"Let me guess," I say, "by linking genes to new chromosomes."

"Partly, boss," Joseph says. "Using artificial chromosomes as a delivery mechanism for simultaneous genetic transfer."

"In cows?"

"To crossbreed Texas bluegrass with the jatropha plant."

"Why?"

"On their application they say it's because jatropha is an exponentially more efficient biofuel sources than bluegrass but hadn't been domesticated enough to grow outside of tropical climates. And if they can bring together the easy production of bluegrass and the energy potential of jatropha through simultaneous mass genetic transfer, they can more quickly turn native bluegrass fields into energy fields on a much larger scale."

"And if the genetics works for plants . . ."

"All life comes from the same source, boss."

Genetically modified bluegrass, biblical red heifer, MaryLee Stock, Megan Fogerty, Maya Armstrong. "Were the patents granted?"

"They're pending."

"But they get patent protection while this happens?"

"Yes."

The synapses fire wildly across my brain. Becker gets the patents but needs more firepower to realize his dream. What does he do? He buys Bright Horizons? He sells them the technology? He makes a deal to give the technology to Bright Horizons in exchange for their help breeding the next messiah? Then how does the government get involved? Where do the Chinese fit into all of this? Where does he get the money?

"Do we know if anyone bought the patent rights?" I say.

"Looking for that but haven't seen anything yet," Joseph says.

"Keep on it," I say, tapping off the call.

My head throbs for three hours, my hands shake as I drive nervously on.

But my mind shifts into gear as I step in the door of Café Aixois.

63

I find him sitting alone in the corner. He had seemed so big, almost godlike, preaching in the sanctuary in Springfield, but here he looks smaller, like a man. I sit, looking him straight in the eye.

"Reverend," I say calmly and authoritatively, "you are going to talk."

"Do you have any idea what you're dealing with?" Becker says, his chest rising.

The sheer power of his presence pushes me back. Then I catch myself. I lean forward. "That's not going to work this time, Reverend," I say steadily, hiding the pounding I feel in my heart.

Becker eyes at me cautiously, a wounded lion, not what he once was, who still knows how to be dangerous. I hold his stare for what seems like an eternity. Becker's eyes are clear and powerful. Then I see them soften slightly around the edges.

"I loved MaryLee Stock," he says with a vulnerability that seems remarkably authentic. "I practically raised her from a child. I would never hurt her. I *did* never hurt her."

"But she was hurt," I say, staring harshly at him. "She was killed."

His neck strains.

"*You* got her pregnant with your child," I press on. "*You* put her in the middle of this mess. *You* are part of her murder and now other women are in grave danger. If there's something I need to know, this is your last chance to tell me. Otherwise, all of this is coming straight at you."

"Where's Henderson?" he says, trying to shift the energy of

our conversation.

"It doesn't matter. I'm here representing both of us. I'm here representing MaryLee."

My words seem to cut Becker. I let the silence settle.

Becker breathes in, turns his head to the side, then squares and faces me. "There's not really that much to tell . . ."

I think of MaryLee Stock and Megan Fogerty, of Maya Armstrong hiding in the motel room and feel a deep anger rising up inside of me. "If you don't tell me everything starting now, I'm going to get up and leave. And I promise, your life is going to start getting a lot worse." I'm not sure where my voice is coming from, but it's angry and it's deep and it's powerful.

Becker's eyes bear aggressively into mine. Then his energy changes. He takes a deep breath. "I met MaryLee when she was three," he says quietly. "She was a beautiful child, an angel."

"Go on."

"She grew up in the church. She was so smart but also so good. I've never met someone with such a pure spirit." He pauses.

"Go on."

"She grew up into a beautiful woman in every way. I loved her."

I glare at Becker.

"Not that way," he says, "in a cosmic way, a Godly way."

"Which is why—"

"It's not what you think."

"So what is it?"

"A woman like that is an incredible rarity. She doesn't come along every—"

"Two millennia?" I say, cutting him off.

He looks into my eyes.

"Life, Mr. Azadian, is not only what we perceive here and now. It is much more. But those secrets don't unfold on their own. We need to seek them out, to uncover them. Jesus was Jesus, but he couldn't have become what he became without Paul. God is

God, but he needs enablers here on earth."

"And you are the enabler?" I ask derisively.

"I'm one of them. All of us have the potential to be if we hear God's voice, if we allow ourselves to be."

"And the red heifer?"

"You know that part already. I've been trying to breed a red heifer at my ranch for years now."

"For if the sprinkling of defiled persons with the blood of goats and bulls and with the ashes of a heifer sanctifies for the purification of the flesh, how much more shall the blood of Christ, Who through the eternal Spirit offered Himself without blemish to God, purify your conscience from dead works to serve the living God," I say from memory, staring him deeply in the eyes.

He looks back at me stunned, as if I'm wounding him with his own sword.

"Hebrews 9," I say, not mentioning I'd ripped the page out of the Gideon's Bible this morning.

Becker flinches. "God doesn't always act on his own. That was the message of Jesus," he says quietly.

My patience has run out. "Tell me exactly what happened," I order. "How did you get MaryLee to go along with this? How did you get the patents? What did you do with them? What was your relationship with Bright Horizons?"

Becker stares at me as if unwilling to let me dictate the flow of the conversation. I glare back.

"We started doing experiments at the lab," he then says quietly. "Our scientists made a lot of progress."

"And your Genesis Labs made three patent applications in January last year."

"Yes."

"For gene transfer onto additional chromosomes and simultaneous mass genetic transfer."

"Yes," Becker says. "Genesis code."

The name doesn't surprise me. "God's will?" I ask in a snarky voice.

Becker doesn't respond.

"So you thought you'd use this to give birth to a superbaby, a messiah?"

"I thought that God had given us the knowledge to pursue God's will."

"And you were the interpreter?"

"I was one of them. Everyone is. Gregor Mendel, as you know, Mr. Azadian, was a monk."

"Go on."

"And I knew, I always knew, that MaryLee was destined to be the mother."

"She was Mary?"

"Maybe not exactly, but as close as we were going to get here on earth."

"And so you—"

"I would never have touched her." Becker leans forward and looks deeply into my eyes. "I *did* never touch her. She knew what we were doing and agreed."

"But you needed her to be the carrier of the messiah and you were the father. What does that make you, God or the Holy Spirit?" I say, spitting out each word.

"Not just me. That's the whole point."

"So someone had to be the father, and it might as well be you, but two humans can't together breed the messiah. Whatever Joseph did, he wasn't Jesus's real father."

"Yes," Becker whispers.

"So you needed to use genetic enhancement to make sure the baby wasn't just a regular mortal, that it had some kind of super-human spark that separated him from the rest of us. Did MaryLee agree to that?"

Becker's eyes tell me the answer is no. "He would be elevated above the rest of us, would help us all realize our destiny, the true greatness within each of us, within all of us," he says feverishly.

"But there was just one problem," I say. "You couldn't exactly get her knocked up in an animal lab in Texas."

My choice of words clearly pains Becker. "Not knocked—"

"I get it," I say, cutting him off without a hint of kindness. "If she's inseminated in a lab, it's technically a sort of virgin birth."

Becker doesn't answer. The words probably don't sound fully biblical coming from my mouth.

"And you needed access to a fertility clinic, but what kind of fertility clinic is going to impregnate someone with a genetically modified embryo?"

Becker physically backs away, pulling his head as far away from me as the backrest of his wooden chair will allow. I move my head forward to close the gap.

"After we applied for the patents," he says, "I was approached by someone from Bright Horizons. A woman."

"Jessica Crandell," I say.

He looks at me surprised. "She said they wanted to purchase my patents and learn more about our processes."

"And you thought this was a sign from God," I say sarcastically.

"You're not a believer, Mr. Azadian, but it was the one thing I, we needed."

"So what? You did a deal? You bought the company?"

Becker looks surprised. "Why would I buy the company?"

"Then you did a deal."

He looks down. "Yes."

"And the terms were?"

Becker seems to pull each word from his mouth. "That I'd give them the patent rights and the knowledge in exchange for their help—"

"Creating for you a genetically enhanced messiah," I say, finishing the sentence. "And MaryLee's test scores were good enough to get her in to the pilot program."

Becker flashes a confused look.

"What qualities did you order for him?" I fire.

Becker flinches. "I don't know," he whispers.

"You don't know?"

"They said they could help with extra capabilities, that they'd isolated some genes that most geniuses seemed to have, that they could help us lift DNA samples off of iron nails from the crucifixion."

"What?" I leave off the additional *the fuck*.

"You wouldn't understand," Becker says, "but the nails were found by Israeli archeologists in the ossuary of Caiaphas."

I stare at Becker, incredulity smeared across my face.

"A funeral box of the priest who presided over the trial of Jesus," he adds.

"You've got to be fucking kidding me," I explode.

Becker pulls back.

"I'm sorry," I say, realizing I've overstepped, "Go on."

"So I sent in my—"

"Your sperm sample," I say, matter-of-fact.

"And I spoke with MaryLee about what I needed her to do."

"And she was on board?"

"She believed, too," Becker says quietly. "She agreed when she was home over the summer. Then she went to Bright Horizons here in Kansas City, and three months later she was . . ."

Becker's face fights the emotion welling underneath.

"Dead," I say coldly.

I feel an almost uncontrollable rage building inside of me. This fucking narcissist tramples on a beautiful young woman who did nothing more than trust him, pulls her into his sick science experiment. I'm disgusted.

And yet.

And yet I can't help but feel that this feverish force of unprocessed emotion did not kill MaryLee Stock. Yes, he put her in the situation that got her killed. Yes, he deserves whatever happens to him as a result. But I now feel I know on a deep, personal level that Cobalt Becker was not the trigger man.

Becker's complete nakedness before his fucked-up values, his God, his love for MaryLee, touches me in an irrational way I'm not completely able to resist.

I am appalled.

But in spite of myself a part of me can't help being touched by Becker's insane faith in the power of dreams, crazy, audacious, impossible, dangerous dreams, dreams that seek to forge a new reality, make a claim against the vast imperviousness and anonymity of time and space, strive to make a dent in the universe. "So who killed her?"

Becker looks up at me with questioning eyes. "I don't know," he says softly. Then his energy begins to change. His body fills with air. A strange power reasserts itself on his face. "But I damn them to hell." His words are laced with dark, vengeful anger.

I stare at Becker for what feels like an eternity.

I have complete contempt for him, yet somehow recognize that in a crazy fucked-up way we may possibly be on the same side. My eyes lock on his. "We're going to find these fuckers, and I need your help."

Becker places his two enormous hands palms down on the table. A fierce determination defines his powerful face. "Tell me what I need to do."

64

My mind tracks options like a cryptographer as I march out the door of Café Aixois.

Becker makes a deal. Bright Horizons impregnates MaryLee. Three months later she and eight other women are dead. I've got most of the backstory, but, my body feels from every pore, who cares? Nine women are dead, and I still don't know who killed them. *Two women are in danger. And what the hell am I doing in Kansas City?*

I don't see Maurice in the church lot across the street but trust he's there. The brick phone rings as soon as I close the door and hit the ignition.

"How'd it go?" he says intensely.

"I don't think Becker killed her. Bright Horizons did a deal with him. They traded breeding him a messiah for the technologies he'd developed down in Texas."

"Hmm," Maurice says, thinking. "So who did it?"

"I don't know, but I need to get back right away. Where's the car?"

"You know the Price Chopper supermarket at Brookside?"

"Yeah."

"Park your car in the lot. Leave the key under the mat. Go into the store. There's a bathroom in the cold storage area behind the fruit and vegetable section. Walk past it and you'll see a door just ahead of you on your right, about four o'clock. Go through that door. There's a fully charged black Cherry Voltero parked just outside the door. It's unlocked. The keys are in the glove compartment."

"Thanks, Maurice," I say, still feeling he's somehow let me down.

He picks up the ambiguity in my voice and responds to it. "I'm here if you need me."

I don't respond.

The drive to Brookside takes five minutes, the car transfer two. I don't make it far before my anxiety forces me off the road. I call Toni's room from the brick phone as I merge onto I-70.

Click, click, click. *Come on.* The phone rings. Once. Twice. Three times. I calculate the size of the room. The phone is reachable from any point within two rings at most. Is something wrong? Does the hotel phone even work? Why hadn't I checked it earlier?

I call again five minutes later. Ring. Ring. Ring. My heart pounds. The decision tree forms in my mind. The Sleep Inn Motel main number is on the key chain. Someone ought to be able to go check. I dial. Ring. Ring. Ring. Ring. With each ring my mind imagines a worse scenario.

I know I shouldn't do it, but I can't help myself. I dial Toni's u.D number.

"This is Toni. So sorry I can't get your call right now, but leave your name and number and I'll get back to you just as soon as I can. Thank you."

My heart sinks. Panic begins to set in.

"I've been calling the hotel, there's no answer," I begin midsentence as Maurice picks up.

"What do you think?" he finally says.

"I don't know," I say unconvincingly, then add what I'm really feeling, "the worst."

My words float in the silence. I'd almost hoped they would become absurd when exposed to the rational sunlight of another person's thinking.

I check my speedometer. Eighty miles per hour. I should be going a hundred but I'll really be fucked if I get pulled over in someone else's car. And then what might happen to . . . ? I banish the thought.

"That's not the only option," Maurice says. "Where are you?"

"On I-70 West," I say, "just passing Topeka."

I can almost feel Maurice's mind laboring. "Where are you going?"

I pause. I've been an idiot this whole time, feeling like I've been secretive while unknowingly broadcasting my every move. "Why?"

"I've got your back," Maurice says. "I'm going to jump in my car now. Will be about an hour behind you."

Can I trust the phone? I have no idea. Fuck it, my panic dictates. "The Sleep Inn Motel, 5403 Huettner Drive, Norman, Oklahoma."

"I'm on my way. Wait for me when you get there," Maurice says.

"Hurry."

The call drops, and there is one more remaining option on my logic tree. A voice inside tells me it's a mistake. I override. Panic has delivered me to the hands of instinct.

"This is Rich Azadian calling," I say aggressively.

"Didn't I tell you—" Gillespie says.

"If anything happens to them, I am going to hurt you. I don't know how exactly you're involved in all of this, and frankly, right now I don't give a shit. But if one finger is laid on either of them, I will never, never rest until I take you down."

"Calm down, Azadian," he says. "I don't know what the hell you're talking about."

"I think you do," I say, not completely sure but desperately needing to hedge my bets.

"Okay," Gillespie says calmly, "then tell me what you think I know."

I'm caught. To say or not to say? Do I trust him or do I not? I don't. "Fuck you," I hiss. My threat has been delivered. Perhaps that's the best I can do. I kill the connection.

Eighty miles an hour feels pathetically, painfully slow. I call the hotel again. Ring. Ring. Ring. Ring. No answer.

I call the hotel again. Beep. Beep. Beep. The brick phone goes dead. They didn't know much about battery life in the fucking 1990s. I slam the worthless phone into the passenger seat.

Emporia, Wichita, Blackwell, my forward progress feels creeping. Maybe everything is okay. Maybe I am overreacting. Maybe, maybe, maybe. The point is that I don't know. The point is that I've promised Maya to keep her safe. The point is that just when I'm realizing what's important to me, I am terrified I could lose it. The point is that racing down Highway 35 South I am desperately alone and realizing that perhaps I don't have to be.

Norman, Oklahoma, fifty-seven miles. Norman, thirty-two miles. Norman, twelve miles. The signs seem to taunt me. Entering Norman, Oklahoma.

My heart pounds.

I know I should think of something clever as I screech into the Sleep Inn parking lot. I also know that everything could be fine, and I'll feel like an idiot banging wildly on the door again or diving in through the window. Maurice may be an hour away but I can't wait another minute.

I leap stealthily up the stairs and pause in front of their door. My heart beats like an overwound metronome.

I try to force myself to stop and think, but I am on autopilot. I gently turn the doorknob. It is unlocked. I hold my breath as I open it a few inches. No noise. A bit more. Nothing. I peer my head into the crack between the door and the wall.

I see it and my mind freezes.

Toni and Maya are lying face up on one of the beds. Plastic

cuffs bind their legs and arms together. Duct tape covers their mouths. They look at me with bulging, frantic eyes.

But their pupils keep shifting beside me.

And before I can figure out why, I feel hard metal pressing against my temple.

65

"Don't say a word, Mr. Azadian," I hear as if through a fog. "That's right. Just relax and step inside. Good, good," the calm voice says. "Now just walk four steps toward the TV . . . One, two, three, four. Good, Mr. Azadian."

I look over at Toni and Maya. Their bodies are paralyzed with fear.

"Now lie on the ground face down. . . . Good, Mr. Azadian. . . . Put your hands together behind your back. . . . That's it. Just like that."

The high-pitched voice sounds eerily familiar. I feel the tight plastic cuffs cutting into my wrists.

"Now put your legs together. . . . Yes . . . Perfect," the voice continues.

I feel the cuffs cutting the blood flow at my ankles. My body twitches between the various impulses—yell, fight, squirm, swear. One impulse overrides them all. Focus.

I breathe in and watch my breath pass from my nose down to my lungs. I breathe slowly out and observe the reverse.

I'm not dead yet, and while I live, with every ounce of energy I have, I will fight to protect the people I love.

My face is pushed into the dust-ridden carpet, but my mind is clear. "The police will be here any minute," I hiss.

"Will they now?" the condescending voice responds.

I feel the metal pressing into the back of my head.

"If you'll just tilt your head back a bit and open your mouth."

The gloved hand on my forehead and knee on the back of my neck compel compliance.

"That's it, Mr. Azadian. . . . Good," the troublingly calm voice says.

My mind shuffles frantically through the options, trying to place the vaguely familiar voice.

The gloved hand stuffs a piece of cloth in my mouth. Then I hear the duct tape being pulled from the roll and torn.

"Good, Mr. Azadian, that's very good."

He rolls me over.

The pasty white skin, the square glasses, the light brown hair slicked across his head, the flinty, unflinching eyes and eagle face take only a fraction of a second to register.

He'd spooked me as Gillespie's menacing sidekick. Now his crooked half smile feels downright terrifying.

Collins holds my mouth closed and slaps on the duct tape.

I stare furiously, as if trying to zap him with the one tool I have left at my disposal.

"I think you'll be a lot more comfortable on the bed," he says with menacing formality.

I squirm as he bends down to haul me up, my mind struggling to reconcile his gentle tone with the ferocious, otherworldly look in his eyes.

"You're not as light as you look, Mr. Azadian," he says as he forcefully drags me onto the second bed.

I stare at him with a rage beyond anything I've ever known as I drop onto the mattress. I am powerless. I twist my head toward Toni and Maya.

"Just lie where you are, Mr. Azadian," Collins says. "No need to make this any more difficult than it needs to be."

The words make me squirm.

Collins leans his face toward me and grins pityingly, as if focused on a vision beyond me, beyond this room, maybe even, I sense, beyond this world. "Sometimes it's hard to tell who the good guys are and who are the bad ones," he continues as he takes Maya's clothes from her small bag and tosses them around the room. "If someone could have killed Hitler, shouldn't they have taken the shot? Would we have called him a murderer with so much at stake? Look at the Israelites coming out of Egypt. Who blames God for the ten plagues, for slaying those firstborns, for wiping out Pharaoh's army? Sometimes bad things need to be done in the name of good. Don't you agree, Mr. Azadian?"

I stare as fiercely as I can.

"All that is necessary for evil to triumph is for good men to do nothing. I can't remember who said that."

Tolstoy, you motherfucker.

Collins looks up reflectively. "Doesn't matter. Sometimes God has big plans for all of us, but he needs us to do our bit here on earth. Sometimes good people need to do things that seem bad in the little picture but a lot different in the big one. Don't you agree?"

He takes out a bottle of Clorox, pours a little on a washcloth, and begins calmly rubbing the door handles and drawer knobs. My body stiffens as I realize what he is doing, why we are all still alive. He is preparing a perfect crime scene, just as, I now realize, he did in MaryLee Stock's apartment. Like MaryLee, we are only to die when he is ready, in the manner he chooses, with little or no evidence left behind.

I am bound and gagged but my mind searches desperately for options. Can the US government really just kill us like this? Why is Collins explaining himself to me? I don't know but latch onto my sixth sense as my only hope. My eyes soften. I nod my head in an oblong motion as if considering the proposition.

"Take her, for example," he continues, looking over at Maya. "She seems like a perfectly lovely girl, somebody's daughter, a daughter of God. Who would ever want to harm her?"

Maya thrashes angrily, a wild animal caught in a trap who still has fight left in her.

"But you know what's inside of her. That, Mr. Azadian, is why you are here. Why you've made my life so much easier by choosing this out-of-the-way place."

The eerie, self-possessed tone of Collins's voice terrifies me as he prepares the crime scene like an artist, moving a plastic glass from one place to another, stepping back to assess his work, then making small adjustments. His moves are calculated, deliberate, professional.

I look over and catch Toni's eye. *I'm so sorry*, I try to say.

A small tear rolls down the side of her face.

Then my self-doubt, maybe even self-hatred, kicks in. What did he just say? I led him here, made his life easier, brought Toni and Maya to the middle of nowhere then left them to rush back to Kansas City. What kind of man am I? I'm tied up, tied down, emasculated, powerless, lost.

"You know," Collins says, "you couldn't tell from looking at this picture, but the world is really a beautiful place. Sure it has flaws, but God created it with the potential to be perfect. We don't have to change God's plan, Mr. Azadian, we've just got to recognize its beauty. Do you follow me? The Garden of Eden wasn't only a garden, it's the space within each of us where pure love for God and his work exists."

Why is the US government mentioning the Garden of Eden?

"God doesn't want us to meddle with the code of life. That's his job," Collins continues, now walking into the bathroom. "At the end of days, God shall overcome," he adds, leaning his head out of the bathroom to look at me. "You know the words."

God shall fucking overcome. The right's marching orders, Eden's Army's fucking credo. I've got to keep him talking.

He peeks his head back from inside the bathroom. "What's your favorite number, Mr. Azadian?"

I try to indicate with my eyes that I'm considering the question.

"Sorry, that was insensitive of me. I know you can't talk right now. Want to know what mine is?"

I widen my eyes, trying to be inviting.

"Forty-six. That's a really good number. If it was good enough for Mary, it's good enough for me."

My eyes remain calm.

"Forty-seven," he says, darkness blanketing his face as he looks toward Maya, "is not God's lucky number. It's a bad number. It's a wrong number." Collins pauses for a moment. He looks at Maya, then Toni, then me. Then he nods his head slightly as if agreeing with himself. He reaches down and picks up a small plastic case from near the dresser and places it on the table near the door. He opens it deliberately. It's only when I see the needles coming out that I begin squirming. Now I fully understand the needle mark on MaryLee Stock's outstretched arm. I start to struggle, but Collins locks me down with his knee.

"Don't worry, Mr. Azadian, it will only pinch a little. I'm really sorry about this. I hadn't wanted this at all. Under other circumstances I could have spared you and your friend here. You both have the lucky number. But you've really left me no choice."

He holds the needle up, flicks it with his index finger, then shoots a tiny amount of potassium cyanide into the air.

"It's probably silly of me to worry about air bubbles at a time like this," he says with a shake of his head, "but I really do want to make this as painless as possible."

I twist my head over toward Toni. *I love you, I'm so sorry*, I try to say with my eyes. All of my emotions—love, regret, fear, anger—roll into one expression that no one, not even Toni, could decipher.

"Just hold still, Mr. Azadian," Collins says, taking my left arm in his left hand.

I stare at him with every ounce of power I have in me, with everything I am as a person, with a life instinct to live and a death instinct to kill. My eyes stay open, sharp, focused . . . desperate.

His fingers stiffen around the needle he holds just below my shoulder as he leans in. I squirm frantically but the weight of Collins's body still holds me. My mind shoots out the two conflicting messages of *good-bye, my love* and *fuck you.*

The noise explodes through the room as the door kicks open.

A hulking body lunges into the room.

"Stop, Collins. Now!"

I recognize the commanding shout. Collins drops the needle and puts his hands in front of him at chest height. He pulls back with his elbows and stands in the space between the two beds.

Gillespie's gun points at Collins's heart.

"Don't *fucking* move," Gillespie shouts furiously.

Collins's torso is now erect. He inches his elbows back, away from Gillespie.

Two streaks catch the corner of my eye. The first is Collins ducking and darting right, pulling his gun from his back belt, and swinging it at Gillespie in one lightning motion.

The second is Maya, hurling herself in a supernatural gymnastic leap off the other bed and into Collins's legs as the room fills with a sound like air darts firing.

Pfoof. Pfoof. Pfoof.

And then silence.

And then groans.

An avalanche of commands flows to my brain as I frantically twist my neck to scan the room. Toni. Toni. Toni.

She looks at me and I know immediately. She is okay.

I wiggle toward the side of the bed. Collins is bloody and not moving. Maya under him.

"Mmm, mmm, mmm," is the only desperate noise I can make through the cloth and duct tape.

Maya uses her head to push Collins aside and peers at me from the valley between the two beds. Her first look is pure terror. Her second an almost unbelieving defiance. The third I might almost construe as love.

I smile at her with my eyes.

Another groan. Gillespie. I twist around toward the door. He is slumped against the TV stand, his eyes glazing over, his shirt a growing blotch of deep red.

66

My body pulls desperately in three directions at once.

I want to hold Toni to shield her, as if that were possible, from what has already happened.

Maya is wiggling out from under Collins's limp body between the beds. I feel the overwhelming drive to pull the body away, to squeeze her by the shoulders, to tell her that it's okay, it's over, she's safe.

But Gillespie appears to be the one in greatest need. And to help him or anyone I have to free my hands. I flop off the bed and wiggle myself toward him.

"Mmm," I mumble, trying to point to my gag with my shoulder.

His eyes look drugged, but he intuits my intent and limply lifts his right hand. I slink around his body and place my mouth near it. He fumbles with the edge of the duct tape. Then I feel him getting a grip on one end.

My face feels like it's ripping as I yank my head backward. His grip holds. I spit out the washcloth and gasp for air.

"Are you okay?" I ask stupidly, still not understanding why he just saved me and killed his colleague when a few hours ago I'd been convinced he was my biggest threat. I stare at him with what I know must be a look of dumb incomprehension.

Gillespie grimaces.

"Baby," I say frantically, rolling my head toward Toni, "are you okay?"

"Mmm," she mumbles. I read her completely, effortlessly. *I'm okay, don't worry about me, focus on the others.*

"Maya?" I bark, twisting my head toward the space between the two beds.

Maya has now fully wiggled her torso out from under Collins's limp body. She lifts her head. Her eyes are still wide and defiant, but they calm when they connect with mine. I smile nervously then turn back toward Gillespie.

"Can you help get me out of these cuffs?"

"There's a jackknife," he says with effort, gesturing with his chin to his front left pant pocket. He twists his torso trying to drag his right arm across his wounded body. His right hand reaches his left pocket after three tries. He pushes out the knife with his palm in a process that seems to take forever. It drops on the floor.

I grab it with my bound right hand, open it behind my back, then squirm backward to hand it to Gillespie. I can't see him but keep moving my arms behind me until I feel the weight of the knife ease. "Got it?" I say. I pull my hands apart behind me. "Can you cut the cuffs?"

"Mmm," I hear Toni mumbling. I look back at her. She focuses her eyes at me and then at Gillespie's u.D, then back at me and again toward the u.D.

"Your u.D," I tell Gillespie.

"No," he groans. "No calls."

I look at him inquisitively.

His face contorts. "No calls . . . Not safe."

I'm too desperate to get out of my cuffs to argue. "Can you cut?" I repeat.

"Move closer," he mumbles.

I maneuver my hands as close to Gillespie's knife as possible, then feel him fumbling from behind me.

Krrr. Krrr. Krrr. The sawing feels weak and inconsequential behind my back.

Toni has now wiggled herself in the opposite direction on the bed, with her head peering over the edge toward me and her feet toward the wall. *It's okay. We'll get there*, she says with her eyes.

I relax my shoulder muscles. *Krrr. Krrr. Krrr.*

I can feel the cuffs beginning to stretch. I strain my arms apart. Nothing.

I pull with all my strength.

Nothing.

I pull again.

My arms go flying to the sides, the blade grazing my hand as it flies away from my flailing arms. I roll over and leap toward Toni. "Hold on," I say, taking hold of the edge of her duct tape. She looks at me calmly. I stop for a moment and look at her, taking her in. Then I put one hand behind her head, kiss her on the forehead, and yank the tape.

"*Mmm*," she mumbles, opening her mouth. I grab an edge of the cloth and pull.

"Baby," I say, moving to kiss her. Her head turns away from the kiss toward Maya. "Maya, honey," she says breathlessly, "are you okay?"

Maya grunts a single syllable. I wiggle toward her.

"This is going to hurt," I say. "Are you ready?"

"Motherfucker." The words fly from her mouth as the duct tape clears.

"You all right?" I say.

She gasps for air. "Think so." She seems to be trying to play it cool, but my hand absorbs the vibration of her bones.

"It's going to be okay," I say, pulling her head to my chest. "You did an incredible thing."

She looks up at me with the wide eyes of a child.

I let go of her, grab the knife, and begin cutting all of our remaining cuffs.

"Gillespie," Toni says in her best caregiving tone from her

perch at the edge of the bed, her face level with his, "you hanging in there?"

"Never better," he grunts softly.

"We've got to get you some help, right away," she orders as I finally cut her free. She jumps over and places her hand on Gillespie's forehead.

Gillespie hoists his head up from its slump. "No," he says with surprising force.

"Look," Toni says with an even greater intensity as she pulls open Gillespie's shirt and begins examining the wound, "every minute counts for you right now. We've got to get you to a hospital."

"Not yet," Gillespie mumbles. "The girl . . . you've got to protect her."

Toni purses her lips, starting to realize that Gillespie is not moving. "We need to put pressure on the wound," she says, taking charge. "Richie, grab a towel from the floor."

I do.

"Fold it in quarters. Hold it to the wound."

Gillespie's face contorts with pain as I press the epicenter of the red blotch on his shirt.

Toni glides her hand gently around his back and rubs up and down. "I don't feel an exit wound. We've got to get you to a hospital."

Maya jumps behind Toni and peers over her shoulders.

Gillespie lifts his head and stares intensely at Maya. "I'm sorry," he mutters.

"We should be calling 9-1-1," Toni says, impatience woven through each word.

Gillespie shifts his head toward hers. "Don't," he murmurs. "The girl . . . won't be safe. You need to get her away."

"I don't understand," Maya says softly.

"I didn't know . . . Collins was Eden's Army," Gillespie says softly. "I don't know . . . who else is. I don't know who to trust, who wants to harm her. You need to know what you're up against." He looks at Toni. "Ten minutes."

Toni shakes her head.

Gillespie focuses his waning strength in a forceful command. "I need ten minutes."

Toni looks at him and then at me then drops her shoulders angrily. "Maya honey, bring me all the pillows."

Toni places them around Gillespie.

"Now put the blanket on top," she tells Maya. "Gently."

Toni holds the folded towel on Gillespie's shoulder and eyes him like a disapproving nun. "Five minutes."

Gillespie leans his head back, gathering his strength.

Then he speaks.

67

"A few years ago we learned the Chinese were secretly enhancing the DNA of embryos."

Maya's body stiffens.

"To breed genius babies and bring glory to the state. Some of our people wanted to stop them . . . but we couldn't. So we needed to match them. If we didn't, how could we compete thirty years from now? Our country wouldn't support a national program, so"—Gillespie pauses—"our front company bought a small chain of fertility clinics."

"But you said—"

Toni digs her nails into my leg. "Bright Horizons?" she asks, bringing Gillespie back to his focus.

Gillespie focuses his eyes on me for a brief moment. Whatever he said at the Hilton coffee shop doesn't matter now.

He turns his heavy eyes toward Toni. "We started acquiring the technology we needed . . . trying to create the . . . extraordinary."

"Becker's technology in exchange for you helping with his own little project," I interject.

Toni's look tells me to shut up so Gillespie can finish.

"Something like that," Gillespie mutters. "And his protégée, MaryLee, was close enough to what we were looking for. Nine more women . . . were part of the pilot project. And then . . ." Gillespie's voice begins to falter. His face betrays surprise as well pain. "They started dying. One by one."

"Thanks for letting me know," Maya says, her voice hovering between sarcasm and compassion.

Gillespie lifts his head with a brief flush of momentum. "We didn't know who, why. We needed to investigate . . . but also keep everything secret." He looks at me. "And then you bumbled in."

I swallow.

"At first, we thought it was the Chinese. The girl from UMKC. Chinese agents in the other cities. They must have hacked us. When the women started dying, the Chinese agents started . . . slipping out. We were looking at everything, at you."

"We?" I ask.

"NCA Operations. You were . . . sloppy."

The words are deflating, but Lord, I know.

"We were trying to protect the program, find the killer, keep tabs on you and the Chinese, and protect the remaining . . ."

Gillespie's voice trails off as he looks at Maya. She is "the remaining." He takes a deep, gasping breath.

"I had a man watching you," he continues, nodding at the heap of a man lying on the floor. The three of us turn to face the body.

"How did you know?" I ask.

Toni looks like she's ready to add us both to the pile.

"After you called me . . . I tried to reach Collins . . . but no answer. . . . Then her u.D activated." He looks at Toni. "I traced it to this place." Gillespie is almost whispering now. "Why hadn't I heard you were here? And then . . ."

I nod expectantly.

"It hit me. I jumped in my car. Tried to call . . ."

"So why—?" I say.

"Figured it out as I drove," he mumbles. "Collins had been against this, but he was a good soldier . . . I thought."

I correct Gillespie. "A good soldier for another army."

"When the letter bombs started three years ago—"

"We don't need a history lesson. Your five minutes are up. We need to get you to a hospital," Toni snaps.

The blood is pooling at Gillespie's waist. He forces out the words. "After the Eden's Army arrests . . . we thought it was over."

Toni can't take it anymore. "That's it," she says pointedly. "Maya, go grab my phone from the floor."

A surprising burst of energy animates Gillespie's voice. "Wait," he orders. "You can't call until she's safe," he says, looking at Maya. I don't know who was involved . . . There are people who'd want to kill her if this gets out."

He looks pleadingly at Toni and me. "She needs to disappear. If I make it, I'll try to zap her name from the files. Take her . . . before anyone comes."

I look at Toni, then Maya. We are all frozen. I have no idea how even to begin.

"But—" I say.

"Figure it out," Gillespie mutters, his eyelids dropping.

"What the hell?"

I turn to see the look of absolute incredulity overcoming Maurice's face as he jumps inside the broken door. I want to hug him. I stand and place a hand on each of his shoulders and fix my eyes on his. "I'll explain everything to you later. The three of us have to leave. You need to get Gillespie to the hospital right away. You need to make sure it seems the girl was never here."

Maurice looks into my eyes, then nods.

"Gillespie saved our lives," I say, glancing down at his crumpled mess of a body. "He's a good man."

Gillespie can hardly move but lifts his eyelids slightly.

I step toward the door. Toni and Maya follow.

"Wait," Maya says. She stops and turns around, then leans down to put her face just in front of Gillespie's.

"Thank you," she says so softly it seems she is only moving her lips.

Everything in the room stops for a fraction of a second. And then it speeds up as Maya, Toni, and I race out into the darkness.

68

It's only after ten minutes of driving that I realize no one has said a word. We're all stunned.

How does the mind, I wonder, absorb shock? I can almost feel new pathways forming in my brain, my mind restructuring itself, recoding.

I glance at Toni and hold out my hand. She takes it.

"Maya," I say, "how are you doing back there?"

"Now what happens?" she asks a few moments later.

It's the thought my conscious mind has been avoiding. The truth is I don't know. I'm just driving. "For now, we need to get you out of the way for a while and see how things play out."

I see her sinking into the backseat through my rearview mirror.

"Maya, honey," Toni says in the same soft voice, "are there people in your family you may need to tell not to worry about you?"

"Not so much," Maya says wistfully. "I talk to my mom every couple of weeks, my dad every few months, so I guess I'd better say something to my mom. Not that she'd much care."

I glance at Toni's pained face absorbing the words and see her as a mother of kids, for a flash, almost, as the mother of *our* kids.

"Okay," Toni says, "you'll probably need to call her one of these days."

"Yup," Maya says in an adolescent tone. The mention of her mother seems to have a devolutionary impact.

"How about your apartment?" I say.

"Rent's due on the first of the month."

"Can we send them a money order?" I say.

"They don't give a shit," Maya responds. The words seem to embody Maya's feelings about most of the people in her life.

We're fifteen minutes from Collins's body, from the dying Gillespie, and already we've sunk into details. Maybe, I think to myself, life *is* details.

"Why do you think he did it?" Maya asks after a long silence.

"Who?"

"Gillespie," she says. "Why'd he send me away when he'd put so much effort into, into this?"

I see Maya in the rearview mirror putting her hands on her stomach.

"Maybe he was a father," Toni says.

"*The* father?" I ask, surprised.

"He was helping create something."

The three of us silently absorb the possibility.

"And so the babies that got killed in their mothers' wombs, the embryos, were his kids?" I ask.

"Maybe not genetically," Toni says, "but in other ways, maybe."

"'He wanted to dream a man, he wanted to dream him in minute entirety and impose him on reality,'" I recite.

"What's that?" Toni asks after a reflective pause.

"A line from Borges," I say. "I'm not sure I fully understood it before now."

Toni reaches across and takes my hand.

I think of Gillespie, picture the ambulance rushing him to the hospital. In a screwy way, I pray for him. I put myself in his shoes. What can any of us leave behind in our transient lives? Changing the human code, improving it, becoming immortal, being God for a few moments. Terrifying, intoxicating. Genesis. "And you think he wanted Maya to have a normal life?"

"I think he understands what's coming. Do you?" Toni asks.

I look straight out the window as I drive. The road ahead is empty. The arc of our headlights fills a passing ark of nothingness.

"So, what now?" Toni says.

The fragments of my mind shift wildly in my head, but I feel them coming together. I feel the pot being remade from the jumbled pile of shards. I look over at her, holding her gaze before looking to the road. "Do you guys mind sleeping in the car tonight?" I ask after a few moments. Neither of them answers.

When we reach Derby, Kansas, I pull into a Walmart and park. Maya stretches across the backseat, and we slide the front seats back to rest just above her body.

"Everybody okay?" I ask as we settle in.

Toni takes my left hand in her right. "Maya, give me your hand, honey," she says. I realize what Toni is doing and pass my free hand through the space between the driver's seat and the door. Maya's meets it immediately.

Maybe it's only now I realize that I've been alone, that my drive for self-reliance has been partly a fear of truly connecting in a way that might reprogram the code of my life. Maybe it's at this moment that I realize I don't have to be alone. Toni squeezes my left hand, Maya, my right. I don't let go. We all drift off to sleep.

The first light and the movement of cars wake us. My mouth still tastes of washcloth and carpet. I feel filthy but alive. I pull over to the ChargePoint station and plug in the car as I fill the reserve tank with gasoline. We take turns in the restroom washing up.

I'm the first Walmart customer at seven thirty. I stop by the electronic device section and do my research, then come back to the car with orange juice, a box of oatmeal cookies, and a bag of apples.

"Ready?" I ask resolutely as I start the car.

Toni swings her head toward me. Maya articulates what Toni's expression asks. "Where are we going?"

"Topeka," I say, matter-of-fact.

"Hmm."

The drive takes two hours.

I place the address in Toni's palm, engulfing her hand with mine.

"You'll figure it out," I say.

She looks at me awkwardly, as if she wants to punch me and kiss me at the same time. I can't blame her for either.

This is the time when a normal guy is supposed to say I love you. We're at the train station and the Southwest Chief is about to board. But the decrepit station is hardly the scene of an old Bogart movie. Somehow it doesn't feel right. We hug desperately, then Toni's arm reaches out from our merged being and grabs Maya's jacket. I feel another arm resting on my back.

In the movies a horn would blow and someone would shout, "All aboard!" In Topeka, the anodyne, prerecorded voice announces in disjointed and disassociated words that "The-ten-thirty-Southwest-Chief-train-is-now-boarding-on-track-two." In Topeka, I don't say the three words pushing up from my subconscious.

As the train pulls away, I head back to my car and drive toward Kansas City. Alone again, I think.

But then again, I wonder, maybe not.

69

"Are you . . . ?" Martina stammers.

"I'm okay. She's okay. We need to meet," I fire staccato from the payphone in Lawrence, Kansas.

"Where?"

"There's a small reading room in the southwest corner of the Plaza library, on Main Street."

"I know it," Martina says.

"Meet me there at two. Park across the street in the BoT Lofts building and come in through the underground walkway."

"Got it," Martina says, taking my lead.

My tone has changed. I have changed. "We're going to need help. Bring Abraham. The two of you should leave separately. Tell him to bring Jerry Weisberg if he's been released."

The line is silent.

"Two o'clock," I say, then hang up.

I begin forming and reforming the story in my head. I mentally draft opening sentences, edit them, scrap them, and start over. I poke holes in the narrative then fix them. My mind is on fire.

I get to the library a little before two. Martina and Joseph enter the reading room a few minutes later. Martina walks up to me, squeezes my elbow, and sits down. Even Joseph's nonchalance conveys an emotional warmth he'd never communicate in words.

I look at each of them with a feeling of appreciation that rises from somewhere deep inside. "Now we need to tell the story." I focus on Martina. "Are you in?"

"Let's hear what you have," she says.

I look at her sharply and let the uncomfortable silence hang.

"Dammit, Azadian," she says, her words clearly a confirmation.

I start with the National Competitiveness Act and the Chinese genetic enhancement program, then I roll through the secret US plan and how Bright Horizons fits into the picture. I veer off to track the Becker story until his quest for the messiah links him to Bright Horizons, then shift to MaryLee, to Maurice and me taking up the case, to the fake autopsy and the stolen tissue. I describe what I know about Gillespie, which, I realize, is not nearly as much as I should about someone who has just saved my life. I go through the Christian right's campaign to save the country's soul, the underground militants it inspired, the Eden's Army terrorist attacks, Senator King's brilliant maneuver to capture all of this energy in the great sail of his campaign to oust President Lewis in the Republican primary. I finish with my arrival here. It's a vast, complicated, interweaving story with such obvious consequences for the future of our country, our world, and our species, but also, obviously, for the specific victims it has swept in its wake.

A profound, momentary silence fills the room after I stop speaking.

Martina is the first to break it. "And the girl, Maya?"

"Safe," I say, then amend my words. "Safe and hidden away for now."

"And you want to—"

"Yes. To deal her out of the story. I insist on it."

"How strong is the connection between Senator King and Eden's Army?" Martina asks.

"Nothing direct. No smoking gun," I say, "but it's hard to deny that the climate of fear and militant righteousness he's nurtured is one of the main catalysts for all this."

"And President Lewis?"

"I hate to sound like Cobalt Becker," I say, "but there is going to be hellfire coming down on his head for the covert genetic enhancement program. Everyone wants this country to be more competitive but not at any cost, not at this cost."

Martina nods. "This could kill genetic research in America and kill the *Star*, you know."

"You know these technologies have enormous potential for good and bad, and if the *Star* can't tell the story it deserves to be killed."

"Let's do this," she says, her battle voice kicking in.

Martina and I dole out the research tasks. Joseph will compile everything we know about the National Competitiveness Act, genetic engineering, and Becker, and reach out to Franklin Chou for help with the science. Martina will run interference with the *Star*, and I will buckle down and begin writing.

Jerry runs in breathlessly, looking a bit worse for wear after police custody. I give him the short version and ask him to nail down the ownership structure of Bright Horizons and to work with Joseph on the multimedia content to embed in the article.

As the team fans out I begin dictating into my u.D. The words flow through me as if the story is being downloaded from my own genetic code. I write until the library closes at ten then sleep for a few hours in my car. I don't trust going home until the story is told.

I'm the first visitor in the library door at eight the next morning. Joseph Abraham is the second. Joseph and Jerry feed me information and check my facts. The story grows longer and deeper, yet I hold to the connective thread, the simplicity on the far side of complexity.

Martina arrives at 2 p.m. to do a final edit.

"Wes Morton is onboard," she says. "I've told him we don't want any edits, that we're going to give them the copy at the last possible minute and it will go straight to press."

"What did he say?" I ask.

"That he needed time to think about it."

"And?"

"I told him if he didn't agree I was resigning and taking this to the *St. Louis Post-Dispatch*. I told him I thought we had enough to bust through the News Protection Act restrictions or go down trying, that if they wanted to take us down for this, then let them fucking try."

I'd never thought I'd view Martina's combative obstinacy so lovingly. How can it be, I wonder, that our best and worst qualities are so closely interlinked? "What did he say?"

"We're going to release the printed version and post the digital story at exactly the same moment early tomorrow morning."

At four thirty the story is ready. It runs almost ten thousand words. We synch it to encrypted files Jerry has installed on each of our u.Ds, and part, separately and in silence.

Martina rushes back to the *Star* to meet the 5 p.m. deadline.

I jump in my car.

There are two places I need to visit before tomorrow morning.

70

Forty-eight hours ago I was an injection away from dead. But the fear gripping me now is of an entirely different sort.

My hand twitches as I reach it toward the doorbell.

My forty-five minutes with Christine Fogerty had been impossibly difficult. I'd left for Springfield feeling that the price of truth might be unbearable pain, that sometimes a comfortable lie might be the more bearable option.

I now wonder for a moment if I should turn back.

I've always seen myself as truth's champion, my mission to track its elusive shadow down its rabbit hole. But who am I to dispel someone else's fantasies? Perhaps I should leave Carol Stock with the story she has in her head. Her beautiful daughter died of terrible but natural causes, God's will. The Lord works in strange ways. The church is his institution here on earth. Cobalt Becker is his helper. The messiah will come and save all believers.

But then what?

Then the story will come out tomorrow. Then someone else will be on this porch in the morning. Then Carol Stock will be even less prepared for what's coming. Then . . .

I ring the bell.

"Mrs. Stock," I say, "it's Rich Azadian."

She pushes the screen door open slightly, as if opening the door to me is opening the door to a dangerous world.

"May I come in?"

Carol nods.

I follow her into her living room. The place is immaculate.

School photos of MaryLee from various ages and framed knittings line the walls. GOD'S LOVE IS THE WAY, JESUS IS COMING—OPEN YOUR HEART, the knittings say.

Who am I, I ask myself, to take Carol Stock's world away from her?

But maybe it's too late. Maybe that world died with MaryLee.

"I promised you I would find out what happened to your daughter."

She looks at me blankly.

"I am so sorry." I begin to tell the story, hoping that someone will be around to pick up the pieces or that Carol Stock will have the power do so herself. As my words unfold, she seems caught between the world she has believed in and the world I am ushering her into. "And then they all started dying," I say toward the end of my story. I stop and rephrase. "They all started getting killed."

Carol slumps back into her chair. Her world of knitted certainties of God's love has not prepared her for this tale. Maybe she had agreed for her daughter to be Mary, but never had she signed on for her only child to have become the red heifer sacrificed on the altar of her beloved Second Coming.

I tell her about Gillespie and Collins. Part of me wants to tell her about Maya just to let her know that death does not always emerge victorious. I refrain.

"And so Collins is dead," I say softly, "all of the women are dead. And the full story is coming out in the *Kansas City Star* in four hours."

Carol looks at me, stunned.

"That's why I'm here. I wanted to be the one to tell you. I wanted you to know what might be coming your way. Reverend Becker and the church are going to be in the middle of this. I just wanted you to be . . ." I'm not sure how to finish the sentence. Safe? Protected? I've hardly delivered either.

"I'm so sorry," I say pathetically. "I'm—"

Carol cuts me off.

"I understand," she says through her soft breath. She lifts her torso slightly then takes my hand in hers. "I understand," she repeats in a slightly stronger voice, "and thank you."

71

Bzzz.

I don't feel the slightest hesitation as I stand outside the door of Cobalt Becker's palatial home.

Bzzz. I press again. *Bzzz. Bzzz.*

A dog barks. Light from a higher floor pierces the 4 a.m. darkness. Footsteps.

The door opens and Becker, in pajamas and a fleece robe, faces me squarely. His golden mane still flows like a lion's.

"I thought it must be you," he says as if he's been expecting me.

"It was a rogue agent in the National Competitiveness Agency."

Becker takes in the information.

"He belonged to Eden's Army. There were eight other women who were part of the same program," I lie.

"And they—"

"Dead. Same as MaryLee."

The mention of her name sucker punches Becker. He holds his chin between his thumb and index finger.

"I never wanted—"

"It doesn't matter."

"I didn't know about the bigger program," he stammers. "I didn't—"

"I know. What you did was despicable, but I know."

"So now what?"

I get the sense his mind is starting to lay out options. His shift to self-preservation mode disturbs me. "You can guess," I say. "The story is coming out this morning. Actually, the papers are being released and the story is going up on the website, well," I look down at my watch, "actually both happened four minutes ago. About the time I rang your bell."

The look on Becker's face makes absolutely clear he understands the personal, professional, and national political implications. "I'm not sure I'd have tried to stop you anyway."

His voice sounds surprisingly human to me.

"Doesn't really matter now," I say with a shrug.

"And the story says?"

I spit out the essentials. Rapture Grove. Genesis Labs. The National Competitiveness Agency. Eden's Army. I state the names of the nine dead women, each word feels like another stab in the great Caesar's wounded body. The Second Coming that never came.

I sense Becker sees his world crumbling, his church collapsing, that he understands the onslaught that will arrive in a few hours, can almost see the television trucks lining up down his street, almost read the headlines in the tabloids, hear the protesters chanting their condemnation. I sense he's already imagining the furious debates in Senator King's office as it becomes painfully clear that Becker has become the poison arrow piercing the heart of the Christian right's political surge, that the King 2024 presidential campaign has crashed to the ground just months before it was set to officially launch.

Becker breathes in as if rising to face the onslaught then pauses. His shoulders drop and he stares at me with his powerful eyes. But in them I see a hint of the unknown, of fear perhaps.

"I'll go write up my resignation," he says as if speaking to himself.

His cool still unnerves me. "And Senator King?"

"What about him?"

The look on my face is clear. *Do you really need me to explain?*

"I don't know," Becker says.

"Without his spiritual advisor, without your people, he's done."

Becker nods.

"There's something else you need to do," I say.

Becker looks at me apprehensively.

"You more than anyone understood the potential of genetic science. You know it can cure disease, prevent disorders, help us face the brutal cruelty of evolution. You saw the potential."

Becker does not seem to get where I am heading.

"Senator King can still choose how he wants to position himself in the coming crisis. He can fight on in the name of orthodoxy that even you don't believe in, or he and your people can finally help foster the national dialogue we need to help our country make smart decisions. This science can do a lot of damage, but it can also save a lot of lives and do a lot of good. You know that."

"So what do you need from me?"

"Call Senator King, call him now. He needs to get ahead of this story, to be the one calling for a bipartisan national dialogue. Only your side can make this happen."

Becker begins to shake his head.

"Listen to me, Reverend," I say forcefully, "God knows I don't want anyone breeding messiahs, we all know the danger of eugenics. I'm not that confident we know enough to start messing with the genetic code, but this science is the key for curing diseases and saving lives. This story will force the country to face up to all of this. You've got to call Senator King."

Becker nods apprehensively.

"Good," I say, "and one more thing. Your church needs to take care of Carol Stock financially."

"How—?"

"That's for you to figure out." I look him square in the eye. My voice is neither stern nor aggressive, but I make my point and it registers.

My mind shifts up a few hundred feet of altitude and looks down at the two of us standing at Becker's door.

"It was a crazy idea, you know," I say.

"Great things sometimes come from crazy ideas," Becker says, beginning to regain his voice.

I let the words settle before responding. "And sometimes people die from them, too."

I don't hear Becker's door close behind me as I walk to my car. I guess he's watching me or maybe just looking out at the abyss we both know is waiting for him.

72

The knocking comes from deep inside a dream, from the middle of my head.

Until I slowly realize it doesn't.

Bam. Bam. Bam.

I press my eyelids down, hoping it will go away.

Bam. Bam. Bam.

I roll over and peer at my clock. Three p.m. I've been asleep, maybe even dead, for the past seven hours. My body aches. I need a shower. I look down at my u.D. *Sleep quality: good.*

I slide on my robe and slink down the stairs. My muscles have not yet adapted to their new reality.

"Yeah?" I say, sounding like a bad guy yelling from an encircled cabin in an old spaghetti western.

"Boss, it's me, Joseph. I've been calling. I came by and saw the car."

I pull open the door and see a brief, awkward smile flash across Joseph's face. He strides in with an alacrity that surprises me. "Have you seen the paper?"

"Yup."

"Everyone's waiting for you at the office. You've got to come in. Wes Morton sent me to get you."

I chuckle to myself about my change of fate. "Give me a few minutes," I say calmly. "I'm going to go upstairs and wash up. Why don't you go into the kitchen and make us some coffee?"

Joseph stares at me with unbelieving eyes. "You don't understand. Senator King is making a statement in thirty minutes."

After all of my rushing around, I am, strangely and not even fully understandably to me, in no hurry at all. "Five minutes," I say with a warm smile.

I walk up the stairs, drop my robe, and float into the shower. The steaming water feels baptismal. I think of Toni and of MaryLee, of Maya and Gillespie, of Kathryn Allison, Dakota Barnes, Megan Fogerty, Celia Guttierez, Louise Osten, Sunita Patel, and Amanda Sullivan, I think of their poor families, I think of Collins zipped up in a bag somewhere, and I think, of course, of me. The person who I was less than two weeks ago seems somehow to have been transcended.

I towel off, comb my hair, put on a clean pair of jeans and a sweater, and walk downstairs a new person.

Joseph stands nervously at the bottom of my staircase, an old plastic travel mug he's somehow found in my kitchen in his hand. I notice the Scooba autobot inching its way across the living room floor.

"Your story is the number one story this morning on the Internet," Joseph says as he speeds downtown, "in the world."

"Wow," I say, uncreatively.

"The Catholic bishops have called this an abomination, Congress is already promising hearings, protests are forming in front of government offices across the country. The conservatives are all over the TV saying that this is what happens when human beings try to play God, when we give too much power to the government."

"And Becker?" I ask.

"Resigned this morning, announced that he's selling Rapture Grove and giving the money to Carol Stock. He gave a statement in front of his house at eight, said he was going to seclude himself in prayer."

The image of Becker at his door in the pre-morning flashes across my mind.

"The police stopped someone with a homemade bomb lurking near his house," Joseph continues excitedly, "and now have the place under twenty-four-hour watch. The press are staked out on his street. I think they'll be there for a while."

Joseph shows me some pictures of the press mob on his u.D monitor.

"Gillespie?" I ask.

"Apparently recovering in a hospital in Oklahoma City. He's in critical condition, but the doctors say he's going to make it. There's a mob of journalists at the hospital, but they're not letting them in. They've also shut down the Bright Horizons clinics."

I'm relieved to know Gillespie is in better shape but nervous about the Bright Horizons files. "I guess no one is threatening anyone with News Protection Act sanctions?"

"Funny you mention that, boss. Martina Hernandez forwarded me the email this morning. The cease and desist order has been rescinded."

I can't help but smile. "And the scientists who've been pushing for more research in the life sciences?"

Sleeping for seven hours has denied me access to a lifetime of knowledge. I feel like Rip Van Winkle.

"A few of them have already been on TV trying to make the case for how important it is to keep going with the good research to cure diseases, but they're having a hard time. People can't really hear them right now. Everything is being lumped together as Frankenscience."

My calm elation turns to sadness.

The government plan to create genetically enhanced babies without telling the mothers was a monstrosity, but I have far more ambiguous feelings about genetic science overall. The master plan of the universe, if ever there was one, cannot have been for humans to live nasty and brutish forty-year lives foraging desperately for food and humping each other in caves. If we are blessed with a passion for knowledge, why shouldn't we use it to tame our surroundings, to enhance our connectivity, to extend our lives, improve our capacities? The concept of God may simply encompass the basic human drive to imagine a better tomorrow, the concept of science the drive to make it so.

"The Chinese Foreign Ministry put out a statement," Joseph says.

"That's interesting."

"Of course, they deny the whole thing. The rest of the world doesn't seem to be buying it. It looks like they had agents across the US spying on America's advanced genetic science capabilities. A bunch of them have been identified and are being deported. Min Zhao was only one. All of this is having reverberations around the world. The UN Secretary General has already put out a statement saying we need to start thinking more about an international treaty to oversee human genetic science."

It's shocking to me that so much has happened in such a short time. It's as if my story has released a spring that was already primed to be sprung.

We reach the *Kansas City Star* parking lot at 3:28. Joseph ushers me up the stairs with a hand pressing against the small of my back. As we enter the newsroom, everyone is standing together facing the giant screen as Senator King steps up to the podium.

"Good afternoon," King says solemnly.

First one of my colleagues turns his head and sees me, then the others follow in a cascade of faces. Joseph ushers me to the middle of the pack. My colleagues close rank around me. I feel hands patting me on the back as I move forward.

"As you know, a story has been released today by the *Kansas City Star* outlining a despicable national effort by the United States government to establish a secret genetic enhancement program and impregnate young American women with synthetically altered fetuses, all in the name of enhancing American competitiveness." The look of disgust permeates King's face. "With everything I am and everything I stand for, I condemn this heinous act.

Today, I call for this program to be shut down immediately and demand that a major investigation be carried out into this program with direct congressional oversight to hold the responsible parties accountable."

The newsroom is nervously silent as King pauses to let his words sink in.

"At the same time, I also have seen preliminary allegations that a member of Eden's Army, the underground terrorist organization responsible for bombings at biotechnology laboratories around the country a few years ago, may have taken it upon himself to murder all of the women who had been impregnated in this despicable manner."

Maybe not all, I think to myself.

"Worse," King continues, "he committed murders in the name of a philosophy that many people in this country have embraced. My fellow Americans, all of us share a desire to make our magnificent country as great as it can be. All of us believe our beacon on the hill must continue to shine. All of us believe our country must find and take a righteous path. But I am speaking to you today because I believe we must find this path together, that the politics of division, if left unchecked, will tear us asunder."

I stand amazed at how King, the ultimate reader of political winds, is repositioning himself.

"And so I come before you today to make the following announcements. First, that I will personally lead the senatorial oversight special committee to review this incident. Second, that I am calling for the reestablishment of the National Bioethics Commission with representation across the American social, political, and religious landscape to help us understand the challenges and opportunities of the genetic frontier. Third, that I will be reaching out to President Lewis to discuss how we can all work collaboratively to bring this country together in this time of crisis. Fourth," King pauses as he slowly scans the small crowd in front of him and the row of cameras behind them, "that I am no longer seeking the Republican nomination for the 2024 presidency effective immediately."

The murmur of our assembled newsroom merges with the murmur of the television crowd and, I am sure, with that around the country and across the world.

"Thank you," King says solemnly. "God bless America and with his help, together, we shall overcome."

73

Perhaps we all have only a few moments in our lives when we really step up. Perhaps we never know when those are, but our lives up to then are preparations for those moments, and our lives afterward are ripples emanating from their wake.

I didn't set up the dominoes, but I did push the first one. And how the others have fallen. Congressional hearings, FBI investigations, the president's speech, the rallies and counter-rallies in Washington, the constant stream of picketers, street protests, it's hard to believe, as far away as Beijing. The *Kansas City Star* actually courting me.

The last month has been a whirlwind. I've done twenty-six television interviews and my picture is everywhere. I've testified before the National Bioethics Commission and the special congressional committee and been grilled by Carlton King, the new great statesmen of the middle ground, himself. I spoke at the KCPD ceremony for Maurice Henderson's promotion to Deputy Chief. I've had seven very long interviews with the FBI team investigating Bright Horizons. I've even been asked, I'm not sure why, for my views on how the National Competitiveness Act should be reformed.

All of this, but my work is not yet done.

I feel the urge to speed, if only the traffic on 101 South would let me. The metaphor of butterflies has always seemed stupid to me, but I can't think of another way to describe how I'm feeling.

How I had come up with the idea, I'll never know. I'm still

struggling between thinking it was my greatest flash of genius and the stupidest thing I've ever done.

My windows are down. The hot air enters along with exhaust fumes. I breathe in. I park a couple of houses down and walk back.

The key is still under the mat as it's been for almost forty years. I'd always thought I started living when I'd exited this house. Now I wonder if the flow is reversing. I turn the key then pull it out and, by painfully instilled habit, place it back under the mat. I turn the knob quietly and tiptoe in.

I'm still charting my announcement when a wildly yelping Shoonig declares my arrival. So much for that.

"Who's there?" I hear in the most familiar voice. It is not friendly.

I don't answer as I walk quickly through the back hallway toward the kitchen. The first thing I see is her rolling pin lifted and ready to strike.

"*Parev, Mayrig. Eendzee mee dzedzer,*" I say with a mischievous smile on my face. Hello Mother, please don't hit me.

The pin drops. She screams. "*Janeegus,*" she shouts, dropping the rolling pin and rushing toward me. I see the other two coming up behind her.

"Baby," Toni says, her voice a mix of tenderness and joy.

Now I believe in butterflies.

My mother and Toni reach me about the same time, pulling the three of us together into a flowing hydra of waving arms coming together in a circle.

"Baby, baby, baby," Toni repeats through her tears.

My mother sniffles.

Toni pulls her head back from the scrum and faces Maya. "And what are you doing standing there like that?" she says sharply but with a smile.

Maya doesn't need much coaxing and we absorb her in the huddle.

Even the damn dog is trying to push his way in.

It's so obvious, yet only at this moment clear. I am home.

The group hug seems to last forever but still feels like it ends before it should.

"Maya," I say after a few moments, noticing how different she looks. "How are you feeling?"

"*Shad lav. Yev took,*" she says, smiling, in broken Armenian. I am fine, thank you. And you?

"This," my mother proudly proclaims, "is one seriously *jarbig* girl."

Toni takes my hand and squeezes.

"We've been having quite a time this past month," Toni says mischievously. "I for one had no idea what a *patuhas* you used to be as a kid. But now that we've seen the pictures . . ." She winks.

I smile inwardly. My worlds are dangerously colliding. I have a feeling I'm going to be heckled with Armenian jabs for years. Squeezing Toni's hand, I sense it might be decades. "Now I'm really in trouble," I say, smiling outward.

"Your mom has been incredible," Toni continues enthusiastically. "Let's see, we've made *bourma,* cooked *lahmajun,* and drank *sourj.* Am I missing anything?"

"*Tel baneer,*" Maya adds proudly.

My mother beams with a joy I haven't seen on her face since, well, before Astrid died.

I'm a little stunned. I'd thought that Toni and Maya could be safe here. I guess I hadn't fully realized that being here would also turn them into family.

I look at Maya again. She smiles at me. She looks different. As if her belt has loosened a couple of notches. As if she is blooming.

My mother sees me watching and puts her arm around Maya. "This is one good woman," she says. Then she reaches over toward Toni. "And she ain't so bad either."

"What have I done?" I ask joyously.

I look down at Maya's stomach. Her eyes follow mine. Then she presses her shirt against herself to reveal her bulge.

"Superbaby is coming," she says mischievously. "I just hope the thermogenesis doesn't kick in before she's out."

Toni picks up on the strange look on my face and steps in. "We've been talking a lot about it," she says. "Maya?"

Maya looks at my mother, then me.

"I'm keeping the baby," she says. I hear the determination in her voice. "I don't know what kind of special qualities she's going to have, but after all this there's no way I'm killing her."

My mind pulls up all kinds of responses. How can I know if Gillespie has fully "zapped" her from the government files? What will the genetic enhancements do? What happens in the next generation? Only one small word escapes from my mouth. "She?"

"We went for an ultrasound," Maya says, "and," she adds, looking over at my mother, "I'm going to raise her here."

"Here?"

"For now, Dikran," my mother says gently, radiating. "She needs a good home. Later will come later."

Later will come later. I play the words over in my head, and all of my philosophizing flies out the window. Later will come later, but now has come now.

I turn to face Toni. We have the conversation without uttering a word.

This scares the shit out of me, but I think we should, you know, kind of almost try to be together, I say with my eyes.

Her eyes mock me. *I can see through you, baby. I know what you are actually saying.*

My eyes respond. *You're right. I'm in. I love you. I'm scared.*

Our hands squeeze tightly together and the deal is done.

I'm not sure what my life to this point has amounted to, but a synapse firing somewhere in my brain tells me that loving, as terrifying as it sometimes seems, could be my little current in the vast stream of the universe.

I'm thirty-nine years, eight months, and sixteen days old. I'm forty-one days older than when I saw MaryLee Stock's body sprawled out on her apartment floor. I am forty-one days closer to my death.

But, I sense, holding desperately to Toni's hand, I have as of this moment already begun to live.

Acknowledgments

I am enormously grateful to the very special people who provided thoughtful comments on earlier versions of this novel. Special thank-yous to Mallika Bhargava, Ming Chen, Deborah Devedjian, Edison Liu, Jordan Metzl, Kurt Metzl, Marilyn Metzl, Elaine Merguerian, Caren Meyers, Fred Meyers, Lindsey Meyers, Samantha Monk, Hasmik Simidyan, Judy Sternlight, Hsu-Ming Teo, and Elizabeth Wang. I'm not quite sure what's the category of appreciation beyond "enormously grateful," but that's how I feel about the assistance I received from my dear friend Rakhi Varma. I also deeply appreciate the many people, too many to name here, who answered specific questions on technical and other issues. Of course, anything seeming inaccurate or objectionable in the novel is entirely my responsibility (I only ask that readers please remember that I am not a scientist, this is not a science book, and the novel is set in the future). My goal in writing the novel is to help spur a broader dialogue about the massive implications of emerging genetic technologies. The novel would not have come to life (outside of my head, notebooks, and computer) but for the invaluable guidance and tireless effort of my amazing agent, Will Lippincott (himself supported by the young and brilliant Amanda Panitch), and the dedication and painstaking hard work of Cal Barksdale at Arcade Publishing. I dedicate the book to four mentors who've had a great and positive influence on my life: Les Gelb, Stephen Graubard, Richard Holbrooke, and Ted Sorensen.